*Her door flung open and Rafe came to her side...*

He encircled her with his strong arms, and she leaned into the seemingly familiar strength of the man with whom she'd felt a connection. This same man she hoped could trust. The man who made her feel every inch a woman when he looked at her.

Who had Rafe Redbourne been in her life?

None of that mattered right now. He was here with her, holding her, keeping her safe. Everything would be okay. His work-roughened hand cupped her head, his fingers entwined her damp curls, and he pulled her closer into the crook between his shoulder and chest.

Tears flowed freely now. Even though she could no longer remember the events of her dream, the effects of it still racked through her.

"Shhh..." His soft baritone voice warmed her.

She hiccupped.

This was the man she'd hoped he would be. This was the Rafe Redbourne she wanted to know. He was familiar, her memory of him so close to the surface she could almost see it, and she struggled to remember.

Tayla snuggled in a little closer, reveling in the warmth of his embrace. His grip around her tightened. She lifted her hand to wipe away a tear and gasped when her fingertips grazed the bare skin of his chest. She flattened her palm over his heart.

He felt good.

When her breathing at last returned to normal, she pulled away from him. She searched his eyes—for what, she was still unsure—but she was grateful for the oversized moon tonight that allowed her to see him so clearly.

Rafe cleared his throat.

"I heard you screaming and couldn't stay away."

Also by KELLI ANN MORGAN

# THE RANCHER
## REDBOURNE SERIES BOOK ONE
## COLE'S STORY

Available from Inspire Books

# the Bounty Hunter

## REDBOURNE SERIES BOOK TWO
### RAFE'S STORY

# KELLI ANN MORGAN

*inspire books*

Inspire Books
A Division of Inspire Creative Services
937 West 1350 North, Clinton, Utah 84015, USA

THE BOUNTY HUNTER

An Inspire Book published by arrangement with the author

First Inspire Books paperback edition March 2013

ISBN-13: 978-1-939049-04-9
ISBN-10: 1-939049-04-0

Printed in the United States of America

# PRAISE FOR THE NOVELS OF AMAZON BESTSELLING AUTHOR

# KELLI ANN MORGAN

"What a great read. The Bounty Hunter draws you in and doesn't let go until the last page! Romances are not usually my thing, but I definitely have to make an exception."

—*David Perry*

"Kelli Ann Morgan paints a wonderful picture of the Old West!"

—*RaeAnne Thayne,*
*USA TODAY bestselling author* on *The Rancher*

"The Bounty Hunter swept me off my feet and into the saddle. I'd ride with a Redbourne any day."

—*Morgan Grant*

"A fun, classic story of a hero coming to the rescue of a heroine you can't help but love. Kelli Ann manages to keep us guessing..."

—*Kimberly Yamashita*

"This was such a fun book. The heroine reminded me of my daughter when she was young—falling and being embarrassed. It made me laugh. Lots of twists and turns. Thanks, Kelli Ann for another great book."

—*Janene Morgan*

# ACKNOWLEDGEMENTS

Every book has many people behind the scenes who help to make it successful. I am very grateful to all of those who've made this journey possible...

To my wonderful fans who constantly inspire me to push forward, dream big, and to enjoy every step of the way.

To my amazing beta readers, Morgan, Dave, Kim, Janene, and Connie who were such an invaluable part of the experience. Thank you for all of your insight and wisdom. You're the best!

To my son, Noah, who likes to pretend he's the hero in my books. You are my own little hero, kiddo, and I love you!

To my aunts, LouJean, Raeleen, Kathy, and Janet for always being so excited to hear about each new book,you're your support, and for always checking in on me.

To my mother-in-law, Janene, and my sisters-in-law, Kim and Jen, for spending hours with me working out the perfect blurbs and tags. You guys rock!

And as always to my wonderful, creative, talented, and supportive husband who has spent countless hours with me talking through plotlines, proofreading, making dinner, doing laundry, and whatever else it has taken to make sure I could have the time to write, edit, design, format, and whatever else it has been needed to get me to this point. And for loving me amidst the chaos that is my busy life.

*As always,*
*to Grant, the incredible and handsome hero in my own love story,*
*and to Noah, my little hero in the making. I love you!*

REDBOURNE SERIES BOOK TWO
RAFE'S STORY

# CHAPTER ONE

*Colorado, Early May, 1876*

"Can we trust him, Father?" Tayla Hawthorne pulled back sheer window coverings to peer at the man who'd provided refuge for her and her father when they'd fled England.

Adrien Longhurst strode through the manor garden at his leisure, his graying hair combed to perfection and his slight limp compensated by an ivory handled cane.

"We have no other choice, Tayla. Besides, if the Redbournes trust him, so will we." Stuart Hawthorne looked up over round spectacles at rest halfway down his nose. "Come away from the window and play for me." He motioned to the beautiful mahogany Steinway situated in the middle of the grand room.

Tayla glanced once more through the window, down at her benefactor, and although she could not shake the feeling something was amiss, she moved to the piano. She set herself in front of the floral padded bench and sat to play.

The music of Paganini always seemed to calm her father. She glanced up to find his chin lifted, his eyes closed, and his head swaying back and forth in short concise movements as if he were conducting a live orchestra. Tayla smiled.

Her life in England seemed a distant memory. Sitting here in the middle of a nearly empty ballroom made her realize just how much she missed it.

A loud splintering crash sounded in the hallway. Her fingers abruptly left the keys and Tayla glanced toward the room's entrance. Two men with guns burst through the closed salon doors. She pushed against the piano and stood up. Her father was also on his feet in an instant.

"What is the meaning of th—"

"Shut up, old man." One of the men with a straggly brown beard pushed at her father's chest. He fell hard against his overstuffed chair.

Tayla gasped and started toward him.

"Stay put there, little one or you'll find a bullet in yer head and his," the man threatened.

The other bloke, the shorter of the two, crossed the room and stopped on the opposite side of the piano. He leaned back to assess her, his belly protruding grotesquely from above his belt. He stared at her for a moment, his eyes roaming her body from top to bottom. His leering smile revealed several missing teeth.

Tayla clenched her jaw, but did not take her eyes from the man's face. How dare he look at her in such a way. Indignation would serve her far better than the fear that lay just beneath the surface.

He whistled and pouted his lips. "Lookie here, Jonas. 'Pears we got us a perty one to boot."

The bearded man joined his cohort and Tayla took a step backward, the piano bench obstructing a full retreat. She dared a quick glance at her father, who now reached for a small ornate box on the shelf just behind his head.

*His pistol.*

He kept his old firearm in that box and her mind raced to think of anything she could do to distract the two lumbering men from turning back toward her father.

"How did you get in here?" Tayla had often felt like a prisoner, living behind the dank dark walls of the manor, and the fact that someone could get in so easily astonished her.

"What matters is that we get what we come for," the tall one countered.

She had to adjust her tactics.

"What can we do for you, gentleman?" The last word left a disdainful taste in her mouth.

"We come to escort ya to the ball, ma'am."

Each man snorted in turn and exchanged sinister looks as if to laugh at some joke between them.

She had to keep them talking.

"I'm afraid I already have a date, but I am sure that we can find two eligible men such as you, suitable matches." Tayla did everything she could to keep her voice even.

The sound of the pistol's box scratching against the shelf sent panic to her chest. Both men jerked toward the noise. She dashed from behind the piano and placed her hand on the thin man's arm, the one who'd pushed her father into the chair.

"Especially you, handsome. I may have to reconsider my choice of suitors." She gagged. Her words were brazen she knew, but she had to give her father time to pull the weapon.

The man, whose arm she touched, raised a menacing brow. The fierce look in his eyes, as his gaze bore into hers, caused her to take a step back. Fear pressed her heart to beat faster. The other man, she'd heard called Jonas, made up the distance between them and reached for her waist, pulling her tightly against his thick belly.

The stench of stale whiskey and old cigars offended her nostrils and she twisted away from him.

"No time for that, Jonas," the first man spat. Then, he turned to Tayla. "Where is it, darlin'?" He took two steps toward her—his face mere inches from hers. His stale breath singed the hairs in her nose.

"Where is...what?" she asked with feigned innocence. She resisted the urge to glance at the black wrought iron vent just to the side of her father's chair where a very beautiful, locked metal box rested.

"Don't play stupid with me, girl. Our orders are *you* or the music box. If you don't give us what we've come for—we take you."

Tayla's eyebrows scrunched together.

*What music box?*

It took a moment for his words to sink in. These men weren't just a couple of thugs looking to steal from Mr. Longhurst or to take the only treasures she'd brought from home. They were there for her.

*Impossible.* He couldn't have found her.

"Come on, Lester. Longhurst will have finished his walk. We should git."

"The box?" His voice was cold.

"I assure you, I do not know—"

Lester grabbed a hold of Tayla's arm and pulled her down to her knees. Sharp pain travelled up her leg causing an involuntary moan to escape. He glanced backward toward her father. Tayla held her breath. When she saw that he had effectively hidden his box beneath a quilt to the side of his lap, she took in a deep gulp of air.

Tayla attempted to stand, but Lester pushed against her shoulders and quickly retrieved a ball of cloth from his jacket pocket. He shoved it into her mouth, then putting his knee into her back, he pulled the handkerchief from around his neck and tied it around her head to keep the balled cloth in place.

She stretched her neck and pushed with her tongue in hopes to calm the gag reflex that resulted from the foreign obstruction filling her throat. It tasted of rancid oil and sweat and a wave of nausea threatened. She turned her focus to the man now handing his conspirator a tightly bound length of cloth.

"Make it nice and tight," he said, making his way around the room tossing over couch cushions, lifting the lid on the piano bench, and scanning the walls in search of something.

Tayla's eyes flitted toward her father and then back to the man intent on tying her hands. It wouldn't be long now. Her father was an excellent marksman.

*Please just focus on me,* she pleaded silently as she closed her eyes for a brief moment. Jonas pulled tighter on her gag, forcing her eyes to open.

Lester stopped his scrutiny of the parlor. His eyes had

become dark and menacing. She followed his gaze to her father. She tried to scream, but the cloth blocked any hope of being heard. She struggled against her restraints in attempt to stand, to make any kind of noise. Her father had pulled the pistol from its resting place. From his position on the couch, he took aim.

All amusement left Lester's face. A slight movement of his arm as it crossed his body drew her attention. His hand wrapped around the butt of the gun tucked snugly in his belt. Before Tayla could grasp what was happening, the man pulled the revolver from its position, straightened his arm toward her father, and without the slightest hesitation, fired.

"*No.*" The scream that sounded in her head was deafening. She writhed fiercely, pushing herself to her feet.

*Father.*

Without so much as a second glance, each assailant took her by an arm. She kicked at them, shaking her head violently, desperately trying to free herself. She stopped long enough to watch her father open his mouth as if to gasp for breath, then he fell limp against the back of the chair. Blood gushed from his chest.

She had to get to him. Had to do something.

"Watcha go and do that fer? Now we'll hafta fight our way out," Jonas whined through his teeth.

The men attempted to bind her feet, but she flailed about wildly, her booted foot knocking Jonas in the jaw.

"Blast it all, Lester. Now I'm bleedin'!" Jonas dropped her feet and dabbed at the blood trickling from the corner of his mouth.

Tayla wriggled from Lester's remaining grasp and lunged forward toward her father. The man reached out, caught her hard by the arm, and swung her around to face him. He dug his fingers into the sides of her face, contorting her mouth into a pucker.

She was forced to look into eyes that betrayed no conscience.

"The boss wants her alive, Lester," Jonas warned. "We must deliver her to Lord Darington in one piece."

Lester let go, albeit reluctantly.

Jonas seized her upper arm in a fierce hold and hoisted her off the ground and over his shoulder before he pushed through the salon doors.

Darington? He *had* found her and now her father was paying the price for her naivety. She reached her bound hands up to where the locket rested beneath her dress and fingered the intricate pattern. How had she not known who he was? What he was capable of?

Tayla pounded on the man's back and tried to kick her feet, but his grip on her legs was too strong. Her heart had already been lost to Dare's bitter betrayal and now, she feared following the seeping trail of blood with her eyes, so had her father. *Live Papa,* she silently willed him. *Live.*

*Silver Falls, Colorado*

"Just give me the baby."

Rafe Redbourne held out his arms as he took a solid step toward the man whose wicked grin spread across his face.

"Nice and slow," Rafe added.

"Stay right where you are, bounty hunter." The man winced at the obvious pain in his side, but he held the child tight to his chest. "You aren't getting your hands on her anytime soon." He leaned up against the back of the overstuffed chair closest to the large stone fireplace.

"Cole!" Abby McCallister Redbourne walked into the room, placed a hand on her husband's arm, and stood up on her tip toes to place a light kiss on his cheek, "don't you think you should let your brother hold his newest niece before he heads out in the morning to catch our preacher?"

Rafe smiled at the short exchange between his youngest brother and his spirited bride—so glad it wasn't him all whooped in love. They'd been through a lot over the past few weeks, discovering the preacher who'd married them hadn't been a real preacher at all, but Rafe's most recent bounty. Then, Cole had gone and gotten himself shot protecting Abby from a crazy woman with a vendetta against their family.

Cole loved his wife. Rafe could see it in his eyes.

He'd tried it once—courting, getting betrothed, the whole bit. Except for the actual marrying part.

*No thank you!*

Music carried in from the large family room followed by the sound of multiple chairs being dragged across the wooden floor. Hannah, his sister, loved to play games and Rafe guessed that she had selected musical chairs for the evening's entertainment.

"Who's your favorite uncle?" Cole scrunched up his nose and wiggled his face back and forth in front of the baby.

A wee little cry erupted from the white and yellow bundle in Cole's arms. From the sheer look of panic on his brother's face, Rafe had a feeling that he would now relinquish his hold on little Eliza Jane.

"That would be Uncle Rafe," he said with a satisfied grin, extending his arms.

Abby laughed as she took the little girl from Cole. Just as she was handing her over to Rafe, Leah Redbourne, their mother, whisked his niece away into the family room. Rafe had always sworn that his mother had ears like a bat. One little whimper from the first grandbaby to be a girl, Grandma appeared out of nowhere to make everything okay.

Rafe threw his hands up in the air with a chuckle and followed Cole and Abby into the commotion.

Jameson, his father, stood in the corner of the room with a fiddle on his shoulder and his foot tapping to the lively rhythm his fingers produced. Musical chairs it was.

Rafe loved Hannah's rules. It was not allowed to simply walk around the edges of the chairs, but everyone had to dance along the circle to the beat of the music, with or without a partner. It kept everyone on their toes. Literally.

He had only been in Silver Falls for a couple of weeks, but had quickly been introduced to the town's population—

especially the girls. Ms. Patterson, the owner of the mercantile, had made sure of that. Ladies of all ages seemed to always stare at him and his brothers and giggle behind raised hands. He guessed it was because they were all over six feet tall and none too wiry.

Rafe was glad there wasn't a gaggle of young women at the SilverHawk tonight. He wanted to spend the last evening here with his family. Those who didn't live here in Colorado would be heading out in the morning. His parents and his sister, along with her husband, Eli, and their new baby, would be travelling back to the Redbourne Ranch in Kansas, while he would resume his search for Harrison Beckett—his runaway bounty.

When everyone started clapping to the music, Rafe broke into a grin and jumped into the circle, grabbing Abby's raven-haired friend, Lily, by the hand and promenading to the left.

They all laughed. When the music stopped, chaos ensued as they all scrambled to find an empty seat.

Thunk.

Rafe found himself sitting on the floor, looking up at his wide eyed dancing partner sitting, with feigned innocence, on 'his' chair. He shook his head, trying to keep the smile from cracking onto his face.

Raine, his eldest brother, burst out with a loud guffaw and reached down to offer a hand. "It's always the little ones you have to watch out for." He winked at Lily, who winked back.

Rafe had to get out of Silver Falls. Something of love was in the air and he wanted no part of it. He still had a bounty to catch. He'd been in one place way too long and it was time to get moving.

The music started again. Rafe stepped outside and took a deep breath. The smell of rain still lingered in the air, but there was no cloud cover tonight. He rested his arm on the porch pillar and looked out at the new barn he'd helped raise.

"It's been eight years." Raine snapped him away from his thoughts. His brother patted him on the shoulder and squeezed. "How long are you going to put your dreams on hold because of her?"

Rafe hated how Raine always seemed to know what was bothering him.

"That was a long time ago." Rafe folded his arms. "I don't even think about it anymore."

Raine snorted.

Silence.

A rider approached and both Raine and Rafe walked to the bottom of the porch steps.

"I'm looking for a Rafe Redbourne. I was told I would find him here." The older gentleman dismounted.

Rafe narrowed his eyes at the man. No one knew he was here. At least, he hadn't told anyone.

"That'd be me." Rafe stepped forward.

The man held out a telegram. "The wife took this message earlier today. Sorry I couldn't get it delivered until now. Said it was important."

Rafe took the paper from the older bespectacled man.

*Levi.*

Their brother had left Silver Falls shortly after Cole and Abby's real wedding to do business for the railroad in Cheyenne and had spotted the fake preacher shaking hands with the mayor of a small town just outside of the city.

"What does it say?" Raine inquired.

As Rafe re-read the message, a sense of urgency welled up inside of him. He wasn't going to wait until morning to leave. He had to get to Tumbleweed, Wyoming.

"Levi found the preacher."

Upon further inquiry, Levi had discovered that the man had been offered a job as schoolmaster in a little town just a few miles from there. He'd sent word immediately.

Rafe tipped his hat to the messenger and headed to the bunkhouse.

"You can't be seriously going after him tonight?' Raine grabbed a hold of his arm and spun him around.

"I have a job to do," Rafe said, feeling a twinge of guilt at having allowed himself to linger with his family this long.

Laughter permeated the courtyard as the party moved

outdoors. As if sensing the moment of tension between brothers, Hannah moved between them, little Eliza Jane in her arms and put an arm around Rafe with a tight squeeze about the waist.

"I think she wants her Uncle Rafe now," she said as she moved the little girl seamlessly into his arms.

He looked down into the wide, searching eyes looking back at him.

He would leave at first light.

Rafe was grateful this job was hired work and wasn't a typical bounty. There was no one else to compete for Beckett's capture and that had afforded Rafe time. But now, time was up.

Harrison Beckett was wanted for kidnapping a British Duke's intended. From what he'd seen, the man was not travelling with any woman and that begged the question—what had happened to her?

*Somewhere Between the Colorado and Wyoming Borders*

Tayla had been sitting on a horse's rump for what felt like hours. After they had removed her blindfold, she'd done a quick assessment of her surroundings, hoping for any glimmer of recognition.

Nothing.

Except for the fact that they seemed to be moving west, she had no idea where they were.

Her wrists, worn red and swollen from the rope binding, had passed aching and now throbbed with want of release. Had she been in this spot under other circumstances she may have actually enjoyed watching how the colors danced in the sky with the setting sun, but now was not the time. She'd been dragged along with Dare's thugs for nearly two days. She was tired and in desperate need of a decent bed.

There had been a few times over the last few days when she

could almost make out what the men in front of her were talking about, but when she'd gotten within hearing distance they'd stopped all serious conversation and resumed taunting her with vile threats.

The only ones who had known where she and her father had been given refuge were William Redbourne and the rest of her family—her mother and sister. But somehow, Dare had figured out where they'd gone and had sent these men to drag her back to him.

He'd been such a devoted suitor and loving fiancé that she hadn't been prepared for his deceit. An imposter who would kill to protect his secret, Dare was not the man she'd believed she'd once loved.

No, Lord Darington was no saint. If anything, he was the devil himself, darkly handsome and devilishly enticing...enough to enable him to strike at will.

"We may just have to hole up here for the night."

Tayla saw the leering smile cross Lester's face before he dismounted and turned to lead both his horse and Tayla's to the riverside for water. The moon was bigger than usual. It sat lower in the sky and offered a good amount of light. She noted that her reins, no longer wrapped around Lester's saddle horn, dangled haphazardly at the horse's side. Lester had bent down onto one knee and cupped his hands into the current of water for a drink.

She had to think of something, and fast. The thought of either man touching her caused a wave of nausea to torment her abdomen and an eerie shiver of disgust trickled through her. Her skin puckered under the chill that had stealthily settled around them.

"Come on, Les, cain't be much more'n an hour or so ride ta Cheyenne. We can git some sleep in a real bed and catch the train tomorrah." The whine in Jonas's voice grated in her head and she rolled her eyes.

"Nah, this here looks like a might perty place. We can get us a fire started and I'm sure this one we'll keep us nice and warm, if we cuddle up real good and tight."

"Lord Darington gave strict orders that she not be touched."

"Eh, what he don't know won't hurt him." Lester walked back to her horse and ran his hand up the hem of her dress over her calf and ankle. "And, you wouldn't go sayin' nothin', would ya, darlin'?"

Tayla kicked out as hard as she could, catching Lester in the chin and sending him sprawling backward. Pain shot through her foot where bone had met bone and it stung from the impact. She wasn't surprised when he whipped back around and faced her with blood oozing thickly from his lip.

"You'll pay for that, girly," he snarled.

Tayla lifted her chin defiantly and darted a glance at the other man when a gun cocked.

"Leave her be, Lester, or you'll be joining her pa in the underworld."

Lester stopped short, spat blood into the dirt, and jerked away from her in a huff.

Emptiness crowded everything else out of her heart at Jonas's words. Her father had come to America to protect her from an evil man, only to die defending her.

"Fine, but we're not moving from this spot tonight," he called over his shoulder as he removed a bedroll from the back of his horse. "We'll start again at daybreak and catch the rails early." His words—forceful and bitter—seemed final and Jonas put his revolver back into its holster and he dismounted.

After leading his horse to the creek and tying the reins to a tree branch, Jonas bent down to the water to fill his canteen. It was now or not at all. Slowly she reached down the right side of her skittish paint pony and was able to pull the reins into her hands. Without much warning she dug her heels as hard as she could into the horse's flanks and tore downstream.

Cussing and yelling ensued and Tayla could envision the chaos of the two men scrambling to re-saddle their horses and smiled a little. She focused her head forward and kept the horse moving as fast as she could. She was grateful for the light the full moon brought with it.

Several times she had to duck away from low hanging branches and on more than one occasion received scrapes and lashes from the whip-like limbs cutting at her cold skin.

After what felt like hours, the rush of her escape started to dwindle and fatigue began to set in. She stayed as close to the river's edge as she dared, but neither she nor her mount would last much longer at this pace. She couldn't hear the men chasing her any longer, but didn't dare stop for long.

Tayla came upon a small clearing in the brush. Her wrists were now sticky with blood and worn raw from her bindings. The quiet hum of the water rushing against the rocks soothed her weary mind and she hoped that its coolness would soothe her aching arms and hands. She dismounted.

As she made her way to the water's edge, it appeared to have a drop off down to the river that was fairly steep, but she desperately needed something to drink and she knew the horse needed watering too.

"Ouch." While looking for a place to climb down to the edge, she hit her shin against a wooden plank protruding from something in the shadows on the riverbank. It looked like a small boat of some sort, but without the light of day, there was no way to see if it was sturdy or safe enough to actually use on the water.

Before she could get a closer look, the crack of a branch sounded behind her. She whipped around to find the paint horse's nose mere inches from her face. Startled, Tayla slipped on the dew-wet grassy bank and her feet betrayed her, sending her sprawling backward into the craft and she caught the back of her head on the bow. Her head flooded with warmth and she realized, as everything started to go black around her, that the boat had dislodged from the bank and had moved into the rush of the river's flow.

# CHAPTER TWO

*Tumbleweed, Wyoming Territory*

"Impersonating a preacher wasn't enough for you?" Rafe Redbourne leaned back against the chair and put his feet on the student desk in front of him.

The man facing the blackboard froze, his arm in midair with chalk resting between his fingertips.

"Now you're a teachin' school to boot." Rafe exaggerated a drawl. "This town must be real desperate to hire the likes of you." He had chased this bounty through three territories and his patience had grown thin. It was past time to deliver.

Rafe watched the tall, blond man from beneath the rim of the Stetson pulled low on his forehead. He rested his hands on the pearl grips of his matching Red Jacket revolvers at his sides and waited for any sign the man would run again.

The door to the left of the blackboard creaked open and a small boy, who couldn't have been a day older than seven, appeared. His patched denims and worn shirt were accented by his unkempt hair and dirt smudged face.

"Mr. Davenport, sir?" The child tugged at the back of Harrison's coat with timid determination.

The new teacher darted a meaningful glance at Rafe, then dropped on his haunches to meet the young boy at eye level.

"What is it, Jimmy?" Harrison's voice seemed kind— something that surprised Rafe. He'd half expected the Brit to grab the kid and use him as a shield as he made an escape.

"You all right, Mr. Davenport?" he asked. "You done sweatin' like a horse," he finished, bewilderment touching his young features.

Harrison pulled a handkerchief from his pocket and dabbed at his forehead. With a reaffirming smile he reached out to touch the boy on the shoulder. "I'm fine, son. I've just been standing a bit too close to the stove this afternoon."

The boy appeared satisfied by Harrison's answer and cleared his throat. His eyes wandered, then fleetingly met his teacher's.

Harrison Beckett returned the handkerchief to the pocket in his trousers and dared a quick glance at Rafe. "What is it you needed to tell me, son?"

Rafe held his breath, slowly lowered his feet from the desk—so as not to alarm the kid—and leaned forward in the seat. His hands remained steady at his sides. This runner would not get away from him this time.

"My pa says we have to get the rest of the field plowed 'fore nightfall, and I can't stay at school," the crack in the child's voice unmistakable. He kicked the toe of his shoe into the dusty wooden floor.

"That's all right, Jimmy." Harrison squeezed the boy's upper arms with reassurance. "Would you like me to send you home with a slate and primer?" he asked the youngster.

Jimmy looked up immediately and met his teacher's eyes with unmasked eagerness.

Rafe shifted uncomfortably in his seat. The creaking noise alerted the youth to his presence and he was met with wide eyed trepidation.

"It's okay, Jimmy," Harrison said as he pulled a slate from the pile on his desk. "Mr. Redbourne is a lawman. There's no need to be frightened. You run along home now." He handed the boy the slate, patted him on the top of the head, and walked him to the door.

Rafe stood.

The sham of a teacher paused at the door, facing the children in the yard.

"I'm tired of running, Mr. Redbourne. I just find it better than the alternative." Harrison leaned against the doorframe and stared outside for a few silent moments.

"I didn't do what they say, you know." He turned around, his hands out, palms up.

Rafe didn't want to hear it. He had been doing this for long enough that he'd heard everything.

"I want your help."

Except that.

"If I tell you the whole truth, will you listen?"

Rafe considered himself a reasonable man. "We can talk," he tugged on his hat, "once I get you over to the jail."

Harrison nodded.

A loud scream came from outside and instinctively Rafe shot to the side of the small, dusty window at the side of the classroom and jerked his head forward only long enough to scan the town boardwalk and the children's play area. His focus fell on two scroungy men in front of the mercantile. One of them had his arm wrapped hastily around a plump woman, holding her from behind while she struggled against his grasp. The other was laughing, his gun drawn.

Rafe glanced at Beckett, who had joined him on the opposite side of the window.

"What is it?" he asked.

"Recognize either of those two men?"

Beckett darted a glance out the window.

"Can't say I've ever seen them before. This is a small town. They're not from Tumbleweed."

Rafe cursed himself.

"Bounty hunters?" Harrison asked with disbelieving accusation.

"Not unless there are other criminals living in town."

Harrison's brows scrunched together.

"Stay here." Rafe took a step toward the door, then paused and turned to look Harrison directly in the eyes. "If you run—pray I never find you."

Harrison nodded his acknowledgement of Rafe's warning.

The town had gone quiet. Even the children had stopped their game of stick ball and watched as one gunman pulled his weapon and fired it into the air.

"I know you're all hidin' her somewhere. We jist want the girl and we'll be on our way."

"Maybe after a little fun, first." The second man chimed in, laughing. He spat into the ground and then leaned in to kiss the struggling woman on the neck.

"Hey, mister." The young boy, Jimmy, who'd had been in the school just moments before, stepped forward and called out bravely to the man.

Rafe's heart sank.

"You'd better leave us alone 'n go back to wherever it is ya come from, 'cause there's a great big lawman inside that there school. I bet he'd love to lock up a couple a scallywags like you."

Rafe snorted at the youth's reference to his size.

The man looked up and squinted his eyes at the kid.

Rafe thrust open the door, hands at his sides at the ready, and stepped out into the courtyard before the men could react to young Jimmy's words.

Where was the sheriff in this blasted town anyway?

"You boys aren't looking for any trouble, now are ya?"

Rafe's head shot to the direction of the female voice.

The sheriff?

The woman leaned against a support column on the porch of the town barber. Her hat was pulled low on her head and she chewed on a long strand of yellow grass. She pulled her duster back and tucked it behind the gun at her side.

A woman sheriff.

He'd heard of one or two, but had never seen one in action. He just hoped she was as good as she played.

Rafe had seen a lot of bad in his line of work, but nothing made him angrier than cowards who preyed on the innocent.

"Let the lady go." Rafe's deep voice resounded in his throat and all eyes turned to him.

The stout man who still stood on the dirt street took aim just a little too late. Rafe drew and fired, hitting his target perfectly on the fleshy part of the man's trigger hand. The gun fell.

"Blast it all, Lester." The hurt man dropped to his knees on the ground in a whimper, clutching his bloody hand into his chest.

Rafe immediately re-cocked the gun and pointed it in Lester's direction.

The lean, wiry man on the boardwalk pulled the woman he manhandled closer into him as if to protect himself from Rafe's wrath. His leer revealed several missing teeth.

Rafe took deliberate steps toward the men, his steely gaze never leaving their intended target.

"Now," he said calmly, but the warning firm and evident.

He took aim directly at the woman's captor. He reached down to the paunchy man in the dirt and grabbed him by the shirt collar, lifting him to his feet, his eyes still fixed on the man on the boardwalk.

The sheriff pushed herself away from her perch and joined him on the street.

"You must be the lawman Jimmy's been jabbering about."

Rafe nodded.

"Sheriff Jess Mallory," she said sticking her hand out in a greeting.

Rafe didn't take his eyes of the man on the boardwalk. She was making small talk. Now?

"Rafe Redbourne," he said, ignoring the extended hand.

The man's eyes grew wider, his eyebrows lifted, as a wild flicker of recognition crossed his features. He stood up taller and a chilling calm passed over him.

"You know me," Rafe stated, feeling confident in his assessment.

Lester spit on the dirt.

"What do you want in my town?" Sheriff Mallory asked the man in Rafe's grasp.

Rafe spoke quietly close to the injured man's ear. "The lady asked you a question."

"We're just lookin' for something we lost is all."

"And you thought you would find it here?" The sheriff rested her hand on the butt of her gun. "I've never seen you before. How is it you lost something in my town?"

"Who are you?" Rafe asked, eyes still firm on the man on the boardwalk. Something just didn't sit right with him and he wondered if he'd be collecting more than one bounty today.

"What's your name?" he asked again, tightening his grasp on the man's shirt.

"Nobody. We ain't nobody." His voice was all a quiver and the whiny intonations grated on Rafe's already taught nerves.

"I will not ask again." Rafe's voice was low and calculated as he spoke with a tightened jaw. He pushed the man away from him and drew his second weapon. With one revolver aimed directly at him, he pulled back the hammer and the gun cocked.

"Jonas," the man began to stutter, "I-I-I'm Jo—onas, Mr. Redbourne."

"I wouldn't," Rafe warned as the revolver in his other hand refocused on Lester, who'd tried to aim around the woman he held.

The sheriff raised a rifle and pointed it at Lester.

"You *do* know me."

"Only by reputation."

"Jimmy," Rafe called loudly, his gaze still firm on Jonas.

The young boy ran up to his side and leaned into him a bit. "Yes, Mr. Lawman, sir?"

Rafe smiled to himself at the thought of how just a few minutes ago this same boy had been frightened of him and was now leaning on him as a protector.

"You got a doctor in this town?"

"Yes, sir."

"Go fetch him. This man's hand will need some attention."

"Yes, sir, Mr. Lawman, sir."

The boy's shoes thudded down the boardwalk and Rafe smiled inwardly at the kid's sudden enthusiasm. He turned to say something to the sheriff, but she was gone. With a brief scan of the surrounding buildings he saw her duck behind the livery and out of sight.

He smiled. She was good. It had been a long time since someone was able to sneak away without him noticing.

"I'll shoot her, Redbourne. I swear. Don't ya take another step."

"I don't think you'll shoot her, Lester," he advanced another pace toward the man, "because you wouldn't live to see her hit the ground. You seem to be a smart man. I know you wouldn't want that now, would you?"

Lester pulled the frightened woman to the left and then back in between him and Rafe, his pistol still aimed at the side of her neck, his other arm crushing the woman just beneath her breasts.

"Jes' let us move along. We wasn't gonna hurt nobody, see? We'll be on our way." Lester's sudden change in speech told Rafe the man was getting itchy and that worried him.

"I don't think this town has what we're lookin' fer anyways," he said, darting his eyes from one side of the town to the other.

"See now, I was ready to do that before Jonas here decided to shoot. That just put me in a bad mood. I don't take well to being shot at. Or to cowards like you who use innocent women as shields." Rafe stepped forward yet again, eyebrow cocked, eyes squinted. "How about you let the lady go...and I won't kill you?"

Lester peered at him from behind the woman.

"Let. Her. Go." Rafe was tired, his patience already worn through.

"Come on, Les. I'm bleedin' pretty good," Jonas pleaded.

"You heard the man, Les." Rafe paused for a moment. "He's going to need that doctor here pretty soon, by the way, if he wants to keep that hand.

"And, you'll let us go?"

"I said I won't kill you, Lester."

"I know youse a man a yer word, Mr. Redbourne. No funny business now." Lester shoved the woman away from him onto the dirt street and shook his head and body as if to straighten out his clothing.

The sheriff stepped out of the mercantile, gun drawn, and placed it close to the back of Lester's head behind his ear.

The sheriff looked up at Rafe and he tipped his hat.

She was good. And pretty too.

Rafe waved his revolver in the direction of the jail.

"After you," he said to Jonas.

The inside of the jail was even smaller than what it looked from the outside. He waited for the sheriff to unlock the cell and then he shoved both Jonas and Lester into the small space.

"Sheriff Mallory," Rafe turned to face her and smiled.

"Jess, please," she asked told him as she sat down in her chair behind the desk.

"Jess," he started again, "Jonas is going to need some attention to that hand. Do you all have a doctor here in Tumbleweed?"

"I think he's out delivering May Henry's baby, but he should be back afore nightfall."

Rafe cursed under his breath. Jonas's hand couldn't wait that long without attention. Nearly three years in medical school had given Rafe the knowhow. He knew it was selfish to make him wait, but Jonas had attempted to shoot him after all. He looked up at the man whose color had started to drain from his face.

Rafe shook his head and turned on his heel without a word.

Lexa was tied to a hitching post in front of the small telegraph office. Rafe reached into his saddle bags and retrieved a small leather bag that he always carried with him. He quickly returned to the jailhouse.

"Would you kindly open the cell, ma'am?" he asked Jess. She raised a brow at him, but stood to comply.

Rafe motioned for Jonas to come out, but when he stood up, all color drained from his face and he fell backward against Lester, effectively pinning him between the bunk and the wall.

Jonas was not a small man.

Rafe rushed inside.

"You stay put," he barked at Lester who looked as if he might take advantage of an open jail cell. Rafe quickly opened his bag where he kept a few medical supplies.

"Jess, could I get some rags and clean water?" he asked over his shoulder.

She didn't say anything, but the door clacked against its frame.

He pulled out a small jar of a white sticky poultice, made up of a variety of wild herbs and liniment.

Jess returned with a bucket of water and a few bar towels he guessed she'd gotten from the saloon next door. She also handed him a bottle of whiskey.

"Thought you might could use a drink," she said with a nervous smile and scrunched shoulders.

Rafe had learned what happened to his senses a long time ago whenever he consumed the foul liquid and had vowed never to let anything like that cloud his judgment or his clarity again.

"Thank you." He nodded and uncorked the bottle. He poured the liquor over Jonas's hand and then spread his poultice over the fleshy wound and quickly finished by wrapping it tightly with a cotton bandage from his bag.

"That should do for now," he said, looking up at Lester. He pulled Jonas's face into his hands and smacked his cheek.

He didn't rouse.

Rafe stuck his head against Jonas's chest, drawing one of his weapons at the same time.

There was still a heartbeat.

Lester's scowl deepened when Rafe's gun pushed a little harder into the fleshy part of his jaw beneath his chin.

"Why don't you just hand over that knife, Lester, and you may still live to tell about this little incident."

Reluctantly, Lester handed him a short black handled blade.

Rafe pulled his gun back and handed the dagger to Jess. "Those are some very interesting buttons you have on that vest there, Lester." The British crown resting on an eagled crest seemed out of place on a thug like Lester. "I don't know that I've ever seen any quite like them around here," he said, waving some smelling salts beneath Jonas's nose.

Jonas sucked in a startled gasp of air. His eyes opened

wildly as his gaze darted around the small cell. With the help of
Lester's impatient shove, Jonas pulled himself into a sitting
position.

"What's it to ya?" Lester spat the question, never taking his
eyes off of Rafe.

Rafe shrugged and stood up. "You're missing one." He
turned to Jess. "I've done what I can for now." He closed his
small leather bag and walked out of the cell.

"You're not going to cause the lady any more trouble, now
are you fellas?" he said, turning back to the two ruffians. He
didn't wait for an answer.

There was no way he was going to lock up Harrison Beckett
in the same cell as these two.

"This the only lockup you have in town?" Rafe asked
Sheriff Mallory.

"You plannin' on arrestin' somebody else today?"

Rafe pulled the wanted poster out of his pocket and handed
it to her. "I'm afraid I will be taking Harrison Beckett into my
custody."

The sheriff twisted her head and jutted out her ear as if
she'd missed something he'd said.

"I think you know him as Mr. Davenport."

"The new teacher?"

Rafe nodded.

"Well, I'll be hornswoggled." She sat down in her chair,
leaned back on two legs, and thought for a moment. "Micky
Jenkins, up the road, has an empty storm cellar we can keep
these two in for the night. You need longer than that?"

"No, ma'am. One night'll do mighty fine. Thank you."

# CHAPTER THREE

*Northern Colorado*

"It's about time I saw those pretty green eyes of yours. You gave us quite a scare." A woman with flaming red hair and a warm smile sat on the end of the bed. "That was quite a knock to your head, honey. How're you feelin'?"

Tayla looked around the cheery yellow room and back to the woman. When she didn't respond, the woman stood up from the bed and threw open the sheer window coverings near the door.

"You just sit there and rest a mite and I'll have Jacob bring you up some breakfast." She paused at the door before leaving. "I'm Maggie, by the way, and I'll be back to check in on you after the morning rush." She disappeared behind the door, leaving Tayla to her thoughts.

She tried to focus. The woman had mentioned a knock to the head, but it was strange that she didn't feel injured. She pulled the sheets away from her and dangled her legs from the bedside. A slight wave of dizziness forced her to grip the edge of the bed to steady herself.

What was this place, and what did Maggie mean by 'the morning rush?'

Tayla gingerly stood up and glanced into the mirror of a small white vanity, tucked in the corner of the quaint little bedroom. When her bare feet stepped off the rug and onto the room's wooden floor planks, a cool shiver worked its way up her body. She briskly scrubbed at her bare arms and walked over to the vanity.

Bandages encircled her head and Tayla reached up to touch them. Her reflection—foreign to her—she pushed at the wrapped material and pulled it off, revealing thick locks of wheat-blond hair.

The wound was not immediately visible. She ran her fingers over her scalp and when she touched a spot just below the crown of her head, she pulled her hand away with a quick intake of breath. It was extremely tender to the touch and had encrusted over as it had begun to heal.

A huge lump rose in her throat and her heart began to race as she tried to remember how she'd been hurt. She couldn't seem to remember anything. Not even her own face.

Nothing.

She looked down at her clothing—a sleeveless flowing nightshift. Nothing was familiar. She looked back into the mirror and just stared at the stranger before her.

On the table sat an intricate ivory handled brush and a bottle of smelling salts. However, her eyes were drawn to a beautiful, square jeweled pendant, lined with deep red gemstones and five short spires that protruded uniquely from the edge.

When she picked it up, the clasp pulled the square up by the corner into a diamond shape and she held it in front of her neck. She drew her eyes away from the dazzling facets of the large center ruby back to her unfamiliar reflection. She sat down on the woven cloth bench and returned the necklace to the vanity top.

A knock sounded on the door. Tayla barely heard it. She couldn't pull away from the image staring back at her from the mirror, but then the loud creek of door hinges startled her and a large, brown bear of a dog barreled into the room with a deep bark. He looked around the room and when he saw her, bounded toward her and sat down—tongue out and tail wagging.

"Bear," a young man of no more than sixteen scolded. He carried a tray of food with him.

"Sorry 'bout that ma'am. Didn't mean to scare ya none." He set the tray down on the bed table.

"Bear, go find Pete," he commanded, and the dog raced off back out the door.

"He loves new people."

Tayla just stared at him.

He nodded his head and turned to leave. "I'll go get some grease and get that fixed." He said pointed at the base of the door. He stopped. "Sure am glad you ain't dead, ma'am."

Her face must have drained of color, because the lad stepped forward as if he would catch her if she fell.

"I'm all right." She tilted her head trying to gain some semblance of those around her, but with no recollection of who he might be. "And you are?"

"Jacob, ma'am. The name's Jacob Miller. I work for Maggie." He shoved his hands into his pockets. "Me and my pa was the ones that found ya in the river. Good thing we found ya when we did too or you'd be... well, you wouldn't be *here*, that's fer sure."

Tayla managed what she hoped would be a warm, sincere smile. "Thank you,… Jacob."

*Breathe*, she had to remind herself. *It's going to be okay.*

"Where *is* here, exactly?" She hated appearing vulnerable.

Jacob stood up a little straighter and announced with pride, "You're at the Smokey Sky Inn. The best bed 'n breakfast this side of the Platte."

"Jaaaacob," a voice called from a distance.

"Coming," he yelled back in two-note syllables over his shoulder. He turned back to face her. "Well, gotta run. Make sure you eat somethin' or Maggie'll have my hide. I'll be back to fix that door." With that, he turned on his heel and ran out the door.

Tayla watched the empty space for a few moments after he left. Her stomach groaned. She glanced over at the food on the nightstand. It felt like it had been weeks since she had eaten anything. The tray was filled with what looked like a first class gourmet meal—bacon, eggs, biscuits with honey, a glass of milk and a small bag of lemon drops. A miniature wreath of flowers and ribbon added a sense of welcome and she smiled a little. She walked over to the side table and sat down on the edge of the bed.

When her stomach grumbled again, she slowly reached out toward the food. The savory scent made her salivate and despite unladylike manners, she shoved a large, slightly crinkled piece of bacon into her mouth and followed it with a quick swig of milk. She sat back on the bed against the wall and pulled the tray of food over her lap in front of her and continued to devour the heavenly meal.

The flakey, buttered biscuit melted on her tongue as she took her first bite. She closed her eyes and pursed her lips. The delectable taste of the food enveloped her in warmth. Her mouth was still quite full when the door opened again. She picked up the folded cloth next to the plate and used it to dab at the corners of her lips.

"Now, that's what I like to see—a woman with a healthy appetite." Maggie smiled as she walked into the room with a simple sage green dress over her arm. "You haven't had anything to eat in days. Glad to see you're up to it."

*Days?*

Tayla finished chewing the food in her mouth and swallowed. "Maggie?"

"Hmmmm?" Maggie responded, her back to Tayla as she hung the dress from a hook in the ceiling.

"What happened?" The tone in Tayla's voice was serious. She needed to know.

Maggie turned around, her forehead scrunched, confused. "I was hoping you could tell us. The Millers found you down by the river, sprawled and unconscious in a little fishing boat that had washed up onto the bank 'bout a mile or so upstream."

Tayla fought hard to recall the incident, but a big black fog had clouded her mind and it wouldn't clear.

"I honestly don't remember."

"Well, your head took a pretty good knock. It'll all be coming back to ya soon, I'm just sure of it." Maggie joined Tayla on the bed. "What's your name, honey?"

Tayla looked into Maggie's pale blue eyes, searching for some hint of recognition. She had no response for the woman. Her past. It was gone.

Maggie narrowed her eyes, but did not take them off Tayla's. After a few moments, she stood and walked over to the vanity. She picked up something from the dressing table and rejoined Tayla on the edge of the bed.

"Maybe this will help, honey." Maggie's outstretched hand held the necklace she had admired earlier. "It was around your neck when Jacob and his pa brought you here."

Tayla reached for the jeweled pendant. When she took it from Maggie, she held it up to the ray of light that shone through the curtains of the bedroom window. The dazzling red gem glittered and sparkled.

Tayla's fingers brushed over the beautiful intricate design and she looked up at Maggie in awe. "This," she started. "This…is mine?"

Maggie nodded.

The necklace was so elegant, so refined. If something this exquisite belonged to her, she had no doubt that there was someone out there, looking for her, even now.

"What's this?" Maggie asked, leaning forward a bit and pointing to a small protruding facet on the side of the necklace.

Tayla brought the pendant in for closer inspection. One of the side jewels had been knocked loose, most likely with recent events. She reached up and when she touched it, the five short spires on the bottom retracted and the catch opened the pendant into a locket. Pictureless.

Curious.

Her eyes trailed the length of the pendant until they reached her wrists, which were chaffed and somewhat bruised. She looked past her obvious injuries into the distance reflection of the vanity. Without an inkling of who she was or what had happened to her, she was faced with a choice.

Fear or hope.

She gripped the necklace tightly in her fingers and pulled it into her chest. There was only one choice.

Hope.

"You said you wanted to talk. I'm listening." Rafe sat down in the sheriff's chair and leaned back far enough that he rested his feet on top of her desk.

"You can let me out of these. I'm not going anywhere." Rafe's captured bounty sat on a thin mattress behind the bars of the particularly small jail cell, his arms extended, revealing the cuffs that adorned his reddening wrists.

"Do you need your hands to talk?"

"Well, no, but—"

"Cole and Abby got married, by the way. Legally, this time—no thanks to you."

Harrison dropped his head. "Your brother's a good man, Mr. Redbourne. I know it was wrong to..." his voice trailed as he fell back against the cell wall. "I'm glad he worked it all out with Abby. They were good together. I don't know that I could face him after all the trouble I caused."

"I'd be more worried about Abby, if I were you." Rafe chuckled to himself as he thought about how his new little sister-in-law would react to the man who'd impersonated a preacher and falsely married her off to his brother.

Harrison groaned.

"We'll stay the night here and head out at first light." Rafe glanced again at the man he'd been tracking for weeks now and wondered if the Brit was truly innocent of the crimes of which Darington had accused him. "You got a horse?" he asked in afterthought.

"Nope. Teacher's don't get paid in advance out here. And I haven't exactly been in a position long enough to acquire one yet, now have I?"

"Guess not."

"I have to tell you, Lord Darington is a very dangerous man. If he's—"

"Excuse me." A young woman behind Rafe cleared her throat, her small voice barely audible over its shaking.

Rafe turned around, dropping his feet to the floor, to find a slip of a girl with plain brown hair and some of the widest and bluest eyes he'd ever seen staring up at him. The dim lamplight accented her youth and he lifted an eyebrow at the basket she held in her hands.

"My mama thought you and Mr. Davenport might want some warm vittles and fresh rhubarb pie."

His stomach groaned in an uninvited response. He hadn't eaten a good home-cooked meal since leaving Silver Falls and both the meat and fruit jerky he carried in his pack were nearly gone. He made a mental note to stop at the general store for food supplies before leaving town in the morning and hoped the folks around here arose early. They'd be leaving just after the sun was up. It had been too long since he'd been home and he reckoned after the payment for this bounty he'd be able to…what? Go home? Settle down? He'd given up on that kind of life a long time ago.

"Why that's mighty kind of your ma. Thank you, Miss…?"

"Dehlia." The young woman lowered her lashes demurely, lifted her shoulders toward her chin and giggled."

"Dehlia," Rafe repeated with a wink and the warmest smile he could muster. He loved women and as long as they understood he wasn't going to settle down and do the marriage thing, they loved him back.

He had grown accustomed to women bringing him food and as soon as folks in small towns like this found out he was a lawman, they generally offered him a decent bed. He wondered if they all would feel the same if they knew he was a bounty hunter and not a marshal or Pinkerton. He brushed away the thought.

Rafe stepped aside and Dehlia treaded into the small jailhouse and set the basket down on the table. She folded the green checkerboard napkins away from the underlying food. The resulting heavenly aroma filled the now crowded building and Rafe's mouth began to water. He peered over the side of the basket and was greeted by a large pot of chicken stew and a half dozen or so hot buttered biscuits.

"It smells delightful, Dehlia. Thank your mother for us, would you." Harrison stood with his cuffed hands holding the bars.

The slight woman bowed her head in polite agreement and started to fill an over-sized tin bowl with the tempting concoction.

Rafe guessed that the whole town had heard about the school master's arrest by now. It wasn't every day that someone in such a respected position was taken into custody—even if he'd only been there a few short days. He was just grateful to be met with foodstuffs instead of pitchforks.

He watched with curiosity while the young woman dished up the remaining food. She glimpsed up at him and then stole a fleeting glance at Harrison. Something wasn't quite right, but he couldn't place the feeling. Maybe she was just sweet on the new teacher.

"Won't you join us, Miss Dehlia? Your mama must be a real good cook. You've been eyeing that pie rather carefully." She jumped back like a frightened little rabbit—her eyes darting between him and Harrison.

It wasn't proper for her to be in the jailhouse alone with two men, but Rafe figured that because the door was open and the whole town could see inside, her reputation would stay intact.

"It's all right little one. We won't tell." Rafe tried to soften his voice to a gentle coaxing. He stepped forward and picked up the knife, cut a small portion of the pie, and held it out to her.

She shook her head. "I'd better run along. Ma's holding my supper for me." She darted another glance at Harrison, then backed out the door and disappeared.

"You hungry, Beckett?"

"Dehlia's mother works for the hotel across the way. In the

restaurant," he said. "I wouldn't pass up her cooking to save my life."

Rafe cocked an eyebrow at this last statement, then narrowed his eyes at the man.

"And the name's not Beckett."

Rafe took the key ring off his belt, unlocked the cell, and passed Harrison a bowl of the steaming stew and a small piece of the pie.

"What do you mean, your name's not Beckett?"

"Thank you." He stared at the food in his hands and looked around the cell. "It's kind of hard to eat with these on," Harrison protested.

"You'll make do," Rafe said, closing the barred door. He turned back to his own bowl, walked behind the worn wooden desk, and sat in the empty sheriff's chair. His feet rested on the top of the desk while he scooped the warm liquid into his mouth with a biscuit.

"Name's not Beckett, huh?" Rafe had mulled over the new information while he finished his supper. "Then just who are you?"

"My name is Harrison Davis."

Rafe barely heard him. One bite of the rhubarb pie and he thought he was in heaven. It was almost as good as his mama's. Almost. Who needed a wife at home when he got this kind of treatment on the road?

"Beckett is my home," Harrison continued. "I grew up on Beckett, a farm just outside of London." He paused. "This is wonderful," he said scooping the last of his stew into his mouth. He closed his eyes.

Rafe shook his head with a bit of a laugh. He set his dish on the desk near his feet and leaned back into the chair, his legs still stretched in front of him. He rested his hands on his full belly. His eyelids felt like lead and his focus started to blur. He tried to process what he was being told, but quite suddenly he wondered if he had trusted the wrong gut.

Pushing through sleepless nights in search of a bounty had become habit and he'd grown accustomed to the bone-tired exhaustion that often accompanied the work. But this was different. This was…drugged.

Rafe tried to stand, however his balance had left him. He glanced to the cell. Through the glaze that crept into his sights, Davis reached out to him through the bars. Rafe's knees hit the floor and he reached out to grasp the table in attempt to break his fall. Everything around him went black.

# CHAPTER FOUR

Whispers clouded Rafe's mind as he emerged from the silence of a deep slumber. A solid ray of light penetrated his closed eye lids, intruding on the peaceful darkness of uninhibited, however restless sleep. As his mind began to clear, the throng of methodic drums in his head grew louder.

He gingerly worked his way into a sitting position. He massaged his temples and tried to open his eyes, resulting in a one-eyed squint.

"Good morning." Harrison Davis handed him a tin cup of liquid. "This should help."

Rafe looked up at the man through narrowed lids. That little chit had gotten the better of him with her seemingly innocent supper. His jaw clenched as he grabbed the extended cup from the man who was supposed to be in his custody, not the other way around. Some of the liquid sloshed to the ground. It didn't help his mood.

"Thanks," Rafe grumbled begrudgingly.

He lifted the beverage to his mouth. The bitter concoction burned his mouth and he spit it out. All he needed at this point was some sort of homemade moonshine to dull his senses even more.

"What the hell happened…Davis?" Rafe set the cup down on the mortar floor and tried to stand. He nearly lost his balance. Harrison stood up to help steady him, but he pushed him away.

"Dehlia's father works over at the apothecary and it seems as if a few of the townsfolk thought they could help me get away if you, uh, fell asleep."

Rafe nodded and even that motion hurt.

He should have seen it coming. Davis may have only been the town school master for a week or so, but teachers were hard to come by in these parts and Rafe reckoned the townsfolk wanted to keep him around.

Even though Rafe had been out cold, Davis's cuffs were off and the cell door opened. He hadn't run. That surprised Rafe. Something had changed. He'd run from Silver Falls the moment he'd seen Rafe's horse, so why stop now?

"Why you still here?"

"I told you. I'm tired of running. If I don't stop now, I will be hiding for the rest of my life and that is not why I came to America. For some reason, I feel like I can trust you, Redbourne. I figure if I tell you the truth, you'll listen."

Rafe groaned.

His head felt like a lead weight and he stumbled toward the door. He was sure he should be angrier than he felt. There must have been a mood relaxer mixed in the girl's vittles along with the sleeping agent that had knocked him cold.

Rafe made his way to the horse's trough and knelt down in front of the water—sure to be freezing. Taking a deep breath, he plunged his whole head into the icy trench.

After a few seconds, Rafe pulled himself out of the trough and shook his hair free of the bitter cold water. The dunk had been invigorating and had cleared his head enough to focus on the town around him and he pulled himself to his feet. Harrison leaned against the doorframe of the jail, watching him with a slightly crooked grin.

"Feel better?" he asked in a low, amused voice.

Rafe reached up to his wet top and slicked his hair back behind his ears. "Much."

"Mr. Davenport," a slight bustled woman called out from across the street. She stopped short of the jail steps and reached out with a small slip of paper in her hands. "This arrived just a few minutes ago." She smiled at Harrison Davis, then gestured toward Rafe. "For your friend," she said, her voice laden with disdain.

"He won't bite you, Harriet. Give it to the man," Harrison encouraged. "And my name is Davis. Harrison Davis."

The woman's jaw dropped slightly, but she quickly regained her composure. When she turned to face Rafe, she scrunched up her shoulders and glanced him over from soaking head to booted toe.

"Arrestin' a teacher. Humphhhh." She stepped toward him with the letter outstretched.

The moment Rafe took the telegram from the woman, she turned on her heel and marched back to the telegraph office across the street without another glance.

He looked down at the simple note.

*Rafe STOP Urgent STOP Longhurst Manor STOP Adrien needs your help END*

Cryptic. No signature.

"Looks like our time gallivanting in this little town is over. We're leavin', Davis," Rafe said, rereading the note. When he glanced up, Harrison still stood with his arms folded across his chest. "With or without the cuffs," he added. "The choice is yours."

Harrison pushed away from the doorframe and headed to the back of the small whitewashed church. Rafe guessed that's where the town had put him up as the new teacher. He watched the man until he entered the church. His gut told him that Harrison was sincere in wanting to stop running, but letting him walk around of his own accord felt out of sorts.

He glanced back down at the note. Whoever had sent it had to be quite resourceful to catch him in a little town like Tumbleweed. Rafe crossed the street to the telegraph office. The small building hardly seemed big enough for Rafe to enter, but he pushed open the door, leaned over the counter, and threw the telegram in front of the startled clerk.

"Where did this message come from?"

The short, greying man adjusted his white visor and put on

his spectacles. "Ah, Mr. Redbourne. This is not the first time something has come in for you, but it is the first time you were in town to get it."

The man raised his nose a little and sized up the note looking down through his glasses.

"This one is from Baltimore. Although, I think the first originated somewhere overseas."

Will. It had to be.

"Thank you," Rafe said as he turned to leave the small office, but was brought up short by Sheriff Mallory standing in the doorway.

"I understand there was some trouble in my jail last night, Redbourne."

Rafe couldn't help the heat that quickly rose in his neck. It was not very often that someone got the best of him. Least of all, a little chit.

"I think the people in your little town are desperate for a teacher." The telegraph office seemed to be growing smaller. He looked past the sheriff and out the doorway. "After you, ma'am."

She turned on her heel and walked back outside onto the boardwalk.

"Well, that's true," she said as she flicked a thumb across her nose. "Teachers have been hard to keep around here. Some might say the town's a little desperate to hold onto one."

That was an understatement.

Rafe looked around the town and spotted a livery next to the mercantile. Like it or not, Harrison Davis would have to accompany him to Longhurst Manor and he wasn't about to share his horse with the man.

"Those two troublemakers give you any trouble last night?" he asked.

"Nothing I couldn't handle."

Rafe smiled and tipped his hat. "If you'll excuse me, ma'am. I've got a few more things to round up before we get on the road."

"Just one more thing, bounty hunter." Sheriff Mallory faced

him squarely and pushed her hat up higher on her forehead. Her tight black curls jutted out in every direction and framed her oval face perfectly. She was pretty to be sure, but he didn't have time for a woman. Especially now.

"Be careful. From what I could tell from their conversation last night, there's something else going on, something big, and I have a feeling it involves you." She pushed on his chest with one finger.

Rafe was accustomed to looking over his shoulder. It came with his line of work. He wrapped his hand around hers and bent down and placed a light kiss on her cheek.

"I'm always careful," he said with a wink.

Longhurst Manor came into view the moment Rafe reached the summit. The name belied the country it was from. Adrien was Pawnee by birth, but had been adopted by an elderly British couple as a child. When he'd returned to America many years later with a young son of his own, Adrien had built a near replica of the family estate in Britain.

Rafe had spent many days in his youth running through the manor with Malcolm, Adrien's son, and now, he looked over the vast grounds with fondness. It had been a long time.

"Are we stopping here?" Harrison's question was simple, but brought Rafe out of his reverie.

"The manor is just over the hill." He coaxed Lexa, his magnificent strawberry roan, faster with a nudging of his knees against her shoulders.

The scent of lilacs grew stronger as they neared the garden where Adrien loved to walk. The man had often spoken of the garden in reverence, always saying that it made him feel closer to his late wife.

The fresh smells of his second childhood home now inundated Rafe's senses. He closed his eyes and let out a deep breath with a sigh. The simple two-mile ride seemed to last for hours and Rafe found himself feeling more excited to see the man than he'd expected.

"Come on, you bloody arse," Harrison swore loudly. The man had proven himself to be an experienced rider, but the small grey gelding they had picked up at the livery was no match for Lexa and he'd had to break into a gallop just to keep up. Rafe slowed and Harrison pulled up alongside him.

As they approached the front gate, the hairs on the back of Rafe's neck prickled to attention. The gate had been left open. That wasn't like Adrien. Something was wrong. He dismounted and walked Lexa through the open archway and tied her to the hitching post behind the gate. Harrison followed suit. In three strides Rafe was at the front door and pounded.

"Adrien," he called in a booming voice. "It's Rafe." He tried the door. It was locked. "Adrien," he demanded again.

The garden. Maybe he was strolling in the garden. Rafe turned quickly, jumped off the step and without thinking, ducked under a tree branch almost without even realizing it was there.

"What's wrong with you?" Harrison had caught up to Rafe, panting. He bent over to catch a breath and rested his hands on his knees.

"Something's definitely not right." Rafe scanned the immense gardens for any sign of Adrien.

Nothing.

Satisfied the homeowner was not on the grounds, Rafe moved with purpose to the back entry. The door was shut, but unlocked. His hand rested at his hip and he slid open the latch of his holster. He nudged the door open.

"Adrien," he called with more apprehension in his voice than he liked. He pushed the door wider. Two barrels of a shotgun greeted him, held by a silhouetted figure in the dark hallway.

"What have you done with her?" The voice was unmistakable. Adrien.

"Adrien, old friend, it's me. Rafe." He stepped a booted foot over the threshold of the doorway, his hands separated in front of him and elevated somewhat.

The darkened figure took a step forward into the stream of light that hit the entryway with noonday force. He held up a hand to the light, his slight limp exaggerated and highly noticeable. The shotgun was still raised, but his head had moved from behind the gun sights to squint at Rafe, who knew the scrutinizing look all too well.

"Rafe Redbourne." A wave of relief visibly washed over Adrien, but the scowl did not disappear from his face. He un-cocked the weapon and lowered it to the floor in place of his cane. He turned around and headed into his study and waved a hand forward, motioning for Rafe to follow. He did.

Harrison gingerly treaded into the house and stepped in place behind Rafe. "Fine greeting," he whispered.

The musty scent of the study was so thick it could have been pierced with a blade. A large half-empty glass of a clear liquid sat on an end table next to the deep red velvet couch. The strong stench of alcohol filled Rafe's nostrils. It wasn't water in that glass.

Adrien leaned the gun up against the table and lowered himself down into the over-sized cushioned chair, motioning for Rafe to sit. Adrien pulled his head back a little and Rafe followed his surprised gaze to Harrison lurking in the open doorway.

"Come in, son. And who might you be?" Adrien picked up his drink and brought it to his lips.

Harrison cleared his throat and stepped forward into the room where Adrien could see him. "Harrison Davis, sir."

He'd started to sweat again and Rafe began to think there might be something seriously and physically wrong with him. Rafe had worked hard in a blazing sun all day before without sweating as much as Davis did now.

Adrien just nodded his head and lifted the drink again to his mouth. "Ah," he forced through a liquor laden groan.

In all the years Rafe had known him, he had never known Adrien to drink alone. He knelt down in front of his friend to meet him at eye level.

"What's happened?" Rafe looked around the house and shivered at the unusual silence. "You asked me what I'd done with *her*. Who is *her*, Adrien?"

The house was usually full of people—most hired-hands.

"Where is everyone? Where is Malcolm?" Rafe could feel the quiet seep into his soul and suck out any hint of happiness. It was so unlike his old friend to be so solitary.

Adrien stared at him blankly.

Rafe took the glass from the older man's hand and returned it to the table. He looked up at Harrison Davis, who stood very still just inside the doorway.

"The kitchen is just down the hall to your left," Rafe directed. "See if you can drum up some coffee."

Harrison nodded and strode out of the room.

"She's gone." Adrien's voice was distant. "I have ridden for days looking for her, but these old bones aren't as strong as they used to be." He turned his focus to Rafe's eyes and spoke, the corner of his mouth upturned dejectedly. "This is the first time I think I've ever let one of you boys down."

"Let us down? Adrien, where is Malcolm?"

Adrien was not making any sense.

"Who is gone?" Rafe asked again, his voice solid yet coaxing. "What happened?"

Adrien slumped back against the couch.

A noise from upstairs reverberated through the ceiling. It sounded like a chair scratching across the wooden floor boards and it echoed through the otherwise silent house. Rafe patted his old mentor on the knee and pushed himself up.

It only took a matter of seconds for him to reach the second floor, taking two steps at a time. A light came from the drawing room at the end of the hall. Rafe marched toward the room, determined to get some answers.

When he thrust the door open, the sight that greeted him was the last thing he'd expected. A balding, bespectacled man with a doctoring kit whipped around to face him. Rafe's eyes shot to the chair just inches away from the bed.

In that instant, the lanky gentleman had drawn a very small

pistol and aimed it directly at Rafe. "What is the meaning of this?" the man demanded.

"Sorry, Doc." Rafe took his hand off his holster. "I'm Rafe," he announced, but the man showed no sign of recognition. "Redbourne," he added.

"Ah. I've heard of you, Mr. Redbourne. Mr. Longhurst speaks very highly of you and your family."

Rafe nodded. "The feeling is mutual."

"The name is Simmons." He carefully returned his gun back into the folds of his bag where Rafe assumed it had been hidden. He then removed his glasses and started cleaning them with a dingy grey rag as he turned to face Rafe squarely.

"Excuse me, doc, but what the hell happened here?"

The physician shifted his weight and turned enough to reveal an older gentleman lying, with his eyes closed, in the bed that had been positioned just below the window.

Rafe scanned the room for signs of anyone else and noticed the dark red stains on the chair beneath the bookcase and the surrounding floor boards. He looked back at the doc.

"Here you are." Harrison had a hold of the door knob of the door and held it open just far enough to peer inside. "I heard the thumping on the stairs and thought there might be trouble."

"No trouble, Davis. Did you need something?" Rafe asked.

"Your friend downstairs is out cold, but I did find a small pouch of Foxgrove's coffee. From the best little coffee house in all of England, I might add." Harrison's gaze moved to the doctor and then to the patient. He stood up straighter, opened the door all the way, and stepped inside the room.

"What's this, then?" he asked, his eyebrows furrowed together and his chin jutted forward.

"Mr. Hawthorne here was shot, poor man, by the ruffians who made off with his daughter." Doc Simmons finished his task and returned the wire frames to his face.

"Hawthorne?" Rafe repeated the name. He swallowed the lump that had just formed in his throat.

"And might I say he is a very lucky man. Most men

wouldn't survive a shot like that," the doc speculated.

"Tessa was here?"

"I believe the lady's name was Tayla."

Rafe's hands balled into fists.

*Of course it was.*

"Maggie, quick!" A young blond cowboy in worn leather chaps yelled when he burst through the front door. "The stage's met up with some trouble. A man was killed and Jake's been hurt real bad!"

The clatter of Maggie's dirty dishes dropping onto the hutch in the kitchen near the entryway snapped Tayla straight out of her chair.

Maggie gathered up her skirts and ran to the closet where she kept her medical supplies.

"Take me to him, Pete."

With a glance back at Tayla, she smiled reassuringly, but spoke in a firm, commanding voice. "Locket honey, go an' grab me a large bowl of water and clean rags, would ya? And hurry." Maggie called back as she ran out the restaurant door.

It had only been a few days since she'd woken in the strange room at the bed and breakfast, but she felt a part of it now all the same. Since she still had no recollection of her past, Jake had taken to calling her Locket, because the only key to her past had been the rather large necklace she'd been wearing.

The name had stuck. Now, Jake was in trouble and Tayla rushed to the kitchen to pump some fresh water as Maggie had instructed. Tayla reached for the small clean washcloths on the shelf next to the windowsill while pumping the water. The tin basin filled quicker than she'd expected.

Tucking the cloths into the waistband of her apron, she reached down and enveloped the bowl with both arms. The weight of it nearly toppled her over and some of the contents splashed out onto the hard wooden floor. She righted herself and with firm determination headed gingerly out to the barn.

When she reached the heavy green door, the blond cowboy opened it from outside. On a makeshift stretcher next to the barn, Jake lay silently while Maggie huddled over him. Tayla saw him wince and her heart ached for him.

Pete looked up, saw her straining to hold the bucket, and in an instant he was up, taking the heavy load from her arms. He set the water down next to Maggie. Tayla removed the rags from her apron and crouched down next to her friend.

Jake's thigh was covered in blood. A sudden flash of a blood soaked shirt invaded Tayla's mind and a sharp pain stabbed at her forehead. Her hands flew to the offending spot as she tumbled over onto her rump in the dirt, pressing her fingertips firmly into her head.

When the pain subsided, she sat up straighter and leaned closer, wrapping her hand around Jake's.

"I can't get the bleedin' to stop." Maggie wiped her forehead with the back of her hand, leaving streaks of blood in its path. "Locket," she called, "run upstairs and grab one of the clean linens." She nodded to the blond cowboy. "Have Pete here help you tear it into strips."

The pain in her head had all but disappeared and with it the disturbing image. She struggled to get her skirt out from under her knees and almost fell face first into the water bucket. Pete reached out a hand to steady her. She took it. Heat rose in her cheeks as he helped her from the ground.

"Thank you."

Pete kept a hold of her hand and pulled her toward the main house. They ran up the stairs.

"Where are they?" Pete was breathing heavy and Tayla had to swallow to find her voice.

She remembered seeing linens in the wardrobe across the hall from her room and she rushed toward the near empty corridor.

Mr. Francis, a businessman from Hackensack, had his nose deep in a green bound book and only looked up when Tayla clipped his shoulder with her own.

"Really," he said in a huff. "Are there are no manners in this part of the country?"

"I'm sorry, Mr. Francis," she called as she continued to run past him.

If the traveler said anything more, Tayla didn't hear because she was already around the corner. She pulled on the small knobs of the wardrobe and inside, found neatly stacked sheets for the beds and pillow casings. She grabbed the top sheet and shook it open.

Shears?

She couldn't think where they might be and her mind ran over several other possibilities. Before she resorted to trying to tear the cloth with her teeth, Pete snorted and reached into his back pocket, from which he withdrew a small folded knife.

He blew out a strong breath and he flipped the blade open and began making cuts every couple of inches in the fabric. Once he had completed one entire side. He held the sheet up in front of him, holding two different sides of one of his slashes and ripped. The material gave way.

Tayla grabbed the opposite end of the sheet and started ripping as well, carefully folding each strip in half and placing it over her forearm. She wanted to keep them as clean as possible.

Within minutes there was a fairly large collection of fabric scraps weighing down her arm. Pete grabbed a hold of the bottom section of the material and together they carried them down the steps and to the barn's edge where Maggie awaited them.

To Tayla's horror, Jake was laying very still, a stick protruding from both sides of his mouth. An older man stood over him hugging his upper body and arms to the ground. Another man handed Maggie a red smoldering branding rod. Tayla pulled Pete behind her, running forward as fast as her feet would allow.

"Stop, Maggie. We've got them."

Maggie didn't turn around. "Go back in the house, Locket." Her voice was steady, but firm. "The bleedin' just won't stop. This is the only way."

Tayla looked up at Pete, whose face had become masked—unreadable. *No.* She shook her head.

Pete took the strips from her arms and set them over the fence railing.

She took a step backward, then another. The realization of the young man's lot pained her.

*Be brave.* A familiar reassuring voice called to her from the recesses of her mind, but it was too much. She shook her head again and turned for the door.

Jake's scream reached her ears with perfect clarity. The stick in his mouth had done nothing to muffle the noise and Tayla found tears pouring down her face and she buried her head into Pete's chest. His arms gripped tightly around her. After a few moments, she pushed him away, threw open the door and tore up the stairs. She didn't stop running until she'd reached her bedroom. Once inside, she locked the door behind her. She fell onto her bed, smothering her face in the down coverings and cried for the young boy who'd found her in the river. And saved her life.

She clutched the locket around her neck and rubbed the stone with her thumb. *He has to be okay. He just has to.* She hiccupped a little.

"Papa, you just have to be okay," she whispered, weeping into the now crumpled bedcoverings.

# CHAPTER FIVE

"Tayla Hawthorne is a conniving, selfish little troublemaker who took everything from me. My soon-to-be bride," Rafe started the list as he took two paces to one side of the couch. "My inheritance." He stomped toward the large bookcases, stuffed with novels and encyclopedias. "My pride." His blood was pumping so hard through his veins he thought one might burst under pressure. "Why the hell would I agree to help her?" He threw himself into the office chair, folded his arms, and crossed his ankles on top of Adrien's desk.

His old friend raised an eyebrow at his feet and Rafe wordlessly dropped them to the floor. He leaned forward with both elbows resting on the desk and clenched his fists together until his knuckles turned white, his jaw flexing and releasing in rhythm.

Hawthornes. His friend knew better than to ask him a favor on behalf of a Hawthorne. And Tayla, above all others.

*Unbelievable.*

"Are you quite finished?" Adrien tsked. "You are a grown man. And better than that," he scolded.

Rafe's face heated in an instant and he lowered his gaze to his hands. He was here and Adrien was asking for his help. But he never imagined the mere mention of her would still sting. Eight years was a long time to carry such resentment, but how could he forget the pain that had cost him so much? Let alone, the person responsible?

"Have you ever stopped to realize what a privileged life you've lead? Being born a Redbourne comes with great responsibility. Determination. Influence. Integrity. All qualities every Redbourne man I've ever met has possessed."

Rafe snorted. "Not so easy to live up to."

He was well over twenty-five years old—the age by which his grandfather had stipulated in his will that by which his male heirs must be married. Without his inheritance, the Redbourne fortune had been lost to him. Payment for his bounties kept him warm and fed, but didn't bring with it a lot of comfort or influence.

Adrien limped over to the desk and rested a hand on Rafe's shoulder. "A woman needs your help, Rafe. Does it really matter what family she comes from?"

Rafe knew Adrien was right, but for the life of him he wished he weren't.

"As I discovered this morning, I am not as young as I once was," Adrien said as he sat down in the large leather chair across from Rafe. "I tried, mind you. For three days on horseback I searched for Miss Hawthorne, but lo, I'm afraid these old, weary bones just can't make the journey ahead."

Rafe had lost.

"How can you ask this of me? I am only a man. Cole and Raine are just a couple of days ride. Anyone could do this—anyone, but me."

Adrien leaned forward and patted Rafe's shoulder twice. "If you won't do it for her…" he paused and tilted his head over his right shoulder to the side—not quite meeting Rafe's eyes, "do it to save the pride of an old man." He grabbed his cane, stood, and walked to the open study door. He stopped at the entryway, then stepped over the threshold without another word.

Rafe had known he would go after Tayla Hawthorne the moment he saw the blood stains on the floor in the parlor upstairs. Even if it was the young woman who'd changed the course of his life forever, no woman deserved what she'd likely seen over the last few days. At least her father was alive—for now.

He stood up, grabbed his Stetson off the end table, set it low on his head and jaunted up the staircase. He cracked the door to the room he and Harrison had been sharing and peered inside. While the man had kept his promise to stay put, Rafe was unaccustomed to putting any kind of trust in the men he captured. And after the pie incident, he was more than a little wary. However, something in his gut told him he could trust Harrison Davis now.

Rafe'd requested the only room in the manor with two beds in order to satisfy his sense of duty, but the reality of it was that unless he was going to keep Harrison Davis cuffed or locked up, there was no point. He pushed the door open a little further.

Harrison leaned against the wall, his bare feet casually crossed along his mattress lengthwise. He looked up from the novel he must have borrowed from the library.

"Make sure to get a good night's rest. I'm still waiting for that talk we were going to have, but we'll have to do it on the road. We're leavin' at dawn and it'll be a good day's ride before we arrive at Maggie's place."

Harrison lowered his book and looked at Rafe with an arched brow. "Maggie's place?"

"The Smokey Sky Inn. Be ready." Rafe shut the door and headed further down the hallway back to the drawing room. He wanted to talk to Stuart Hawthorne. He wanted to find out exactly what had happened.

Doc Simmons pulled the door closed behind him as he left the room. "He really shouldn't be disturbed, Mr. Redbourne."

"He may know the men who took Tayla or at least why. We're heading out in the morning and I need as much information as Mr. Hawthorne may be able to provide."

Doc sized up Rafe in one roaming glance. The wiry little man squinted his eyes at him while lifting his nose a few inches. "Two minutes. I just gave him another dose of laudanum. He'll be asleep shortly."

Rafe pushed past the doc and strode over to the bed. With an abundance of bedrooms available in the manor, Rafe wondered why they'd set Hawthorne up in the parlor. He glanced about the room, and his eyes fixed on the specialty Steinway piano in the middle of the room. It was a beautiful piano that had been commissioned from the German master craftsman out of his shop in New York and Rafe remembered how much Tayla had loved to play. He guessed it was the reason for the odd accommodations.

Mr. Hawthorne didn't have much strength when Rafe stepped up the bed, but he did manage to get out a few raspy words before he drifted into a seemingly restful sleep.

"Rafe." Stuart Hawthorne managed a weak smile. "Locket." His hand shook as he pointed at his neck.

Rafe repeated the word.

"Keep her—" Stuart swallowed with difficulty, "safe."

His eyes fluttered shut, but one more word formed on his breath.

"Darington."

Rafe's jaw tensed and his teeth clenched together as he ground out the name. "Darington."

Mr. Hawthorne didn't look good. He was far from the spry man he remembered. Rafe stood up straight and narrowed his eyes at the splintered doorframe. Coincidence? Rafe didn't believe in coincidences. Lord Darington had placed a bounty on Harrison for kidnapping his betrothed. If the same man had something to do with Tayla's disappearance, that would make Tayla...

Rafe shook his head. He was anxious to meet his most recent employer. Too many things weren't adding up and he wanted answers. He didn't take kindly to being played the fool. He was not going to be a pawn in anyone's game.

"I'll find her," Rafe whispered, unsure whether Stuart Hawthorne could hear him. He turned to leave and kicked something across the floor. He bent over to pick up the small round metal trinket. It seemed to be a button of some sort and he walked closer to the shortening wick of the lamp. A gold button with a British crown resting on an eagled crest peered back at him.

Damn.

"Tayla Hawthorne," Rafe nearly shouted when he walked into the room where Harrison still sat reading his book in the dim lamplight.

"Excuse me," Harrison looked up at him, chin jutted, and eyebrows squished together.

"Tayla Hawthorne, how do you know her?" Rafe took off his hat, threw it onto his bed and sat in the hardwood chair against the wall by the door and began removing his boots. He did not take his eyes off of Harrison's for even a moment.

"You mean Lord Darington's fiancée, Tayla Hawthorne?" Harrison sat up on the bed, his finger holding his place in his book.

Rafe couldn't believe his ears. He stared at Harrison, his blood beginning to boil. Harrison tilted his head back a little, then his eyes grew wider. The novel he'd been reading fell to the floor in hapless disarray.

"Impossible," he said more to himself than to Rafe. "Then, that man down the hall is…"

Rafe made it across the room in a matter of seconds and had Harrison up against the wall to the side of the bed by the shirt front.

"You want me to trust you? Start talking. I want to know how on earth you are acquainted with Tayla Hawthorne," Rafe demanded.

"I don't *know* her at all. We didn't exactly run in the same circles." Beads of sweat began to form on Harrison's forehead.

Rafe growled.

"You said you'd listen, remember?"

"Talk."

"If you'll kindly let me down, I would be happy to tell you what I know."

Rafe relaxed his hold of Harrison's shirt with a push and took two steps away.

Harrison smoothed out his shirt and sat down on the edge of the bed and ran his fingers through his disheveled hair. With his elbows resting on his knees and his hands now folded together he looked up at Rafe.

"Lord Darington was engaged to a Miss Hawthorne."

Rafe folded his arms. "Go on."

"I left England over three months ago. The night I left, two thugs chased me onto the ship, claiming that I had taken something that belonged to Lord Darington. I had no idea to what they referred until I saw a poster with my face on it. Here. In America." Harrison shifted uncomfortably. "Imagine my surprise when I discovered I had kidnapped the Earl's fiancée."

His unmasked sarcasm did not help Rafe's mood.

"Why would I do that? I came here because America was supposed to be the land of opportunity, a place where a man could make something of himself. Kidnapping Tayla Hawthorne wouldn't have gotten me any closer to that."

"There's something else going on here. Out of all the lawmen and bounty hunters in the west, it cannot be a coincidence that Lord Darington hired *me* to find you. I have history with the Hawthornes. What aren't you telling me, Davis?"

"Wait, you have history with the Hawthornes? What kind of history?"

Rafe shot him a look that he hoped would quell any questions for now. His eyes narrowed and he took a step toward Harrison.

"Okay," Harrison said, holding up his hands. "Honestly, I've never met the woman, but on the night I left, my brother was going to see Lord Darington."

"Why?" Rafe sat down on the bed across from Harrison and met him at eye level.

"Well, funny story that. I only learned who my grandmother was shortly before she passed. I didn't want the life she offered, but my brother…"

"What are you trying to say, Davis?" Rafe had had enough of this and just wanted the point.

"Lord Darington is not the rightful heir of Darington."

Rafe waited for the punch line.

Harrison just stared at him expectantly.

"And you are?" Rafe snorted.

Harrison didn't respond.

*Impossible.*

"The Earl of Darington was my father," Harrison's voice grew louder as he spoke. "But my brother and I were hidden from him after our mother died during childbirth."

Rafe whistled. *Now* he'd heard everything.

Harrison stood and walked to the window, gazing out at the darkened countryside.

"Imagine a woman you'd known all your life as a kindly old neighbor turns out to be the Dowager Countess of Darington and your grandmother."

He wasn't joking. Rafe took a deep breath and listened more intently.

"It was a bit of a shock to learn that our mother had been beaten so badly that she actually died giving birth to us and we were taken from that life to protect us from such an abusive father. The Earl's own mother hid us, his firstborn children, from him. Told him we had died." Harrison's voice quieted at the last and he turned to face Rafe. "What kind of a monster was he?"

Rafe was still trying to process the information he was learning. He'd seen a lot of bad in his line of work, but his own father was a strong, God-fearing man who loved his wife and children. He felt for the man standing in front of him.

"Finn was excited to discover that we were more than the simple peasants we'd been raised to believe we were and that we had another brother, another family. He couldn't wait to step into a new life, with a fresh start, but I..."

"You didn't want the restricting life of society," Rafe finished for him.

Harrison nodded.

"And Tayla, where does she fit into all of this?"

Harrison leaned back against the windowsill. "Truly, you must believe me when I tell you—I've never met the woman. I knew her name. Everybody did. When their engagement was announced, it seemed the whole countryside was humming about it. Lord Darington is a recluse. There aren't many who've been personally acquainted with the man."

Rafe snorted at the thought that he was once engaged to a high society Hawthorne.

"A few months ago, the Dowager Countess came to our home and invited us to attend a dinner at the Darington estate. She said she was dying and Dare, I can only assume she meant Lord Darington, needed to know the truth before she was gone. She wanted us to be a family. She told us of a music box that contained proof of our birthright and an heirloom that would unlock the family's darkest secrets." Harrison folded his arms across his chest.

"Where is this box?"

Harrison shrugged. "Still in her safe at the Darington estate, I'd imagine. See, she died before we could attend her dinner. I didn't want to expose any dark secrets then and I certainly didn't want to be any part of ruining someone's life, but Darington has made it rather difficult to be cordial."

"What did Finn think about all of this?"

"Like I said, he went to see Lord Darington the night I left for America. He wanted everything the Dowager promised. I have not heard from him since. I have tried to contact him multiple times over the last few months, but have had no luck reaching him."

"Why does Darington think you kidnapped Tayla?"

"I have not a clue. When I discovered who had ordered the bounty, I was mystified I'm afraid. I had wanted to clear the air with the man, so I turned myself in," Harrison said as if that were the most logical thing in the world.

Rafe admired that.

"But after spending a few damaging moments with him," Harrison lifted his shirt to reveal a long jagged scar just above his naval, "I realized the error of my ways and ran the first chance I got. I have been running ever since."

Rafe was beginning to question this job. He hated being made a fool of and he hated working on the wrong side of the law.

Rafe awoke before the sun. Clouds continued to shadow the moon and he could barely make out the silhouette of a man sleeping across the room. He'd broken nearly all of his rules with this bounty and had begun rethinking every decision he'd made on this trip. He'd never before dreamed of allowing a bounty to sleep either unrestrained or outside of a cell. However, something inside of him said that Harrison Davis was telling the truth. And a Redbourne, most of them anyway, always trusted his gut.

He sat up, yanked on his boots, and shoved his arms into his black shirt, leaving the tails dangling at his sides. Rafe picked up his leather pack and made his way along the dark corridors to the stairs. He wanted to get an early start and to have plenty of energy for the short journey ahead. A stop by the kitchen was just what he needed.

He knew his way around the place blindfolded and he cringed when the stair beneath him creaked loudly in protest. How could he have forgotten about the stair? It had been way too long since he'd been here he realized and a twinge of guilt edged in on him.

He reached the bottom of the staircase without another sound.

"You're up early."

Rafe whirled to face the voice, guns already drawn.

"Adrien, you scared the hell out of me. What are you doing lurking around your own house in the dark?" He returned his revolvers to their holsters.

Adrien rotated the key on his lantern. The flame grew enough to illuminate nearly half of the small sitting room outside the kitchen.

"Trouble sleeping?" Adrien inquired.

"Just want to get a jump on the day. As soon as Davis is up and ready, we'll be headed out."

Adrien tilted his head in unfeigned interest.

Rafe noted the gaunt shadows beneath Adrien's eyes and wondered if they were cast from the dim lighting of the lamp.

"Adrien?" he asked, moving closer to the man who'd been like a second father to him. His brows furrowed together and he knelt down on one knee next to the big black chair where Adrien sat. "Are you all right?"

"I couldn't sleep, either." A half-hearted smile touched his sallow face and he patted Rafe's hand.

It was cold.

"I didn't get much of a chance to speak with Miss Hawthorne or her father before this whole ordeal. When Will told me they were in trouble, I was pleased to be able to provide a temporary home for them."

Wait. Will knew about this? Of course he did. His brother had been living in England for a while now and would be someone the Hawthornes could trust if they'd needed something. These 'coincidences' just kept piling up.

"I didn't realize just how grave a situation they were in," Adrien continued. "I should have called on you earlier."

"I wouldn't have come," Rafe stated matter-of-factly.

There was a long stretch of silence between them.

"Where is Malcolm, Adrien? Why wasn't he here to help?"

"Ah," Adrien nodded knowingly, "my son. He's returned to England I'm afraid. He just couldn't let the past be."

"I understand that. My past pushed me so hard away from my humanity that the thought of helping someone just for the sake of helping seemed a distant memory—at least until all the trouble out at Cole's place in Silver Falls." Rafe moved to the chair opposite Adrien.

"How did it feel? Helping someone?"

"I realized just how much I've missed my family. My brothers."

For the first few years, tracking bounties had provided the necessary distraction that allowed him to forget about Tessa Hawthorne. He'd used the skills he'd learned with the Pawnee tribe, and his name had become one to reckon with. Being a bounty hunter was a solitary life, but he'd given up on dreams of having something more a long time ago.

Adrien stood up, balancing on his cane. "Let's get something to eat. Tildy made some fresh biscuits yesterday morning and I think there are still some peach preserves next to the ice box."

"Tildy's here? What about Jethro?" Rafe had always loved the Longhurst's cook and gardener. Of course he found that he loved most women—of all sizes and shapes. And Jethro, well, what was there not to like? He was a cranky old buzzard who knew more about flowers and growing things than anyone Rafe had ever met.

When the sun finally rose up over the distant hills and the cock in the yard sounded his morning wake-up call, Rafe leaned forward on the table, where he'd enjoyed a comfortable silence with his good friend.

"Adrien," Rafe cleared his throat, "who took her?"

The relaxed smile that had lazily rested on Adrien's face vanished. "I was in the garden when I heard the shot. By the time I made it back into the house, they were gone, and Mr. Hawthorne was near death." He turned sad eyes to Rafe. "I'm sorry, I didn't see anyone."

Stuart Hawthorne had been too weak to answer any questions and then his last word crept back into Rafe's mind. Darington. He reached into his pocket and rubbed the button he'd found on the floor upstairs. He needed to get a message to Jess Mallory. If the two heavies they'd run into in Tumbleweed were working with Darington...

They'd said they'd lost something valuable and Rafe wondered if they had been referring to someone.

Tayla.

It all made sense and he cursed himself for not questioning them more at the time They could double-back to Tumbleweed and find out, but Rafe figured that if Tayla had gotten away from them, she wouldn't be headed to the small town, but to someplace familiar. Redbourne Ranch was the only place that made sense—unless she tried to come back here to check on her father.

"Adrien, we have to go. If Tayla comes back, send word immediately to Redbourne Ranch."

"You think she would come back here?" he asked, his eyes wide and glass-like.

"Her father is still here. I think she'd risk anything for her family."

"Find her, son. Be safe."

Rafe patted Adrien's forearm and pushed away from the table. "Thank you, old friend. Take care of yourself."

"And don't be gone so long this time. I'm tired of getting scolded by my own help that they never see you." The wrinkles around Adrien's eyes became more pronounced when he smiled. He stood.

Rafe hugged the man—noticing how small and frail he had become. Worry knotted his brows and he pulled away, but still held Adrien's arms. "Are you sure you're okay?" he asked.

"It's nothing a bowl of Tildy's chicken stew won't cure. Go on, now. The sun's up and you best be on your way."

Rafe nodded. He didn't want to lose any time. He squeezed Adrien's arms and strode from the kitchen, grabbing a couple of biscuits from a basket on the counter.

He found Harrison sitting on the bottom step tying the laces on his boots. Harrison looked up and removed the belt from between his teeth.

"Almost ready, Mr. Redbourne," he said. He stood and strung the belt through the loops on his trousers.

"Might as well call me Rafe." He tossed Davis a biscuit.

Harrison grinned at him as he clipped past him through the open doorway.

Rafe followed him to the stables where he could saddle Lexa. They needed to get to Redbourne Ranch. The sooner, the better. Tayla was out there alone and he had no idea if she had any money for shelter or food, or if she'd been hurt. All he knew was that he had to find her—if only to say his peace and be done with her.

He'd start at Maggie's place.

# CHAPTER SIX

Tayla opened her eyes to the cheery yellow tones of the smallest of Maggie's guest rooms at the inn. It took a moment for her to remember why she'd retired so early in the day. Jacob's muffled scream stabbed at her mind with haunting clarity and her heart ached for the young boy who'd endured the searing heat of a branding iron against his leg.

The sun spilled behind the mountains and brilliant hues of orange and gold played with the horizon. All outside seemed quiet, but from downstairs she could hear the soft hum of murmuring patrons in the restaurant. She sat up and wiped her mouth. Her stomach grumbled when the savory smell of Maggie's chicken pie wafted under her nose.

She jumped up off the bed and as an afterthought turned to smooth out the covers. Embarrassed by the wet splotch on the blanket where she'd drooled in her sleep, Tayla noticed the decorative pillows that adorned the reading chair. She picked one up and tossed it onto the bed in just the right spot.

"There." She placed her hands on her hips and nodded. Satisfied, she turned back to the door and took a quick glimpse in the vanity mirror. Tayla picked up the locket from the table top and fastened it around her neck. Glancing again at her still unfamiliar reflection, she brushed out the wrinkles of her dress with her hands, pinched her cheeks, and headed downstairs.

"Maggie Malone," a deep booming voice sounded in the restaurant downstairs.

Startled, Tayla backed up against the wall.

"If you aren't a sight for a man's weary eyes."

Tayla peered around the corner, over the second landing railing into the dining room.

A tall man—with a physique from the gods—had Maggie in a bear hug. He spun her about, evoking girlish giggles. Between Tayla's position on the stairs and the man's wide brimmed, low-riding hat, she couldn't quite make out his face, but his resonant voice warmed something inside of her. He set Maggie down and kissed her smack on the mouth.

Tayla gaped with a dropped jaw.

"Why, Rafe Redbourne, you are lookin' better than ever," Maggie said as she pushed on the man's shoulder playfully. Tayla noted the pleased color that tinted the inn owner's cheeks.

"How long you around this time?" Maggie asked.

The stranger glanced up toward Tayla and she sucked in a startled breath, pulled back, and again plastered herself against the wall. *Redbourne*, she repeated the name in her mind, hoping for some sense of recognition.

Nothing.

After her breathing slowed some, she peeked once again around the corner.

He hadn't seen her.

"Ah, Mags." He wrapped his arms again around the woman standing half his size, but this time he didn't lift her. "It's good to see you." He let go when she protested.

"I'm afraid we're just passing through."

Tayla did not even remember her own name, but she could tell handsome when she saw it. And Rafe Redbourne was handsome.

"We?" Maggie inquired.

Rafe nodded at the door where another man, equally as tall, but not nearly as broad, stumbled through the open doorway with an over-sized pack over his shoulder and a bedroll tucked under his arm.

He was familiar somehow.

"This," Rafe said as the man righted himself in front of

Maggie, "is Harrison Davis."

The man set the bedding on the floor and reached out a hand to take hers.

"It's a pleasure to make your acquaintance," he coaxed and bent to kiss her hand.

Tayla perked up at the sound of his British accent. Certainly, there had to be a lot of people from England who'd immigrated to America. Was it just a coincidence or had someone really come looking for her?

Maggie looked up at Rafe with creased brows.

"Let's just say he's... a business acquaintance." Rafe picked up the bedroll and elbowed Harrison Davis in the side. "Just need a couple of warm beds. Any available tonight?"

"For you?" Maggie looked at Rafe, let go of Harrison's hand, cleared her throat, and wiped her hands on her apron. "Anything." She hurried to the counter where the room keys were kept.

Tayla took the three steps that separated her from the top of the staircase.

"Hey, Mags? We're looking for a girl who mighta crossed by here in the last few days. Name's Hawthorne."

Maggie dropped a key into his open palm.

Tayla couldn't help wonder if this Rafe was Maggie's beau. She'd thought that Maggie and Pete were sweet on each other, but now, she wasn't sure of anything at all. The British man was handsome too, but something about him unsettled her.

"Hawthorne, huh? Can't say as anyone has passed through here by that name." Maggie shook her head. "Although," she glanced to the top of the stairs and met Tayla's eyes.

Hawthorne? The name didn't sound familiar, but she could be the girl to whom he referred. Couldn't she?

Tayla took the first step down. She chastised herself for the fireflies dancing in her stomach. She was drawn to him. Rafe. Whether it was simply attraction or if someone deep inside of her knew him, she was unsure. Something in his voice drew her closer and she realized her hope was for the latter. Part of her was scared to uncover her past, but if he held the keys, she *needed* to know. She leaned forward in attempt to catch a better look at him.

"Her name is Tay…" Rafe started.

The floor boards resonated as a deep, rich bark reached her ears just moments before Bear came bounding down the hallway behind her.

"…la," he finished as he turned toward the sound.

The most beautiful smile Tayla had ever seen greeted her. His teeth were whiter than most men she knew and the crinkles in his cheeks endeared her.

The huge dog knocked Tayla forward as he bounded down the stairs and she lost her balance.

"Bear!" The large man boomed. Then, his eyes caught hers and his smile disappeared.

She wobbled and could not right herself. There was no time to catch her footing. In an instant Tayla found herself at the bottom of the stairs on her rump and she was sure she'd broken bones. Her knee ached and her head throbbed, but that was nothing compared to what had been done to her pride. She couldn't force herself to move. Wouldn't. The damage had been done.

"Tayla," she heard him breathe the unfamiliar name. The man's firm grip on the dog loosened. His expression transformed in an instant from loving recognition to scornful disdain.

He let go of Bear and pushed himself away from the excited animal. Without taking his eyes off her, he strode toward the stairs with purpose. Moments later she felt the warmth of work-roughened hands brushing the hair away from her face. She looked up searching hopefully for kind eyes, but instead his gaze was cold, almost angry. She was scooped up into Rafe's arms and he carried her to the velvet fainting couch in Maggie's study, followed by Maggie and Harrison.

"Thank you," Tayla managed through a weak smile.

He didn't return the gesture, but turned away from her and walked back out into the dining room. She could still see him from the doorway. Puzzled, she felt like crying. He knew her, she was certain now. But what had she done to warrant his cool treatment? She looked up at Maggie whose eyebrows had scrunched together.

"Locket honey, you took quite a fall. Are you all right?" Maggie sat on the edge of the couch and took a hold of Tayla's hand.

"I'm fine, Mag—" she stopped before her sudden emotions bubbled over. She refused to cry—especially in front of him. She swallowed the lump that had formed in her throat and sat up taller. Tayla could still see Rafe from the doorway. He ran his hands through his hair and said something to his friend that she couldn't hear.

"Let me see her, Mags," he said, pushing Maggie aside on the couch.

Maggie slid further down, anxiously watching as Rafe took Tayla's face in his hands and stared into her eyes. His fingers roamed through her hair, massaging her scalp and she closed her eyes unwittingly. A soft moan escaped her lips. Her eyes flew open wide.

Rafe jerked his hands away from her like they were on fire and cleared his throat. Tayla lowered her lashes, the desire to cry returning stronger than before. She bit down hard on her lip.

"She doesn't have a concussion, but she should probably rest for bit. There is a lump on her head, so you'll want to watch her closely over the next few hours to make sure she doesn't vomit."

"That bump is probably not new. She had some sort of an accident earlier this week."

Rafe narrowed his eyes at Maggie. "What kind of accident?"

"We don't know really. Ev and Jake found her—"

"I am sitting right here," Tayla announced. "I can hear you."

Rafe shot a look at her that could have frozen hell, but she didn't back down. She lifted her chin and stared at him, daring him to continue treating her like a child.

"Well, Miss 'I'm right here,' try taking the steps one at a time next time and we'll all be the better for it." Rafe's words bit. She dropped her jaw. He had to be the devil himself.

Maggie huffed and even though she was a good foot shorter than Rafe, forcibly turned him around by yanking his upper arm toward the dining room and pushed him right out the door.

Rafe glanced back in the study at his traveling companion who'd started to follow them. "You stay in the house. And take those bags up to your room," he barked.

Maggie pushed him again out of Tayla's sight.

Tayla glanced up at the blond man who arrived with Rafe. He turned to offer a polite smile and started to say something, then stopped as his eyes trailed down her body. Tayla had the sudden need to cover the exposed flesh at her neck.

Harrison Davis took a step toward her. All cheerful façade had left his face and reached out toward her. Tayla leaned back away from him.

"Excuse me, but may I?" he asked, glancing at her briefly for approval.

She hesitated, then nodded her consent.

When his knuckle brushed her skin and clasped the locket, stabbing pain seared streaks of white light directly above her eye. She gripped her head and fell forward into the man. A vivid image of his face flashed before her, bloodied and breathless.

"Are you all right?" Harrison dropped to his knee in attempt to keep her upright.

"Do I know you?" she asked through the pain.

"I don't believe I've ever had the pleasure. Maybe you should lie down."

Tayla shook her head gingerly. "You're British," she stated the obvious.

He smiled and a little huff of laughter escaped him. "Yes, I am. So are you."

She managed a smile. Harrison Davis was so congenial, so what was he doing with someone as disagreeable as Rafe Redbourne?

"What in heaven's name has gotten into you?" Maggie whirled on him the moment they entered the kitchen.

"That," Rafe pointed to the closed kitchen door, "is Tayla Hawthorne."

"I think you've made that perfectly clear. But that doesn't tell me why you are acting like a horse's backside."

"Hawthorne. Think about it, Mags. You might remember a certain man who was left at the altar by a lovely young Miss Tessa Hawthorne."

Maggie leaned back against the counter, resigned. "Ah, *that* Hawthorne. So, Locket is the culprit behind your wounded pride and restless nature."

"Who the hell is Locket?"

"For all your charm and good looks you really have a lot to learn," Maggie said as she pushed herself away from the counter and stepped into Rafe's personal space. "That young woman in there, the girl who you've spent the last few minutes badgering, has no memories of who she is or how she got here."

Rafe glanced at the door then back at Maggie. "What do you mean she doesn't know who she is?"

"Ev and Jake found her down by the creek, wet and unconscious. She'd been hurt. Her head was bleeding and she was cold as ice."

Rafe flexed his jaw.

"They brought her here. It took a few days, but she finally woke up, but didn't know her own name. Now, I understand that you're upset about your little faux pas that day at the altar, but it happened a long time ago, Rafe. She doesn't remember anything about it. I expect you to be civil."

How could he just pretend that Tayla Hawthorne hadn't ruined his life? His eyes bored into Maggie's as he fought the urge to unleash his tongue. Maggie could hold her own and Rafe had seen first-hand what happened when she was crossed.

"Locket?"

Maggie nodded her head. She walked to the stove, wrapped her hands in her apron and pulled out the hot pan of dried berry muffins that had just finished baking.

"When Jake and his father found her, the locket around her neck had gotten caught up in her hair. It's the only personal item she had on her and we thought it might be a family heirloom that could give us some idea of who she is. So…"

Maggie set the pan down onto the wooden countertop and reached up on her toes for the basket on top of the indoor icebox. She couldn't quite make it. Rafe plucked it from that height with ease and handed it to her with a smirk.

"So," he urged.

Maggie slapped him on the shoulder in mock affront at his teasing. "So, Jake called her Locket, and it stuck." She shrugged her shoulders. With her hands still wrapped in the apron, she tossed the baked goods into the basket and turned around to grab a bottle of cordial.

The smell of the muffins drifted across the bottom of Rafe's nose and he snatched one from the basket and took a bite before Maggie could object. The steam seared the roof of his mouth and he opened his mouth and blew around the small piece of muffin to allow some of the heat to escape.

When she turned around, his mouth was closed and he smiled, then swallowed. She appeared as if she might scold him, but instead burst out into a loud guffaw. Rafe's grin widened and he finished enjoying the rest of the muffin.

"We need to get back out there." She looked up at Rafe with narrowed eyes. "Be nice."

Rafe placed his hand over his heart. Maggie picked up the basket, but before she could open it, he grabbed another warm treat and grinned.

"Redbourne," Harrison shouted from the other room. "You better get in here." There was something urgent in his voice.

Rafe tore through the dining room to the study, Maggie close behind him, to find Tayla huddled over, arms supported by her knees and her hands clenching the sides of her head.

Tayla exhaled. The pain in her head had already begun to subside when Rafe and Maggie came bounding into the room. The image of Harrison's face had disappeared, but the lingering ache still throbbed at her temples.

Rafe knelt down beside her. His strong hands encircled her wrists in attempt to pull her hands away from her head.

"Leave me alone," she spat. She didn't want his help. Her eyes squinted against the evening sunbeams that would disappear behind the mountains at any moment. She forced herself to open her eyes enough to look up at Maggie. "Can I just go to my room?"

"Locket, honey, Rafe just wants to help."

"Let her go," Rafe said matter-of-factly. He stood and swept at the air with his hand toward the door in invitation to leave.

"Go on, child. I'll bring some supper up to you in a bit."

Tayla gingerly pushed herself off the fainting couch. She smiled politely at Harrison and Maggie, but it fell when her eyes met Rafe's. She walked out into the dining room, where a room full of curious spectators awaited. She looked at the stairs, but decided against returning to her room. She needed some fresh air and thought a walk down to the pond would do the trick.

The sun had fallen behind the mountain peak, but the colors of the sunset still danced on the sky in darkened tones. The cobblestone path circled the inn and wound through a small thicket of Aspens to the pond. She breathed deeply. Fragments of thought and vision played with her mind as she made her way down the path.

"May I join you?"

Tayla glanced up to see Pete leaning against the stone encased waterwheel holding out a small gathering of freshly picked wildflowers.

"Maggie thought you might could use some cheering up."

Tayla smiled. There were so many questions in her mind, so

many thoughts, but Pete's presence seemed to calm her some.

"Of course." She took the extended flowers and sniffed at their heavenly scent.

"Lilacs," Pete said quietly. "They were my mother's favorite."

"Were?" Tayla inquired.

"Lost her in an Indian raid a few years ago."

"I'm sorry, Pete."

Tayla felt comfortable talking to Pete. He was strong and large physically, but something about his gentle demeanor put her at ease. They walked comfortably down to the water's edge and sat on the carved wooden bench surrounded by a garden of wildflowers. Her headache was gone.

"So, you remember Rafe, huh?" Pete asked.

"Remember him?" Tayla's heart fluttered a little. "Should I?"

"If you are Tayla Hawthorne, you should."

"Well, maybe I'm not this Tayla person. I don't know him. And I don't want to. He's mean and cruel and I would do better without knowing the likes of him."

"Nah, Rafe's a good man, just too stubborn and proud for his own good."

"Seems *you* know an awful lot about him."

"He's been a regular around these parts for a long time. Met him a few years back when I came to work for Maggie. We used to be real close."

"Used to be?"

"I'm afraid it's too long a story to tell you tonight," Pete said with a hint of a smile playing about the corners of his mouth.

Tayla suspected it had something to do with Maggie. She'd seen the way that Pete often looked at her. And by the way Rafe had kissed her when he'd arrived, Tayla wouldn't be surprised if she is what had come between them. She just had to figure out how to get Rafe out of the picture and push Pete and Maggie closer together. She needed to believe that there was a happily ever after for someone.

"How's Jake?"

"That kid's got a stubborn streak too, but he's got a lot of fight in 'im. Doc said he doesn't think there'll be any permanent damage, but we'll have to wait 'til morning to see." Pete rested his arm behind her on the bench, but didn't touch her. "It's a beautiful evenin'."

Tayla sensed he was done talking.

"I'd better head back in. Thanks, Pete. For the flowers. And the company."

Pete stood with her and they walked back to the inn in silence. When they reached the front door, they found Rafe sitting on the short retaining wall leading up to the entrance.

"Pete." Rafe's face brightened some when he saw his friend. "It's been a long time." He stood up and reached a hand out to take Pete's.

Tayla slipped behind them to the door, but before she could open it, Pete was there.

"Goodnight, Miss Locket." He leaned over and kissed her cheek.

Heat rushed into Tayla's face. She glanced over at Rafe who raised an eyebrow and flexed his jaw.

"Goodnight, Pete." She closed the door behind her with a disturbing sense of satisfaction.

"Goodnight, Rafe," she whispered.

Rafe pounded a fistful of moistened clay down onto the wheel. He was grateful for the distraction the potter's tool provided. He pulled the crusty pinstripe apron from its hook in the barn and straddled the wooden platform, which had been made for someone much smaller than him.

His muscles were tired, but his mind would not relent. He grasped the metal disc firmly and spun it harder than he should have. It only protested momentarily before easing into a gentle spinning hum as he kicked at the rotator wheel under his feet.

His palms cupped the clay firmly, thumbs on top, carefully coaxing the clay to open beneath his touch. The excess material seeped through his fingers. It had been too long since he'd created anything new. He missed working with his hands. As he coaxed and molded the rounded mound, the raw materials began to rise at the edges.

*Tayla Hawthorne.*

He'd had no idea the affect seeing her would have on him. He dipped his hand into the small water bucket on the side table and wet the clay.

"Thought I might find you out here." Maggie leaned against the barn door and watched him work. "Don't know why I've held on to that old thing. I guess I always hoped it would keep bringing ya back."

"It worked. Here I am." He kicked the wheel again, unsmiling.

"Here you are." She pushed away from the frame and walked toward him. "What's eaten at ya, Rafe?"

"What makes you think something's eating at me?" In order to avert Maggie's scrutinizing stare, he intentionally kept his eyes focused on the clay. He didn't feel like answering her questions. He just wanted to throw a piece.

"Well, it's been a long time since you've worked out here. Always in such a hurry and all." She paused for a moment. "It's Locket, isn't it?"

Rafe's hand slipped, ripping into the thin sides of the pitcher he'd been forming. The top layers of the clay collapsed onto the wheel.

"Not a word," he grumbled.

Rafe gathered the broken section up into a ball and slammed it on top of the remaining portion of clay. He splashed the haphazard clump with water and started the process again.

"What are you going to do?"

"About what?"

Maggie pursed her lips, but did not speak. When she started tapping her foot against the floor, he stopped the wheel and looked up at her.

"She's coming with me," he said, half expecting Maggie to protest. She didn't.

"There are bad people after her, Mags. I need you to be safe. Just having her here puts you at risk. I need to take her to Redbourne Ranch until I can get this mess straightened out. What other choice do I have?"

Maggie remained quiet, but sat down on the stool in the corner next to Lexa's stall. "I don't know all that's going on with you. Not sure I want to, but it's not me you have to convince." She got up off the stool, walked over next to him, reached out her hand, and placed it carefully on his forearm. "You haven't been very nice to that girl and without a past to rely on, I don't know that she'll trust you enough to go with you."

"I'm trying," he said with more aggravation in his voice than he'd intended. "But my memory seems to be a little longer than hers." He managed a smile and Maggie hit him playfully on the shoulder.

Rafe needed to just think of her as a bounty. That way, they could both walk away unscathed. He still couldn't believe his luck at finding Tayla unexpectedly at Maggie's place, and almost without incident or injury. Well, except for her little fall down the stairs, and a complete loss of memory, she was safe...for now. If she really was unaware of her identity, she couldn't stay here.

"What's going on between Pete and Tayla?" Rafe cursed himself for the hint of jealousy in his voice.

The moment Pete had leaned over to kiss Tayla tonight, a lump had formed in Rafe's throat. His jaw was beginning to ache from clenching it. It irked him that he would care what the likes of Tayla Hawthorne would do or who she was with. The worst was that he was beginning to feel less like an older brother and more like a fool suitor.

Damn it.

Maggie didn't say anything, but she raised an eyebrow at him and the corners of her mouth upturned.

This was going to be more difficult than he'd expected. Wounds he'd thought had healed a long time ago returned to the surface to inflict new damage on the wall he'd built around his heart.

He kicked at the wheel. "We're leaving as soon as she can be ready to ride. Me, Davis, and Tayla."

# CHAPTER SEVEN

"Tayla," Rafe knocked softly on her bedroom door. It was getting late and he didn't want to disturb any of the other inn patrons. He realized, with some irritation, that she had no idea that *she* was Tayla.

"Locket," he tried again, "will you please answer the door?" Hawthorne or not, his mama would have tanned his hide had she ever heard him talk to a woman the way he had spoken to Tayla all day.

The lock on the bedroom turned and she opened the door just enough that he could see one eye peering at him. She slammed it shut.

"Go away. I have no desire to talk to the likes of you."

"Locket, please. I have to talk to you. It's about your father."

He waited.

The door swung open wide.

Rafe stood in the doorway of her room frozen. The neckline of Tayla's nightshift plunged low and hugged her breasts. Her locket dangled between them. She held a brush in one hand and her hair fell in loose tendrils around her face and down her shoulders. He opened his mouth to speak, but nothing came out.

She pulled her robe more closely around her. "What do you know about my father?" Tayla crossed her arms, hiding his distraction from view.

Rafe needed something to wet his dry throat.

"He's alive," Rafe croaked.

"I don't understand. Do you know me? My family?"

"Your name is Tayla Hawthorne. The rest we'll talk about later."

"I don't want to wait until later. If you can't provide me with answers then this conversation is over." She started to close the door again.

Rafe's patience was growing thin. He put his boot between the door and the frame.

"You're not safe here. If they find you, they'll take you again and I can't let that happen."

"Who will find me? And why do you care? You hate me."

Rafe felt a twinge of guilt twist in his gut. "I don't hate you." He took a deep breath. "There is no excuse for my behavior today. I-I'm sorry," he choked out. "All the same, I'm staying here with Maggie and Jacob. And Pete."

The muscles in Rafe's jaw flexed involuntarily. Pete. She wanted Pete. He was tempted to just walk away and never see her again. He motioned to leave.

Tayla uncrossed her arms and nearly flew out after him. When her fingers touched the skin of his forearm, he froze. She pulled her hand back as if she'd been bit.

She narrowed her eyes at him. "What about my father? How do I know *you're* not dangerous?"

"Oh, honey, I'm dangerous all right, but a chit like you has nothing to worry about from me."

"Don't call me honey. My name is..." her eyes roamed the doorframe.

"Tayla," Rafe filled in. "And we're leaving first thing Friday morning so you'd better get used to the idea. Be ready."

"No. I am not going anywhere with you."

"Wanna bet?"

Tayla slammed the door.

"And my name is Locket," she screamed from behind the closed door.

"Well, that went well," he muttered under his breath. "Friday," he yelled back and turned around to his room, which was directly across from hers.

A man peeked his head out from a room down the hall.

Rafe just smiled and tipped an imaginary hat to him. Then, he opened the door to his room and plopped down on the patchwork quilt of his bed to remove his boots.

*Davis.* Rafe had been so distracted by finding Tayla at Maggie's he'd nearly forgotten the Brit, but the man knew the consequence if he ran again—not that Rafe thought he would. He'd made himself perfectly clear and somewhere along the way, he'd chosen to trust the man. Trust didn't come easily.

The door of the adjoining room was blocked by a six-drawer dresser and Rafe didn't feel like moving it, so he walked down the hall, his thoughts still on the woman in the room across the way. She made his blood boil, but it was hard not to notice how much she had grown up. Her wheat blond curls were a stark contrast to Tessa's raven locks. Tayla's cheekbones were higher and her lips fuller. He tried to conjure the image of the young fourteen-year-old girl she'd been the last time he'd seen her.

Rafe cursed himself for the direction his thoughts had taken him. Tayla had certainly grown into a woman. Despite her trespasses against him, he couldn't deny the attraction he felt now.

"Enough," he demanded of himself aloud.

It had been a long time, but the love he'd once held for Tessa and her baby sister had faded long ago and in its place had grown disdain, distrust, and apathy toward any kind of long-term romantic entanglements.

He rapped his knuckles on the door. He reached for the doorknob, but before he had a chance to open it, it swung wide and Harrison stood there grinning from ear to ear.

"What's gotten into you?" Rafe asked with lifted eyebrows.

"Look at this room. Besides the decent décor at Mr. Longhurst's place, I haven't slept in a room this elegant since England. I'd forgotten how wonderful it is."

Rafe snorted. "I hadn't realized you were such a woman."

"Mock me all you like, Rafe, but it is perfectly acceptable for a man to like nice things and enjoy the comforts of home," Harrison shot back at him as he placed himself in an oversized armchair at the edge of the room and propped his un-booted feet on the stool in front of him.

Rafe had to admit, it was nice to stay in a place with somewhere to sleep other than the hard dirt ground.

"Don't get too comfortable," Rafe cautioned and then closed the door behind him as he walked further into the room. "We're leaving first thing Friday morning. And Tayla's coming with us."

Harrison sat bolt upright. "Was she still wearing the necklace?"

"Yes." Rafe's voice squeaked a little as he thought of Tayla in that locket.

"I think there's something you should know," Harrison told Rafe.

"What do you mean?" Rafe eyed him warily. He'd thought Harrison had already told him everything.

Harrison smiled weakly and Rafe could see beads of sweat already formulating on the man's brow.

"That locket is one of a kind. I've seen it before," Harrison tried to explain. "It's a Darington family heirloom."

"Well, she *was* Lord Darington's fiancée." Rafe was getting impatient. He was tired and wanted sleep before their journey tomorrow.

"You don't understand. That locket belonged to my grandmother. She was wearing it the night she came to visit me and Finn. It could be the heirloom my grandmother had referred to and if Tayla is wearing it..."

"If that locket belongs to you and Finn, we'll figure it out. But for now, we're going to stick around here one more day. One!" Rafe said curtly and turned to leave the room.

Harrison jumped onto the bed and threw his hands behind his head.

"Okay by me, mate."

Rafe rummaged his fingers through his hair. "I don't know what it is about you Davis, but I believe your whole cockamamie story."

After a good night's sleep, he, Harrison, and Tayla would all sit down and have a nice little chat. He wanted to get to the bottom of this goose chase he was on and then get back to his life.

When he reached his door, he heard an odd sound coming from the room across from his. He leaned in a little closer. Tayla was crying. He shook his head and walked into his bedroom, trying to ignore the sounds coming from the other room. He removed his shirt and tossed it onto the chair next to the bed. He needed sleep

When he crawled into his bed, Rafe swallowed hard, but ignored the pang of guilt that stabbed at his abdomen. He wanted to be happy he'd made her cry, but unfortunately he'd always had a soft spot for women of all shapes and sizes—even the little ones. As much as he tried to deny it, it still extended to this girl he once knew and loved. Could he forgive her and forget the past? Did he even want to?

Tayla awoke to the sound of her own screams.

"No, papa. No!"

She sat bolt upright, beads of sweat trickling down the sides of her face. Ragged, shallow breaths had her whipping her head from one side to the other. Within moments her door flung open and Rafe was at her side, encircling her with his strong arms, and she leaned into the seemingly familiar strength of the man with whom she'd felt a connection. This same man she hoped could trust. The man who made her feel every inch a woman when he looked at her.

Who had Rafe Redbourne been in her life?

None of that mattered right now. He was here with her, holding her, keeping her safe. Everything would be okay. His work-roughened hand cupped her head, his fingers entwined her damp curls, and he pulled her closer into the crook between his shoulder and chest.

Tears flowed freely now. Even though she could no longer remember the events of her dream, the effects of it still racked through her.

"Shhh..." His soft baritone voice warmed her.

She hiccupped.

This was the man she'd hoped he would be. This was the Rafe Redbourne she wanted to know. He was familiar, her memory of him so close to the surface she could almost see it, and she struggled to remember.

Tayla snuggled in a little closer, reveling in the warmth of his embrace. His grip around her tightened. She lifted her hand to wipe away a tear and gasped when her fingertips grazed the bare skin of his chest. She flattened her palm over his heart.

He felt good.

When her breathing at last returned to normal, she pulled away from him. She searched his eyes—for what, she was still unsure—but she was grateful for the oversized moon tonight that allowed her to see him so clearly.

Rafe cleared his throat.

"I heard you screaming and couldn't stay away." He looked down at her, his brows scrunched together and his face jutted forward as if waiting an explanation.

Tayla blinked. He was so handsome in the moonlight. Especially now, in the middle of the night, with his hair tousled, shirtless, and his guard lowered from the effects of sleep. But, what could she say?

She'd been having nightmares since she was brought to the inn. The only thing she could remember from them was the sound of a gunshot and blood seeping through a shirted man's chest. She still couldn't see the man's face from her dream, but had a feeling it had something to do with her father. She wished she could remember the dream, and the rest of her past. She wanted to understand why Rafe had been so cool to her this evening and yet her lifeline tonight.

Tayla's damp curls spilled about her shoulders and she realized her night shift was bunched all around her middle. A nervous giggle escaped and she pushed at the garment until it covered her completely.

Rafe's nearness threw her off kilter and she was glad that she was already sitting down.

"You said my father is alive," she whispered, inching closer to him. "Have you seen him?"

Rafe nodded.

"What's he like?"

"Shhhh."

He placed a warm finger on her lips and she began to tremble. He rubbed her bare arms vigorously. "We'll talk about it in the morning. Go back to sleep."

"Thank you. I'm okay now." She forced a reassuring smile and placed a hand over one of his.

Rafe narrowed his eyes at her and then glanced down at their hands. In one swift movement, he pulled his hand from beneath hers and pushed himself up off the bed and to the door. His large frame seemed to fill the space there.

"Maggie's put me just across the hall," he said without turning around and then he closed the door behind him.

Tayla fell back against the bed and exhaled loudly. Try as she might, sleep eluded her. She lifted her hand to the locket and held it close to her skin. Her fingers trailed over the blunt facets again and again as she caressed it, hoping it would help her find answers.

She was afraid, she realized. Rafe wanted to take her away from the only place, the only people she knew. Maggie. Jake. Pete. They had all been so good to her. She was grateful for the warm bed and comfortable night shift Maggie had provided her to sleep in. The playful company she had enjoyed with Jake, and the strong shoulder Pete had been for her over the last few days.

She snuggled down under the blankets and stared out the window. Moonlight spilled through the sheer curtains. A gape in the window coverings allowed her a glimpse at the moon, which looked bigger than she'd ever seen it.

Her father was alive. She smiled. She couldn't picture his face and she wondered what had happened to him. Was he the one she was seeing in her dreams? Questions filled her thoughts and she pondered on the new information she had obtained tonight. Sleep still eluded her.

Dawn was nearing.

Tayla couldn't stay in her room any longer. Her stomach growled. The thought of Maggie's biscuits would not relent. Maybe a glass of warm milk would help to calm her nerves.

The moment her feet touched the floor, she shivered and rubbed her hands together. She felt around the wooden planks for her slippers, but could not find them in the dark recesses under the bed. She stepped across the room and pulled the gossamer robe from her vanity post and threw it around her shoulders.

The door creaked when she pulled it open and she winced, glancing down the hall for any indication that someone had heard her. Rafe's door was shut and only a soft blue glow came from beneath it. She held her breath for a few second before venturing out down the stairs to the kitchen.

The lantern was on the counter table just inside the door, but Tayla was unsure where Maggie kept the matches. She'd never thought to ask. She bent over to feel around on the shelf for the heavy wooden matchbox. The kitchen door swung open, hitting her square on the behind, and knocked her to her knees on the floor.

Rafe needed air. Tayla's screams had awakened him and his first instinct had been to run to her side. However, his conscience had warred with his pride. She'd made a fool out him and he'd vowed to never let that happen again. Tayla had only been fourteen years old the last time he'd seen her, but now she was a woman—a woman who needed his help.

His conscience won.

He'd thought he would be able to walk away, but after holding her in her room and seeing the fear in her eyes and feeling the speed of her heart under her sleeping gown, he knew it would be an impossible task to leave without her.

He didn't bother to put on a shirt when he walked down the stairs. The crisp night air would do him some good. He picked up the lap blanket that Maggie had strewn over the back of the couch and walked out onto the back porch. He sat down on the wooden bench that overlooked the lake. The moonlight danced with the smallest movement in the water and Rafe took a deep breath.

He was becoming soft and in his line of work, soft wouldn't cut it. After only a few minutes, the chill started to penetrate his skin and he shook the blanket out and threw over the length of his body. His bare feet stretched out in front of him. The sun would rise at any moment.

Rafe heard a noise coming from the kitchen. Maggie didn't usually get up until just after dawn. Curious, he stood up and went back into the house, using his hand to ease the front door shut behind him, careful to not make any sound. He tiptoed to the swinging kitchen door and looked around for something he could use as a weapon, should he need it. A set of tall, metal candlesticks reflected the light from outside. He grabbed one and shoved the door open, hand raised and ready to strike.

Thump. He'd knocked someone to the floor. The scream that met his ears belonged to a familiar voice and he scrunched down closer to the huddled form on the floor.

Tayla.

She whipped her head around and met him with a fire in her eyes that sent him backward. He reached out a hand to help her up, but she just blew a stray lock of hair from her face and turned onto her bottom.

"What is wrong with you?" she asked, fighting the strand of her hair that just would not stay put. "You just blow hot and cold, don't you, Mr. Redbourne? One moment you are mean and cold and bitter. The next you rescue me from my nightmares in the middle of the night. And now, look at me.

Which is it to be with you? Hot or cold?"

How could he answer that? Hot *and* cold. Was that an acceptable answer?

He couldn't help himself. Tayla pushed the hair out of her face again. When it fell back down to cover her eye, a bubble of laughter spilled out in a loud guffaw.

"Argggggh," she squealed and threw her hands up in the air.

"You are a sight," he said, laughter still filling his voice.

Tayla pouted her lips and then he saw it, the curve of her lips until she too started to giggle.

"Come on," he said, reaching down to help her.

She took his hand this time and he pulled her up. She stood mere inches from him. He reached up to the stray lock that had fallen over her face in disarray and carefully tucked it behind her ear. Their eyes locked and for a moment he thought he might kiss her.

*What are you doing, Redbourne?*

She felt good and memories from holding her in her bed earlier made his muscles tense involuntarily. He quickly set her away from him and her robe slipped away from her shoulder.

He groaned inwardly. He'd stayed away from romantic entanglements with women for good reason. This was no time to get involved. *Especially not with a Hawthorne. Not with Tayla.* He turned around and faced away from her.

"Better go get dressed," he said to her. "Wouldn't want Pete or somebody else to get the wrong idea." He regretted the words the moment they left his mouth. What was she doing to him?

"And I'd had the idea that you might actually be a gentleman."

She didn't back down. He liked that.

Rafe lifted his head, but refused to look at her. "I think I dispelled that notion a long time ago. Now, go on. Get on with ya. We're leaving in an hour."

"Not with you, I'm not," she said right up close to his ear before she pushed through the back kitchen doors and walked out.

"I hope you're packed," he called after her. He'd planned on giving her an extra day to collect her things and say her goodbyes, but he just couldn't risk more time with her. The sooner they got on the road, the sooner he would be rid of her. Away from her intoxicating eyes, her nearly irresistible curves. He was only a man and he wasn't sure how long he could stay away from her. She was not a part of his plan.

*Women.* He shook his head.

The door creaked open behind him. She'd returned. How could he resist her supple mouth?

"What do you exp..." he stopped short when Maggie's face appeared. She smirked.

"I just saw Locket running up to her room." She winked. "Everything all right?"

He growled and walked past her up the stairs. He stopped on the top landing and dropped the blanket he'd been carrying onto the chaise below. It landed perfectly on the top corner of the back and draped the arm. Satisfied, he walked into his room and slammed the door.

What had he been thinking? Beautiful or not, protecting Tayla would take a lot of patience and expended energy and restraint—and not the kind he normally displayed.

He and Mr. Davis should be on the road for Kansas right now. He wanted to just leave Tayla here with Maggie. Heavens knew Maggie would be happy to have another woman around to talk to, but he still didn't know the extent of the demons that haunted her. And as much as he hated to admit it, he didn't like the idea of her being here with Pete.

Besides, he'd given Adrien his word he'd find her and protect her. He just hadn't considered that it might be him from whom she'd need protecting. He just hoped he could find a way to focus on his job instead of her mouth.

He yanked open the wardrobe and took out a clean black shirt. He sat down on the bed and pulled on his boots, grumbling to himself.

Harrison Davis peeked in the door. "Um...Did I miss something? Miss Hawthorne told me goodbye and good luck? Is she not coming with us?"

Rafe couldn't decide if he liked Mr. Davis or if he should strangle him. He'd never let a bounty have any leeway, but with this man his defenses were down and he'd started to look at him more like a friend than a bounty.

Rafe put on his hat and picked up his belt. "Yes. I told her we're leaving in an hour. Why?"

"An hour? Okay. Well, I just saw her heading into the stables."

Rafe threw his arms through the sleeves on the unbuttoned shirt and grabbed his hat.

"Be ready to go in a half hour."

"Oooo!" Tayla squealed the moment she walked into her room, her hands curled into fists at her sides. A single tear found its way down her cheek and she wiped it away with one brisk movement. "I will not let him affect me."

She changed into a simple blue dress. Rafe thought he could tell her to leave with him and be ready in an hour. Well, wasn't he going to be surprised? She may not remember much, but she was sure she would have never let Rafe Redbourne tell her what to do.

Part of her wanted to go with him. But if she really were in danger, she didn't want her newfound friends to get hurt on her account. Tayla opened her bedroom window. The birds chirped and the gentle soothing sound of the creek rushing toward the pond provided her with a sense of calm. She leaned against the windowsill. A soft whinny of a horse reached her ears. A good ride is just what she needed. She pushed herself away from the window and headed down to the stables.

The barn housed stalls for six horses. Only four were occupied. As she stepped inside, a brown and white paint nudged her on the arm and she rubbed his nose. Maggie stood on the other side of the horse, brushing him down.

"Good morning." Maggie smiled and patted the gelding on the side. "Locket, meet The General."

She picked up and apple and fed it to the paint. "He seems to have taken a liking to ya." She resumed her grooming.

"He's beautiful."

The General nickered and rubbed his face up against Tayla's.

"Maggie, how long have you known Mr. Redbourne?"

"Rafe? A mighty long time. He's a good man, that one. A bit hard headed, but good."

"He's infuriating."

Maggie laughed.

"Oooo!" she squealed again. Tayla wanted to stomp her foot, but refrained. "He said I have to leave with him, no matter what I want. How dare he *demand* I do anything?"

"For as long as I've known him—and, that's been a long while—he's always adhered to a sense of duty and responsibility. He feels responsible for ya is all." Maggie set the brush down and picked up the red bucket full of oats from the corner of the stall.

"He's as stubborn as they come, but you won't find a better sort," she stated with a firm nod of her head. "But Locket, if you really don't want to go, you're a grown woman and that's up to you. You are welcome to stay on here until your memory returns. Heaven knows I could use some help around here."

Tayla plopped down in the chair outside the stall and leaned back against the wood.

Maggie patted the horse and grabbed the reins from their place on the wall. "He's normally full of charm and humor."

"Rafe or The General?" Tayla smiled.

"You are wicked." The older woman grinned back.

"What happened, Maggie? Why is he so angry with me?" Tayla turned to watch her new friend tack her horse.

"Oh, honey, it's not my place to say, but that man was hurt something fierce. Be patient. He'll tell you when he's ready—if your memory doesn't recover before then."

After her encounter with Rafe in the kitchen, she'd gone to

her room, looked around, and had realized that not one thing in there had belonged to her—though she was very grateful for the fresh underthings and clean dress that Maggie had provided.

Rafe would be going up to her room at any moment and as much as she hated to admit it, he scared her a little. Not scared for her life or her safety, but scared of what he did to her. The reactions he caused just by being close to her. She didn't want to go.

Maggie led the gelding from his stall and Tayla followed them out into the corral.

"You remember how to ride?"

Tayla looked from Maggie to the horse and back again. A grin spread across her face. She took the outstretched reins from her new friend.

"Maggie, thank you," she said sincerely, "for everything you have done for me here." As much as she hated to admit it, she knew that leaving with Rafe was the best chance she had at getting her life back, her memories. But she was even more grateful that Harrison Davis would be there with her. She couldn't help but wonder how it would look—one woman travelling alone with two men without a chaperone.

Maggie smiled at her knowingly.

"I'm just going to go for a quick ride up the ridge."

"How about you just say goodbye to Maggie here and we'll be on our way?" Rafe walked up beside the horse and rubbed his hand across the bridle.

The spans of his chest caused Tayla's breath to catch in her throat. She took a deep breath, determined not to let him get under her skin. She smiled.

"I don't know what you think you know about me, Mr. Redbourne, but I must not be the same girl you knew as I have become accustomed to doing as I please and will not be bossed around by some overindulged bully just because you have a nice face." She arched her back slightly and straightened her spine. "You are not in charge of me and I do not have to do your bidding simply because you demand it. Now, if you'll excuse me." Tayla turned back to Maggie. "I'll be back in time to help with breakfast." She climbed up onto The General, grateful for the extra material in her skirt that allowed her to sit comfortably, clicked her heels against the horse's flank, and rode out of the stable at a walk.

As much as she wanted to, Tayla resisted the urge to glance behind her. He didn't call after her and she smirked, imagining him standing there gaping. When she finally rounded the edge of the hill and would be out of sight, she released the breath she'd been holding. Why did he get to her so? Any hope she'd had of simply asking him about her past now seemed out of reach. Rafe Redbourne was stubborn and arrogant. The less she spoke to him, she decided, the better.

She had only been at Maggie's for a week, yet somehow, she felt at ease here. Little snippets of her memory continued to invade her thoughts, but nothing coherent enough to really piece together. Every time Rafe's face flashed through her mind, he wore a smile, and she was sure he was someone else altogether.

She finally reached the top of the ridge. The sun had risen just above the mountains and cast a long ray of shimmering light across the lake. The soft mist that rose from the water added an air of beauty to the already brilliant hues of morning and the distinct scent of rain still lingered on the breeze.

The General snorted and his step faltered.

"What is it, boy?" Tayla coaxed him forward, but with the next step the gravel gave way beneath his feet and his front legs paddled against the mud to keep on solid ground. Tayla leaned forward, clinging to his neck, the saddle horn protruding into her hip.

He reared. Tayla squeezed her knees even tighter together and to her surprise and relief, was able to remain saddled. She wondered if she'd always been clumsy or if whatever was wrong with her head had affected her ability to balance. The General backed a few feet away from the ledge and stopped. Tayla dismounted. Maybe she would just walk him back to the inn.

She grabbed a hold of the dangling reins.

An animal's scream sounded in close distance. Tayla took a

step toward the noise, The General following close behind. This time it sounded like a hollow cry and she squinted her eyes into the small copse of trees just a few feet ahead.

At the base of one of the larger walnut trees, a small bear cub struggled to loose itself from some sort of snare that twisted around the trunk. Tayla smiled. He looked so cute, big round eyes, and a short little snout. A small beehive dangled from the lower branch and swarms of the creatures collected around the base of the hive and near the bear cub's head.

"Honey will do it to you every time." Tayla shook her head and giggled.

In order to free the cub, Tayla would have to get past those bees. An image of an old woman in masked garb flashed through her mind, but this time, there was no pain. The image was gone in an instant, but it left her with the idea she needed to use smoke to distract the bees.

Tayla glanced around for something she could use to start a fire. With all of the rain they'd had over the last few weeks, the chances of finding something dry enough to light was slim. She just needed to create smoke, not a fire exactly. She walked around The General to look in his saddle bags. Nothing.

The baby bear whined again, but this time a searching roar sounded from somewhere higher in the hills. Tayla sat up straight and a sense of urgency overtook her. Mama bear was looking for her cub and if Tayla didn't free the small animal, there would be trouble. The bees seemed to be getting more agitated and a few had started to swoop down to the bear cub's ears.

As the loud roar of the mama bear got closer, The General started to prance about. He was getting anxious, as was Tayla. While she had no intention of coming face to face with the threat, she couldn't leave the young cub trapped in the snare. She took another step forward and froze when a group of twigs snapped behind her.

# CHAPTER EIGHT

"She's been gone way too long," Rafe said, leaning forward on the porch bench he'd built just last year.

It had been everything he could do to stop himself from riding after Tayla when she'd ridden out of the stable. He had to admire her backbone though. Not many men dared talk to him the way she had done.

"Why, Rafe, if I didn't know any better I would say that you were feeling a bit protective of the Hawthorne lass." The redheaded inn keeper laughed as she kicked at the base of the outer kitchen door and pushed through to hand him a steaming mug of spiced cider.

"You don't have to remind me who she is, Mags." He nodded a thank you and leaned down to take a sip.

The animal's roar was unmistakable around these parts and Rafe jumped to his feet, spilling hot liquid on the back of his hand.

"Damn it all," he cursed himself as he quickly moved to set the clay mug on the railing. He shook his hand and then brought it into a fist. "You had bear trouble lately?" he asked Maggie.

"Ev and Jacob spotted a mama and her three cubs up at Winder's Peak a couple weeks back. There's still quite a bit of snow up there. I wonder if she's come down looking for food."

Rafe grabbed his Stetson from the seat and jumped down off the porch. He'd already brushed and packed Lexa this morning. He'd wanted to get an early start, but it seemed that

Miss Hawthorne was going to make that difficult. He whistled and ran to the pasture gate. Lexa was running and frolicking with some of Maggie's horses. She perked up her ears and ran over to the gate. He checked the rifles hanging on either side of the horse.

Lexa snorted when he pulled himself up and with a short nudge to her sides, Rafe left the stable at a canter. When the bear roared again he urged Lexa to a run. The bears around here seemed particularly fierce and if the one he heard now had cubs, the situation would become dire in moments.

Tayla would be up along the ridge. He just knew it, and he turned Lexa in that direction. His blood rushed through his veins as his heart pumped faster. He had been in the middle of a chase more than once in his line of work, but somehow, the idea of chasing after Tayla invigorated him and he pushed himself harder. However, he wasn't quite sure what he was going to do with her once he had her.

The hillside was still slick with mud from the torrents of rain they'd seen over the last couple of days and more than once Lexa lost her footing on the slippery slope of the terrain.

*Fool woman.*

He pulled Lexa to a stop and swiftly dismounted, lifting one of the rifles from its mount. He carefully made his way through the brush, figuring he would be able to get there more stealthily on foot. Once he reached the woods, he stopped to look for the telltale signs of a trespasser. Broken branches and scattered leaves on the ground directed him toward her. A soft nicker pulled his attention toward the cliffs above the lake.

He finally caught glimpse of The General through the checkerboard of trees and a splash of blue whooshed through a small thicket of aspens. Tayla was distracted and didn't hear him—until a twig snapped beneath his feet.

He dropped his head.

*So much for stealth.*

The last thing he'd wanted to do was startle her, but to his relief, she didn't scream. She met his gaze head on, but instead of walking toward him, she took a step toward a small bear cub that looked to be caught up in a hunter's snare.

"What are you doing?" Rafe demanded in a whisper.

Tayla glanced back over her shoulder, but kept walking.

"I have to free this cub," she said just before catching the toe of her boot on an elevated tree root and fell forward onto her hands and knees.

Another roar sounded. It was much closer now. They didn't have much time.

"We have to leave. Now!" Rafe's words came out more harshly than he'd intended, but even in a whisper, the meaning was still the same. He did not want a confrontation with a bear today. He'd done that and didn't want a repeat experience. His hands moved to his side where two very large, crooked gashes had long since healed.

*No bears today*, he reiterated silently.

Tayla crawled across the wooded floor until she reached the trapped animal. The cub just stared at her with large, round eyes that seemed to plead for help. It didn't appear to be afraid of her at all, which Rafe deemed odd.

She quickly loosed the snare from the youngling's foot, but instead of running away, he stretched his leg and sat down next to her.

She giggled and reached out to scratch behind his ears, seemingly oblivious to the danger headed their way. The bees that had been frantically buzzing about had gone back about their tasks and even the morning breeze had quieted.

"The Pawnee would call you a witch woman," Rafe said, annoyed at the woman who now ignored him.

Tayla didn't look up, but pulled herself to her feet. She reached out for The General's reins, the cub still dancing at her feet.

Rafe glanced back over the hillside and there, amidst the tall yellowed grasses and wild paint brush, the curved hump of a lumbering black bear appeared.

"We have to go, Tayla. Before that bear gets any closer."

Tayla glanced up and searched the hills.

*She can't see her*, Rafe thought. The fur of the mama's coat was lighter and blended well with the surroundings.

A loud yelp came from the small bear cub and Rafe's head darted back in his direction. The small animal was staring up at the beehive and Rafe guessed he was getting frustrated that he could not get to its contents.

He looked back in the direction of the bear. She'd disappeared. Rafe's search spanned the vicinity. Nothing. Lexa was grazing on some of the foliage at the base of the hill. He had to get Tayla out of here. And now.

In two strides he was standing beside her. He swept her up into his arms and put her down, none too gently, on The General's back. The bear cub squealed again. Rafe took a hold of the horse's reins and started down on foot toward Lexa.

An onslaught of water thrust down on top of them as the rain started to fall. It had been a long time since Rafe had seen this much water fall in such a short period of time. The lake was already very full and the terrain would become even more dangerous the wetter it got. The deafening sound of the mama bear's roar broke through the methodic humming of rain. A dense coppice of aspens was all that separated her from them. She lunged, her teeth bared and dripping with foaming spit. The trees were too thick for her to penetrate and she wildly thrashed her head about. She turned toward the base of the thicket.

Rafe spun around. They would not be able to reach Lexa before the bear caught up to them. They were trapped between the bear and the ridge. He looked at the bear cub still swiping at the air below the beehive. If he could just get the baby to run to his mama, she may leave without incident. He picked up a small rounded rock and threw it a few feet behind the small animal.

"Stop. You'll hurt him," Tayla protested. She still hadn't seen the danger they were in.

The General's hooves were getting bogged down in the thick mud that lined the ridge. He shook his head with a snort and tried to lift his front legs in a prancing motion to avoid getting stuck. They needed to get off the ridge.

The bear cub stopped flailing his arm to look behind him. He glanced over to Rafe and Tayla, but did not move. His little head reverted back up to the hive. Rafe leaned over and picked up another stone.

The mama bear had found her way around the dense grove and was headed with purpose in the direction of her cub. In their direction.

Rafe lifted his hand to throw the rock and in one smooth movement, Tayla dismounted and grabbed a hold of his arm. The rock only flew a few feet. Rafe whirled around to face her. He half expected her to cower, but she simply lifted her chin defiantly and took a step backward.

Before Rafe could grab her, the ledge gave way and she disappeared down the side of the ridge. In attempt to get her in his sights, he took a step and leaned forward, but the floor fell out beneath him too and he slid on his backside through mud, falling rocks, and debris. There was no time to think. He flexed his heel and reached out to grab onto something that would help stop his rapid decent. Finally, his foot caught on a small side growing tree trunk. He quickly scanned for Tayla and let out a deep breath when he found her. She clung for dear life to a branch that protruded from the side of the hill.

He eased himself lower, trying to control his movements by grasping at firmly rooted branches. When he was positioned close enough to reach out to her, he made the mistake of looking out over the lake and realized just how high they were. His vision seemed to play tricks on him, and he had to look away.

Why did it always have to be heights?

He forced himself to focus on the water. It was then that he remembered a little fourteen-year-old girl who had refused to get into the swimming hole out of a deep seated fear. Tayla couldn't swim.

Would she remember that? He hoped not.

"Take my hand," he called out to her, the wind and rain making it difficult to hear.

She looked up at him, the whites of her eyes popping out against the deep rich brown of the mud that smeared across her face. She hugged the branch tightly and seemed downright terrified. Only water could bring out this kind of fear in her. She'd always been strong.

"Tayla," he cooed, "it's going to be okay." Rafe stretched his hand even farther.

If she would work her way toward him and he could grab onto her hand, they might be able to reach the overhang a few yards behind him together. At least they would be able to gain solid footing and he would have a moment to catch his breath.

Debris and mud still fell around them. Rafe's foot slid a little and he repositioned it. He didn't know how much longer he could keep steady. The overhang would give him the needed time to assess their location above the lake, but they would have to work quickly.

"Give me your hand, Tay." Rafe used the familiar name he'd called her so often in the past, hoping it would help her trust him.

She looked up, a blank expression draped across her face. Then, she tightened one hand around the straggly branch in front of her and slowly lifted the other toward him. Her fingertips brushed across the ends of his, but she was still too far away. Rafe clenched his jaw and with new determination leaned forward and stretched until he felt the slippery whole of her hand catch in his. He yanked. The whole of her body clashed against his. He held her firmly against him, but almost wished he wasn't. Yes, Tayla had certainly grown up.

Excess mud made it difficult for Rafe to hold on to her. Tayla slipped a little and Rafe felt his grip on her loosen. She grasped the front of his shirt and as he secured his arm more tightly around her waist, the support beneath her feet gave way.

She screamed, but held resolutely to his shirt. The buttons popped. He tried to regain his hold on her, but the material started to tear, increasing the pressure on his shoulders. He lost all footing and slipped. Tayla screamed again. And with another ripping sound they plunged over the edge of the cliff and into the cool water of the lake.

The moment they hit the water, Tayla was jerked out of Rafe's grasp. Her arm flew upward and her elbow connected with something very hard, sending a jolting pain through her arm and up into her shoulder.

She opened her eyes and saw the sun reflecting through the few feet of water that separated her from the surface and pushed her arms down to help get her more quickly to the top, but the strap of her chemise caught on a large stick of some sort and held her down. She looked up to see Rafe's feet kicking beneath the surface.

He'd already made it to the top.

Her chest started to constrict. She needed air. Tayla tried to reach the offending stick, but it was at her back. She twisted and squirmed, but to no avail, and darkness began to encroach around the edges of her vision. Suddenly, she was free.

Rafe had her around the waist and dragged her to the surface. When the water tension broke, she opened her mouth, gasping desperately for the air that would fill her lungs with much needed relief.

"Come on, Tayla," Rafe whispered. She was amazed that he was able to keep them both afloat. He was worried and that realization spread warmth throughout her body. She forced herself to open her eyes—to look up at him.

She wanted to let him know that she was okay, but the words just would not come out. Rafe's chin rested just above the water and on occasion bobbed below the surface. She reached a hand up to his arm and grabbed a hold, her feet moving slowly beneath her. His nose was swollen and bleeding.

"Rafe," she managed, raising a finger toward his face.

He wiped at his nose with the back of his hand. The blood was gone.

"Rafe," she tried again. It was all she could get out before he pulled her closer to him. His lips were so close she could almost taste them.

"Who's out there?" a man yelled from the shore.

Rafe pulled her out to arms-length and looked from one eye to the other. The moment had been broken.

"Can you swim?" he asked, concern lacing his words.

Tayla nodded and pushed through the water, dividing it with her hands beneath the surface. She was surprised that she was able to move so freely.

Rafe swam behind her. She guessed he wanted to make sure she could make it. While it wasn't that far, she found herself tiring and her muscles ached. The more she kicked, the more she realized that something was wrong with her foot. Pain started to radiate into her leg.

Once they reached an area shallow enough for Rafe to stand, he pulled her up out of the water and into his arms. It took a moment for Tayla to realize she was missing her dress. She glanced over Rafe's shoulder to the cliff they'd fallen from and saw the blue material of her dress dangling from a protruding branch. She snuggled tighter into Rafe in hopes of hiding her unsuitable state.

Droplets beaded down Rafe's bronzed chest and Tayla felt herself relax against him. Despite the cool water they'd just emerged from, he was warm to the touch and she took comfort in his strength, leaning her head into his muscled shoulder. She wanted to run her hand across his chest, but thought better of it.

"You know this is private property, don't you son?" An older gentleman with a straggly gray beard, said to Rafe as he walked down the bank and onto the shoreline.

Tayla wondered where the man had come from and what he was doing out here in the rain.

"Couldn't be helped." Rafe shrugged. "Have you seen my horse?"

"That monstrous strawberry over there? She's a real beauty. Wondered where she came from. You interested in selling?"

"No," Rafe said coolly.

"Too bad. She'd make for some good breeding stock."

Rafe whistled and Lexa strode up next to him and nudged him with her nose.

Tayla wondered at the intelligence of the horse. She must have followed them along the ridgeline.

"You folks staying at Maggie's place?"

Rafe set Tayla in the Lexa's saddle, walked around the back, and retrieved a blanket from his bedroll. He pulled himself up behind her and wrapped the woolly warmth around Tayla's shoulders. The rain fell in rivulets and the wet cloth of her under things was beginning to chill. She was grateful for the warmth the blanket provided.

"She all right?" the man asked.

"She'll be fine." Rafe rubbed her arms briskly. "Tell Mr. Lancaster that Rafe Redbourne says, hello."

Tayla was fine letting Rafe take charge. She'd heard Maggie talk about the man who owned most of the land around here, but wasn't sure she wanted to meet him. Right now, she was tired and had no desire to make small talk. It was obvious Rafe knew the man.

"Wait. Rafe?" The man paused a moment and scrubbed at his chin. "You're the bounty hunter, ain't ya?"

Rafe's patience had apparently started to grow thin with the man as Tayla felt his muscles tighten against her.

"I am."

"Mr. Lancaster has been looking for you. Says he's got some important information for ya."

"Tell him I'll visit." Rafe tipped an imaginary hat at the man and pulled away. "Now, if you'll excuse us. I'd like to get Miss Hawthorne here back to the inn."

Tayla wondered where his hat had gone. He'd been wearing it when he'd reached for her on the ledge. Now, rain dripped down his face and he blinked a few times to rid his eyes of the water.

More than ever she wanted to know who Rafe Redbourne had been in her life and the reason he'd left. She felt safe in his arms. Loved even. What had she done that had made him act like he'd hated her before?

With her still wrapped in the confines of his arms, Rafe gently nudged the mount forward. When they hit the main road,

The General was eating the long grass along the wayside. Tayla listened closely to the sounds of the morning, but she didn't hear any hint of the mother bear or her cubs. She was grateful that Maggie's horse had had not fallen prey to the mama protecting her wee cub. Rafe leaned down, grabbed The General's reins, and wrapped them around his horse's saddle horn. The General didn't seem to mind.

Rafe cut across the field back to the inn. She supposed he didn't want all the patrons to see them in their half-dressed state. Especially Maggie. What would she think? Then, the idea occurred to her. Maybe Rafe and Maggie were more than friends. A sinking feeling started deep in her stomach and somehow she hoped she was wrong.

Rafe dismounted first and then reached up for her. She slid into his arms like she'd done it a thousand times before.

Pete came whistling around the corner of the main house and froze when he saw the two of them. His face turned a dark shade of red.

"What the..." Pete ran up to them and assessed her appearance.

The blanket fell away from her shoulder when Rafe set her down on the ground and Pete sucked in a surprised breath. She looked down and realized that the strap of her chemise had dropped down the length of her arm and her shoulder was completely bare for everyone to see.

"Rafe?" Pete turned to the man who'd saved her for answers.

"Bear trouble," was all Rafe said, as if that answered everything. "She's safe. There's nothing to worry about."

Tayla took a step forward and her ankle collapsed beneath her. Both men reached out to steady her. If Rafe hadn't been standing so close to her, she was sure that she would have fallen flat on her face.

Rafe and Pete stood on either side, supporting her. She didn't miss the cool exchange between the two men.

"It's nothing," she told them. "I think I just twisted my ankle on the way down the mountainside.

Rafe swept her up into his arms again.

"Pete," Rafe said with an air of control, "will you bring some ice up to Miss Hawthorne's room?" Rafe's voice was rough, but not unkind. "And some extra blankets," he added.

Pete continued to stare. "Doesn't look like it's *nothing* to me. Why are you both half naked and soaked?" He obviously wasn't in the mood for mincing words.

"I'm all right, Pete," she said in a soft voice that she hoped would reassure her blond friend. Tayla pondered for a moment the difference in the two men. Pete was sweet and caring, while Rafe was...well, she wasn't sure what he was yet.

Rafe opened the back door and carried her into the warmth of the inn.

"Good heavens," Maggie squealed. "What's happened this time?"

"Mud slide. We slid down the backside of Lancaster Cliff and landed in the lake. Somehow, she's twisted her ankle in the process."

"And her dress?" Maggie asked, hands on hips. She couldn't hide the smirk that touched her lips.

Rafe looked down at her with a mischievous grin. "I guess the mountain wanted to keep it."

Tayla's heart skipped a beat.

Colored flooded Rafe's neck and cheeks. He cleared his throat.

"Take her on up, and I'll get her some ice." Maggie swatted at Rafe as she turned toward the back door. "Looks like you might be needin' some for your face too." She reached up to touch his face.

"I'll be fine," Rafe said seriously. "Pete's gone to collect the ice, but she'll need some dry clothes, Mags."

He took Tayla up the stairs, followed closely by Maggie. When they reached her room, Rafe tapped the bottom of her door with his boot to open it. He set her on the bed with her back against the headboard and pulled a pillow from behind her to place beneath her foot. He lifted her ankle very gently and gingerly squeezed the slightly swollen area around the bone.

When he seemed satisfied, he laid it back on the pillow, looked at her, and smiled. But when his eyes found the locket at her chest, all expression left him. She lifted her hand to her neck and gripped the pendant.

Without another word, he turned and left the room with her staring after him.

"Hot and cold," she muttered under her breath.

"What was that, dear?" Maggie asked.

Tayla barely heard her. She was still staring at the door.

*Enough.* She was done worrying about Mr. Rafe Redbourne, and she determined it was time for her to focus on getting her memories back. The distinct feeling that Rafe's friend Mr. Davis could provide her with answers made her take a mental note to ask him what he knew. Rafe certainly didn't want to talk about it.

Maggie retrieved a simple lavender dress and a new set of underthings from the wardrobe across from the bed. She helped Tayla remove her torn chemise and change into the clean, dry clothes. She had only been resituated on the bed for a couple of seconds when a knock sounded on the door.

"Here is the ice you wan..." Pete opened the door and looked around the room, "...ted." He set the brown paper wrapped package on the table next to the door and walked over to the bed.

"Where's Rafe?" he asked.

Tayla shrugged. She was tired and she didn't want to care where the likes of Rafe Redbourne had made off to, but the way he'd retreated still irked her.

Maggie took the tray from her night table and set it on the vanity and Pete sat down on the edge of the bed next to her. Tayla smiled at him. He was certainly a very attractive man. She guessed him to be near Rafe's age and though Maggie was a little older, Tayla thought they would make the perfect match.

"Are you okay?" Pete asked, concern etched in his beautiful green eyes.

"Yes, Pete." She took a hold of his hand and squeezed. She tried to focus on him, but somehow her thoughts could not leave the man who'd just walked out her door. Something drew her to him. Rafe Redbourne was a mystery she was determined to forget.

"Yes, Pete—what, exactly?" Rafe walked into the room, the look on his face anything but pleasant.

# CHAPTER NINE

Rafe had barely been able to hold himself together. It had been too much to ask of any man to see Tayla, her wet body close to him, and not have his thoughts betray him. Once he'd set her down on the bed where he'd held her so closely the night before, he could not bear to stay. His heart had beaten wildly and his breaths had been shallow and uneven in rhythm. He'd had to separate himself from her bewitching presence. Once he'd collected himself again, he'd walked into her room only to find Pete holding her hand.

"Yes, Pete," she said, smiling into his face.

Her words hit him like a flying dagger. A hundred different thoughts grazed through Rafe's mind at what she could possibly be agreeing to.

"Yes, Pete—what exactly?"

The last thing he needed was for her to get involved with Pete. It would make it that much harder to protect her. Maybe it would be better for him though. And her.

"Just what happened out there, Rafe?" Pete's voice held a hint of accusation.

"Watch your tone with me, friend." He put a hint of warning in the last word. Rafe did not have to explain himself, especially to Pete Haversham. However, he could not deny that the man was strong and stable. He would be a good husband and father. A suitable match for most any woman. Just not Tayla. *She* was a Hawthorne, he reminded himself.

He stopped.

Fresh waves of that fateful day lingered and rolled through his mind and he remembered why it was that he hadn't seen Tayla in nearly eight years. It was her fault Tessa had left him standing next to the preacher, brideless and ridicule-worthy.

No. Pete could have her, just as soon as Rafe had fulfilled his promise to Adrien. When she was safe.

"Why don't you two go downstairs and get Locket something to eat?" Maggie excused them both, shooing them out the door.

"Both of us?" the men asked in unison.

Maggie pushed against Rafe's chest, attempting to turn him around and shove him out the door.

Pete tapped the front of his hat and nodded. "Good day, Miss Locket. Maggie," he said before turning to leave.

Reluctantly, Rafe conceded. There was nothing to be accomplished by sitting in Tayla's room anyway. He marched down the back staircase with Pete just ahead of him. The last thing he wanted to do was to get into it with Pete, but he wasn't going to justify his actions to his old friend or anyone else for that matter.

He'd overcome his moment of weakness when he'd fought the overpowering impulse to kiss her and now Tayla was safe in her own bed, away from him. That was all anyone needed to know.

Pete waited for him at the bottom of the stairs.

"Why do you always get the girls? You don't even want them most of the time."

"Excuse me?" Rafe wasn't sure whether to be offended or flattered. "I don't ever remember you lacking feminine attentions. Just what makes you say that I'm the one who gets the girls?"

"You just don't see it, do you?" Pete threw up his hands and pushed through the swinging kitchen door.

"If it's Tayla you want," Rafe called after him, "you can have her."

He stood there, dumbfounded. What had just happened?

He pushed against the swinging kitchen door and followed his long-time friend into the kitchen. Before he could question him further, the opposite door swung open from the dining room.

"It's Jacob," the boy's father hunched over, gasping for breath. "He's burning up and his leg is swelling. I can't find Doc." He stood up straight and looked at Rafe. "I can't lose him too."

Rafe had been in town when Ruth, the man's wife, had passed away. It had been really hard on her husband and young son, and now Jake was all the family Ev had left.

"What's wrong with Jake?" Rafe's brows furrowed together as he inquired. "What's wrong with his leg?"

"There was an accident with the stage and Jacob ended up with a stick protruding from his leg. We got it out, but couldn't stop the bleeding," Pete informed him.

"I couldn't think what else to do, and then I remembered something you'd taught me years ago." Maggie dropped her head and spoke softly. "We seared it with the branding iron."

Rafe's stomach lurched. He'd had to use a soldering iron on a few occasions at medical school and each time, the acrid stench of burning flesh had embedded so deeply in his nostrils that he could smell it, even now.

"We have to do something." Ev Miller was breathing very quickly and Rafe knew that if he didn't sit down shortly, there would be more than one patient to deal with.

Since Rafe had dropped out of medical school, there had only been a handful of times he'd found need of his medical training, and generally, that was for bounties who'd tried to get away—wounds he'd inflicted. Yet, since the Hawthornes had come back into his life, he'd needed those skills almost on a daily basis—reluctant though he was to practice.

"Rafe. Please?"

"Where is he?" Rafe relented after a few moments of awkward silence between them.

"I'll take Locket up something to eat and then join you...with more ice," Pete said as if everything were back to normal. If that is what normal was.

"Fine."

Rafe nodded to Ev, who walked back out through the dining room and across to the stairs that led to the quarters above the barn. Rafe followed. He walked into the room. Jacob tossed his head back and forth, thrashing in small movements on the bed. His exposed leg was bulging at the center of the seared flesh and the area had a green tinge. It was infected.

"Bring me some brandy," Rafe urged Ev.

He walked over to Jake and set his hand on his arm. The heat emanating from the boy's body was excessive.

Rafe walked over to the wardrobe and opened it. Clean towels and linens filled the cupboard. He smiled. Maggie was thorough. He pulled out a few and set them on the table in easy reach.

He pulled his bowie from his boot and laid it on the surface next to the washbasin in the room. He was glad to see that the pitcher was already full of clean water. He poured a little on his hands, picked up the lye soap, and proceeded to rub them until he reached a thick lather.

Rafe retrieved his knife and washed the handle with the lathered soap, then rinsed it along with his hands. He dried them on the small hand towel he'd draped over the side of the bin's railing.

Ev returned and shoved the bottle of liquor at him.

Rafe retrieved one of the clean towels and set it on the bedside table next to Jake and placed his knife on top.

"Open it," Rafe told Ev.

The man's hands shook, but he managed to pull the cork free from the thick, clear bottle.

Rafe picked up the knife and walked over to the water basin.

"Pour it over the blade," he instructed.

Ev was quick to do as he was asked.

Now, go over there and pour some of it over the wound on Jacob's leg."

Ev nodded.

Rafe's heart went out to the man who stood to lose

everything if the kid didn't make it, and he tried to reassure Ev with a look and a nod. He sat down on the chair next to the bed, hovering just above the wounded limb.

Ev walked to the other side of the bed and wiped his hand across the boy's forehead. Then, he braced himself against Jake's shoulders in attempt to hold the young patient still. To no avail. Each time Rafe touched the wound with his knife, the kid would thrash about, making it nearly impossible for Rafe to make a clean incision. He wished he had some ether to help Jake relax and stop moving.

"Can we help?"

Rafe looked over his shoulder to Pete standing in the doorway propping Tayla up, her sore foot gingerly resting at the toes on the floor. The man in him wanted to punch Pete in the mouth, but the doctor in him was glad for the extra hands.

"Pete, bring her over here," Rafe directed.

He stood up and slid the chair closer to the top of the bed with his knee. As he watched Pete ease Tayla down into the chair, a pang of jealously shot through him, but he quickly dismissed the monster.

"Pete, help Ev hold him down. Tayla, I need you to talk to him softly. Touch his face. Reassure him. Let him know you are here."

She smiled.

"I don't know if I'll ever get used to that," she said.

Rafe scrunched his eyebrows together.

"The name."

He tried to smile back with understanding, but the fact was, if she remembered who she was, he could no longer pretend things were different than what they were. Though he hated to admit it, he liked this Tayla.

Rafe nodded toward Jacob and Tayla immediately turned to the youth and started to caress his cheek and to tell him about her day.

"I fell down the side of the mountain this morning," she started. "Can you believe it? Me, Locket, the most nimble person ever, who never ever has accidents." She giggled to herself. "I landed in the water and lost my dress and had to swim to shore and..." She looked up at Rafe and then to Pete. She didn't finish her thought.

Tayla brushed at a stray strand of hair that had fallen in her face and tucked it behind her ear.

Rafe sucked in. His mouth went dry and he made a mental note not to look at her again until the procedure was complete.

"I brought these," Pete held out a few sturdy looking straps of cloth.

Rafe nodded at him and he threw one end under the bed. It was time to focus on a very unpleasant task. He wished the doctor were here, but there was no more time to wait. If Jacob's wound didn't get drained and treated, he could lose the leg or worse, his life.

He touched the blade to the top of the seared tissue and made a short incision downward on the leg.

Jacob screamed.

Rafe worked quickly to clean and disinfect Jake's leg and then wrapped it with a clean towel.

"Thank you." Ev placed a hand on Rafe's shoulder.

"There's nothing else I can do. But Ev, he's not out of the woods yet. Find the doc and get him over here quickly. We'll have to keep a close eye on him over the next couple of days."

Rafe allowed himself to look over at Tayla, who quickly wiped a tear away from her eye. He started to reach a hand out to her, but snatched it back. Pete was there. Pete could comfort her. He stood up and walked out of the room. He didn't drink, but if he was going to start, now would be the perfect time.

Bang.

Tayla awoke with a start. She sat bolt upright in bed and fought to remember the dream that had already begun to fade. It slipped into the darkened recesses of her mind just beyond reach. Dawn was near and she longed to sit and watch the sun as it rose in the eastern sky. She grabbed a blanket from the overstuffed chair in the corner of her room and quietly made her way downstairs to her favorite little bench outside the kitchen door.

It had been a few days since their fall. While Rafe had originally been in a hurry, he'd decided to stay at the inn for a few more days until she could get around better. Her foot was still sore, but it seemed to be healing nicely. She was trying not to use the walking stick Pete had found for her.

Tayla's gaze spanned the beautiful countryside. She liked being up before most of the guests at the inn. She wished she could capture the beauty in her memory forever, but knew all too well how fickle the mind could be. All was quiet, except for a few early morning birds and the distinct sound of wood being chopped somewhere in the distance. It soothed her.

Jacob was also on the mend. Tayla glanced up to the room above the barn where he was sleeping. Rafe had worked a miracle with that boy and she had felt a closeness to him that she couldn't explain. Rafe had worked so hard to make her believe he hated her, yet his actions betrayed an entirely different story.

Her memory seemed to be within grasp, but just beyond reach, and her frustrations grew at not being able to remember her life. She couldn't remember him. She wanted to know what had happened between them, but he still refused to talk about it and Maggie had told her that it wasn't her place.

Movement came from the bunkhouse and she spotted Pete walking across the lawn toward the stable. He caught her stare and lifted a hand in greeting. She smiled at his unkempt hair and scruff that now outlined his strong jaw. Pete was a good man and she felt comfortable with him.

The door behind her opened and Maggie stepped out onto the porch. She leaned forward and set another steaming pie she'd cradled in her towel-covered arms on the railing to cool for the town's box social. It had been the topic of conversation for weeks around this place, but Tayla had no idea what to expect.

"Games and watermelon. Music and dancing. The fishing pond and lots of booths where you can buy things. You'll love it," Jacob had told her when she'd gone to visit him yesterday. "At least I do," he'd thrown in. "And all the fancied up baskets…"

His eyes had been all aglow as he'd spoken and Tayla was sure he would have gone on and on about it had Rafe not walked in and told her he needed to clean Jake's leg. She'd understood that it was time to leave and had managed her way back down the steps without the aid of her thickly carved walking stick.

Tayla smiled and returned her gaze to the morning glow of the fields. The light from the sun gleamed off of a figure walking toward the house. Even though the air still bore a morning haze, she knew instantly it was Rafe. His strong stature and the confident way he carried himself was hard to miss. He held something in his arms in front of him.

"It's beautiful country, isn't it?" Maggie said with a smirk and then pushed herself away from the doorframe she'd been leaning against. She skipped down the steps and headed toward the stables.

Tayla sat a little taller and pulled the blanket tighter around her. When Rafe approached, she could now see it was a stack of chopped wood he carried. She smiled to herself that it had been Rafe creating the rhythmic sound that had brought her comfort in the otherwise quiet morning. As he approached the porch, his eyes caught hers, but he didn't smile. He set the wood in a pile next to the house and stood up straight to stretch.

He lifted his shirt, already wet with perspiration, from the bottom to dab at his face and forehead. While Tayla tried to ignore the tingling sensation that had developed in her belly, she could not deny the appreciation she had for the hard plank of flesh at his naval. Rafe's exposed abdomen brought heat to Tayla's cheeks and her mouth went dry. She knew she should look away, but couldn't. He was a beautiful man—even if he was a little rough around the edges.

"How's that ankle today?" he asked nonchalantly as he

walked up to the porch and rested his arm above his head against the railing looking at her.

"Just fine," she croaked. "I mean, it's still a little tender, but I can get around." She chastised herself for the voice mishap.

"Think you'll be ready to ride out tomorrow, Miss Hawthorne?"

Tayla was still terrified at the idea of leaving behind everything that was now familiar to her and starting over again, but more than anything, she wanted to keep her friends safe and hopefully get her memory back in the process. The best way to do that was to immerse herself in her life before the accident as Tayla Hawthorne. If Rafe and his family *had* known her, as much as it pained her, she needed him and his help.

Still, she didn't want to leave Maggie or Jacob. Or Pete. She smiled as she thought of the young blond cowboy who had been trying to earn her affections since she'd arrived at the inn. He was playful and handsome and kind. Her brain told her she should stay in this place and marry someone just like him. She was sure he would make her happy. But her heart yearned for something more. Besides, Pete was better suited for Maggie.

Tayla looked up and met Rafe's eyes. Somewhere in the recesses of her mind, she knew him, remembered him. Loved him? She was sure everything would work out just the way it was supposed to, but her impatience grew by the minute. She wanted to remember so that, one way or another, they could get on with their lives.

"Well, Mr. Redbourne," she teased back, "my ankle will be fine. It's the mind that might need a little convincing." The exchange had become all too familiar. Tayla loved the light banter between them. It had seemed over the last couple of days that Rafe had forgotten his anger toward her and was acting more like the man she'd first seen when he'd picked up Maggie and had twirled her about.

However, he had certainly kept his distance and had made no secret of the fact that he would be taking her with him when he and his friend, Mr. Davis, left. The purple and blue bruises under his eye and around the bridge of his nose were not as pronounced this morning.

"I'm sorry about your nose," she said quietly.

"This is nothing. You should have seen the other guy." He managed a smile. "Tayla, I—"

Pete walked up to the porch all friendly like, effectively cutting off all serious conversation with Rafe. "Maggie tells me that you're putting together a boxed dinner for the town party tonight."

Heat flooded Tayla's cheeks and she could feel the electricity that had instantly ignited the air between the men standing in front of her.

Rafe didn't say another word. He just turned on his heel and walked back toward the fields.

Tayla had to force herself not to watch his retreat and to focus on Pete instead. "Are you going to bid on it?" she asked more loudly than she had anticipated.

"For the chance to eat alone with the most beautiful girl in the entire territory, you bet."

Tayla smiled and exaggerated the batting of her eyelashes. They both burst out into laughter.

"Be warned," Tayla said, "I am still learning a thing or two about cooking. I burned two batches of biscuits yesterday and churned the cream so long it turned to butter."

"Come on, darlin', Maggie is a great teacher. I'll bet your basket will be one of the best in town."

A sharp white pain seared through Tayla's temple, the word 'darling' echoing in her ears. Then it was gone. In the beginning, each new memory recollection had brought a significant amount of pain, but over the last few days, pieces of her memory had started to return with no pain at all. So, why this time?

Pete's face drained of color and before she could right herself, he was kneeling down next to her, his hands cradling her cheek.

"What is it, Locket?"

Tayla closed her eyes. An image of a dark stranger haunted her like a ghost in the wind, smiling and reaching a hand out to her. *"Come on, darling,"* she felt the man calling to her more than she heard the words.

The pain subsided and with it, the image disappeared. She looked up into the face of a very concerned cowboy.

"I am fine, Pete. Really," she added when his eyebrows stuck in their furrowed position. "I'll bet Maggie's basket will be filled with some wonderful delights. Maybe you should bid on hers." She mentally ironed the wrinkles from her brow and smiled at him, reaching her hand out to his arm to reassure him that all was well.

Maggie returned with a few dozen eggs in a bucket and a tin—which Tayla could only assume contained fresh milk.

"What's going on up here?" she asked glancing back and forth between the two.

Pete hopped down off the steps and took the bucket from Maggie's hands. Stepping in front of her, he opened the screen door and waved and arm in a sweeping gesture, bidding her inside.

"Ma'am" he said as he tipped his hat.

Tayla stood.

Maggie would need some help with breakfast and then preparations for the box social would begin. They were in for a long day and Tayla wanted to be as much help to them as she could. She liked feeling needed. Wanted.

# CHAPTER TEN

Rafe ducked just in time. Pete swung the last of Maggie's bags over the edge of the buckboard and it landed with a heavy thump.

"What does she have in there?" Pete slapped the top of the wagon with both gloved hands.

"Who knows what Maggie takes to these things? I didn't hear any glass break, so I'm betting it wasn't her lot of preserves." Rafe chuckled as he pushed the last milk tin, full of lemonade, up against the seat.

By the size and the bulk of the bag, Rafe guessed it was the patchwork marriage blanket Maggie had been working on all winter. Every year she gave away one of those things at the town's box social.

He decided right then and there that he would not be attending the festivities tonight. He would stay far away from the social where every unmarried man was expected to bid on and eat a dinner made by one of the town's eligible young ladies. He'd enjoyed enough of these meals to know that every one of them came with strings attached. Vivid images from last year's social still haunted him and his friendship with Pete still felt the strains.

Rafe certainly appreciated a good woman, but the idea of courting one scared the hell out of him. A small red corner of the blanket peeked out from the large potato sack. He'd guessed correctly. Yes, he would stay away tonight. *Very far away.*

Maggie came rushing out of the inn followed by Harrison Davis, who was loaded to the hilt with pies and other confections. Rafe was amazed that he hadn't been told to juggle the watermelons as well. By the looks of the wagon and the two men who'd been assigned to take her to town early, it appeared as if Maggie was supplying everything for the event. Most of the townsfolk contributed, but Maggie always did more than her fair share.

"I'm hopin' this weather holds," Maggie said as she looked up at the sky and scrunched her nose. "Smells like rain. I can't believe all the water we've gotten this year. I know Ev must be thrilled about it for his crops, but can it just hold off until the social's over?"

Rafe and Pete both laughed and helped Harrison unload.

At first, Rafe had been reluctant to let Harrison go into town. While he felt like he could trust the man, Davis was still technically his charge. However, Maggie had been very convincing when she'd reminded him of what had happened at last year's social. She'd threatened to make him come along. He'd rolled his eyes and had finally agreed. Better to let Harrison be her lackey than him. Besides, Pete would be there, and Rafe had already informed him of the situation.

It didn't take long before the entire wagon was packed to capacity. Rafe stood back and leaned against the porch's stair railing. Maggie walked out of the kitchen with her red hair down loose about her shoulders and fancied up in a dress bluer than cornflowers.

Rafe whistled, then pushed himself away from the railing. He picked Maggie up by the waist. In years past, hell even just last week, he would have kissed the woman smack on the mouth, but somehow things were different with Tayla around.

"Where you going to fit Tayla in with all that stuff?"

"Oh, honey, didn't I tell you? The boys are taking me into town ahead of time and well, Miss Locket isn't quite finished making up her dinner basket." She looked away from him and set a booted foot up onto metal stepping plank to the buckboard. "The poor man who has to eat that girl's cooking...."

She shook her head and smirked.

Rafe knew better. There was no way Maggie would let Tayla fail. He had watched the two women over the past couple of days and was pleased to see how Tayla was adapting to life out West. Of course, once her memory returned, she'd probably want to return to her fancy life in London society.

Tayla came from a life of privilege and even when her family had come to visit his in Kansas, she'd not been expected to do the same chores he and his siblings had to contend with. Even though they'd had a cook growing up and someone to look after the house, Leah Redbourne had insisted that her children learn to cook and clean for themselves, and his father had taught them to work hard for what they had. The Redbournes had money, but each of them had developed a strong work ethic to go along with it.

Rafe didn't think he'd ever seen Tayla as much as wash a dish, let alone cook a whole meal.

"Anyhow, you'll be bringing Locket to town this evening," Maggie announced matter-of-factly as she scooted onto the seat of the buckboard next to Pete.

"Maggie," Rafe hoped there was enough warning in his voice to make the point that she was sorely mistaken.

"Oh, Rafe Redbourne, Cassie Underhill will certainly have recovered by now. I expect to see you no later than six." She curtly nodded her head.

Maggie handed the reins to Pete, who clicked his tongue and the horses moved forward and out of the courtyard. Harrison waved at him from the back of the buckboard.

Rafe groaned. Maybe he could stay and watch over the inn and Ev could take Tayla into town. That is just what he was determined to do. He walked into the inn. As he passed the kitchen doors, he saw Tayla standing over the sink peeling a potato. Now, that was a sight he'd thought he'd never see. Looking at her in a simple green dress and her hair pulled back, she looked much more innocent than he knew her to be. A part of him wanted to put the past behind him, but another part remembered all too well the last eight years he'd spent keeping his heart far away from any possibility of being hurt.

She set the potato down on the sink and wiped her hands on her apron. Glancing to the top of Maggie's cupboards, Rafe suspected that she was eying the large picnic basket that rested there. She pulled a stool over to the cabinet and stood up on her tip toes, stretching herself as high as she could to reach the prize at the top. He worried that her foot wouldn't be able to take the strain. The stool teetered and with a quick jump and a stride, Rafe reached out and caught her just before she fell.

"You shouldn't be doing that with your ankle the way it is."

"My ankle is just fine, thank you very much," Tayla said as he set her upright on the floor. "Not so sure about my pride though." She smoothed her dress and when she lifted her head her eyes were still closed as if she were trying to summon some patience. "Thank you," she said when she opened them.

Rafe smiled.

"Let me get it for you." He reached up to the oversized wicker basket that was adorned with a big red and white polka dot bow. "Is this what you were after?"

When he looked a little closer, he could see a tear threatening to spill down her cheek and she bit her bottom lip. He wished he hadn't noticed that.

"I'm sorry," he said. "I'll go."

She reached out a hand to stop him.

"Please don't."

He reminded himself that Tayla was different—at least for now—and he should be able to treat her like any other woman. He loved women. This shouldn't be too difficult.

"What in heaven's name are you burning?" He pointed with his chin at the concoction bubbling over the pan on the stove.

"Oh, no," she gasped. Tayla picked up the wooden spoon from the counter and rushed over to the stove. She viciously started stirring whatever mixture she had brewing in the pot.

Rafe glanced around the kitchen and found a small scribbled card. She was attempting to make a meat pie. He thought of his mother. He remembered well the first time she'd attempted to teach him and three of his brothers to make the difficult meal. It had been less than successful, but since that time, he'd spent a lot of time in the kitchen and had learned a few recipes that had kept him from starving over the years.

"I just can't catch a break," he muttered under his breath.

Rafe rolled up his sleeves and pulled a knife from the caddy at the edge of the counter.

"Did you choose this recipe?" Rafe asked over his shoulder.

She looked up from the pot with a resigned look on her face. "I don't think this is going to work."

Rafe picked up the towel that dangled from the edge of the stove and pulled the pot full of burning liquid off the heat and onto the countertop.

"Well, not if you had your heart set on meat pies." He walked over to the cupboard and pulled out the tied knapsack where Maggie kept her bread crumbs.

"We're going to need some eggs." He pointed to the far edge of the counter where the bowl of this morning's collection sat.

"You cook?" Tayla asked as she wiped her eyes, sniffed, and quickly went to retrieve the ingredient he'd requested. "You?"

"Why not me?" he asked, his own pride feeling slightly wounded.

Without another word, she picked up four eggs, two in each hand, and started to walk over to where he stood in front of the counter. She tripped on a loose tile jutting up on the floor. Rafe instinctively reached out to catch the eggs that flew at him. He caught the first, but an instant later another slammed against it and they both cracked, instantly dripping down his hand and forearm onto the floor.

He took a step toward Tayla, who still held an egg in her hand, and realized immediately it had been a mistake. The egg whites had pooled just beneath his feet on the floor. In an instant he found himself on his hind end on the floor.

Tayla looked down at him, her eyes wide and her hands covering her mouth. After a few moments, she snorted and Rafe realized she was laughing. Pride crept in, followed by a smidge of anger, but seeing Tayla's poor attempt at concealed humor, he couldn't help himself. The hilarity of the situation hit him and all irritation washed away. A loud belly laugh burst out of him and he reached up to the counter with his clean hand to pull himself to his feet.

When he stood at his full height, Tayla removed her hands from her mouth and craned her neck backward to look up at him. She rolled her lips together in an effort to stop the laughter. He winked at her, a smirk still on his face, and walked on his heels, careful to go around the mess on the floor, over to the new water spigot Maggie had had installed in the kitchen. He pumped water over his hands and wiped them dry on the clean hand towel.

"Thank you for that." Rafe sat down at the table and removed his boots. After rinsing off the soles, he set them just outside the kitchen door to dry.

Rafe was grateful for the thick woolen socks he was wearing. The floor was cold.

"I'm so sorry, Rafe," Tayla finally managed to say without her voice cracking. She picked up a small woven basket from the hutch in the corner of the room and placed a few more eggs inside and slid it across the countertop to where Rafe now stood.

"Come here," Rafe said, trying to ignore how cute she looked in the little white apron. "Let's get to it. I'm supposed to have you there in less than ninety minutes and at this rate, we'll miss the celebration all together."

She didn't hesitate. "I'm afraid I don't remember anything about cooking," she said. "Maggie tried to show me what to do, but I'm afraid I've ruined everything."

"Don't worry, that has nothing to do with your memory. I don't think you've ever cooked anything in your life." He bit his lip. *Think before you speak, Redbourne.* "I mean, you never really had to. Your family has money and you hire people to do the cooking for you."

"Tell me about my family," she asked sincerely.

Rafe realized how hard it must be to have a void as your

past and he understood that she needed to hear about her life, but he wasn't sure he was ready to share his part in it.

"I'm not sure you want to hear about it from me." He bent over to get a bowl from the lower cabinets.

"Why do you hate me?" she asked point blank.

Rafe felt the heat rise under his collar, but he turned to face her. Her soft mossy green eyes, adorned with the longest eyelashes he had ever seen, distracted him and at the moment, the anger, resentment, and fear he'd held onto for so long seemed a distant memory.

"I don't hate you," he resigned. "I hate the old Tayla Hawthorne, the one who ruined my life."

"How did she do that?" Tayla asked as if speaking of another person entirely.

Rafe didn't want to play along. He beat the eggs in the bowl and opened the knapsack of crumbs.

"The hampers are supposed to be made by the pretty girls. I'm certainly not going to be the one who has to sit and share the meal with the unlucky fella who buys this basket." He had to contain the smile that threatened.

She stared at him with narrowed eyes.

"Come here," he said without leaving much room for argument.

He picked up the knife and nearly laughed when she hesitated. She couldn't really think he would hurt her. Could she?

"I'm not going to hurt you. I just want to show you how to cut the chicken."

She moved closer and he positioned himself behind her. She fit perfectly in the spans of his chest. Carefully, he placed the knife in her hands and reached to the sink and pulled the chicken in front of them. He guided her hands, holding firmly to direct the knife as they sliced through the different sections of the chicken.

Piece by piece the chicken gave way. Rafe had to concentrate on his task, but the honeysuckle scent of her hair distracted him. He stepped back, releasing her rather abruptly.

"Ouch." Tayla shook her hand and sucked the side of her thumb.

Rafe groaned.

"Let me look at that," he said, pulling her hand into his.

She pulled away.

"No, thank you," she said curtly. "It's only a little cut. We need to get this done. What's next?"

Rafe had her wash her hands and then showed her how to roll the chicken in the eggs and then the bread crumbs. Then using his grandmother's secret frying technique—using a culmination of the cast iron pan, a pie pan, some oil, and good timing, the fried chicken was done.

They sliced and fried up the potatoes she'd already peeled and grabbed a few of Maggie's corn muffins from the basket on the table. Together they filled the large wicker basket with food.

"We need to get this loaded. Are you ready to go?"

She took off her apron, laid it over the back of a chair, and brushed at the imaginary wrinkles on her dress.

"How do I look?"

Rafe cleared his throat. Words would not come. He reached out to brush a lock of hair from her shoulder, but quickly pulled his hand back when it touched the skin at her neck.

"You look...um, good."

*Idiot.*

Tayla dropped her hands to her sides. "Give me just a moment and I will be ready." She turned and left through the dining room door.

Rafe turned around and put both hands on the counter. He took a deep breath.

"I can do this," he said aloud.

Tayla walked into her room, closed the door, and leaned against the backside of it. How was she supposed to avoid him and close herself off from any interest in him if he was going to always stand so close to her?

Something had changed in him since that first day. Her memories of him were gone. There was nothing she could do about that now. She only wished she knew what she'd done to 'ruin his life' as he'd put it. Then, they could focus on making new memories.

They were headed to the town's annual social. From what Jacob had told her, tonight promised to be one of the biggest events of the year. She was excited to get out. While she loved being at the inn, she felt confined. In the last couple of weeks she hadn't been any farther than the ridge and for some reason, she felt stifled.

She wished Rafe would talk to her. She desperately wanted to know about her family. About her life. Why couldn't he just take her to them? He'd said her father was alive. What about her mother? Did she have any siblings? So many questions flooded her mind and she hoped that the drive into town would prove more fruitful than their encounter in the kitchen had been. Then again, she couldn't imagine a more perfect memory.

Tayla pinched her cheeks and smoothed the stray hairs that had fallen down into her face. She wasn't sure how far it was into town, but she grabbed a blanket and an old faded brown coat Maggie had given her for the chilly evenings. Today had been the first in many where the sun had come out from behind the clouds and scared away the rain.

The idea of riding alongside Rafe in the dark scared her a little and she wished the sun would stay up and keep her company. Maggie knew and trusted him. Why shouldn't she? She apparently had once, but for some reason, he kept himself at a distance. Maybe Tayla wasn't so sure she wanted to know the truth anymore.

With the blanket and coat draped over her arm, she walked out of her room and down the stairs to where Rafe stood, basket in hand, waiting. He didn't want to share, fine. But Tayla determined that she wasn't going to make avoiding her any easier.

Rafe took the load from her arms and tucked it under his

own. A wave of gooseflesh descended down her arms to her toes when his fingertips brushed the exposed flesh at her wrist. Regardless of whether or not she remembered him, she realized she wanted to know him.

Why did Tayla have to look so good? The last thing he needed was this kind of distraction, yet here he was, escorting her to the town's social. Maggie had to be pleased with herself. While their relationship had been far from platonic, they'd both moved past that time and Maggie seemed more determined than ever to find a woman he'd settle down with.

He'd seen too much of that lately. He didn't want to go backward. And allowing himself to feel like that again—allowing himself to really commit to someone—was not an option.

A little half smile touched his lips, and while he knew he should just turn and walk out the door, he couldn't help himself. He held out a crooked arm for her. The moment her hand touched his elbow and her forearm rested against his, his entire body tensed at the realization he didn't hate her anymore.

Oh, he wanted to. She sure helped him make a mess of his life, but for now, she wasn't that Tayla, but an innocent, beautiful woman with eyes that sparkled like gemstones in the light. He dared another glance at her. Her head was bowed, but there was a soft smile on her lips.

When they reached the wagon, he helped her up onto the seat. Then, he reached into the back for his hat. Rafe missed his new Stetson, but luckily Maggie'd had one of his old brown ones lying around. He shoved it on top of his head and climbed up onto the seat. When he looked over at her, he cleared his throat. He seemed to do that a lot around her.

Rafe wanted to say something, but didn't know what. This was the first time he could ever remember being at a loss for words around a woman and the idea disconcerted him.

What was it about her that made him feel so strange? It

wasn't the same way he'd felt with Tessa, his once intended. He knew what love felt like. Or, did he? This was different than what he'd felt as he'd waited like an idiot at the altar.

His gut twisted inside. No, Tayla had always been like a little sister to him. Almost had been his little sister, yet the feelings he was having toward her were anything but brotherly.

He dared another glance at her and when she caught his stare, he slapped the reins.

"Hi-yah!"

The buckboard lurched forward with a jolt—a little harder than he had anticipated, and Tayla grabbed a hold of his arm to steady herself.

Once she righted herself, she looked at him again and smiled. Not a shy or embarrassed smile, but a real, honest, and heart demolishing smile.

He had to get away from her. The sooner the better.

Tayla wasn't sure what she had expected, but the rows of fire-lit lamps strung from draped ropes and the masses of people that had gathered in the clearing behind the mercantile, was not it.

Rafe held out his hand to help her off the high wagon seat. She rested her hand in his and caught his gaze and held it. As she stepped up over the wagon's side lip, her foot caught on the edge of the wood and she fell forward against the broad expanse of his chest.

He held her tight into him and slowly lowered her to the ground. She smoothed the edges of her dress and, despite her best intentions, giggled.

When she looked up at him, she noticed the smirk that grazed the corners of his mouth and wondered what it would be like to have his lips claim hers.

The thought surprised her. She knew she should be shocked by it, but instead she welcomed it.

The ride had been quiet. She had been building up the courage to ask him all of the questions that plagued her mind, but just when she'd found her voice, they'd reached town.

"I thought you'd gotten lost somewhere." Maggie appeared from around the backside of the wagon.

"Rafe, grab Locket's basket and follow us," Maggie instructed as she grabbed a hold of Tayla's hand and pulled her toward a large booth where dozens of beautifully decorated baskets adorned multi-level tables and haystacks.

Panic rose in Tayla's throat as she thought of eating the impromptu meal she'd made with Rafe with a complete stranger. All of a sudden she wanted to go back to the inn. She wanted to be as far away from this place as possible.

"Maggie, stop."

How had she let this happen?

Maggie turned around, but did not loosen her grip on Tayla's hand.

"I don't think I can do this," Tayla said. As much as she hated to admit it, she felt vulnerable and out of place. She needed to get back to what would be familiar in Tayla Hawthorne's life.

*This*, she thought, *is not it.*

"Locket, honey, you've been cooped up in that inn for weeks. It's time you got out and started to meet new people."

"Maggie, you don't understand. I don't want to meet new people." She hesitated. "I want to…"

"Remember the ones from her past," Rafe filled in for her. He set her basket next to one with a large green bow with wildflowers protruding from the center, and turned around to face them.

"You two are so serious. Tonight is about having fun." Maggie tugged on Tayla's hand again. "Come on. Pete and Harry have both been waiting to dance with you all afternoon."

Tayla looked back over her shoulder to Rafe who stood stock still. She gave him a look that she hoped portrayed gratitude for his attempt as well as the hopelessness of trying to contradict Maggie.

"Who's Harry?" Tayla asked from behind as Maggie dragged her along.

Maggie pulled her up close and tucked Tayla's hand under her arm in answer. Tayla brushed at the tendrils of hair that had fallen into her eyes. Rafe's friend, Mr. Davis, stood next to Pete. He bowed and Pete nodded.

"Do you have room on your dance card for another, Miss Hawthorne?"

"And one for me, Locket?"

Tayla didn't know what to say. She glanced at Maggie, who handed her a small folded card with lines and numbers on it. Tayla was sure she should know what it was, but for the life of her she had no idea how to respond. She wasn't even sure she remembered how to dance.

Music started to play. The two gentlemen stared at her expectantly. Her eyes darted about the party and rested on Rafe's. His eyes were dark, but for once he didn't seem to be brooding. He made his way toward them.

"This dance is mine," Rafe said as he took her by the hand and led her into the middle of the street where others had already begun to dance.

He skillfully spun her around and into his firm embrace. It was as if he understood her fears and was there to help her through it.

"A dance card is simply a way for you to organize with whom you agree to dance each selection. I," he paused, "am your number three—as the first two dances are already over."

The sheer feeling of panic must have shown clearly on her face because Rafe dropped his head a little toward her and demonstrated a deep breath. "Just follow my lead and you'll be fine," he whispered close to her ear. "This dance is called a waltz."

His right arm locked in position with her hand held firmly in his left hand hooked under her shoulder, supporting her arm.

Try as she might, his instructions to let him lead her around the makeshift dance floor did not reach her feet. She faltered and tripped over pebbles on the road, over Rafe's foot, and more than once she stumbled over her own feet. After what felt like eternity, Rafe's hand at the small of her back tightened and he pulled her tightly against him, lifting her off the ground.

"Just stand on my feet and hold on." A mischievous grin spread across his features as he whirled her about and around all the townsfolk. Though strangers to her, many of them nodded approval, patted Rafe on the back, and before long, she felt the apprehension drain out of her and anticipation take its place.

The song ended all too quickly. Rafe deposited her on the boardwalk next to Maggie and walked to the other end of the street.

Along with Harrison Davis and Pete, four other men rushed up to her and asked if they could claim one of her dance slots. Before she knew it, her entire card was filled. She couldn't help the twinge of disappointment that lingered with her as she filled the last slot. Her only dance with Rafe was over.

After the first couple of dance disasters, a rotund man with thinning white hair stood up on the back of a wagon and announced that it was time for the bidding on the baskets to begin. Butterflies invaded Tayla's stomach. She scanned the town center for any familiar faces. Pete stood near the livery with one booted foot resting on the edge of a water trough. She couldn't see the woman he was talking to, but the deep purple trim of the woman's dress skirt swayed behind him in the light evening breeze. Tayla smirked when Pete threw his head back and laughed loudly. He was obviously sweet on the gal. She expected to feel a pang of jealousy, but she didn't feel that way about Pete. What about Maggie? Maybe she'd misread them afterall.

A few of the inn's patrons adorned the streets, including Mr. Francis who wore a dark green bowler hat and matching tie. She nodded in his direction, but he didn't see her. When her gaze reached the bank, there was no mistaking the large and chiseled form of Rafe Redbourne. He leaned against one of the porch railings, his arms crossed in front of him. Harrison Davis sat on the bank steps a few feet from him and it appeared they were in casual conversation.

She lingered a little too long on his face. He met her stare with a look that sent fire to her belly. She lowered her lashes and looked away. Where was Maggie?

"This first basket here is a mighty perty sight. Smells like a sweet treat inside. Do I hear two bits?"

Men started raising their hands.

"Four," a gangly cowpoke called out.

"One dollar," yelled another.

One by one, girls paired off with the gentlemen who'd purchased their boxed dinners. Tayla stared at the big basket with the large red and white polka dot bow, now just a foot or so from the auctioneer's feet. The knots in her stomach tightened as the man picked up her basket.

"Isn't this exciting?" Maggie linked her arm with Tayla's and squeezed.

Tayla started to nod her head, but when the auctioneer started the bidding on a large wicker basket with a polka dot bow, she quickly shook it back and forth.

"I don't know any of these men, Maggie."

"Don't worry, Locket," Maggie whispered, "you know Pete. Look, he's bidding."

Tayla relaxed a little. Then another man she'd never seen before called out a higher bid. The price of her basket was quickly climbing.

"Two dollars and three bits," yelled an older man wearing a black leather vest with a pocket watch protruding from his pocket.

"I'll be right back," Maggie said and let go of her arm. Tayla watched as her friend made her way over the gentleman who'd just bid. She whispered in his ear and pointed to another basket that had yet to be sold.

"Come on gents, smells like fried chicken. A new schoolhouse ain't gonna build itself. Do I hear three?"

"Three," Rafe's voice boomed over the crowd.

# CHAPTER ELEVEN

Seven dollars and twenty-seven cents was everything Rafe had left with him. The majority of his funds was split between a small bank in Kansas City and his hiding spot at home. Until he delivered his bounty to Lord Darington, it would have to last him.

Three dollars? How could he bid nearly half of his earnings for a meal that he'd helped prepare? He was out of his mind and it would do him some good to have someone—anyone—knock some sense into him right now.

"Three fifty," a man called out.

Rafe scanned the crowd. The voice was familiar, but Rafe couldn't place it. Mr. Lancaster, one of the town's most wealthy land owners and the judge, had stopped bidding once Maggie had gone over and spoken to him. He'd thought Pete would be the biggest competition, but it seemed he'd stopped the moment Rafe had bid.

"Three dollars and fifty cents going once, going twice—"

"Three dollars and six bits." Rafe couldn't walk away. He pushed himself away from the bank's porch rail and walked into the small crowd that had gathered around the auctioneer.

Rafe realized that he was putting the last pittance of his self-imposed stipend at risk for the woman who'd caused him to lose his inheritance. The irony was not lost on him.

"Four dollars," someone called.

*Who is that?*

There were only a dozen or so men left standing around to bid on the baskets and only a half dozen boxed dinners to go around. Most of the others had already paired off to one section of town or another.

Rafe watched as dozens of lovesick farmers swooned over their gals. The thought brought him up short. Let him have it, he thought to himself. I cannot go down this road again. Especially with a Hawthorne.

He caught Tayla's hopeful glance. She still hadn't remembered their falling out, but he couldn't forget. As much as he'd tried. He turned around, walked back to his previous spot in front of the bank, and leaned against the pole.

Harrison opened his mouth to speak.

"Not a word," Rafe warned.

Harrison closed his mouth, his eyebrows creased and his jaw clenched.

"And sold for four dollars to the gentleman in the fancy braided vest."

Rafe shot upright and froze. He only knew one man who wore a braided vest. Mal Brewster. He was the kind of bounty hunter that gave them all a bad name.

Rafe stepped forward in hopes he was wrong, but his stomach turned when he saw the straggly haired brute walk to the front of the crowd to claim his prize.

Mal Brewster was good at his job, but only in the same way a mountain lion was a good hunter. And even then, Mal did not have the same grace or finesse as the beast. He always shot first and asked questions later and generally only took on the job if the poster read, dead or alive. Mostly because he liked them dead. And when they weren't gracious enough to die, he treated his bounties like animals.

Now, because Rafe had been so worried about protecting his heart...

"You're an idiot, man." Harrison interrupted his thoughts.

Rafe barely glanced at him before stomping over to where Mal held out his hand to Tayla in a slight bow.

He pulled money from the hidden pocket in his belt and

pushed himself between Tayla and his nemesis.

"Not this one, Mal."

"Ah, Redbourne," he said, his crooked smile distorting his otherwise stoic face. "Won the girl fair and square."

"Here's your money. You can even keep the meal, but Tayla will not be eating it with you."

"Don't ya think you should let the lady speak for herself?"

Rafe stepped aside, sure what he would hear come from her lips.

"You heard the man, Mr. Redbourne. He thinks I am worth at least four dollars." She turned to Mal. "I would be pleased to eat with you, Mr..."

"Brewster. But you can call me Mal, ma'am." He tipped his thick black hat and held out his arm.

"I don't think so." Rafe led with his left foot and slammed his fist into Mal's jaw, throwing Tayla off balance. She landed on her rump. He didn't have time to feel bad about it. Mal had already come up swinging.

Rafe knew that Mal played for keeps and if he didn't stop this quickly, it was going to end badly.

He shoved his rival with all the pent up energy he could muster and Mal tumbled backward. Rafe drew his revolvers and aimed both of them directly at Mal's head, but Brewster's guns were also drawn. The crowd had dissipated and now formed a circle around them. The people that stood on either end moved to the sides. A stray bullet was never friendly.

Boom. A very loud shot fired into the air. Rafe didn't take his eyes off Mal. Their stares locked.

Rafe was sure it was the sheriff. Mac wouldn't put up with any gunplay in his town. Movement to his left told Rafe that someone was approaching.

His heart pumped faster. The only sound he could hear was the rushing in his ears.

"Gentlemen," Mac said, "this is not going to happen today. Put your guns away."

Rafe held his steady, unwavering.

Mal carefully got to his feet, his aim still on target.

"Deputy," Mac called to a gangly kid near the mercantile, "will you please help the stranger re-holster his weapon?"

The deputy took each step slowly, as if approaching a box of TNT.

Mal wiped away a trickle of blood that dripped from the corner of his mouth and broke into an ugly grin.

"This wasn't your day to die, Redbourne." He flipped the trigger guard around his forefinger and slid his pistol into his holster.

"I think it's best you leave town, friend." Mac turned his back on Rafe, but still held his shotgun at the ready.

"It's all right. I was just passing through." Brewster leaned over to pick up his fallen hat, dusted it off, and headed for the livery.

Rafe didn't move until he watched Mal ride out of town. He wouldn't go far and that made Rafe nervous. Mal wasn't the type to give up or be told what to do.

It was time to get on the road. Rafe had made many enemies in his eight years as a bounty hunter and he wanted to get Tayla somewhere safe. Somewhere that no one would think to look for him. Home.

"Of all the bullheaded, arrogant, asinine things to do." Tayla's head hurt. Harrison and Maggie had been there to help lift her off the ground the moment Rafe punched the man who'd won her basket.

She'd held her breath as she watched Rafe's steady aim focused on the stranger and decided she couldn't fall for a man whose life would hang in the balance every day.

When she'd seen the stranger hit the ground, a memory flashed in her mind, replacing the man's face with Harrison's. Now her mind was filled with memories she couldn't explain. She'd seen Harrison fall to the ground before and she'd heard shots.

"Locket," Maggie nearly yelled at her.

"I'm sorry, did you say something?"

"Are you all right?" Maggie repeated.

Tayla tried to focus on the memory. If Harrison had been killed, how could he be standing here in the middle of town with her? Maybe he had some answers that Rafe refused to give her. She made a mental note to talk to him about it once they got back to the inn.

"Yes," she said, "I just remembered something, but it doesn't make any sense."

"Looks like I get that basket of yours. Care to join me?" Rafe walked up to them, handed Tayla her jacket, and held out an arm.

Charming? He was going to be charming after practically throwing her to the ground and calling out the man who'd dare bid on her boxed dinner?

Part of her wanted to leave and pretend she had never heard of Rafe Redbourne. But she didn't want him to know that he'd gotten to her, so she would put on a smile and act like it didn't matter.

"Sure. I can't wait to hear the story."

He could have been killed, yet here he was, playing it off as if nothing had happened. "What story?" Rafe asked with a smile.

"How you became such a pompous..." It was on the tip of her tongue, but she couldn't say it.

His smile dropped and she turned and walked back toward the surry.

"What were you thinking?" Maggie backhanded Rafe's shoulder.

Foreboding still pumped through his veins. Every instinct shouted that they should leave, yet he'd suggested they eat dinner as if nothing had happened.

"I wasn't," he responded.

White light streaked the sky followed by the booming sound of thunder.

"I don't think the weather is going to hold much lon…" a fat droplet of water hit Rafe's forehead, "…ger," he finished.

Within moments, torrents of water fell from the sky and party goers dashed into buildings and under the protection of the covered boardwalk.

He glanced across the street and saw Tayla laughing with Pete behind the window of the mercantile. She brushed the sopping strands of hair from her forehead and threw her hands up in the air. Then, she caught his stare through the glass and the merriment left her face. She stood there, looking more beautiful than he had ever seen any woman. And if he wasn't careful, all of his intentions to avoid commitment might be lost on her.

"Come on," Maggie called as she dashed across the street to join the others.

"Why Rafe Redbourne, is that you?"

Rafe closed his eyes at the familiar voice he'd hoped he'd never have to hear again.

"After last year's social I didn't think you'd ever show your face in this town. Daddy still carries his shotgun at the ready."

Rafe slowly pivoted on one foot until he was face to face with his biggest reason for not wanting to come to the dance.

"Gertrude." Rafe removed his hat—out of respect or because of nerves, he was unsure. "You're looking mighty lovely this evening."

*Careful, Redbourne*, he warned himself. *The last thing you need is her daddy's shotgun helping you make decisions better left unmade.*

"Why thank you, kind sir." She bowed her head and made a slight curtsy. "You always were quite the charmer."

"Listen, Gert," he started. Heat rose in his neck and he felt like a foolish teenage boy.

"Shhhh." She placed two fingers over his lips. "I got married. Did Pete tell you?"

Rafe stared at her, willing his eyes to avoid her ample bosom. He'd taken a liking to her last year and had bid on her basket. The dinner hadn't quite turned out as he'd planned. Rafe wasn't surprised that Pete hadn't mentioned her.

He shook his head when he realized she was still waiting for his reply.

"Just like my brother to avoid sharing the good news."

Rusty Porter, the town physician, appeared out of nowhere, still holding a dripping newspaper over his head, his shoulders scrunched, even though the rain was beginning to let up and the hotel balcony provided a roof to the boardwalk.

Rusty had been in the class behind him in medical school at Harvard and had moved back here to his hometown to take over for his father when he graduated. The familiar twinge of regret twisted inside Rafe's belly.

"Rafe," she placed a hand on his forearm, "you remember the good doctor?"

Rafe held out his hand and nodded a greeting.

They shook. Firmly.

Rafe understood.

"How's the foot?" he asked, sincerely hoping there had been no permanent damage after he'd landed on it last year. Pete packed quite a wallop.

"Oh, it only hurts when it rains or snows." She smiled.

Rafe looked out into the street at the downpour now attacking the ground. He gave her a half smile.

"I should be grateful to you, you know. Rusty here took good care of me while it healed and, well, here we are."

"Come on, darling, we really must get inside. We were lucky to get the last room for the night." The good doctor was done talking, it seemed. He curled his arm about Gert's waist, but stopped reluctantly. "You did good, Rafe. With the boy's leg, I mean. Had it not been for you, young Jacob would have lost that leg for sure." He pursed his lips, nodded, and ushered Gert inside the hotel lobby.

The offhanded compliment couldn't have been easy for Rusty to say, but a reluctant sense of satisfaction planted deep inside of Rafe.

Gertrude looked back over her shoulder and smiled.

"Goodbye," she mouthed at him.

He raised a hand and waived.

The rain still fell, though just a trickle, and the moon finally broke through the thick cloud covering that had blanketed the sky all evening. He reckoned it was time to get back to the inn. The festivities would be done for the evening and the sooner he could get everyone away from town and safe from a reckless, revenge monger bounty hunter the better. He had no idea where Mal had gone, but the hairs standing on end at the back of his neck told him to be careful.

Rafe slid his hat low on his head, shoved his hands in his pockets, and walked across the street to the mercantile.

"Looks like the social's over," he said as he peeked his head in the door. He saw Tayla's basket sitting on the floor next to her and suddenly his stomach reminded him loudly just how hungry he was.

"What do you say we get on the road and have some of that dinner I paid four dollars for?" He was itchy and that meant trouble, but he didn't want to alarm the others.

Everyone stared at him blankly. This is why he avoided romantic entanglements. A bounty hunter was his own man and his only expectations were self-imposed. Those he loved would always be in danger if his enemies discovered them. That was unacceptable.

"What?" he asked when no one said anything. He looked from Maggie to Pete and then over at Tayla.

Maggie was the first to break the new silence. "Pete, honey, will you go fetch my blanket? I'm sure Hetty will have another social when the weather clears up and we can auction it off then."

"Moon's out. We should take advantage of the light and get back to the inn," Rafe said.

"We'll just get us a couple of roo—" Maggie started.

"Hotel's booked. Just spoke with Doc Porter and his new bride. They just got the last room." Rafe turned with a raised eyebrow at Pete, who effectively avoided his stare.

"Well then, Rafe is right," Maggie said as she turned to him.

"Now, don't you go and let it go to yer head," she warned with a slight twinkle in her eye. "Who knows how long this weather is going to hold. I don't want that quilt to get all muddied up and wet sitting in the back of the wagon, so I figure Rafe and Locket can take it back in the surrey."

"You don't really expect me to ride back with him, do you?" Tayla took a step closer to Maggie. "Please don't make me."

Rafe was beginning to get the idea that Tayla was a little upset.

"I'm standing right here," Rafe said, feeling bad that she seemed genuinely scared to be alone with him. He cursed himself. Never before had he reacted to a woman the way he reacted to her. It was time to figure it out—one way or another.

Tayla sat as far to the opposite edge on the seat as she possibly could. Rafe had loaded the back seat with some of Maggie's things—the quilt, Tayla's boxed dinner, and a few other supplies—leaving no room for a passenger. She still resented the fact that she had to make the short trip back to the inn with him. He was such a frustrating man and she was getting tired of his games. He either hated her or didn't, it was that simple.

The surrey lurched when it hit one of the many wet ruts in the road. She nearly fell off the seat. Rafe reached out and cradled her around the waist with one swift movement and pulled her close to him on the seat.

"I don't bite," he said in a low, calm voice.

In a matter of minutes the moonlit ride home became dark—almost black—as the moon tucked behind the murky storm clouds. Rafe stopped the rig.

"Why are we stopping?" Tayla took a deep breath and held it.

"Can't see where we're going. I'm sure these horses could

find their way back, but I'd rather not leave it to chance."

A light came to life as Rafe lit a fair-sized lantern and hung it from a hook just to the upper left of his seat. It illuminated the path a few feet in front of the horses. She hoped that Pete was as prepared. Maggie had left with him and Harrison in the wagon just a few minutes before they had.

Tayla's stomach grumbled and she realized they still hadn't had any supper. The Smokey Sky Inn hadn't been too long of a ride when there was light outside, but Tayla worried how long it might take them to get back in the darkness of a storm.

Tayla rubbed her arms. The night was proving to be chillier than she had expected it to be. When Rafe climbed back up onto the front seat, he must have noticed because he reached behind them to the back seat and pulled out Maggie's blanket. Without a word, he wrapped the quilt around her shoulders and tucked it around the rest of her.

They hadn't been moving for long when a thunderous cracking sound jolted the rig. Tayla screamed as the front corner of the surrey crashed forward onto the ground, throwing her from the seat. She tumbled out.

Splash.

Tayla landed in a puddle of water that had collected in one of the deep grooves of the road. Her arm connected with a hard surface and sent a jolting pain through her arm and up into her shoulder. This time, she didn't think it was Rafe's face she'd hit. She was grateful for the blanket he'd wrapped around her shoulders as the thick material cushioned what might have been a nastier blow.

Rafe was next to her in a moment.

"Are you all right?" he asked as he set the lantern down on the ground next to her.

She heard him, but didn't answer immediately. A brief flash of another starless night invaded her memory and a deep seated fear took root. She remembered the desperate need to escape and a horse knocking her into a boat. She remembered her accident.

"Tayla," Rafe prodded again, holding her face between his

open palms, "are you hurt?"

"I remember," she told him, not meeting his face and grateful that there was no searing headache to accompany the memory this time. "I remember my accident." She looked at him.

He pulled back away from her—just a little. He grabbed the lantern and held it up to her face, looking at her eyes, not into them.

"I think you've had one too many falls," he said, shaking his head. He stood up and held out a hand for her. Her arm was sore, but there were no more stabbing pains.

"I don't know if I have ever met anyone as prone to accidents as you." He smiled a little, but there was something else behind his eyes. "Come on," he said. "The wheel is broken. I need you to hold up the light while I try to fix it well enough to get us back to the inn."

She lifted the bulk of the quilt into her arms and tossed it back into the backseat of the surrey.

Rafe handed her the lantern and moved the front of the rig. He knelt down in front of it and calculated the damage. A low whistle accompanied his assessment.

She held the lantern up a little higher and took a step toward him, only the ground was not level and her ankle buckled beneath her. She fell. Glass shattered and the light went out.

"What the—"

Warm liquid slid down Tayla's hand. It stung. What had she done now? Hadn't he just finished telling her she was a clumsy dolt?

The moon peeked out from behind the storm clouds again. Rafe swooped her up in his arms and walked a short distance before he set her back down under what looked like an overhang in the rocks.

"Stay," he ordered.

A wolf howled in the night. She had no intention of defying the order. It was cold. She was tired. And her hand had started to throb in a pulsating rhythm.

Tayla squinted against the darkness. The shadows were hard to distinguish, which scared her more than a little.

She pulled her knees tight and hugged them to her.

She knew the moment Rafe had joined her. His presence filled the small space under the rock covering. Heat emanated from him. She shivered and longed to feel the warmth of him near her.

"Hold this tightly against your hand." He placed a soft cloth against the skin of her palm.

She did as she was told.

Rafe moved about the small area as if searching for something.

"What are you doing?" she asked quietly.

"Looking for something in here we can use as kindling," he responded. "Everything out there is too wet to help with a fire."

Tayla remembered earlier that morning when she'd seen him carrying the chopped wood back to the inn and her face warmed when she thought of the way his taught muscles had glistened with perspiration behind his open shirt. She was glad he couldn't see her face.

After a few moments of silence, a small fire came to life. He must have been able to collect enough dry grasses to get it started. She saw in the very dim light, a small bundle of firewood he'd brought in with him from the surrey.

"It was supposed to be used at the social tonight. Luckily, I hadn't unloaded it before it started to rain. It'll keep us warm for a bit." He sat down next to her and pulled a little brown pouch from his back pocket.

"Now, let me take a look at that hand," he said as he pulled it into his own. He removed the cloth she'd held there and leaned closer to the light of the fire.

With expert hands Rafe cleaned the wound and applied a sticky poultice to the area.

"It's pretty deep. If we don't stitch it up, it could get worse and even infected."

*Stitch it up?* He wanted to sew her hand?

She shook her head. "I don't think that will be necessary."

She pulled her hand away. The stinging had stopped and it no longer throbbed.

"Tayla, trust me," was all he said as he picked up her hand again and rubbed the edges of her palm with his thumb.

His soft touch felt intimate somehow and she realized that if he'd told her he needed to stitch her fingers together she would have let him do it.

She nodded. "Okay."

"You might want to look away."

She shook her head again.

Carefully, and with a precision that surprised her, Rafe began to seal the wound that Tayla could now see had been a gaping gash in her flesh.

She winced.

Another flash of memory exploded in her mind. She remembered sitting on top of a wooden counter with her knees bent. Rafe stood over her with a needle and thread, much like he was doing now. He'd rubbed something on her knee and had blown on it. She couldn't have been more than fourteen at the time.

"You've stitched me up before," she said matter-of-factly.

He didn't say anything. When he finished his task, he cut his thread with the smallest pair of shears she had ever seen.

He tied a thin bandage around the area and released her hand before he sat down next to her, his feet extended in front of him.

"Seems your memories are returning more quickly now," he said as he replaced the shears, thread, and needle in the small leather pouch.

"Some," was all she could think to respond.

Silence.

"Thank you," she managed with a tight throat.

"Any chance you can ride bareback?" Rafe asked.

Tayla didn't know what to say. She thought that riding bareback meant no saddle, but she couldn't be sure she would be able to ride at all, let alone without the contraption created to keep her upright. Rafe must have taken her silence as an answer.

"There's not enough light to see how to fix the wagon wheel, and without a lantern," he threw something into the little fire, "I'd rather not walk the rest of the way tonight. I'd say we could ride together, but let's face it, it's dark and wet, and I'm worried about being able to keep you on the horse. We'll just have to stay here until the others realize we didn't make it back and come looking for us."

Tayla's eyes widened at the thought. She lowered her head, feeling like a fool for having broken their only real light source on such a dark night.

"They will come back for us though, yes?"

"Pete won't let a heathen like me be alone with a fancy British heiress like you all night. They'll be back."

Tayla wasn't sure if her feelings were relief or disappointment. She shivered again.

Rafe stood up.

"Where are you going?" Tayla didn't want to be any farther away from him than she had to.

He didn't respond, but she could hear the creaking sound of the broken rig's door being opened. When he returned, he had Maggie's quilt and her box social basket.

"I unhitched the horses. Don't want them getting startled by another bout of thunder and lightning and bolting with the surrey. Maggie'd have my hide for sure." He carefully laid the blanket over her lap and then opened the basket. "Thought we might as well get something in our bellies while we wait."

The aroma from the fried chicken sent her stomach into spasm. She realized she hadn't had anything to eat since breakfast and was starving.

Rafe handed her a cloth napkin and pulled out the knapsack that contained the meat. He unfolded it slowly, to her irritation. Without thinking, she reached into the pile and grabbed the first piece she touched. He'd called himself a heathen, but she felt the heathen now as she stuffed the fried food into her mouth.

The meat was tender, moist, and tasted like a little bit of heaven. Tayla closed her eyes and reached up and wiped her mouth with the back of her hand.

Rafe burst out in laughter.

"Hungry?" he asked.

Tayla gave him a little half smile and took another bite of her chicken. "Aren't you?"

Boom.

Thunder rolled across the sky, followed by another flash of light. Tayla screamed.

"Sorry," she said feeling silly that she startled so easily. She put her hand to her heart and realized that Rafe's guns were drawn and pointed in separate directions. He was fast.

A wolf howled again and the rain started to fall. She took a moment to look around her at the little cave Rafe had found them for shelter.

"How did you know this place was here?" she asked.

"I saw it on the drive in. Luckily, we weren't too far from it or we'd be out in that."

Silence.

"So," Rafe started in a low voice, "what do you remember about your accident?"

Tayla had been sure that he hadn't heard her before. Although the memory wasn't crisp and clear, she knew she'd been on the run from something—or someone.

"It was dark, much like tonight, and someone was chasing me. I remember being on horseback and riding very quickly through some trees."

He sat up and leaned in close to her, listening.

"I remember stopping to allow my mount to drink from the river. I stepped down near the bank, but when I turned around, the horse's face was so close it caused me to stumble backward and I fell into a boat. I hit my head on the edge and then it all went black."

Rafe didn't say anything. He just continued to look at her.

"Rafe?"

"Shhhh," he warned in a hushed voice.

It took a moment for her to realize he was looking past her and staring at something in the same direction as the tilted surrey.

"What is it?" Tayla squinted into the darkness.

Rafe drew his guns and pushed himself to his feet.

Tayla hadn't heard anything except the rain as it pounded the ground. She actually found the sound quite relaxing and with the warmth the oversized quilt provided, she was surprisingly comfortable.

"The fire could have drawn any number of creatures toward us."

"Rafe, what's going on? You're scaring me."

"Just stay here." Rafe stepped out from beneath the shelter the rock overhang and stone walls provided with his shoulders hunched forward and his hat low on his head.

She didn't hear anything for a few minutes and then Rafe reappeared. He removed his hat and turned it upside down, allowing the water to drain over a pile of rubble at the far end of the overhang. He picked up another chopped log and set it on the dying embers of the fire, then placed his hat a few inches from the heat on a rock to help it dry.

A slight breeze wisped past them and Tayla pulled the blanket closer around her and pushed herself tighter against the back wall of the shelter.

"There's no sign of the others. Try to get some sleep. I'll wake you when they get here," Rafe said as he stirred the embers with a stick.

"You are soaked through. You'll catch your death." She knew it was brazen, but he had to be cold. "Do you want to share the blanket?"

Rafe glanced over at her and cleared his throat.

"I'll be fine."

Tayla suspected that his reasons had nothing to do with how cold he was or wasn't—at least physically.

# CHAPTER TWELVE

There was only so much a man could take and Tayla Hawthorne was testing his restraint. Her memories were coming back to her more quickly. He had to keep his distance.

She'd betrayed him once. Even as he thought it, he knew it was a weak argument. Whomever Tayla had been, she was different person now, a woman.

The night held a damp chill, but in his line of work, he'd endured worse. Of course, there hadn't been a beautiful girl sitting next to him offering to share her warm blankets either. He was a fool. And he knew it.

He rubbed his hands together over the flames of the fire. They had enough cut wood to last them through the night. It would keep some of the animals away, but he was more afraid of what animals it might attract. The human kind. Mal Brewster was out here somewhere and it would be best if Rafe remembered just how dangerous of a man he was. And after their encounter in town, Rafe knew the man would be agitated and looking for a fight. Forgiveness was not his style. There weren't many places around that a man could lay his head.

Rafe highly doubted that Mal had moved on to the next city. It was a good couple hour's ride and with it being dark and storming, his immoral rival could be lurking anywhere. Rafe would have to stay alert.

He glanced over to where Tayla sat huddled in the large blanket.

Maggie would be none too excited when they showed up and the quilt had been literally dragged through the mud. At least it would keep her warm.

They would be sitting targets out in the open, and worse so under this ledge, but with the rain and cold settling in for the night, there wasn't much choice.

Tayla had been right that he would catch his death if he stayed in his wet clothes. That blanket looked mighty inviting, especially with the prize that now sat beneath it. Tayla had leaned back against the back wall of the makeshift cave. She watched him, which made him feel off kilter.

A wisp of wind curled itself around Rafe's shoulders and danced with the short flames of their fire. He shook his head, pride be damned, and removed his wet shirt. His trousers were dry enough that he could keep them on, but the shirt had been soaked through. He avoided her gaze as he threw another log onto the fire. It took a few minutes for it to light, but soon the fire was big enough that it warmed him. At least one side at a time.

When he turned around to warm his back, he faced Tayla, whose eyes were now closed and he breathed a quick sigh of relief.

He took a moment to admire how her lashes laid against the smooth planes of her face. Her lips were pouted and pink and a desire to capture them with his own wove into his thoughts. He looked away. Why did she have to be so beautiful?

Suddenly, Tayla's brow furrowed and she began to toss from one side to another.

"Shhh," he coaxed from afar.

Her breathing became heavier and labored. She was having a dream and by the way her face had scrunched up and her hands balled the blanket into her fists, he guessed it wasn't a very good one.

Rafe laid out his shirt and moved his hat so it wasn't too close to the fire. The last thing they needed was to be trapped by an unintentional blaze. He moved to the edge of the blanket, debating his next move, when Tayla shot up and screamed.

"Nooooooo."

Within seconds Rafe had her snuggled into the crook of his arm, her head on his chest. The words to a familiar hymn coursed through his mind and he started to hum. He pulled the blanket over his legs and tucked it up under Tayla's chin, then gently brushed her hair with his fingertips.

Enough time had passed, that he guessed Pete and the others would not be coming for them tonight. He hoped they were all right. He and Tayla would probably have to make the trek back on foot in the morning. He wasn't about to go back on his own and leave her out here all alone with Mal out there somewhere.

Glad she was sleeping peacefully now, he decided that he should probably get some shut eye as well. But he kept one hand at his side, resting along the butt of his revolver.

Rafe awoke with a start. Tayla was nestled loosely under his arm and was sleeping soundly. Maggie's blanket had proven to be very warm. He glanced over at what was left of the fire. White ash and orange dying embers stared back at him and he smiled. That was one of the better nights he'd spent on the ground.

Carefully, finger by finger, he unwrapped his hand from her arm and lifted away from her. He reached into his pocket to retrieve his grandfather's pocket watch. He was surprised no one had noticed they hadn't returned yet. It would be another couple of hours before the sun would be up and they would need to be heading back. He gingerly pulled the blanket away from him, careful not to let the crisp early morning air beneath it, and tucked it up against Tayla's sleeping form.

His shirt was still damp, but the sun would help to dry it. He pulled it over his shoulders and shivered once at the cold material against his warmed skin. He should put another log on the fire.

"Rafe," someone called from a distance. "Miss Hawthorne."

It had to be Harrison. Everyone else around the inn called Tayla, Locket. He peered out into the countryside. The clouds had all but disappeared and Rafe could make out two figures on horseback riding quickly toward them with lanterns lit. He got to his feet.

As soon as they reached the broken down rig, both Harrison and Pete dismounted.

"Rafe," Pete stepped forward holding his lantern high enough to lighten Rafe's face, "there's trouble."

"Maggie?" Rafe asked.

"It's that Brewster fellow. He was waiting for us when we got back to the inn," Harrison said.

"Waiting for *you*," Pete nearly spat out the last word.

No wonder the shameless bounty hunter hadn't found their little makeshift camp. He'd ridden on ahead. One thing was for sure, he'd done his homework.

"Rig's wheel is broken. Why did it take you so long to come back for us?"

"When you didn't show up after a couple of hours, Brewster realized we weren't just playing him. He told us to come and fetch ya," Pete said. "Wouldn't let me stay."

"Pete, you stay here with Tayla and I'll ride back with Harrison."

"I'm not staying here, Rafe." Pete was adamant. Then, his voice became pleading. "He has Maggie."

It hit him like wind in the face. Pete was in love with Maggie.

The last thing Rafe wanted to do was to let Tayla get in harm's way, but he couldn't leave her out here unprotected. He wasn't comfortable enough with Davis's abilities, not to mention his loyalties, to leave him out here with Tayla alone. He figured they could ride to the stable at the edge of Maggie's land and leave her and Harrison there until it was over. At least she'd be hidden, but close.

"Well, let's go then." Rafe motioned them to the horses.

Luckily, the horses from the surrey were still tied up right where he'd left them. Tayla may not be able to ride bareback, but he could. As much as he didn't appreciate the idea of her riding behind one of these men, it was better than the alternative.

Tayla was glad to see the Smokey Sky Inn come into sight only after the better part of an hour.

She had awoken during the night to find herself snuggled into Rafe's bare chest, warm and safe. She was still a little unsettled over having slept so close to him and knew she should feel shame or sorrow or something for not having moved the moment she'd realized the comprising position they'd been in, but she couldn't have willed herself to leave. She'd loved having his arms around her. Loved feeling the rise and fall of his chest as he slept. She hadn't wanted it to end, but she'd fallen back asleep all too quickly.

Now, Maggie was in danger, and she wondered if the patrons of the inn knew or understood the peril that surrounded their proprietor. Rafe seemed more anxious than she'd seen him yet. He rode one of the rig's stock horses alongside her and Harrison.

They sky was starting to lighten, but Tayla guessed the sun would not rise for another hour or more. Her muscles were sore and her hand had started to throb again.

"This is where you get off," Rafe pulled up next to them and motioned to a small rundown stable to the west.

"You're just going to leave us here?" Tayla asked incredulously.

"Davis, don't make me regret trusting you." Rafe acted as if he hadn't even heard her. He handed Harrison one of his pearl-gripped revolvers, then turned around and dug his heels into his horse's flanks.

"Well, come on then," Harrison said as he dismounted and held his hands up to help her down.

For a brief moment she debated riding off on her own and leaving Mr. Davis alone, but thought better of it. This would give her the chance to talk to him about some of the memories she was having that included him.

Once her feet hit the ground, she smoothed her dress.

Harrison led the horse into the stable. She followed. From what she could see, it looked as if the building hadn't been used in ages.

She thought she'd prefer to stay outside unless it started to rain again. No telling what kinds of animals had taken refuge in the old place. She sat down on the log in front of the door that hung by only one hinge.

"So," she said.

"So," Harrison responded.

"Did we know each other? In England, I mean." Tayla wasn't sure how to approach the conversation. She couldn't very well tell him that she saw him get killed. He'd think her crazy for sure.

"I knew of you. But like I told Rafe, we hardly ran in the same circles."

"What do you mean?" Tayla drew a circle in the dirt with the toe of her boot.

"You were," he started, "excuse me, *are* a Hawthorne, engaged to the Earl of Darington," he told her as if it had been obvious.

"Did you know the Earl?"

"Not exactly."

"What do you mean?" She knew she was bombarding him with questions, but he was a real connection to her life in England.

Harrison sat down on the log beside her and bent over with his elbows resting on his legs.

"It's a long story," he said casually.

"We appear to have some time."

Silence.

"Let's just say we got some news recently that will change our status among London society."

"We?"

"My brother and I. We grew up on the outskirts of town in a humble, but nice home. We'd always known we were adopted, our mother hadn't kept that secret, but..." He paused and looked at Tayla.

"Ah, never mind."

"No, please continue. Tell me about your brother." Tayla realized she wasn't sure if she had a brother. What if she had a whole gaggle of siblings that she couldn't remember?

"Finn is a whimsical bloke. More of a dreamer than I. It gets really annoying sometimes, really. It's the reason we got into this mess in the first place."

"What mess?" Tayla didn't know anything about the man, but his comfortable demeanor made him easy to talk to. She shifted on the log to be able to see him better.

"You really want to know?"

Tayla nodded. She really did. He had insight that could help her piece some of her past together.

"A few days before her passing, the Grand Duchess came to my home for a visit."

Tayla felt her eyes widen. "The Grand Duchess? Did you know her?"

"Very well. She was a dear family friend, only this time it was different."

"Different how?"

"This time she visited us as The Grand Duchess."

Tayla didn't respond because she didn't understand.

"We had always known her as Mrs. Potts, but she came to tell us that she was dying and didn't want to die with her secret."

Tayla's curiosity heightened and she moved forward on the log until she was barely sitting on it at all.

"She had a secret? And she wanted to share it with a farm boy? Why?"

"We *were* her secret." Harrison breathed out a deep sigh.

Tayla scrunched her eyebrows together.

"How can I put this delicately?" he asked, then turned to look at her directly.

The catch lights from the moon glimmered in his eyes. Tayla felt a sudden urge to reach out and touch him, to comfort him somehow.

"She was our grandmother."

Tayla wasn't sure what she had expected, but that was not it.

The sun peaked over the mountain before she could formulate a response. "You mean you are relat—"

"I know you don't remember, but you are engaged to Lord Darington. The Earl of Darington."

Tayla was floored. Royalty? Her? She didn't feel like royalty.

Crack. The piercing echo of shots being fired reverberated in Tayla's ears as vivid images of her father being shot in the chest were replaced by a scene where she watched as Harrison, lying on the floor, scrambled backward and Dare aiming a gun at him in the garden and firing. She hunched over, her hands boxing her ears away from the sound.

What was happening?

"Miss Hawthorne, pull yourself together. We've got to get to the inn. Rafe wanted to keep you away from it, but I'm afraid they may need some help."

Tayla took a deep breath, sat upright, and nodded. She shoved the images and newly acquired memories from her mind. She'd analyze them later. For now, the people she cared about the most in this world right now were in danger and she had to help.

Harrison grabbed the reins of the gelding they'd been riding and in moments, both were saddled and moving quickly toward the Smokey Sky. When they pulled into the yard, Tayla did not miss the anger that flashed in Rafe's eyes when he exchanged looks with Harrison.

Mal Brewster had Maggie by the hair. She was hunched over and fighting, her arms flailing about in concentrated jabs, but the misguided bounty hunter didn't seem to notice.

"Where is he, Redbourne?" Mal Brewster yelled across the yard.

Curtains opened and closed in the windows of the rooms

facing the courtyard, but none of the inn's guests were outside.

"I want Harrison Beckett!"

Harrison stood up a little straighter. In the dim light of the morning, Tayla could see beads of sweat formulating across his forehead and down his neck.

Rafe shook his head at them.

"No," Tayla whispered and reached across him to block Harrison, but to no avail as he quickly dismounted and took a step forward.

The look of warning in Rafe's eyes was unmistakable.

"What do you want with me?"

The man whirled Maggie about, evoking a scream and earning him another punch to his gut. He winced slightly, but did not let go. He righted himself and spun Maggie in front of him, his arm around her neck, and pointed his gun at Harrison.

Tayla could not watch him get shot again. Her recent recall of the memory was already too much. And she needed him to be alive to explain it. She darted a glance at Rafe.

"What do you want with him?" Rafe shouted his question, inching his way closer to the man.

"Let's just say you weren't working fast enough, Redbourne," Mal looked down at the ground, but did not turn to face Rafe. "The man who wants him upped the stakes. Dead or alive. You know that's my favorite kind." He turned back to Harrison. "So, what's it gonna be, Beckett?"

Harrison swallowed hard. Tayla could not watch this happen. She wanted to do something. Had to *say* something. She moved astride the gelding between Mr. Davis and the man and dismounted.

"My name is Tayla Hawthorne and I am Lord Darington's fiancée. I'm sure he will pay you handsomely for my return, but I will only come with you if you let this man go."

"I guess I'll just have to take you both," he said with a wide malicious grin. He licked his lips and moved a little closer. "Yer that pretty little filly from last night. Redbourne's girl."

"Leave her be, Mal," Rafe warned, taking another step toward the bully.

"I suggest you stay right there, Rafe," Mal said, spitting at the ground. "I've got her in my sights."

Crack.

Mal went down.

Rafe's guns were drawn, but he was scanning the yard. He hadn't made the shot.

Jake stepped from behind a corner of the house with a rifle in his hand. He reached behind him for his walking stick and took another step forward.

Rafe re-holstered his weapons, nodded at the boy, and quickly made his way over to the wounded bounty hunter.

"You're a fool," Rafe whispered loud enough for Tayla to hear. He removed his shirt and wadded it up, pressing it tightly against the man's chest.

"Maggie, we need to move him." Rafe looked down at the man whose eyes were closed and whose face was quickly losing its color.

"You're gonna try to save him? After what he did?" Maggie asked disbelievingly.

"Rafe, you can't expect her to—"

"Maggie," Rafe cut Pete off, speaking in a very firm and commanding voice, "a man is going to die if we don't help him."

Maggie seemed to snap out of it and she nodded. She looked at Pete with a little smile and disappeared into the inn. Rafe scrunched down onto his haunches and lifted an unconscious Mal into his arms and headed toward the kitchen door.

"I'm sorry, Rafe," Jake said, limping alongside him. "But he was hurting Maggie and was gonna kill that British man you were travelling with." His voice held a hint of desperation. "And I've seen him before."

They had precious little time, but Rafe stopped for a

moment. He handed the dying man to Pete. "Take him to Maggie," Rafe instructed.

Pete turned with his cumbersome load and with help from Harrison, took him inside.

Rafe put his hands on the boy's shoulders and hunched down enough to look Jake square in the face.

"Where did you see him?" Rafe inquired.

"The day I got hurt. He was there. He had something covering his face, but his hat, his jacket...it's him. He shot a man. I saw it. He would have hurt Maggie and your friend too.

"You did the right thing, Jacob. You understand?"

The young man nodded.

"You protected the people you love and showed compassion for a stranger. You should be proud of that, but you need to remember that life is worth something. I imagine even his."

Truth was, Rafe was proud of the boy. Over the years when he'd passed through at the inn, he'd taught him how to conduct himself in fight. He'd worked with him on his shot and helped him to understand the consequences of having to use the skills he learned. He was impressed by the calm the kid had demonstrated today in being able to make a shot like that in his condition and, although he was shaking, he still had a cool head.

The little boy, Jacob, had grown up into a man and Rafe realized just how much time had passed. As for now, there was a man lying in a bed upstairs in desperate need of medical attention.

He would have preferred it if they'd had time to ride out for Doc Porter to come and help, but Rafe doubted that Mal Brewster had even a few minutes, let alone an hour or two.

Tayla was shaking like a leaf, standing at the edge of the fenced courtyard. Rafe tried to smile, but was sure it looked more like a grimace.

He turned quickly on his heels and ran the distance up the stairs and to the empty room where Maggie stood waiting at the door.

She shook her head. Not the kind that was disapproving,

but the kind that told of bad news.

Mal was already dead.

Rafe thrust open the door. The familiar stench of death greeted him. He stepped into the room and removed his hat. Pete patted his shoulder and left, leaving the door open behind him. Rafe sat down in the chair next to the bed.

He felt like he should pray over the man, but it had been a long time since he'd really talked to God. Sure, he went to church occasionally in the hopes of finding some sort of redemption for his transgressions, but his pride had kept him away for too long.

Harrison had pretended to be a preacher. Maybe he'd know what to say. Rafe stood to leave, but came up short when he glimpsed Tayla standing in the doorway.

"We've got to get on the road," he said. "Go get your things together. We're leaving in an hour." He knew she wouldn't love the idea, but Mal had been looking for Harrison. He'd been told that finding Davis had been a solo job. Someone was not being straight with him and he didn't like it one bit. The sooner he got Tayla and Harrison to Redbourne Ranch, the better.

Tayla didn't say anything. She just turned around and went to her room.

When he finally found Harrison, the man was reluctant, to say the least.

"I've never given a eulogy. The man was going to kill me. I have no idea what to say. Why would you think I would?" Harrison said.

"Um, you married my brother and his wife—illegally true, but you said the words all the same."

Harrison raised an eyebrow. It was something he'd seen his brother, Cole, do on many occasions. But he took a step toward the table the dead man laid on, bent his head, and offered as good a prayer as Rafe'd ever heard.

A knock on the door brought his head about and his attention focused on the short man with the green bowler hat standing in the open doorway.

"Excuse me, but I have a few questions for you, Mr. Redbourne," the man said. The stern look on his face would have been comical had his hand not been resting on the colt he had tucked in his belt.

"Have you no respect, man?" Harrison asked from behind him.

The man pulled his vest jacket back to reveal a dull marshal's badge. It was Rafe's turn to raise an eyebrow. A glimmer of irritation grew quickly into anger as Rafe realized this marshal was a guest here. Where'd he been for the last few hours while they'd all been terrorized by a rogue bounty hunter?

Rafe didn't give the man the chance to walk over to him. With two strides he had the man's shirt bunched between his fists and held him a few inches off the ground against the wooden door.

"You. Are. A coward." Rafe had to remind himself that they were supposedly on the same side.

"Mr. Redbourne, I assure you—"

"What? That you, a man of the law, couldn't stand up to a reprobate bounty hunter like Brewster? Just where were you when he started waving his gun in the air?"

"Rafe," he heard Harrison saying his name, but couldn't stop himself.

"Where were you when he took Maggie by the hair? Where were you when that kid put a bullet in his chest?" Rafe knew he needed to calm down or he was going to put his fist through the man's face.

"Rafe," Harrison nearly screamed. He placed a hand on Rafe's arm at the shoulder. "Let him go."

With a firm shove into the door, Rafe let go and the man fell to his feet.

"Did ya get it all out, son?" the marshal asked as he straightened his vest.

Rafe said nothing.

"I wanted to let you know that Ev Martin rode into town this morning when all the rucus started to come and get me at the Morning Glory hotel—where I stayed last night on account of the rain."

He took a step farther into the room—a move which Rafe thought pretty bold considering. "He said no one could find you and I was the only other 'man of the law,' as you called me, around."

"Just who the hell are you?"

"Name's Dylan O'Leary, and up until two weeks ago, I was a territory marshal."

"And you're not now?" Rafe huffed as he sat down on the overstuffed chair in the corner of the room.

Harrison leaned against the arm of the chair with his arms folded, also staring at ex-Marshal O'Leary.

"I have been appointed as a territory judge and am on my way to Denver to be sworn in. I arrived just as Mr. Brewster called you out, looking for a Harrison Beckett, I believe he said. I'm guessing he was referring to Mr. Davis here."

Harrison nodded.

"You want something with Davis too?" Rafe asked as casually as he could. He didn't want to put any more heat on an already hot subject.

"Nope. You can tell me about that later. For now, we do need to deal with this." O'Leary pointed to the corpse on the table. "I think we can get it cleared up real quick. Seein' as I arrived in time to see what happened."

Rafe shoved his hands into his hair and out again. Jake was a good kid, trying to do right by the people he cared about. Wouldn't seem fitting to have him hauled off to some jail to await a trial.

"Go on," Rafe said in a low voice.

"I figure that now I've been sworn in, I'll just declare him not guilty. Will you be witness to that, Mr. Redbourne?"

"Yes, sir." Rafe was relieved that Jake wouldn't have to go through that nightmare.

"Now, let's go downstairs and find Ev's boy."

Rafe nodded and stood from his chair. He motioned for Harrison to follow the judge and he trailed behind long enough to place a yellow sheet over the dead bounty hunter.

# CHAPTER THIRTEEN

"Not guilty," Judge Dylan O'Leary called from behind the table where he'd conducted a brief hearing.

Jake turned and hugged his father and then Maggie.

"I just couldn't watch him terrorizing everyone. He shot that man on the stage, threatened Rafe at the box social, and with him waving that gun about, pointing it at Locket and Mr. Davis, he woulda hurt somebody for sure."

"Shhh," Maggie insisted as she tucked his young head into the crook of her neck.

Tayla crossed her hands over her chest. Her heart felt so big that it might burst at any moment. While she was delighted that the gruff Mr. O'Leary had turned out to be a judge and was able to expedite a hearing, she'd been afraid for Jake. He had a lot of people here who loved him, but taking a life was no light matter. He was so young and she hoped he would be okay. She wished for a moment she could stay and just start over here. Start a new life. But until this moment, she hadn't comprehended what she was missing to not have her family around.

"Now it's over," Maggie said. "Let's not spoil it."

A small group of the inn's guests had gathered in the dining room to watch the proceedings.

"What do you say we all have some pie?" Maggie hooted.

A murmur of agreement crossed the room and she disappeared into the kitchen. Rafe followed. He'd told Tayla to be ready and as much as she wanted to cling to the only real place familiar to her right now, it was time that she did what she could to remember...everything. She needed to be with her family. She *needed* to know what had happened between her and Rafe.

"Maggie, I know you all are celebrating and it's real great that everything worked out here, but we have to be going."

Maggie stopped slicing the cooled blackberry pie on the counter to stare at him.

"Well, at least you stayed longer this time than usual," she conceded. "I can be glad for that. Are you taking Locket with you?"

Rafe nodded. "I am."

"She's agreed to go with you?"

Rafe hadn't really thought about asking her permission, he'd just told her to be ready to go. He hoped she'd see the logic in it, but until this moment hadn't really entertained the idea that she wouldn't go.

He wasn't sure she'd be safe here. Something had happened to take her away from her fiancé in England and brought her to America. Lord Darington had placed a bounty on Harrison for her kidnapping, but he'd watched the man around her and he believed he hadn't known her before they arrived at the Smokey Sky.

Rafe bent over and placed a light kiss on Maggie's cheek.

"You should give the first slice to Pete," he said with a smirk on his face. He stood up straight, smiled hard, and walked out the swinging kitchen door.

"Rafe Redbourne, whatever do you mean by that?" she called after him.

Maggie deserved a little love in her life and he knew Pete to be a good man. He would treat her well and if his friend was indeed sparking over her, they'd do well to be together.

He glimpsed Tayla refilling a glass of lemonade for the

judge. When she met his eyes, she glanced over at the stairs where he saw a very small suitcase.

She was ready to go. No questions. No fighting.

Rafe smiled. Then he worried. It wasn't like the Tayla he knew to just go along with it. Either she was cooking up something in that brain of hers or she really wanted to go. Something inside of him hoped it was the latter.

Within the hour, Rafe had three horses, Lexa and two of Maggie's team horses, saddled and ready to go. Maggie stood in the doorway leaning against the frame. She had a jar in her hand, playing with the lid.

"Thanks again for the horses, Mags. I'll send back what money I can get for them in Denver." Rafe crossed the yard, climbed the porch steps, and leaned against the tall railing directly across from her.

"No need," she said as she handed him a small canning jar with money in it.

"What's this?"

She shrugged. "Sold some of your pieces to a few of my guests over the last few months."

"What? You mean the big mugs and things I threw on that old wheel?"

Maggie nodded.

Rafe opened the jar. There was nearly sixty dollars inside. "I can't take this, Mags."

"It's yours." She shrugged.

Rafe could feel a lump forming in his throat. He wasn't sure what to say.

"Thanks, Mags. Let me pay you for the horses."

"No need. I already took my share." She winked at him and he laughed.

Maggie was a smart business woman. Maybe he should have been surprised that she had turned his stress release into a profit, but he wasn't. It wasn't as if he were poor. His family was very wealthy, but he had a pot of his own. While a small portion of his funds were in a bank in Kansas City, in his line of work he'd seen too many of them robbed and had chased his fair share of thieves. He had no desire to make the job personal and had decided to keep the majority of his money hidden at his place on Redbourne Ranch.

He looked down at the bills in his hands.

While it wasn't near the amount he would have received for turning Davis over to Lord Darington, it would be sufficient to cover the cost of the horses, a train ticket home, and a few other things.

Home.

It wouldn't be long now.

Tayla's rear end ached. She was grateful to Maggie, who had given her a pair of trousers to wear for the trip.

They'd been travelling for what had seemed like an eternity, although the sun was still high in the sky and it could have only been a few hours since they'd left Maggie's. She hoped Rafe would let them stop before long.

As if in answer to her inward plea, Rafe led them down to a small inlet in the river to water the horses.

"We'll rest a bit," he said as he tipped his hat at her.

It was the most he'd said all morning.

Harrison Davis had been quite talkative, but they hadn't spoken of anything of importance. She'd wanted to ask him more about his family, about her supposed fiancé, and about herself, but the moment she'd mentioned his family, he'd changed the subject.

Tayla didn't think she was going to be able to move. She was sure that she was familiar with horses, but by the pain in her behind, it must've been a long time since she'd ridden for so long.

"Here, let me help you down." Rafe reached up, his large hand spanning the length of her side.

Tayla slid down to the ground with Rafe's assistance, but her legs felt like she hadn't been on solid ground in months and she faltered slightly against him.

His strong arms stiffened around her and kept her from landing on the hard dirt floor.

It took her a moment before she dared look up at him, but when she did, her breath caught in her throat. His features were stoic and hard, but there was something in his eyes that warmed her.

"Thank you."

Rafe cleared his throat. "Are you okay?"

Tayla nodded.

Rafe slowly let go of her and reached for the reins of her horse. "We'll stop here and rest for a bit. Maggie packed us a lunch. Would you mind retrieving it from Lexa's saddle bags?" he asked as he led her horse to the water.

"Of course," she replied, testing out her footing by putting pressure on one foot, then the other. When she was sure she could trust her legs to make it the short distance without falling and making a fool of herself, she made quick work of it.

"Would you like some help?" Harrison offered as he took the saddle blanket from her arms and spread it out on the ground.

"What's your story, Mr. Davis?"

"My story?" He sat down on the edge of the blanket and motioned for her to do the same.

"What brought you to America?"

"My mother used to regale us of tales of the place where a man could own acres of his own land, without royal blood, and I dreamed of coming here and building a place of my own— being my own kind of royalty. I guess when I found out that I stood to inherit land in England, I'd already made up my mind to discover dreams of my own in this new land of opportunity—as it's been called."

"So, why are you here with Rafe and not out finding your dream?"

He seemed to ponder the question for a while before responding.

"Let's just say that I love a good mystery."

Tayla still didn't understand, but before she could question Harrison further, Rafe appeared with two canteens. He handed one to her and the other to Harrison.

After their meager little meal, Tayla excused herself for a moment.

Rafe wanted to reach Denver by nightfall, which meant a few more hours in the saddle. She rubbed her derriere and elongated her stride as she walked behind a clump of brush and out of sight, trying to stretch the soreness out of her legs in the process.

She was determined to make the best out of the rest of the trip and get Rafe to talk to her. She needed to remember and it seemed he was the only one with the keys that would help her to unlock the past.

The hairs on the back of Rafe's neck stood on end. Something was amiss. He'd shaken out the blanket they'd sat on in the dirt, had folded it, and was about to return it to the back of Lexa's saddle when a sudden feeling had him whip his head around in search of something out of place. Harrison stood next to his gelding, rubbing the horse's neck. Rafe scanned the trees and water's edge for any sign of Tayla, but he couldn't see her. He closed his eyes and took in a deep breath, trying to distinguish the scent of mischief that surrounded him. Something was definitely wrong.

Just as he reached up to lay the saddle blanket over Lexa's back, a shotgun cocked, shattering the near silence of the trail. Slowly he turned around, careful not to startle whoever had crossed their way.

Dread filled his gut as recognition flooded him. The two ruffians he'd dealt with in Tumbleweed, Jonas and Lester, faced him. Lester wore a crooked grin that sunk Rafe's stomach even lower. His mind raced. Reaching for his guns with that shotgun only a few feet away would be deadly. His mind had to work quickly. He darted a glance at the empty handed man astride his horse and raised an eyebrow at the white bandage that still wrapped the man's hand.

Tayla was gone, but by the looks of it, they did not have her and he prayed that she would stay out of sight.

"What do you want, gentlemen?"

"A little retribution, don't you think, Jonas?" Lester asked his cohort without removing his eyes from Rafe's.

"We sure is lucky running into y'all out here in the middle of nowhere. Who'd a thought we'd have the pleasure of seeing you again, bounty hunter." Lester spat into the dirt, his grin turned into a snarl.

"Did you ever find what you were looking for in Tumbleweed?" Rafe asked, hoping to buy them some time. He chastised himself for not being aware of them sooner. He was slipping and he had a feeling it had everything to do with a certain Tayla Hawthorne. She distracted him and now, his lack of focus could very well be the death of him.

"Naw, but we see you've got something, or should I say someone, just as good." He pointed to Harrison Davis, who watched every move with keen understanding.

"What you want with him?"

"There are wanted posters up all over the territory with his face splattered all over them. Reckon he'll bring a good price to the boss in Denver." Lester laughed, an ugly, heartless sound.

Rafe slowly started to lower his hands. He had to get to his guns.

Lester shook his head. "I don't need another reason, Redbourne. You've given me plenty. Why don't you just take off that belt. Slow and careful like."

If Lester were just standing on the ground he'd have a chance without his guns. He hoped instinct would provide him with some recourse.

Gingerly, he unbuckled his gun belt and with slow and steady movements he raised his weapons out in front of him.

"Toss them over here," Lester directed.

Rafe did as he'd been instructed.

"Jonas," Lester said from the side of his mouth, "go get the man's guns."

Jonas hopped down off his horse and scurried over to the leather belt. He pulled one of Rafe's prized pearl handled Red Jacket revolvers from the holster and aimed it at Rafe.

There was a slight rustle in the bushes a few yards away, but it seemed Rafe was the only one who heard it.

Tayla. It had to be. He hoped she would have enough sense or wits about her to keep quiet.

"Not today, Jonas," Lester said.

"Aw, come on, Les. Look what he done to my hand."

"I said no!" Lester nearly shouted.

Jonas lowered the revolver and with his head hung low walked back around to his horse and with the gun still in his good hand, pulled a dingy rope from his saddle horn.

"As for you, Mr. Beckett, you'll be coming with us."

"The hell I will," Harrison said mockingly.

Lester's eyes still fixed on Rafe, his aim unfaltering. Jonas on the other hand, with a rope dangling over his shoulder turned the gun on Harrison and pulled back the hammer. It cocked.

"Get your horse," Jonas told Harrison. "We're leaving, and yer comin' with us."

Harrison only hesitated for a moment longer before he collected his gelding's reins. Jonas tied his fists in front of him, a feat Rafe found impressive given the state of the man's palm.

"Oh, and Mr. Beckett..."

Harrison and Rafe exchanged glances at the name Beckett.

"...if you try anything, I'll kill Mr. Redbourne here."

Harrison glanced at Rafe again, this time through narrowed eyes. "What makes you think I care about that? He was planning on turning me over for the bounty."

For the first time, Lester's gaze flinched—surprise evident on his face.

Rafe moved a step forward and Lester shot the ground in front of his feet.

A quiet gasp came from behind the trees. To keep Tayla

safe, he would have to let them be for now. He'd find Harrison quickly. After all, he was considered one of the best bounty hunters across the plains. He snorted at the description he'd heard of himself in the past. If he were one of the best, these two bumbling idiots would not have gotten the drop on him.

"Now, your boots."

Rafe stared at him as if he hadn't quite understood what the man was asking.

"Your boots. Take them off."

Heat rose in Rafe's face, his jaw clenched tight, and his hands balls into fists, then opened again. He darted another look at Harrison, who was now sitting atop his gelding.

A muscle twitched in Harrison's face, but Rafe shook his head in warning. Jonas and Lester may not be the smartest idiots he'd ever encountered, but they were shifty and had proven unpredictable.

Rafe bent over and removed his boots, setting them on the ground next to him.

"Now bring them to me," Lester said smugly.

Hope caught in Rafe's chest. If he could get close enough to Lester, he could end this whole thing without jeopardizing Tayla or Davis. Harrison nodded slightly to indicate he understood.

"Stop," Lester said right before Rafe reached his horse's nose. "Why don't you just go and put them in the saddle bags on that beaut of a horse over there." Lester motioned the tip of his gun at Lexa.

Oh, hell no. Rafe was not going to let them take Lexa. A man is these parts was nothing without his horse.

Rafe didn't move.

"Come to think of it, why do y'all have three horses? Is there someone else out here with you?" Lester's eyes widened and he frantically looked about, his eyes wild and fearful.

Rafe could not let him discover Tayla's presence.

"We bought the horse to pack all of the supplies we're carrying," Rafe said through gritted teeth.

He raised his hands, his boots in his grasp, and slowly made his way over to the horse Tayla had been riding. The ground was hard and stubs of weeds jabbed at his mere stocking covered feet. He stuffed his boots into the horse's saddlebags.

He slid the knife from the inside pocket of his boot and hid it in his hand. Rafe preferred his revolvers. Knives were too intimate a weapon and the likelihood of getting hurt was much greater. However, at this point, he had no other recourse. He just needed to get close enough to use it without Lester or Jonas being able to get off a shot. This time he had more than his own safety to worry about.

Lexa snorted and shook her head briskly. She was on edge and seemed to sense the danger that surrounded them. Jonas tried to approach the roan, but Lexa reared and pawed at the air. He backed away quickly.

"She's not going to let us take her, Lester," Jonas stated the obvious.

"I am not leaving a horse for Mr. Redbourne here. If she won't settle down and come along…shoot her."

Rafe looked hard at Lester's face. There was no jesting behind his words. He meant to kill Lexa if she didn't go with them.

Jonas lifted a rifle and took aim.

"No," Rafe yelled and stepped in front of his horse. He raised his hands in the air in front of him, palms forward to show he wasn't going to try anything.

Jonas smiled when he lifted his head from the sites. Rafe guessed he was simply waiting for the word from Lester. For the first time in a very long while Rafe was out of options. He would have to let them take her.

# CHAPTER FOURTEEN

"Damn it all," Rafe bent down to pull another stick from his socks. When he stood up, he looked at Tayla. "Excuse me, ma'am. That's no way to talk in front of a lady."

Tayla had no idea what was going on. He'd not yelled at her or made any snide or rude comments since the men had ridden away with his boots. She almost wished he would. This new nice Rafe was starting to worry her a little. Beyond the rise, just above his head, delicate swirls of smoke entangled the low riding clouds.

"Look, Rafe." Tayla pointed.

When they reached the top of the hillside they looked down onto a quaint little farmhouse just beyond a blanket of newly tilled rows.

He adjusted his hat.

"Let's just hope they'll be willing to help us get to the nearest town. It's getting on dark and most folks settle in for the night. Don't know how they'll feel about strangers encroaching on their evening."

The sound of a wagon approaching caught Tayla's attention and she turned to get a look. Rafe reached down and took a hold of her hand as they continued forward, walking down the hillside toward the house. Tayla liked the feeling of her hand in his.

"Rafe?" she asked hesitantly.

"Hmmmmm?"

She hesitated, afraid to ask questions she might not like the answers to.

"What happened between us?" Tayla didn't know when she'd have another opportunity to ask him. And he seemed to be in a much better mood than before.

Rafe stopped, but did not let go of her hand.

"I don't hate you, Tayla." He paused. "Our families are friends. Have been for a long time. I knew you eight years ago, but I've found it seems I don't really know you at all anymore."

Before long, the wagon was near on top of them.

"Whoa," the driver yelled, pulling his team to a stop. "Can I help you folks?"

Rafe reached a hand up to the man. "Name's Rafe Redbourne, sir. This your place?"

The man nodded as he shook Rafe's extended hand. "Landon Thomas."

"Well, Mr. Thomas, we've found ourselves in a bit of a situation and were hoping you might be able to help."

Mr. Thomas eyed Rafe speculatively.

"What did ya have in mind?"

"I noticed your wood pile is getting a little slim and can see that your rows are ready for planting."

"You new around here?" Mr. Thomas asked.

"No, sir. Just passing through."

"Can't afford to hire anyone right now, Mr. Redbourne. I'm real sorry for you and the missus, but you may be able to find some work in town."

Missus? Did Mr. Thomas think she and Rafe were...were married? Why didn't Rafe correct him?

"How far is it into town?"

"On foot? A few hours. It's getting' a might late tonight. Why don't you jump on back? I'm sure Rena's got something real tasty a cookin'."

"That's mighty kind of you, Mr. Thomas." Rafe jumped up onto the back of the buckboard and reached down for Tayla. He pulled her up as easily as if he were tossing hay. That made her a smile a little.

"What happened to your boots?"

"Some ruffians a ways back made off with my guns, my boots, and our horses."

"Where ya headed?"

"Kansas City. We were hoping to catch the train in Denver tonight, but now we'll just have to make do."

The kitchen was full of heavenly aromas. Tayla didn't realize how much she'd miss the inn after such a short time. While some of her memories were returning, the Smokey Sky Inn was still the most familiar place to her. She had to remind herself again why she'd decided to come with Rafe. The fact was, no matter how comfortable she felt at the inn, she had a family that was probably worried sick about her. She had a life somewhere. Most of her memories still created more puzzle pieces than a complete picture, but she hoped that with time—with Rafe—the gaps would soon fill in.

"Landon, is that you?" A shorter woman with plump curves and rich brown hair rounded the corner with a grin on her face. She stopped short when she saw Tayla and Rafe standing in the doorway with her husband.

Tayla nearly giggled when the woman's head travelled Rafe from toe to head with surprise touching her soft features.

"Well, Landon, what have ye brought home with ya?" The Scotswoman's hair had been woven into a braid and cascaded down one side of her body and she self-consciously played with the thick strand.

"Found 'em on the trail with nothing but the clothes on their backs." Mr. Thomas unexpectedly pulled his wife into an embrace and kissed her directly on her mouth. Then he pulled away as if it were nothing unusual and sat down on a wooden straight back chair next to the door and removed his boots. "They're needin' a warm meal and I reckon a bed for the night."

Tayla darted a glance at Rafe. They couldn't share a bed.

"I don't think—" she started.

"Well, now. I have some hot stew on the stove and some fresh biscuits in the oven. Good thing my Landon has a hearty appetite, there's plenty to go around." There was a twinkle in her eye as she put her arm around Tayla. "You're welcome to sit with us a while. Ye can wash up over there," the woman said to Rafe as she pointed to the basin on the far edge of the counter.

"This is might gracious of you, ma'am. Thank you kindly." Rafe tipped his hat and walked toward the water pump.

"Mrs. Thomas—" Tayla wanted to explain.

"Rena, please," she said as she squeezed Tayla's upper arm and looked directly into her eyes. "I'll go and fetch some clean linens and make up the room. My Landon builds some of the most beautiful pieces of furniture. But I'm afraid the bed is not large," she said sizing up Rafe once again, "but it's a chilly enough night that I don't suppose that will be a problem." She winked at them and then turned a smile on her husband.

Rafe laughed out loud and Tayla felt the flush enter her cheeks.

"Rena," Tayla tried again, but the woman wouldn't let her finish.

"It's our little Teddy's room while my brother is away, but I'll pull him in with us for the night."

Tayla scrunched her eyebrows together and for the first time, noticed a small bassinet in the corner next to the fire ablaze in the hearth. They had a baby.

"Well, don't just stand there, my dear. Get yourself washed up for supper." Rena made a shooing motion with her hands and disappeared into the room at the far end of the house.

Tayla dropped her hands and walked over to the basin, where Rafe was drying off on a small woven towel.

"We can't stay in the same room," Tayla whispered in his direction, lessons of propriety screaming alerts in her head. Heat rose in her cheeks as she recalled the nights she spent in his arms—once at Maggie's place and again in the cave.

"Would you rather sleep out there?" Rafe shook his thumb toward the window. "Nights still get chilly around here."

Tayla looked out the window. The sun was finally beginning to set and while there were some soft pink and gold hues coloring the sky, she knew the warm tones were not a reflection of the temperature outside. She turned back to look at the fire.

Warmth won.

A wee cry sounded and Mr. Thomas jumped from the chair and had scooped up the child in his arms before Tayla could blink.

"There," Rena said, wiping her hands against her apron. She peeked over the blanket in the bundle Mr. Thomas was holding and then quickly moved to the kitchen and pulled two additional bowls from the hutch in the corner.

"Sit. Please," Rena said as she set the large pot of boiling stew on a cloth pad in the middle of the well-used table.

They each took a seat and waited for the couple to join them.

"Thank you, love," Mr. Thomas said, cradling the baby in one arm as he bent over and kissed his wife on the top of her head and squeezed her close to him.

Tayla dared a glance at Rafe, whose face was unreadable. He didn't look the least bit uncomfortable, like he'd seen that kind of affection his whole life, but there was something about his expression that told Tayla that whatever had happened between them had something to do with love.

*No.*

It was impossible that he'd loved her once. Or was it? She found herself hoping, more than just a little.

Rena took little Teddy from Mr. Thomas and set him back in his basket before joining them at the table.

Tayla felt the knots in her stomach expand when Mr. and Mrs. Thomas set their hands out on the table face up. She looked at Rafe again, who had taken Mr. Thomas's hand and was extending his out toward her.

With a quick attempt at a smile, she slid her hand into his, reveling in the feel of his warmth against her chilled skin, then took Rena's hand into her other. As grace was said, Tayla bowed her head, but she didn't close her eyes. She wanted a moment to look at Rafe without him knowing it, but when she glanced at him, his eyes met hers with simple understanding. With a smirk, she quickly closed her eyes—just in time for Mr. Thomas to say, "Amen."

The meal was humble, but delicious. Tayla couldn't help but think how well Rena's stew would compare with Maggie's. They were both very good cooks and suddenly she felt a weight settle in the pit of her stomach. It had been all she could do to help Rafe prepare her basket for the town social. She'd quickly learned that she was not a cook by any sense of the word. How would she ever be able to care for a family of her own if she couldn't even make a simple meal by herself?

Her thoughts were interrupted by the scratching of the chairs against the wooden floor. Tayla quickly began to gather all of the dishes and followed Rena into the small kitchen.

"He's quite a handsome man, your Rafe, isn't he?" she asked without reservation. "And big." Her eyes grew a little wider.

"Yes. Rafe is handsome, but as I have been trying to tell you, he is not—"

A howl sounded in the night, closer than Tayla would have expected and she jumped at the boom of a shotgun being fired. A stricken look of fear hit Rena's normally soft features. She grasped at her skirts and both women hurried into the living room. Mr. Thomas stood at the front door, shotgun in hand.

"What in heaven's name?" Rena rushed over to her husband and looked out the door over his shoulder.

"Wolves," Mr. Thomas said to Rafe. "They're gone for now." He curled an arm around his wife and squeezed her close to him before letting her go. He turned to face them. "They must be herding cattle through here again. Can't afford to lose another ox. Just replaced one last month. Blasted wolves always come out when the drives pass through. Those fellas sure have their work cut out for them."

"It's tough all right. But with a good boss and trained drovers, it's honest work."

"Sounds like you know something about it." Mr. Thomas hung his shotgun back on its perch next to the door.

"I've been on my fair share of drives," Rafe said nonchalantly. "Redbourne Ranch herds cattle and horses from Texas to Kansas, Colorado, and the surrounding territories."

"So, you're a rancher?"

"No, sir. I mostly round up people who run from the law."

Mr. Thomas whistled. "A bounty hunter."

Rafe nodded.

"Why aren't you a rancher anymore, Mr. Redbourne?" Rena asked.

"Ranching and wrangling, well, that's for my father and a few of my brothers."

"A few...of your brothers?" Mr. Thomas nearly choked with surprise. "How many you got?"

"Six. And a sister," Rafe replied with a grin. "But, her husband works in carpentry. You and Eli would get along just fine," Rafe said as he pointed to one of the smaller tables next to the couch. "This yours?"

"Isn't it lovely?" Rena crooned.

Tayla enjoyed the exchange. She'd learned more in the last five minutes about her handsome cowboy than she had in the last few days.

After a while, Landon looked down at Rafe's feet. "Maybe you should take it up again. Ranching, I mean. Seems a might safer than dealing with these outlaws a yers."

Rafe opened his mouth to say something, then closed it again. "Let's just say there are a lot of things I plan on changing once we get home."

Rafe didn't know how he was going to make it through the next few hours. Sleeping in a room alone with Tayla proved to be more challenging than he'd expected. Grateful for the chair he assumed was used to rock little Teddy, he sat with a blanket haphazardly strewn about him and watched as a sleeping Tayla tossed about on the bed. He wondered if she'd had a decent night's sleep since her accident. He kept trying to remind himself that Tayla Hawthorne took everything away from him, but somehow it no longer rang true.

Why did she have to be so beautiful and sweet? It had been easy to hate the idea of her—when she was far away across an ocean and he didn't have to see and talk to her every day. Things were different now. He realized he was the one who'd given up on his dream. It had been him who'd dropped out of medical school. It had been him who'd taken the job as a bounty hunter. True, there had been nothing he could do to salvage his inheritance, short of marrying someone just for the money, but he mused, maybe it was time he confronted Tayla with the truth.

"She's lost her memory, you fool," he said to himself just above a whisper.

Tayla screamed out in her sleep. She sat straight up in the bed and started sobbing. Rafe was at her side in an instant, cradling her close to his chest. He ran his hands over her dampened wheat tresses and spoke to her in soft resonant tones.

"Shhhhh," he coaxed.

She nestled into him and hiccupped.

Her breaths came in gasps, but after a few minutes she calmed. She held onto him so tightly he didn't dare let go. He started to hum, hoping it would help her to relax. He leaned back against the wall with her wrapped comfortably in his arms. He pulled the thick blankets up around her to help keep her warm. The feel of her next to him sent shivers through his body, though not from the cold. It felt so natural to have her there. So right. He smiled as he drank in the heady scent of peaches and cream that infused her hair.

His face rested against her forehead, but before long all was quiet and he felt himself falling asleep alongside her. It felt good.

The cock crowed. Rafe awoke with a start. Landon had offered to drive them when he headed out to get some supplies. It was time to get up. There was a lot of work to be done on the little farm, and Rafe intended to help as much as he could over the next few hours.

He looked down at a sleeping Tayla, who was still nestled in the crook of his shoulder. Suddenly, he didn't want to move. He thought about his brother Cole and how he'd thought him crazy for marrying a woman he'd just met. However, he realized, Tayla was a stranger to him now and he wanted nothing more than to have what Cole and Abby had found together. He wanted to forget the past and have Tayla be a very real part in his future.

As much as he'd wanted to stay, he gently eased Tayla off of him and tucked the blankets up around her chin. Her hair was mussed and her cheeks flushed, but she looked like she was resting peacefully.

He opened the door and walked into the kitchen. Landon sat at the table holding his son, all bundled up in cloth. He looked up when Rafe entered.

"I thought I'd give his mama a reprieve this morning. Don't know how much longer it will last though. He seems a might hungry."

Rafe smiled.

Landon pointed with his nose toward the front door. "I set out a pair of Rena's brothers boots. Not sure if they'll fit, but I'm hoping they'll suffice."

Rafe wanted to get started on whatever projects Landon had for him. The field needed planting, the barn was only half finished, and the wood pile was dwindling to near nothing. There was plenty to do, but Rafe knew he didn't have the time to see everything completed. He would just have to do what he could. He was grateful for the boots, regardless of their size, they would be better than working in his socks.

"Thank you," he said, his voice still scratchy from nonuse. He walked over to the door and sat down on the chair to pull on the worn brown boots that laid there in a heap. While he was able to get his foot inside, his quickly discovered they were a size or two too small. They pinched a little, but fit well enough to work. That was all he needed.

He wanted to let the man know he would kindly repay him, but somehow the words weren't enough. He had money in the bank back home—and some hidden in the house—but for now, he had to do something more.

He hoped Harrison Davis was holding his own. At least it wasn't Mal Brewster, rest his soul, who had him in his clutches. That offered some comfort. And now, with the delay, it would take a little longer than Rafe had expected to find him.

It irked him that he'd let Jonas and Lester get the drop on him. Tayla certainly had been a distraction, but he was beginning to realize that she wasn't the only one. When he'd taken care of Jake, back at the inn, it had reminded him of the reasons he had chosen to study medicine in the first place. He liked fixing things and fixing people—or what ailed them. It was one of the most satisfying feelings he'd ever experienced. He missed it.

"Can I get some breakfast started?" Rafe asked, not wanting to overstep his welcome.

Landon raised an eyebrow. "You cook?"

"Not as well as I shoot, but yes, I can cook."

Landon burst out with a loud laugh and then quieted quickly when little Teddy started to fuss.

It took a few minutes for Rafe to orient himself to their kitchen and fixings, but within a short time he had some flapjacks whipped up and scrambled eggs cooking.

Rena walked into the room, pulling her hair up behind her and fastening her robe.

"Why, Mr. Redbourne, aren't ye just full of surprises?"

"Ma'am," he said in a low toned greeting, the hint of a smile touching his lips.

"Landon Thomas, ye are the sweetest man alive," she said as she walked over to her husband, took their baby from him, and placed a kiss lightly on his lips.

Once all the food had been prepared, Rafe walked into the room he had shared with Tayla to find her making the bed.

He cleared his throat.

She looked up at him with eyes that were nearly his undoing. He had the sudden urge to pull her into his arms and kiss her straight on the mouth. He quickly regained his wits about him. He couldn't be with Tayla. At least not until she had regained her memory. Not until they both knew the truth of what had happened once and for all. He thought he would just be able to let it go, but the more he tried, the more thoughts of Tessa invaded. He had to know.

"Breakfast is ready," he said more abruptly than he intended.

Tayla's eyebrows furrowed and she tilted her head. He turned and walked out. If he couldn't explain his actions to himself, how the hell was he going to explain them to her?

Rafe ate quickly and was outside before Tayla joined them.

Landon handed him a pair of gloves. "I'm mighty grateful to have an extra pair of hands today," Landon said as they walked toward the half-finished barn.

"I'm grateful you happened on us when you did," Rafe pulled his hat more snuggly onto his head. "Thank you for putting us up for the night and feeding us. I'm in your debt."

"Not after today," Landon smiled and patted him on the back of the shoulder.

They both laughed.

When the sun hit near the high point in the sky, Landon suggested they turn in for some lunch. Rafe wiped the sweat from his brow and looked toward the house. That meant facing Tayla again and he wasn't sure he wanted to do that quite yet. He stood back to look at what they'd been able to accomplish.

After they'd planted the first few rows, they'd started to work on the remaining section of the barn. Rafe understood how much easier it was to hang the boards when there was someone else to steady it. He'd help put up many a barn, but usually it was along with a team consisting of his family, all six of his brothers, Eli, and his dad. Too bad Landon didn't have that kind of support to help now.

Rafe needed to focus. Harrison Davis was out there somewhere with the two men who'd taken Tayla and shot her father. He patted his denim pocket where he'd kept a little brass button. Harrison Davis was innocent of the charges that had been brought against him and if Mal Brewster had been right about this Lord Darington wanting him dead, there wasn't much time. He had to get Tayla safe to Redbourne Ranch, so he could track down Harrison and the two brutes who'd taken him. He needed his boots, his guns, and his horse.

Rafe realized he'd come to a crossroads in his life. It was time for a change, but there were still things left undone that he needed to take care of first.

"Let me just grab that ax there and get some wood chopped for the pile. Then I'll be in."

"Nonsense. We've been working all morning and by the looks of you, you need some refreshment as much as I do." He held open the barn door. "Well, come on."

Rafe removed his gloves and slapped them against his hand. There was no use putting it off any longer.

# CHAPTER FIFTEEN

Tayla pulled herself away from the window coverings the moment she saw Rafe emerge from the barn. He looked hot and tired and by the looks of his limp, she guessed that the boots he wore were pinching his feet more than a little.

"Ye must not've been together long. Though, I sometimes still watch my Landon like you're doin' there to your man. And why wouldn't ye? He's a fine lookin' man," Rena said with a wink, bouncing her son on her hip. "Looks like they're comin' in for some food." She smiled and turned back to the kitchen.

"Rena? Can I ask you a question?" Tayla asked as she followed the woman at a close distance.

"Of course'n ye can." Rena set Teddy in a tall wooden high chair Tayla guessed Landon had made for the boy.

Tayla sat down at the table, leaned forward, and rested her chin on her fists. "I—"

"Something smells mighty fine," a male voice called from the entryway.

"I'll bet it tastes pretty good too," Rena said in response. She turned back to her. "My apologies, Tayla. What were ye sayin'?"

Tayla opened her mouth just as Rafe walked in. She closed it again, shaking her head slightly at Rena.

"It's amazing how much faster it goes out there with more than one set of hands." Landon leaned over the table and kissed his wife.

"Are ye sure ye have to be leavin' today?" Rena asked Rafe without looking at him, her cheeks slightly flushed.

When Landon pulled away, he stared at Rafe expectantly. "Well?"

"Well, what?" Rafe stood still in the doorway to the kitchen.

"Well, that's no way to greet your woman," Landon said with a smirk.

Rafe hesitantly stepped forward and leaned down to place a kiss on her cheek. She was unprepared for the jolt his warm lips would send through her back. She sat up a little straighter and felt the heat rise in her face.

"You don't have to feel embarrassed to show affection in this house. If you haven't noticed none, we kinda like each other around here. Now kiss her."

Tayla's heart seemed to grow inside her chest as the gentle rhythm quickly turned into a vibrant pounding. She had a hard time controlling her breaths when she met Rafe's eyes—hot and fierce. She wasn't afraid of him, and there was no denying that she had to have loved him before. Her body remembered, even if she couldn't.

Rafe reached out and pulled her to her feet.

Tayla bit her lip. He was really going to kiss her. She swallowed.

He placed a firm hand along her jawline and brushed a strand of hair from her face with his forefinger. He moved closer. She closed her eyes.

Boom. Boom. Boom.

The firm, rapid knock on the door made Rafe pause and he dropped his hands to his sides. Tayla's anticipation deflated as she watched him follow Landon out into the living area.

Tayla stepped out of the kitchen in time to see Landon reach for his shotgun, then swing the door open wide with it already pointed at the entry.

"Whoa there. We don't mean no harm."

"Ethan?" Rafe asked as he stepped closer to the door, opening it enough that Tayla could see two men carrying a third between them.

The man in the center was bruised and barely conscious.

"Rafe?" Ethan scrunched his eyes together and a huge smile broke onto his face. Relief seemed to wash over him. "I'd ask what you're doing here, but Marty's gotten himself hurt and he needs help."

There was something familiar about him.

Rafe lifted the unconscious and bleeding man they'd called Marty into his arms.

"Landon, go get the doc," Rena said frantically as she worked to clear the decorated table behind the couch enough for Rafe to lay the man down.

"What the hell happened to him, Ethan?" Rafe leaned down and held the hurt man's head between his hands, carefully opening his eyes.

"Landon," Rafe called before Mr. Thomas reached the door. "It'll take too long for you to ride out for the doctor. Will you just grab me a couple of boards, a little shorter than your arm?"

Landon looked confused. "I thought you was a bounty hunter."

"I'll explain everything, but I really could use those boards."

"Rafe, had we known, we wouldn't have brought her along."

"Brought who along?"

"The pregnant heifer."

Rafe darted a glance at Ethan, then at the other cowboy.

His attention quickly returned to the man lying on the table in front of him.

"Marty," he said firmly.

The man barely moved his head.

"Marty," Rafe said again even louder. He gingerly worked his hands over the man's arms, legs, and ribs. Tayla guessed he was looking for broken bones.

"Aaaaa," Marty finally called out in pain when Rafe's hands moved over his left leg.

"Ethan," Rafe called, "help me get him to the floor. Easy now," he said as they laid him on the wooden surface. He grabbed a decorative pillow from the couch and placed it between the man's legs. "Okay, little brother, I need you to sit down and put your foot up against this pillow. Try to keep his leg straight."

*Brother?*

Tayla tilted her head a little to look closely at the man who sat on the floor, quick to do as Rafe instructed.

Ethan held Marty's foot, one hand on top and one on the bottom.

"Now, keep holding it straight and lie back all the way."

Ethan just looked at him, skepticism lining his already worried features. "That's going to hurt."

Rafe shot him a look that allowed no room for questions. "Just do it. Now."

"Okay," Ethan said and he lay back with the foot held tightly in his hands.

Everyone in the room watched with bated breath as the crooked leg straightened.

Marty screamed, then visibly relaxed.

Rafe closed his eyes and let out a deep breath.

"Tayla," he called her name without looking at her, "go with Mrs. Thomas and bring me some rags, a water basin, and some rope or twine."

Rena rushed to follow, but turned when the injured man spoke.

"I must be dreamin', Ethan. I see Rafe." Marty's voice was ragged and skipped a few tones as he spoke.

"You're not dreaming, buddy." Ethan knelt down next to the couch and spoke coaxingly into Marty's ear. "Rafe's here and he's going to take real good care of you."

Tayla slipped into the kitchen to help Rena gather the supplies Rafe had requested.

"I'll run out to the barn for some rope. You finish filling this bin and take these rags into him," Rena said, reaching for the back door. "Don't you let that man go," she said before disappearing outside.

When the basin was full, Tayla draped the rags over her

arms and carefully made her way into the front living area with the bowl hugged into her chest. Rafe looked up and attempted a smile.

"Here," he said, "let me take that." He stood up and relieved her of the heavy basin. With the absence of weight in her grasp, she folded her arms across herself and rubbed them. She wasn't chilly, but she didn't know what else to do with them.

Rafe dipped the rags in the water and gingerly began to clear dirt and blood from the man's face.

The front door burst open. Landon carried a variety of boards in different shapes and sizes. "I wasn't sure what you needed, so here's a few to choose from." He laid them on the floor next to Rafe.

Rena joined them again a few moments later with rope and a ball of twine. She kneeled down next to the boards. "What can I do?" she asked.

Rafe nodded. "Thank you, ma'am," he said with a smile. "If you'd cut a few lengths of string that would be most helpful."

Landon handed her a knife and she made quick work of it.

Rafe picked up a few of the boards and tossed them aside before he found the ones he wanted. He set one on each side of Marty's broken leg and, with Ethan's help, he lifted the leg enough to get the twine wrapped around the makeshift splint.

"I'll just go get some fresh water for him to drink," Rena said before disappearing back into the kitchen.

Tayla wished she'd thought of it. She wanted to help, but had no idea what to do or even where to stand. She backed up against the wall near the fireplace to watch.

"No you don't," Rafe looked right at her and motioned for her to sit next to him.

"Sorry, Rafe," Marty said through parched lips. "The calf got stuck. I was only down for a minute when..."

"Now, you listen to me, Marty. You are going to be just fine," he said. "You'll be good as new in no time, but for now, I want you to meet this pretty lady. This is Tayla and she's going to help you take a few sips of water, all right."

His encouraging smile sent warmth through Tayla's body. Rena handed her a cup full of water.

"You're not going to be able to finish this drive, I'm afraid."

Marty tried to sit up, but Rafe pushed him hard back to the floor.

"Lucky for you, Miss Hawthorne here and I can help out. Just lay there, Marty. I'll be right back." Rafe stood up and immediately pulled Ethan into a firm hug.

"It's been too long, big brother," Ethan clapped Rafe on the back and pulled away. "What on earth are you doing here in this little farmhouse, and why," he glanced at Tayla, "is Tayla Hawthorne with you?"

Rafe glanced at Tayla and pushed his brother and the other man farther into the corner of the room.

Marty seemed more alert now and looked as if he were trying to listen in on their conversation. Tayla leaned sideways, straining her ears. She couldn't hear what they were saying, but when all three of them turned to look at her, she pulled the button down shirt she wore a little closer around her. What could they possibly be saying about her?

Why was she waiting here to find out?

"Excuse me for a moment," she said to Marty and pulled herself up off the ground.

She dropped her hands to her sides and marched up to their little circle. Before she could say anything, Ethan stepped forward and pulled her into a tight hug and lifted her off the ground.

"I can hardly believe it. It has been way too long since we've seen you, little girl. How have you been?" he asked with hearty enthusiasm. He set her down and grasped her shoulders. "Although, you aren't so little anymore, are you?"

Tayla didn't know what to say. She smiled. She liked him immediately. She wondered if all of Rafe's brothers were this friendly. "It's Ethan? Right?"

Ethan looked confused and...injured.

"Don't take it personally, brother. She doesn't remember me either. It's a long story, but Tayla got a little bump on her head and has little recollection of her past. She is getting some of her memories back, but they seem to be sketchy at best."

The look on Ethan's face was beyond shock as he looked from Rafe to Tayla and back again. "So, she doesn't know—"

"No," Rafe said firmly and with a look of warning.

The other man extended his hand. "You don't know me, just to be clear. Name's Judd. I'm new to Redbourne Ranch."

Tayla took his offered hand and nodded. "Locket," she said as she fumbled with the trinket about her neck.

"Like I said," Rafe clapped his brother on the shoulder, "it's a long story. "Now, tell me what happened out there."

Taking Tayla on the trail was a risky choice, but Rafe couldn't see any other way. He had to make sure she got to Redbourne Ranch safely and the only way to see to that was to take her there himself.

Rafe leaned back against the walls of the humble farm house and looked out over the fields that had yet to be planted. He glanced toward the still unfinished barn and wished he had time to stay and help. He'd speak to his father about sending back a team of men to help as payment for all Landon's help.

Ethan hadn't liked the idea of taking a woman along, but the stretch from here to home would only take a few days. He guessed she could handle it that long. And he hoped the men could too.

The Thomas's had offered to let Marty stay with them until he could be sent for. There was no way he would be able to sit astride a horse, let alone work as a drover on the drive. His leg needed to stay perfectly straight or the cowpoke would be in danger of losing it. As it was, he would probably have a slight limp even after it had healed.

Marty had refused to stay and, so, they made up a place for him in the back of the short chuck wagon with Griff, the cook. Rafe pushed himself away from the wall and over to the barn where Ethan and Judd were brushing down and watering their horses.

The wagon was usually full of foodstuffs for the drive, but they were down to the last leg of the return trip and most of the supplies had been diminished. Both men agreed that they would be able to work it out without much delay.

Along with a broken femur, Marty had suffered several broken ribs and a fractured forearm. Rafe suspected he had also cracked his cheek bone, but couldn't be sure. The swelling in his face was pretty severe and he was covered in bruises. Being kicked and stomped on by a bull was never a good idea. The man was lucky to have made it through the experience without a cracked skull.

"Need a lift?" Landon asked when he emerged from the barn.

Rafe extended his hand and his new friend gripped it firmly. "Thank you for all you've done."

"Thank you," Landon said. "I got ahead on my planting and am a lot closer to finishing that barn, thanks to you. If all it cost me for your help was to put you up for the night and offer a warm meal or two, I'd do it more often." He grinned.

"I'm just sorry we can't stay and do more. I will take you up on that ride, though. If you'll take us as far as camp, I'd be much obliged. It'll be easier on Marty to be able to lie down in the back of the wagon."

Tayla stepped out of the house and when he caught her stare, something inside of him warmed. Her hair looked wet and Rafe wondered if she'd bathed while he'd talked with the menfolk. He realized all too quickly that he needed to change the direction of his thoughts or this trip was going to be a lot longer than he wanted it to be.

Why did Maggie have to have given her a pair of trousers to wear instead of a dress? As if his concentration wasn't already suffering, just with her being around, the denims weren't helping matters much. Maybe they could pick up a dress for her in town when they reloaded with a few extra supplies.

Tayla hugged Rena and joined them at the barn.

"The trail, huh?" Tayla rocked back and forth on her heels. "Have I ridden along on one before?"

"I doubt it," Rafe said with a grin. Ethan snorted and shook his head.

"What does that mean?" Tayla insisted. Instantly, Rafe recognized his error. He needed to give Tayla a new beginning and if he kept treating her like he thought the old Tayla would be, it would be him who ended up losing.

"I just meant that riding the trail isn't generally the kind of work a lady enjoys." *Except maybe Abby,* he thought with a smirk how Cole's wife would have liked riding along. "It may take some adjustment, is all. Luckily, we're only a couple days ride from home."

"Are we not going to look for Mr. Davis?" she asked out of nowhere.

"After I get you safe to Redbourne Ranch, rest assured I will find Mr. Davis, my horse, and the brutes who took them." It still got under his skin to think about Jonas and Lester getting the drop on him. He hated to admit he was worried about Harrison and Lexa, but he hoped he would be able to pick up on their trail soon.

Rafe went in to get Marty. Ethan and Landon followed. When they got into the living room, Marty was sitting up on the couch with his leg resting on the low riding table.

"You are an angel, Mrs. Thomas. Mr. Thomas is lucky to have the likes of a woman such as you. I'd snatch you up in a moment if you ever had the idea of leaving him." He winked. Rena giggled as she disappeared into the kitchen.

"Well, you seem to be feeling a might better," Rafe stated matter-of-factly.

Marty snapped his head to look at him, his grin retracting into a somber expression. "It was the leg, Rafe. Whatever you did eased the pain enough for me to think straight. I can't tell you how grateful I am you was here."

He still looked a sight. With his leg in the makeshift splint, his arm bound with a sling, and his face purple, swollen, and puffy, Rafe reckoned that most people would have had their spirit knocked out of them. But not Marty. He was as happy-go-lucky as ever. By the look on Landon's face though, if he didn't stop flirting with the man's wife, he just may end up with a few lost teeth to boot.

# CHAPTER SIXTEEN

It took them just over a quarter hour to reach camp. There were only a handful of cows—both bulls and heifers and less than a dozen horses, including the drovers' mounts. When Rafe jumped down off the wagon, he nearly lost his footing as sharp, stabbing pains shot through his foot. He needed a pair of boots that didn't pinch his feet if he was going to be any good to anyone.

There were six fellas in all riding along this time, including Griff, and Rafe introduced Landon and Tayla to each of them. They were all very surprised to see him and he didn't blame them. It had been a long time since he'd associated with the teams and even longer since he'd actually be on a drive. While this part was the easiest, as they didn't have a herd of thousands to control and lead home, it still required skill and hearty resourcefulness. Rafe could recognize a prize bull, and the one they kept separated from the others definitely fit the description.

"Is that the one that got Marty?" he asked Rigg, one of the flank riders.

"Sure is. Mean as spit, that one."

"And the calf?"

"If it weren't for Marty, she'd a been done for. She's right over there, behind her mama," Rigg said, pointing to one of the other improvised enclosures.

After familiarizing himself with the animals and the route map Ethan had given him, Rafe turned to look at his new friend.

"How far is the town from here?" Rafe asked Landon. They would need a few things before heading out, including a new pair of boots.

"Another half hour or so. I've got to go there myself. I can take ya, if'n you'd like."

"Thanks, Landon, but I think we'll ride. This has to be out of your way and we've already inconvenienced you enough."

"Nonsense, but suit yourself. I'll lead the way."

Rafe nodded.

Ethan still had money in the cash fund—though not a lot, and handed a small roll of bills to Rafe. "There should be enough there to get a fresh horse for Tayla, a pair of boots for yourself, and maybe even a new pistol. Just to be safe."

Rafe had explained everything to Ethan, who was now itching to find Jonas and Lester almost as much as he was.

They'd only had enough broken horses for the riders. While Rafe could take Marty's mount, Tayla would need a calm horse that would make it an easy ride for her. He hoped the town had a livery with horses for sale.

It took less time than Rafe had expected to reach the small, dusty town of Mapleton. The townsfolk seemed friendly, but the hair on the back of Rafe's neck stood on edge. Something told him to be careful and alert.

Landon pulled up in front of the mercantile, but Rafe wanted to see about getting another horse before anything. He scanned the streets. Nothing appeared off, but he felt itchy and he didn't like that feeling one bit. The sooner they were away from here and on the trail, the better.

Loud music and raucous laughter came from the saloon between the livery and the blacksmith shop. Rafe generally avoided such places. He hated to see women in such a degraded fashion and he'd learned a long time ago what liquor did to a man's senses. In his line of work, he couldn't afford the repercussions of losing himself in drink.

Rafe reached up and helped Tayla dismount. He took her hand in his and together they walked toward the livery. He wanted her as close to him as possible. Something was amiss, but this town was unfamiliar to him and he wasn't sure what dangers may be lurking around the next corner. Without his guns, he had to rely on instinct and brawn—both of which he had plenty.

The livery stable doors were closed, which Rafe thought odd in the middle of the day. He looked around and caught sight of a man staggering out of the saloon and toward them. He wasn't a short man, but was far from meeting Rafe's height.

"You needin' to stable your horses?" he asked, placing a hand on Rafe's chest and gripping his shirt for balance.

"This your place?" Rafe asked.

"Yes, sir. Still mine. And I won them here boots, fif-ty dollars," the balding man bent in half and pointed down at his feet with his free hand, "and a blasted mare I've got tranque'd in the back stall."

Rafe didn't have a lot of patience for drunks. He'd seen too many of them and it seemed every town had one or two who were in a constant state of intoxication. He gripped the man's fist in his own and squeezed enough to get his attention as he pried the livery owner's fingers away from the buttons of his shirt. The stable hand stood upright, his eyes glazed and bloodshot, and craned his neck up to look at Rafe.

"Hey, whatcha do that fer?"

"I'd like to buy a horse," Rafe said evenly.

"Well, why didn't ya say so?"

Rafe let go of his hand and the man snatched it back and shook it out before he turned to open the stable doors. The pungent mixture of horse manure and sweat insulted them and Rafe had to turn away for a moment to collect himself. When the light hit the horses to his left, he recognized them immediately and instinctively reached for his guns.

They weren't there.

Damn.

The gelding Harrison had been riding neighed and Rafe stepped forward to rub his nose.

As the stableman opened the far side of the livery, Rafe noticed a light clacking sound as he walked and haphazardly glanced down at the man's new boots. The deep red leather band with a carved R in the side of the spur straps unmistakable.

His boots.

It was everything he could do to hold himself back from picking up the stranger and slamming him into the now open stable doors. As if sensing his restraint, Tayla walked up behind him and rested her palm over the inside curve at his elbow.

He breathed.

"Where'd you say you got those new boots of yours?" Rafe asked as calmly as he could.

A loud nicker stole his attention to the back of the livery.

"That's what I was trying to tell ya. I won them off these fellas over at the saloon. I also got this devil of a horse. Wanna see her? She's real perty." He guided Rafe and Tayla to the back of the livery where Lexa paced the oversized stall. "She near broke the doors when we first got her in here. I'm afraid she's the only one left for sale."

Tayla looked up at him with a horrified expression on her face. "Rafe. That's… That's—"

"Lexa. I know," he said in low tones so the stableman would not hear.

The mare raised her head. She always did have great hearing. She must have recognized his voice and grew more restless.

Rafe had to get her out of there, but there was something he had to take care of first. Lexa whinnied and reared onto her hind legs. She was a magnificent horse, normally standing about fourteen hands, but Rafe noticed she didn't rise as high as usual. Upon further inspection, he realized that his mare had been tethered to an old metal post that had been buried in the ground. He clenched his jaw.

"We need to find Landon," Rafe said as he turned to leave the stable. Then he turned back to the livery hand as he stuck his hand deep into his pockets. "I'll give you three dollars for those boots."

"These old boots?" The man thought for a moment. "Five."

"Done." Rafe paid him and grabbed Tayla's hand, pulling her toward the open door.

"Too big a horse for ya, is she?" the man called after them.

"I'll take her too," Rafe called back without turning around. He had to find Landon because there was no way in hell he was going to take Tayla into a saloon and brothel. Landon was loading a sack of flour onto the back of his wagon when they approached. Rafe sat down on the edge of the boardwalk and traded his boots for those Landon had given him. He tossed the latter into the back of Landon's wagon and pulled the shotgun his new friend kept next to the seat.

"Can I borrow this?" He waited just a moment for a confused Landon's nod. "Don't take your eyes off of her," Rafe charged as he headed toward the saloon. "I'll just be a moment."

"What's going on?" Landon called to him. "You find one of your criminals in this little town?"

*If he only knew the truth of it.* Rafe cocked the gun one-handed. He preferred a rifle or his revolvers to the clumsy weight of a shotgun, but it would do in a pinch. If Jonas and Lester were in this town, then Harrison Davis had to be around somewhere and Rafe intended to find him. The Brit had information that would help him protect Tayla, and as much as he hated to admit it, he liked the man.

It felt good to be in his own boots as he strode steadily toward the saloon. For the first time since he'd found Tayla, he felt back to his old self. His heart beat faster and he had to work to keep his breathing steady. Anticipation threaded its way through his veins and he clenched his teeth.

When he reached the doors, he glanced inside and scanned the room. It didn't take long before he saw the men he was looking for sitting at the table, playing a game of cards. Lester leaned back on the back pegs of his chair, one of Rafe's Red Jacket revolvers hanging loosely from his belt. Jonas sat to one side watching the game intently.

Rafe pulled the front of his hat lower on his forehead and slowly opened the doors. He had a clear path to the poker table and with each step felt his anger grow. He knew he had to keep it in check, for all of their sakes. When he reached them, he lifted one booted foot onto the empty chair on the opposite side of Lester and leaned down with his arm resting on his knee. Everyone at the table looked up and stopped. Lester looked down at his boots.

"What do ya want now, Farley. I told ya we was go—"

"What are you planning on doing with that Ace in your lap, Lester?" Rafe said in a low, threatening tone.

The gambler across the table with a shiny silver and black vest stood up and pushed at the table. "You cheatin' at cards?"

Lester slowly looked from the gambler, back to the boot on the chair next to him and then his eyes trailed upward until his sight rested on Rafe's face—the fear in his eyes unmistakable.

"I wouldn't," Rafe said, effectively relieving Lester of his weapon and pinning his arm behind his back. "Where's the other one?" he asked, pulling tighter.

"What Ace? He's lyin' fellas. I wouldn't cheat ya." Lester pushed away from the table and stood up, but his attempt to catch the extra card failed, and the evidence floated to the floor next to the fancy dudded man.

Jonas's eyes darted from one man to another as if searching for help, but no one seemed willing to comply.

"The other revolver?" Rafe asked again, slowly, his words highly annunciated.

Jonas touched his empty belt. "Must've left it in with Davis and the horses," he said, then sat up straighter as if it had been the wrong thing to say.

"Jonas," Lester spat. He turned to Rafe. "You can't kill us here, Redbourne. Being cold blood and all. From what we hear, that's not your style."

"Well, you are right, Lester. However, if I'm not mistaken, this town has a sheriff and last I heard, horse theft is a hanging offense. Not to mention, stealing a man's guns and his boots, leaving him out in the wilderness to die. Although, you left me the pretty lady for company, and for that, I'm grateful."

Lester turned as much as he could to face him. His confusion quickly turned his expression dark and menacing.

Rafe laughed out loud. "What? You didn't see her bathing in the river behind us?"

Lester attempted to scramble from the chair, but Rafe shoved him to the floor, face first, and knelt on his back. Before Jonas could retaliate, Rafe grasped his revolver and aimed it at his heart.

"Do you really want to play this game again, Jonas?"

Jonas looked down at the bloodied bandage on his hand and then back at Rafe. He put his hands out in front of him.

"Now, tell me about Mr. Davis. Where is he? And where is my gun?"

Jonas shrugged his shoulders.

"You left a bounty alone?" Rafe asked with a snort of derision.

"Course not. He's still tied up over at the livery."

Rafe had just come from there and there had been no sign of his friend.

"Shut up, Jonas," Lester screeched from the floor, the sound barely audible between his squished cheeks.

"We was just havin' a little fun, Mr. Redbourne. You got yer boots now, and yer gun. No harm done." Jonas attempted to placate him.

"No harm done? You left me in the middle of nowhere without boots, a horse, or a weapon. You let my bounty get away. You tried to kill me, and no harm done?" Rafe could feel his anger rising, but he managed to keep his hands steady.

He stood up and pulled Lester to his feet.

"The boss isn't going to be none too happy about this, Lester," Jonas said when Rafe pushed his cohort toward him.

"Storm's a comin'!" A young man burst through the saloon doors, breathing hard and frantic. "Everybody better hunker down real quick. It's ugly."

Rafe glanced outside at the grey clouds that hurled forward from the horizon. The wind that twisted the surrounding air up into a funnel looked like it was heading toward the town. As much as he hated to let them go, Jonas and Lester didn't matter right now. He had to get back to Tayla and Landon.

He hoped and prayed that the twister would miss the Thomas's home and the camp where Ethan and the rest of the team were settled. Rafe ran from the saloon and into the windy street toward the mercantile. Tayla gripped her hair in her hands, standing next to the wagon, waiting for him to return. Landon was by her side.

"We need to get inside. Fast," Landon yelled over the wind that had picked up speed over the last couple of minutes. He quickly guided his wagon to the space between the two buildings.

A tall, thin man Rafe guessed was the shop keeper ushered them inside and led them down to an underground cellar. Tayla slid her hand into Rafe's. She was shaking. He wanted to gather her into his embrace to keep her safe from the storm, but instead he squeezed her hand and guided her down the cellar steps to where a dozen or so other townsfolk anxiously waited.

"Who's your friend, Landon?" A woman, whose graying hair was pulled up tightly into a bun on top of her head, asked as if trying to lessen the tension in the small room.

Landon cleard his throat. "I'm sorry, Mrs. Applegate. This is Rafe Redbourne and his wife Tayla."

Rafe smiled through the new awkwardness he felt. He should have been honest with Landon from the beginning, but at the time it had seemed the right thing to do to keep up the ruse. 'Round these parts, folks didn't take too kindly to a single man and single woman travelling together across the country. The last thing he wanted was to soil Tayla's reputation.

Rafe smiled at Mrs. Applegate and then at the others in the room.

A loud crash interrupted the awkward pleasantries and everyone went stock still. Listening. The normal whistling sound of the wind had turned into a fierce screech as it burst through the tiny crevices in the cellar door and attempt to lift the wooden planks, violently trying to pry it off its hinges and the chains that bound it shut from the inside.

It was over in minutes. When the howling finally stopped, the unnatural calm left an eerie feeling in its wake and Rafe feared what they would find outside. The twister had been headed straight for the town. Heavy winds were one thing to get through, but a twister was a whole other story entirely.

Tayla looked up at him with wide eyes. Her hand rested at her neck, caressing her locket between her fingers. She still clung to him. A feeling he rather enjoyed.

The shopkeeper brushed past them and up the stairs. Rafe and Tayla weren't far behind. He unlocked the cellar door and pushed it wide.

Boxes full of goods were strewn in disarray, but other than a few squished fruits and vegetables, it looked as if the store had gotten off rather lucky. The wind still blew some outside, but the worst of it seemed to be over.

The rest of the store's patrons emerged from the basement one by one, looking around and surveying the damage.

They walked outside, the path of destruction certain. Half of the livery had been demolished. Rafe let go of Tayla—for the first time since the storm had started—and he ran for the building where he'd last seen Lexa. Landon and Tayla were both on his heels.

Most of the horses were just gone. However, two lay trapped beneath a collapsed support beam and the drunken stableman was crouched in a sobbing heap in a corner of the still standing portion of the building. Rafe hardly dared glance at the stall where Lexa had been. He couldn't see her, but a distinct and frightened snort came from the back of the livery. He breathed relief.

Landon had already rushed over to the downed horses and a relieved Rafe quickly joined him, along with a few others who had seen the problem. They all worked together to lift the beam away from the mounts.

The chestnut pulled himself to his feet, but when the grey gelding attempted to right himself, he collapsed back to the ground. By the way the horse's front flank sat at an angle, Rafe suspected that his leg had been broken in several places. There was nothing that could be done. The horse would need to be put down.

A pained moan came from the stableman and an odd gurgling sound accompanied his sobs. Rafe rushed over and discovered that a stray piece of debris had lodged itself in the man's side and had pinned him to the wall behind him. He was huddled over because he could not move.

"Is there a doctor in this town?" Rafe called out to anyone who could hear.

"Hey, Doc, they need ya over at the livery," Rafe heard a man yell from the street outside.

An older gentleman, with hair that looked a mixture of salt and pepper, came to his side with a black bag very similar to his medical kit. The doc knelt down beside the stableman and looked long and hard at the wound. They tried to figure out how to get the man free without ripping out his innards in the process.

The doc figured the chip of wood had lodged through his liver. "Ironic," was all he said, but after having met the man in his inebriated state, Rafe understood.

The doc motioned for a group of men to come over. "Get Farley over to my office. He's in a real bad way," he instructed the others.

Rafe, seeing that his help was no longer needed with the stableman, nearly ran to Lexa.

"Good to see you, girl," he called, but when he reached the stall, all that greeted him was a frightened black and brown pack horse.

Lexa was gone. Rafe stared in disbelief at the pole where she'd been tethered. His heart dropped. It had been broken clean through. He'd heard of cattle being carried away in a twister, but Lexa? How could he have let this happen? She had been his best friend over the course of the last eight years. She had always been there for him and he hadn't been able to protect her when she needed it most.

He fell to his knees and looked heavenward. A single tear fell down his hot cheek, followed by another. Lexa was gone.

# CHAPTER SEVENTEEN

There was blood everywhere. Tayla watched the men pull the livery owner off of the wall and trails of blood followed them out into the street. Flashes echoed through her mind.

Her father. He'd been shot. She remembered. Panic threatened to flood her mind, but she refused to let it in. Refused to think about it.

Boom.

At first, Tayla thought she was hearing her father get shot again in her mind, but quickly realized that the men who'd come to help free the trapped horses from the downed beam must have found the owner of the grey gelding and had just put him down.

She glanced over at Rafe, who had fallen to his knees.

Something was terribly wrong. The shot hadn't even fazed him.

The sight of his wet cheeks burned into her mind and she walked over to him and reached down to touch his shoulder. He grabbed ahold of her and hugged her into him. She ran her fingers through his hair, trying the same type of soothing motion that he used when comforting her after her nightmares. She didn't ask what was wrong, she just let him hold her as he buried his face into her belly.

A man cleared his throat behind them. Rafe pulled his face away, his forehead still against her stomach for a moment before he pulled away from her completely.

"I'm sorry to interrupt, but I'm sure you'll understand, Rafe. I'd like to get home to my wife. It didn't look like the storm was headed to my place, but with these types of winds, I'm sure she's worried something fierce."

Rafe stood up and the two men gripped each other by the forearm.

"Thank you, friend. I'm not sure how long it will take me to finish up my business, but if you ever need anything, send a wire to the ranch. I'll get it."

Landon nodded.

Rafe's demeanor changed in an instant. His cheeks still bore the stained pathways of his tears, but his jaw was clenched tight and his voice was even and steady.

"Time to get a move on. Ethan'll be wondering where we are," he said without quite meeting her eyes.

*What just happened?* she asked herself as she stood alone in the middle of the splintered debris. She turned around to look about her and saw the broken metal post where Lexa had been tethered. Everything made sense now.

A flash of memory took her back to another time when Rafe had first gotten his beloved horse. The memory was incomplete, but she remembered the pride he'd had when he'd showed it off to his brothers. He had six of them, brothers that was, she now remembered. She clung to the images in her mind, desperately trying to hold onto them as they wistfully dissipated into nothing more than sheer imprints, fading into a blank slate.

"I'm sorry," she called after him. "About Lexa."

He stopped for a moment, but didn't turn around. Then he started back out again.

She knew she should follow, but she just stood there, mourning for him.

Heavy footfalls sounded against the dry dirt road and Tayla looked up to see Rafe coming back toward her with purposeful step. He grabbed a hold of her, took her head in his hands, and kissed her with more passion than she'd likely experienced in her life. Even her toes seemed to be on fire. She wrapped her arms up around his neck and combed her fingers through the hair at his nape. His kiss deepened and Rafe groaned. She gripped his hair and pulled him harder and closer to her—if that were even possible.

After a short while, he pulled away enough that his lips no longer touched hers, but his forehead still rested against her. Then he pulled her closer into him and delved his head into the crook of her neck, his arms encircling about her.

He felt good. This felt right.

After a few more minutes, he pulled away, finding her fingers and lacing them with his own.

"We have to go," he said in a whisper before he dropped her hand and walked over to the frightened horse that had been pulled from beneath the fallen beam.

"It's okay, boy," he coaxed, his voice calm and soothing. The horse tossed his head at first, but within moments Rafe had him composed.

"There is a runt pack horse behind what's left of that stall over there. Will you go get him?" he asked Tayla. "We should probably take them outside. Who knows how much longer some of these rafters will hold and I'm sure their owners will be worried."

Tayla quickly made her way into the stall where Lexa had been kept and unlatched the door behind the stall where the pack horse pranced about nervously.

Tayla tried to imitate Rafe's actions with the gelding and sure enough, the pack horse calmed enough to allow Tayla to lead him from the otherwise deserted livery. She followed Rafe over to the hitching post that had been built just in front of the saloon. It seemed as if half the livery, the cobbler, and a few of the small town's shops had taken the worst of the damage. It appeared as if the small unpainted church house and school building had just missed the same fate. The rest of the buildings in town appeared to remain structurally sound.

Rafe took the horse from her and tied him to the railing alongside a dozen or so other horses that were tethered there, including the chestnut he had guided from the livery. "I'm sure their owners will find them here."

Tayla scanned the street where townsfolk, business owners, and saloon patrons alike were busily working together to clean up the aftermath of the windstorm. Wagons had been overturned and horses injured in the process. Signs had blown off buildings and broken against the hard dirt roads. The street was littered with all manner of debris.

Landon guided his wagon and team of horses from the slim alleyway between the mercantile and the bank, and Tayla realized just how lucky it had been that he'd moved his team there before they'd taken shelter in the cellar at the back of the mercantile. She figured the direction of the wind must have been blowing in a cross pattern that hadn't been able to gain enough momentum to overturn the wagon in such a small space.

"Are you sure I can't drop you back at your camp?" Landon said as he sat astride the tall seat of his buckboard.

Tayla wasn't sure how else they would get anywhere. It was doubtful that people would part with their horses after so many had been lost or injured in the short windstorm. She knew that Rafe was anxious to get on the road, but something was holding him back.

He hesitated.

"I just need to send a quick message at the telegraph office. Then, we would be much obliged for a ride back to camp."

Tayla breathed out with relief.

"If it isn't too much trouble," Rafe added. He nodded curtly and headed to the small shop on the opposite side of the bank.

Landon helped Tayla climb up onto the tall seat. It certainly helped that she had on a pair of britches instead of a dress. She was sure that the people in this town thought her scandalous, but at this point, she didn't care.

Rafe returned shortly and jumped up onto the back of the wagon with a paper wrapped package and a potato sack full of food and other items from the general store.

*How did he manage that?*

They sat in awkward silence for a long time. Tayla had no idea what to say to either of the men, so she just sat in the seat and stared ahead. As they approached the pass, it looked as if a rock slide had been triggered in the storm and a few mid-size boulders and debris blocked the way. Rafe and Landon both jumped down off the wagon and stood in front of the rock pile. Tayla could sense the dread coming from the men. There was no sense staring at it. If they were going to get to the other side, they were going to have to dig themselves out.

Tayla sucked in a breath as a lone wolf walked the ridge just a few feet above the men.

"Rafe," she yelled.

He whipped around and she pointed at the predator looming overhead.

Rafe pulled his weapon and fired.

Click. The chamber was empty.

"Tayla, nice and slow, honey, I need you to reach behind the seat and get Landon's rifle," Rafe said with a deep, calm voice

Tayla immediately reached behind her and felt around the back of the bench. Her fingers closed around the cool steel barrel and she tugged, but it did not come free.

"You have to undo the latch," Landon called from his position. He took a step toward the wagon and the wolf jumped down onto the ground separating her from the others. He faced the men. Tayla could hear her heart beating in her ears and worked frantically to unfasten the rifle from its perch.

Boom.

A shot echoed through the air. It had come from somewhere behind her.

The wolf went down in an instant and Tayla whipped her head around to see Harrison Davis astride a horse with a rifle of his own.

"Thought you might be able to use some assistance," he said with something akin to pride lining his voice.

Tayla breathed a sigh of relief and jumped down off the wagon. "Nice shot," she said turning back toward him. It was then that Tayla noticed that Harrison had someone tied up and strung over the back of his horse.

"Yes, it was," Rafe added. "Very nice shot indeed." He picked up a stick on the side of the road and nudged the wolf. It didn't move.

"I never said I couldn't shoot," Harrison said with a wry grin.

When it appeared that Rafe was satisfied the predator was dead, he walked over to the wagon, pulled a package of ammunition from his potato sack and proceeded to load his revolver. He shook his head and muttered something under his breath.

A horse whinnied, but it came from behind Harrison. Tayla stepped around to see where the sound had come from.

"Oh," Harrison said as if he'd had an afterthought, "I thought you might be missing something." He pulled a lead forward and a beautiful roan horse appeared next to him prancing about and shaking her head.

Lexa. The mare pranced about and lifted her front hooves into the air with a nicker. Another man, whose eyes were as round as saucers, was tied up and strung over her saddle. Tayla darted a glance at Rafe. She saw the moment his set eyes on his horse. She was alive. A huge dimpled grin appeared on Rafe's face and in two strides he picked Tayla up, whirled her around, and laughed out loud before he set her back down and ran to his horse.

Tayla giggled.

"There's my girl," he said as he ran his hands enthusiastically along her face and neck. "Davis...how? Where on earth did you find her?" Rafe asked Harrison.

"They left me alone in the barn when they went over to the saloon." Harrison threw Lexa's lead rope to Rafe. "It didn't take too long to free myself of the ropes. Jonas had left your gun and money pouch in the saddlebags on his horse." Harrison reached into his belt and pulled out one of Rafe's revolvers and a small leather pouch.

Rafe squinted one eye when he looked up at the man who'd just saved his life.

"Lucky for me, the liveryman thought I was their friend and

I rode out of the stable on Jonas's mount, and none were the wiser," he said as he handed the gun down.

"Lucky for all of us."

"The wind started something terrible and when I saw the twister hit the ground and head for town, I knew we needed to get somewhere safe, and fast. We were around some rather large red cliffs a few miles back. Old Bessie here and I took shelter in a cave until the wind died down. When we came out, a handful of horses were running up the pass."

Tayla watched Rafe as he groomed his horse with his hands. He felt each of her flanks, rubbed over her shoulders and down each leg as he listened to Harrison's tale.

"I turned around and there she was, Lexa, dragging her reins behind her." Harrison leaned down so his elbows were resting on his saddle horn. "Craziest thing. It was like she was telling me something." He sat up straight, swung a leg over the side of the horse, and dismounted. "Anyway, I headed back into town. Jonas and Lester here sure weren't expecting to see me."

"And just how did you get them in such a...compromising state?" Rafe asked, standing up after checking Lexa's shoes.

"Well, now, that's an interesting tale. You see, they were already like this when I got there and a nice fella offered me twenty dollars to take them out into the plains and leave them."

"City slicker? Black and silver vest?"

"Yes. That's the bloke."

"Well, what do you say we have them help us move enough of these rocks to get the wagon through? Then, we can drop them wherever you like."

"That's a right fine plan," Harrison said as he walked to the back of his horse and cut Lester loose. When he was upright on the ground, he shook his head free from the binding that had been secured there. He looked straight at Tayla and his eyes got wide.

There was something about those eyes. Cold. Distant. The study at Longhurst manor came crashing into her mind as it replayed images of the man standing before her shooting her father.

"You!" She rushed forward and pounded on the man's chest. "You shot him. You shot my father," she screamed. Tears stung her eyes, but she refused to let them fall.

It took a moment before Rafe's arms were around her. She continued hitting the air as he pulled her away from the vile man who had shot her father and taken her away from him. Rafe turned her in his arms to pull her close. She couldn't help herself. She started to cry.

"It's him, Rafe. It's him."

Rafe set her at arms-length and craned his head to look into her face. He stuck a crooked finger beneath her chin and lifted until her eyes met his.

She hiccupped a little and exhaled.

"He's the one who took me from Adrien's and..." she hesitated, "shot my father."

"I know. Wait. Are you saying...you remember?"

The wet rims of her eyelids clouded her vision and she blinked hard and thought. She'd been remembering a few bits and pieces of her life, but this was the first time a full scene had returned in context.

"Not everything." She shook her head. "I remember being at Longhurst Manor, but I'm not sure why. And I remember him." She strained her eyes to look at the man without turning her head.

Rafe pulled her into his embrace and held her tight for a moment. Then, he walked her over to Landon.

"Stay," he ordered, but not unkindly. He met her eyes and held them for a moment. Then he turned and headed back toward Harrison and Lester.

Without hesitation, Rafe walked right up to the man and punched him in the face.

He went down like a felled tree and was smart enough to stay down.

Rafe reached into his front denim pocket and pulled something out to show Lester. The man narrowed his eyes at Rafe and a sneer formed on his lip.

"I think a territory marshal would be real interested to

know what you two boys have been up to." Rafe pulled Lester
to his feet.

Jonas was still tied to Lexa's saddle. Harrison cut him down
and he struggled to get to his feet.

"I hate to get in the middle of all of this," Landon walked
up behind Rafe and placed a hand on his shoulder, "but I've got
to get home to check on Rena and the baby."

The two horses on Landon's wagon were starting to prance
about anxiously.

"You're right. Let's get to it." Rafe motioned for Harrison,
who dismounted straightway and joined him next to the blocked
pass.

"Jonas and Lester here, are going to help dig us out of this
predicament, now aren't ya fellas?"

The two men looked at the rocks, at Tayla, and back at
Rafe. The expression on Lester's face was murderous.

"Well, git to it," Rafe pointed to the rocks that blocked their
path.

Harrison handed Tayla his rifle. "Do you know how to use
this?"

"I think so," she said as she took it from him. She set it up
against her shoulder, aimed at a cluster of weeds next to Lester's
feet, and pulled the trigger.

The shot made the man dance about. His scowl deepened
and he shot her a derisive look that chilled her to the core.
Despite that, she smiled with a small sense of satisfaction. She
wished it had been his foot.

"I guess so," Harrison said with pride.

"We're going to help clear these rocks," Rafe said, his hand
resting at her elbow. "Landon needs to get home to check on
Rena, and we have got to get on the road. We'll have a nice little
chat with Jonas and Lester once Landon is on his way." He
smiled at her. "They won't hurt you," he added as if sensing her
apprehension. "But don't shoot 'em until these rocks are
cleared."

She couldn't quite tell if he was joking.

When it came down to it, Tayla didn't think she could

actually shoot a man—kill a man. No matter how angry she was.

"You said my father is alive—back at the inn. You said he didn't die."

Rafe nodded. "He was under a doctor's care the last time I saw him. Adrien will make sure he is taken care of."

The sun had crossed near half the sky by the time the men were almost done. Luckily Landon had a small barrel of water he'd filled at the mercantile in the back of the wagon. Tayla filled two empty canteens and offered the refreshment to the men as they worked. Rafe handed the first canteen to Jonas, who slurped at the water as if it were his last breath.

She'd been charged with protecting the others by keeping the gun on Jonas and Lester, but her attention was drawn away from them at times as she admired how Rafe's arms strained against his shirt as he lifted and tossed the rocks. Sweat lined his neck and brow and she honestly couldn't remember a time when he looked more appealing.

She needed a little of that water herself.

At long last, their task was complete. Landon jumped up onto the seat of the buckboard, grabbed a hold of the team's reins, and guided them through the narrow pathway.

"Landon, you should get home to Rena. I am sure she is beyond worried," Rafe told him.

"It's only another quarter hour to your camp. I'm sure she'll be fine that long," Landon responded. "Besides, she'd have my hide if she learns that I left all five of you to share two horses."

"Jonas and Lester can walk," Rafe said flippantly.

"Naw, tie 'em up and get 'em in the back. I'll cart ya'll as far as your camp and then I'll get myself home to that beautiful woman of mine." He smiled. Tayla loved the twinkle Landon got in his eyes when he spoke of his wife. Her gaze moved to Rafe. She hoped that one day maybe his eyes would sparkle when he looked at her. When he met her stare, she quickly glanced away, but could feel the heat rising again in her cheeks. She cursed him silently for having such an effect on her. Then, shamelessly, she looked at him again...and smiled.

All seemed right in the world.

Horses and cattle ran in every which direction. The cattlemen had been able to corral them into a circle, but the animals didn't seem to want to settle.

"Ethan, what the hell is going on here?" Rafe rode Lexa up next to his brother and asked.

"Wind kicked up something fierce and knocked down two of the temporary corrals. Nearly took Griff's wagon and hell, nearly took some of us. The animals were restless, but it wasn't until that blasted wolf," Ethan pointed to a lifeless carcass at the edge of the perimeter, "pounced the heifer that they all got riled up."

"And the heifer?"

"Didn't make it."

"The calf?"

"Griff has her tied up to the wagon." Ethan flung his whip and it snapped in front of a beautiful brown and white paint gelding that tried to escape the perimeter. "Problem was, we no longer had somewhere to contain them, and we couldn't very well move out without you."

"Sorry about that. Had some trouble of our own. A twister set down in town, a rock slide blocked the pass on the way back, and we had a wolf of our own. The rest is a long story that I'll have plenty of time to tell once we're on our way."

Ethan let a low whistle escape. "It'll be good to get home. I miss Grace and the boys something fierce."

"Get everybody ready to ride. I'll just be a minute." Rafe headed back toward the others.

"Looks like it's time to part ways," he said to Landon. "Thanks again for all your help, friend. And remember, send word if you need anything."

Landon tipped his hat and pulled out.

Jonas and Lester stood with their hands tied behind them.

In Rafe's line of work, he usually was after one bounty at a time. He'd had a few occasional incidents where he'd had to take in a few at once, but it was usually on his terms and in places he could control. It would be hard enough protecting Tayla from everything else they could encounter in the few days on the road, but now with two ruffians along, his job would be made even harder. He was grateful to have Harrison and Ethan to help.

Rafe had been tempted to leave them bootless and without horses in the middle of the plains, but he couldn't bring himself to do it. He still wanted answers and he had a feeling they had much more to tell. After he learned what he could from them, he would turn them over to the territory marshals, who he suspected would be happy to take them off his hands.

His dilemma now was where to put his charges. Tayla could ride Marty's mount and, thanks to Harrison, he now had Lexa back, but that left the question of Jonas and Lester.

The bray of a pack mule caught his attention. There were two mules along for the trek, each carried a few supplies, bedrolls, and water. With the chuck wagon being nearly empty by now—except for Marty—he could transfer the haul into the wagon from the two mules. He debated, if only for a moment, making them walk, but he knew that the group was anxious to get home.

The pack mules would suffice. They were used to trotting along behind the wagon and should be able to keep up speed, even with riders.

Nightfall came all too quickly. Rafe glanced over to Tayla, who'd ridden the last few hours without complaint. She looked up and met his stare with a weary smile. She was so beautiful. He didn't know how he'd missed it before. The memory of her lips succumbing eagerly beneath his suddenly made his ride a little more uncomfortable.

The last three days had been awful. Tayla had watched Rafe's every move and had been all too aware when he'd ridden close to her. They'd slept on the hard ground, mere feet away from one another, but he hadn't as much as touched her since that first night.

A large homestead came into view as they peaked the last blanket of rolling hills. Horses dotted the grounds and cattle grazed in the surrounding fields. The chime of metal clanging against metal reached Tayla's ears. She squinted against the horizon and down at the house. A woman stood out on the porch.

"Ah, suppertime," Ethan took a whiff at the air.

Surely he couldn't smell the food from here, but he closed his eyes and smiled all the same.

"I'll bet it's fried chicken," Ethan spoke longingly.

"Or stew," Marty called from the back of the chuck wagon.

Harrison pulled his horse up onto the ridge and then Rafe rode in between them, alongside her.

"This," he waved his hand across the vastness of the land, "is home."

Tayla half expected all of the cowpokes she'd gotten to know over the last couple of days to tear down the hillside whooping and hollering, but they all stayed together with their small herd of cows and horses, and casually made their way onto the stead.

"Get on up to the house. I'll be there after we finish up," Rafe told her, then rode over to where Judd and Ethan were guiding the bull into a pen of his own.

"They're home," an older, very beautiful woman called from the porch steps into the house. Tayla suspected she was Rafe's mother.

Two young boys darted from the house, the smaller of the two nearly tripping over his own feet. They ran down the steps and over to the corral, where the men herded the few horses they had brought home with them, then jumped up onto the fence planks and watched with awe.

Tayla laughed at their unmasked eagerness. That earned her the attention of both women, who now stood on the porch, and they descended quickly to greet her.

"Hello," the older woman said, holding a hand up to help her down.

Tayla was certain that she had not spent this much time on a horse's backside in a long time. Her derriere ached and her legs were stiff and sore. When she dismounted in front of the porch steps, she wasn't sure she could trust herself to stand up straight without support and was grateful for the help.

"Thank you," Tayla said sincerely. She looked at the two women who now stared at her and suddenly longed for a hot bath and a clean dress. She was sure she stank. The men sure did.

"You can tell how anxious the boys are to see their daddy." The younger woman looked over her shoulder and smiled at the two youngsters who still perched the fence.

"Come to think of it," the younger woman said in a lower, sultry tone, "I'm pretty anxious to see him myself."

They both laughed.

The older of the two stared at her expectantly for a few moments, then, as if jostled from her thoughts, she stepped forward. "I'm sorry. Where are my manners? I'm Leah Redbourne," she placed an arm around Tayla's shoulders, "and this is Grace."

"Hello," she responded looking back and forth between the two women. "I'm Tayla," she said, testing out the name. It was the first time she'd actually spoken it aloud. "Hawthorne."

Leah's jaw dropped and she pulled Tayla away from her just enough to get a better look at her face. "Tayla Hawth—"she breathed out a laugh and pulled her into a hug. "My you have grown up." She laughed again, then her face became serious as her eyes trailed Tayla's body.

"I know I must look a sight," she said, playing with some of the loose tendrils that had found their way down her neck and onto the front of her shirt.

"Dear heavens. Were you on the trail? I thought you were in England, just about to get married to a handsome Earl—or so your mother told me. What are you..." she shook her head as if not knowing what to ask next. "What...?"

Tayla didn't know what to say. It's true, Harrison had told her that she had been engaged to marry an Earl, but didn't remember anything about it.

"There will be plenty of time to ask the questions later. Let's get you inside and cleaned up at bit. It's a good thing Rafe isn't here. I know it was a long time ago," she said putting her lips a little closer to Tayla's ear, "but I'm afraid my son still hasn't forgiven you."

"Forgiven me for what, exactly?" Tayla hoped that she might be finally able to learn what had caused the rift between her and Rafe.

"For wha...?" Leah pulled her head back, her forehead creased and her brows crumpled together. "Tayla, has something happened? Are you all right?"

Tayla opened her mouth to tell her what she remembered.

"Mama," Rafe called as he and Harrison walked toward them from the stables with Jonas and Lester a short distance behind them, still astride the pack mules.

She closed it again.

Leah's eyes grew wide and she motioned for Grace to take Tayla into the house. Leah winked. "Go," she mouthed before she turned around.

"Rafe? Have you caught that dreadful preacher already?"

Harrison cleared his throat and Tayla smirked.

"You are a braver woman than I," Grace said with a hint of admiration. "I wouldn't have lasted five minutes on the trail with Ethan. He drives those men pretty hard."

Tayla smiled.

When they walked into the kitchen, the spiced scent of apples baking filled her lungs as she breathed deeply. She had to be dreaming. She hadn't been surrounded by so many pleasant aromas in days—not since they'd left the Smokey Sky Inn. In seemed like ages since Jake and Ev had found her in the river and taken her to Maggie's place.

A grey-haired woman stood next to the open stove with her apron gathered in a bunch as she collected what looked like small loaves of bread. When she looked at Tayla, there was surprise in her eyes, but they were warm and inviting. She immediately liked the woman.

"Lottie," Grace started, squeezing Tayla's shoulder, "the men have returned from the Wyoming drive and they brought a few more mouths to feed, including Miss Hawthorne here."

The smile that spread across Lottie's weathered face was contagious.

"Señorita Hawthorne," she greeted, "it has been too long. Siéntete!"

Tayla had no idea what the command meant, but she smiled back at the woman and nodded.

"Grace," Leah said from behind them as she bustled into the kitchen, "will you show Tayla to my washroom?"

Grace grabbed her gently by the arm and nodded toward the hallway with a smile. "Come on," she said, her voice a little higher than before, "you'll love it."

They wound through multiple corridors until they reached a room at the back of the house. Grace opened the door to a very large and delicately decorated washroom. Tayla glanced from wall to wall, basking in its entirety. When her eyes landed on a large, white, cast-iron bear claw tub in the corner, lit perfectly by the afternoon sun coming in through the shaded windows, she nearly melted.

Grace giggled. "Isn't it beautiful?"

Tayla reached up to touch the lace frill curtains that covered the window shade, but quickly retracted her hand for fear of getting them dirty. "It's exquisite."

She stepped inside and found herself in front of a beautifully carved, full length mirror. When she caught her reflection, she groaned. Streaks of dirt lined her face and her hair was matted and looked as if she'd lived through a tornado. She smirked a little. She had.

An empty water pitcher and a small folded towel adorned the table next to the mirror. She picked up the cloth and tried to wipe away some of the grime on her neck and face. All she managed to do was smear it.

Rafe cleared his throat.

"I'll just get you some towels," Grace said, excusing herself from the room.

He stood at the door holding a fresh pitcher, but instead of moving to exchange them, he leaned against the door frame and watched her with a smirk of his own.

"Here, let me," he said, pushing away from the frame and setting the full pitcher of water on the table. He took the cloth from her hand. His fingertips brushed against hers. A bolt of fire started in her hand and quickly spread upward into her cheeks.

Rafe dipped a corner of the cloth into the cool water and with one hand under her jaw, he gently wiped at the smudges on her face. She wanted to look up at him. Wanted to see the man she feared she'd fallen in love with, but her lashes wouldn't cooperate until she felt the hand towel drop to the floor, and his bare thumb caress her wind-chapped and sunburned lips. Her eyes snapped up to meet his and she felt herself melt into him. She'd waited for too long to feel his kiss again and lifted her head expectantly.

"Hmhhmmh."

Rafe pulled away from her to reveal Harrison Davis standing at the doorway, sweating, with a large steaming bucket of water. He stepped forward and dumped the sumptuous water into the tub.

"You forget yours, mate?" Harrison asked Rafe, who smiled and followed him out of the room.

They returned a short while later, along with Ethan, carrying more buckets of hot water and continued back and forth until the tub was filled.

"You may want to wait a bit before getting in," Rafe said, dropping his bucket in one hand and taking a step toward her. "I imagine the water will still be a little warm."

Tayla reached up to her locket and bit her lip.

"I'll save you some supper," Rafe said with a throaty and roughened edge to his voice. He pulled away, winked, and disappeared around the corner.

She walked over to the door to close it, but a booted foot

stopped it from shutting. Rafe pushed the door open and handed her a small paper wrapped package, then he was gone.

*Hot and cold.*

# CHAPTER EIGHTEEN

*What the hell are you doing?* Rafe asked himself as he marched from the washroom.

Tayla Hawthorne was the most beautiful woman he had ever seen. He could admit it, but she was betrothed to another man. He'd kissed her once and the memory of her lips responding to his made him ache to touch her. A part of him hoped she never remembered her past, yet another part of him knew she'd never be his until she did—at least until she remembered enough to choose.

Lord Darington, rightful Earl or not, still held the title of fiancé for now. He had to get to the man and settle this once and for all. If Harrison was right about him, he wanted nothing more than to expose the truth.

*What if he was wrong?*

Rafe couldn't think about that possibility. He'd taken a chance on love before—with a Hawthorne no less—and had been burned. As hard as he'd tried to keep his distance, he couldn't help being drawn to her. He shoved his fingers through his hair as he sat down at the table next to Harrison.

"Uncle Rafe," a little voice squealed and he turned in time to catch young Luke who had launched himself from the doorway. The five-year-old boy squeezed Rafe around the neck.

Rafe laughed. It felt good to be home. He set his nephew on the floor and tousled his hair. A short tug on his pant leg directed his attention downward to where a dark-haired toddler with the bluest eyes stared up at him. He held a small trinket in his hand and held it out to him.

"Ollie bug, what do you have there?" He reached down and picked up the small object and realized it was a rough little mug that had been molded out of clay. The handle drooped and it was full of lumps, but it was perfect.

"Did you make that all by yourself?" Rafe asked.

He beamed up at him. "Like Wafe," he said proudly.

Rafe picked him up and nuzzled his neck, earning him a delighted giggle. The youngster pushed at his face and writhed with joy.

The back door opened. Jameson Redbourne marched in with Ethan at his heels.

Rafe stood and set the little boy down next to his brother.

"I heard that you rode in with the team," his father said, clapping Rafe on the shoulder. "I'm glad you're home, son." He pulled Rafe into a firm embrace with a laugh.

Ethan nodded at him, then bent down to pick up his children. His brother was far from being the oldest, but he was the only one who'd been willing to stay on at the ranch and follow in their father's footsteps. "Who are those men you've locked in the cellar?" he asked.

Before Rafe could respond, the door opened again and Malcolm Longhurst strode inside.

"Malcolm?" Rafe was taken aback. "What are you doing here?" It had been a long time—nearly six years.

"Nice to see you too, old friend."

Rafe snorted and pulled his friend into a quick embrace. "Of course, it's good to see you. I just didn't expect to see you *here*. Your father told me that you'd moved back to England."

Harrison coughed and when Rafe turned back to look at him, he scrambled backward in his chair, nearly falling to the floor. Rafe shook his head and returned his attention to his friend.

"That's true," Malcolm responded. "I came into town a few days ago—is he all right?" he asked craning his head to see who was behind Rafe.

Rafe turned again. Harrison was hiding behind a hand on his forehead.

"He'll be fine."

"Well, your parents were kind enough to put me up and I have been helping out around the place—just like old times." He gave an appreciative nod to Jameson, then turned back to Rafe. "I actually came to see you. I need your help."

Harrison coughed again.

"You boys can talk about business later," Leah said with a smile. "Come in. Sit. Let's just enjoy the company for now."

"Of course, Mrs. Redbourne. My apologies," Malcolm said with a tip of his Stetson.

When she stared at him expectantly, Malcolm quickly removed his hat and Leah winked at him. Rafe smirked. His mother was anything but subtle.

As soon as he sat down, Harrison grabbed him firmly on the forearm.

"Can I speak with you for a moment?" he asked in a whisper through the side of his mouth.

"Later," Rafe said dismissively.

"We got a telegram from Will. It seems he will be coming in tomorrow on the train with a friend. It will be nice to have so many of you home for a spell."

Will was coming? Rafe hoped that he would bring answers with him.

"Speaking of that, where's Hannah?" Rafe asked. His little sister had been staying at the family ranch with her husband so that Leah could help her with the baby for a while.

"She took the little Eliza Jane over to the Parkers. Eli should be back with them anytime now," Leah said.

"I guess you caught that Beckett fella pretty quick," Jameson said to Rafe.

Harrison coughed again.

Rafe smirked and handed him a glass of his mother's lemonade.

"You going to be home for long or are you headed out soon?" Jameson asked.

"I'm afraid it won't be for long. *Davis* and I," he pointed at his new friend, whose brow was now damp with perspiration, "are headed out to meet Tayla's betrothed in the city."

"Rafe, I really need to speak with you." A bead of sweat collected over Harrison's brow.

Odd. There was nothing for the man to be anxious about right now.

"Tayla?" his father's head perked up, interrupting Rafe's thought.

"Hawthorne," he supplied.

Jameson's brows furrowed even closer together and his jaw dropped.

Rafe put up a hand. "It's a long story, but I was hoping I could leave her here for a few days. Maybe a week."

"Tayla's still engaged?" His mother's face fell.

Rafe knew exactly what she'd been hoping. And if he were honest with himself...well, he couldn't think about that right now.

"Tay-la," his father boomed, and all eyes fell on the door where she stood with her hands together in front of her.

She was beautiful. The rich, earthy brown of the dress he'd purchased at the mercantile complimented the soft pink glow of her cheeks. He imagined they were still warm from her bath.

Hell. Rafe needed to change the direction his thoughts had just taken and quick.

Jameson pushed away from his seat to stand and motioned to the empty seat next to Rafe. "Join us, won't you?"

She took her seat and spanned her gaze across the faces of everyone sitting at the table. When she glanced at Rafe, he cleared his throat. Again.

"Tayla had a little accident a few weeks ago and there are some things that she is struggling to remember."

"Like names, faces, events, you understand. Not much," she filled in with a sheepish smile.

"That explains a few things," Leah said with a quick wink.

Rafe realized just how strong Tayla had been through all of this. He couldn't imagine how frightening it must be for her and yet she chose to be optimistic. Admiration brought a smile to his lips.

"Tayla," Rafe placed a hand on her upper back, "I know you won't remember him, but this is my longtime friend Malcolm."

When she looked at Malcolm, a shadow crossed his friend's face and Tayla's expression went blank, her brows furrowed together. She blinked a few times and then turned to Rafe with a faint smile.

In an instant, the need to protect her from Malcolm surfaced. But why? Jealousy?

Clank-crash. The sound stole everyone's attention. Rafe, Ethan, and Jameson all jumped from their seats. Lottie had tried to pick up the oversized pot of lentils and had knocked the serving utensils to the floor.

"Let me get that," Ethan took the pot holders from Lottie and lifted the large pot to the table.

"You look a little tired, Lottie." Rafe reached out an arm to steady the older woman. "Are you feeling all right?"

"Oh, yes," she said with a weak smile. "It just got a little too warm for me. I think I'll just go sit down for a moment."

Rafe helped her to the couch in the living room. Ethan and his father waited in the doorway.

Her skin looked pale and sallow and her eyes bore heavy sacks.

"Let me get you a glass of water."

"Don't be fussing over me, Señor Rafe. I just need to catch my breath a bit."

Rafe walked into the kitchen and pumped out a cool glass of water.

"Rafe!" Ethan called loudly in urgent tones.

He ran back to the living area, spilling half the cup of water he'd gotten for her on the ground. Lottie's head fell back against the couch and her eyes closed. Rafe nearly dropped the glass before he set it on the end table and rushed to her side. Her skin was warm. He leaned down with his ear against her chest.

Relief washed over him. Her breathing was shallow, but her

heart still had a strong beat. He picked her up and curled her up in his arms. Lottie roused enough to lift her head.

"Maybe I'll just lie down for a while," she said through a tired smile.

Her quarters were at the back of the house and he would have to pass through the kitchen to get there. Rafe carried her robust form through the wide opening to the kitchen. Everyone at the table stood.

"Good heavens," his mother exclaimed, "is she all right?"

"I will be fine, Señora Leah. No te preocupes."

Rafe's mother looked to him to confirm that there was nothing to worry about.

"I honestly don't know. Is Doc Richards still in town?"

"If he's not out visiting folks," Ethan said with a head nod.

"It might be a good thing to have him come take a look at her." Rafe set the cook down on her bed.

She looked past him to the door. When he turned around, Tayla slipped into the room with the glass of water he had filled for Lottie.

"I thought she might need this," she said, making her way over to the bed.

Rafe took it from her, and holding Lottie's head, placed the cup against her lips.

"I am feeling much better now." The woman took the water from him, sat up straight, and took a sip. "See? I am fine."

Rafe raised a quizzical eye at her. Her color had started to return and she seemed much more alert. "I still think you should lie back down."

"Okay, doctor Rafe." She winked at him.

He took the cup from her and handed it to Tayla before opening the large patchwork quilt on the edge of her bed and tucking it around her.

"Descansate, querida Lottie," Rafe said, unsure if he'd pronounced the words correctly in her native tongue. They'd all learned a bit of Spanish growing up with Lottie, but it had been a long time since he'd actually used it. Unlike some of his other brothers, Rafe had never mastered the language.

Tayla turned to walk in front of him and it felt natural to place his hand at the small of her back. He almost wished that she was still in those britches—she filled them out very nicely—but he remembered all too well how much she'd liked to dress up in fancy dresses.

When supper was nearly over, a wagon approached the house.

"They are finally back," his mother said, glancing toward the curtained window. "Hannah will be so pleased to see you, Tayla."

Rafe recognized a flash of fear on Tayla's face and then it was gone and she smiled.

"Something smells mighty fine in here," Eli's voice carried in from the hallway.

"Come on in and see who's joined us," Leah called to them.

Hannah walked through the archway with Grace, laughing. Little Eliza Jane must have fallen asleep on the way back because she rested peacefully in her mother's arms.

"Mama!" Luke shouted and he jumped up and ran over to his mother, followed closely by little Oliver.

"Rafe?" Hannah rushed over to his side and gave him a sort of one armed hug. "I didn't expect to see you back here so soon. You do work fast. How long did it take you to catch that no good pretend preacher?"

Harrison nearly choked on the biscuit he was eating.

"I can't wait to hear all about it."

Rafe stood up and wrapped his arms around his little sister and her little yellow wrapped bundle.

"Sis," he pointed at Harrison, "this is my new friend, Harrison Davis. Or…as you so aptly called him, the pretend preacher."

Harrison picked up his glass and drank until it was empty. Everyone turned their eyes on him and Hannah jerked her head back a little, color flooding her cheeks.

"Well, aren't you full of surprises?" she said to Rafe with wide, accusing eyes. She turned to Harrison. "Mr. Davis, you sure created a mess of trouble for my brother and his wife." She eyed him speculatively, then offered a slight smile.

Harrison stood in front of his seat and wiped the corners of his mouth with his napkin. "Yes, um...sorry about that," he said, the sweat already started to bead on his forehead.

Rafe rolled his eyes. How the man could sweat so much every time there was the slightest bit of conflict was beyond him. There had to be something to fix it.

"Hannah, dear," their mother interjected, "did you see that Tayla Hawthorne is here visiting?"

Hannah looked around the table until her eyes fell on Tayla on the opposite side of Rafe. She shoved the baby into Rafe's arms and quickly pulled Tayla into a firm hug.

"It has been so long since we've seen you. How have you been? Where is the rest of your fam—"

The last question stopped Hannah cold and she darted an apologetic glance in Rafe's direction.

"Let the girl breathe," Jameson said with a chuckle. "She just came in with Rafe and the team."

"The team? But you look so...so refreshed."

"Mama's tub," was all Rafe said and by the look on Hannah's face, it was all he needed to.

The baby's eyes opened and she stared up at Rafe. He fell in love all over again with that little girl. She didn't cry, but her lips contorted slightly as if she didn't recognize him. Of course she wouldn't. He wasn't around enough for her to know him and the thought pricked at him again that something had to change.

"I'm so sorry, Tayla," Hannah said, rubbing Tayla's arm. "I'll let you finish your supper and then we'll have to catch up." Hannah turned to Rafe. "You and I are going to have to talk, big brother. It sounds like there is a lot you have to tell me."

She took Eliza Jane from his arms, bent over and kissed her father's cheek, and sat down next to Eli at the other end of the table.

When Grace reached Ethan, he stood up and kissed her. She giggled and blushed from his affection.

Tayla fell forward onto her elbows on the table, her fingertips massaging her temples.

Rafe leaned over and put his arm on Tayla's shoulder. "What's wrong?"

"I remember," she whispered close to him. "I remember why you hate me." Tayla turned to look at him, a tear in her eye. She looked up across the table. "You…" she started, loud enough to stop the conversations amongst the others. "You kissed my sister." Her voice seemed a mixture of accusation and wonder.

*Wait. What did she just say?* Rafe stared at Ethan, watching for a reaction. It took a moment, but her words finally registered.

"I'm sorry," she gasped. A hand flew to her mouth and she looked between the brothers. "Excuse me. I think I need some air." She pushed herself away from the table and ran through the archway into the living room. When the front door slammed shut, he turned to Ethan who stood there with a blank expression on his face.

Tayla had had a memory and it was of his brother kissing Tessa. Rafe's hand balled into a fist. His jaw clenched.

"Ethan, would you like to step outside?" he asked as coolly as he could. "I'd like a word."

Memories of Redbourne Ranch and the people who lived here filled her mind. She'd remembered exactly what had happened the night before the wedding, but had to get away from the disbelieving stares of everyone at the table boring holes into her. She'd needed air and so she'd fled outside and nearly tripped on the stairs. She sat down. The cool evening air filled her lungs and she fought to keep her tears at bay.

"Rafe," Ethan's voice carried to Tayla's ears, pulling her instantly from her thoughts. "I have never kissed Tessa."

Tayla stood up off the front porch, moved to the edge of the woodpile, and peered around the corner of the house. Ethan stood in front of Rafe just outside the kitchen door, his hands pushing lightly against Rafe's chest. "Rafe, I swear..." his voice became steady, low, and very serious. "I have *never* kissed Tessa."

"But I did." Malcolm stepped out into the yard from the kitchen and closed the door behind him. His head was bent low and it took a long time for him to meet Rafe's deadly stare. "Well, that is, she kissed me."

Tayla stared at Malcolm. There was something very familiar about him and she couldn't shake the feeling that he was more a part of her past than just her memory of him in the barn with her sister.

"Did you love her?" Rafe's question directed her attention back to the men's conversation.

"Hell no!" Malcolm countered.

Tayla knew what Malcolm said was true. Tessa had kissed him. She had seen the incident in the barn for herself and had later confronted her sister about it. She'd threatened to tell Rafe if Tessa didn't, and now Rafe hated her because she'd taken away from him the woman that he'd loved and had wanted to marry.

She knew she should back away, that their conversation was private, but she couldn't tear herself from that spot. Rafe glanced toward her position and she stepped backward onto a loose log. She lost her balance and fell back into the pile. Split cuts of wood came crashing down and rolling into the yard with her on top of them.

Tayla's heart jumped from her chest. So much for being quiet.

The pain in her derrière was nothing compared to her aching pride. Rafe and Malcolm stood above her within moments. Both reached down and took a hold of her hands, and helped pull her to her feet. When she looked up at Malcolm, another memory flashed through her mind—a faint image of him, reaching out to her from a garden.

*"Tayla, you need to get as far away from here as possible. If Dare sees you or knows what you've just seen, he'll kill you. Do you understand? You have to run. Now."*

It took her some time to process the memory, then the realization dawned on her. Malcolm was the reason she'd fled to America. He'd been trying to protect her from something. Or, someone.

"I know you," she said to Malcolm. "You tried to tell me he was dangerous and for once, I listened."

"Is this true?" Rafe asked. "Do you know her?"

"Yes," Malcolm said, "but Rafe, you have to let me explain. That's why I'm here. Remember, I said I needed your help?"

Rafe looked at Tayla, but she was unable to read what he might be thinking.

"Malcolm, go wait for me in my father's study. We need to discuss this. I'll be in in a minute."

Malcolm looked between Tayla and Rafe, then nodded before walking up the front porch stairs and into the house.

"Rafe," Harrison stepped outside from the kitchen and walked toward them. "May I have a word? It's about your friend, Malcolm."

Rafe continued to look at her, concern etched on his face.

"It's okay," she told him. "Go."

"Can you give us a minute?" Rafe asked Harrison.

"Sure thing, mate. But I think you'll want to know sooner, rather than later." Harrison turned back for the kitchen.

"Tayla."

She stood still, staring into the colorful sky as the sun fell behind the hills. Rafe's voice sent shivers through her body and she wrapped her arms around herself to protect from the chill.

"I don't hate you," he said quietly.

She didn't know what to say, how to respond, so she just continued to stare forward. That was the last thing she'd expected him to say.

"I hated the way she left, and I needed someone to blame," he said softly.

Tears brimmed her lashes, but she didn't care.

"Now that you have your memory back, I guess you'll want to go home. To your life in England. I mean, once we know it is safe for you to return."

*What life?*

There was nothing for her there. Nothing she could recollect.

"I remembered why I told Tessa that she couldn't marry you. And I remembered the look on your face when you saw me again at Maggie's." She had wanted to be quiet, but didn't know if she could stop herself from speaking, from telling him everything she was thinking...and feeling.

He turned her to face him.

"I don't know if I will ever remember everything. It all comes in bits and pieces. Sometimes those pieces fit together and I see a whole pictures, but most of the time my memories are only fractions of what they were." She met his eyes for the first time tonight. "Except for you. For some reason, I have very vivid memories of you."

"Like what?" he asked with a chuckle.

"Like the time when everyone was jumping off the rope swing over the pond and I was too scared." Tayla smiled as she remembered him in his cut off trousers and very tanned chest. "You held onto me and we went in together."

"You remember that?"

She nodded.

"I remember the day you received your acceptance post from Harvard and the party that your parents had at the house that night. Everyone was dancing, but I didn't know how and you pulled me away from the wall and taught me."

She smiled, but then she realized that in all of her memories she had only been a child who had fallen in love with her sister's beau.

"What did you just think of? Just now?"

"Why?"

"Because the light fell from your face."

"I remembered how much you loved Tessa and how angry I was with her when I saw her kiss your best friend."

She looked up at him. He stood so close to her she could hardly think straight anymore.

"I'm sorry I took her away from you, Rafe. I'm sorry I

made her leave."

"Shhh. It's taken me a long time to realize that you didn't make her leave—"

"But I—"

He placed a finger over her lips.

"She was a grown woman. She could have told me she was unhappy. She could have told me that she wanted out, but instead, she left me standing there..."

Tayla felt his body tense a little.

"...in front of the whole town. Our friends. Our families. Without even saying goodbye."

"She didn't say goodbye?" Tayla distinctly remembered Tessa telling her she'd already spoken to Rafe.

"All I had," he reached into his vest pocket, "was this." He handed her a small, yellowed note.

When Tayla opened it up, she recognized the handwriting as her own.

*It's for the best, Rafe,* was all it said.

"You still have it?"

"I kept it to remind me of everything I lost that day."

"Rafe, I'm so—"

He grabbed her face and pulled her close to him, enveloping her in a kiss that sent tingles to her toes.

"Now, I'll keep it to remind me of everything I've gained."

Something caught Rafe's attention behind her and he squinted his eyes into the darkening horizon.

"Who the hell let the horses out of the corral?"

Gunshots sliced the air. Rafe threw a protective arm around her and they crouched low to the ground. Within seconds livestock crashed through the fences and into the yard.

Rafe nearly picked her up as he ushered her to the house.

Jameson, Harrison, Eli, Ethan, and Malcolm all ran from the house and dodged the animals that encroached the drive. Leah stood in the doorway holding a shotgun. She fired it into the air when the bull they'd brought in on the drive looked as if it was going to run through the front door.

Tayla stepped up further onto the porch. The yard was in

chaos. She scanned the area looking for Rafe and her heart lifted a little when she found him. He and his brother, Ethan, had mounted horses and had ridden out to the outside of the broken fence line. They each had guns and started shooting them in the air to distract anymore animals from barging through. Hired hands appeared from the bunkhouse and barn, working to get a handle on the rambunctious crowd.

The sun had already begun to set and the light was diminishing quickly.

Tayla backed up again when two men on horseback whooshed past the porch.

Jonas and Lester. Where did they come from? She hadn't thought much about them, but was sure Rafe would have made sure they were locked up somewhere. Now they were free and Tayla feared they had started the stampede. In this light, she couldn't see if they had weapons, but fear gripped her heart. Rafe would be distracted with the herd. Tayla looked up to the spot where Rafe had been moments ago. He was gone. She had to warn him.

"Mrs. Redbourne," she stepped next to Rafe's mother, "have you seen Rafe?"

"No, dear. I'm sure he is riding along the perimeter with Ethan and Malcolm." She must've sensed Tayla's apprehension because her brows furrowed together and she placed an arm around her shoulders. "What is it, Tayla?" she asked.

"Do you remember the two men that Rafe wanted to lock in the shed?"

Leah nodded.

"That's them." Tayla pointed at the two riders who didn't seem too intent on leaving. She worried that they may try to hurt Rafe now. What if they tried to...to kill him?

She had to find a way to get to him before Jonas and Lester could. The small pack mule Rafe had made the two brutes ride, was tied up at the edge of the barn. It didn't look as if the chaos had perturbed him one bit.

"Tayla, where are you going?" Leah demanded in a higher pitched voice than was normal for her.

Tayla didn't look back. She ran to the small mule and untethered his reins. It was easy enough for her to mount, but she wished she still had on Maggie's old riding trousers. She pulled the horse around and carefully made her way to the edge of the fence. The animals seemed to be running in circles at this point and were mostly contained inside the fenced structure, however, Tayla noted, there were a few cows and horses that had escaped and had become mere dots in the darkened distance. At last, she saw Rafe. He had dismounted and it looked as if he were working quickly to repair another portion of the damaged fence.

Lester and Jonas had separated. Jonas was riding away from Redbourne Ranch, but Lester slowly made his way toward Rafe and was now merely a few feet from him.

Tayla didn't think. She just dug her heels into the horse's sides. Her mount wasn't pleased and she quickly found herself nursing a sore rear end from the ground. She ignored the pain and jumped to her feet, running as quickly as she could toward Rafe.

A large black and white paint rounded the house running straight for her and she dodged it just in time. The haunting yell of the bull came at her side and she tripped over a rock, landing face first in a mud puddle. As she pulled herself from the ground, she was grateful she hadn't fallen a couple more inches to her right as there was a large pile of fresh steaming dung.

Boom.

She froze.

Harrison held a rifle up to his shoulder and aimed. Lester's left side jerked backward and he cursed loud enough for her to hear. He'd been shot, but he'd managed to remain astride his horse. He turned the reins and quickly headed out toward Jonas.

Tayla couldn't breathe.

Harrison didn't move. He focused the rifle on Lester until he was nearly out of sight.

Rafe was all right and headed straight for her. Tayla dropped to the ground in a heap.

"Fool woman," Rafe chastised as he pulled her off the

ground in a run and all but threw her onto the porch.

How did he get to her so quickly?

He didn't say anything else, but turned on his heel and headed back to where Lexa awaited him by the broken fence.

Tayla wanted to do something. Needed to do something to help.

"There's not much we can do at this point," Leah said knowingly. "Don't you fret none. They've almost got it under control. My boys are good at what they do," she said proudly.

Tayla nodded.

"My son cares deeply for you, you know?"

Tayla blinked up at the woman who stood leaning against one of the porch pillars and frowned. "What makes you say that?"

Leah pushed herself away from her post and sat down on the step next to Tayla. "Oh, he was angry for a while. Tessa hurt him, bad. Stripped his pride. And if there's one thing these Redbournes cling to, it's their pride."

"What makes you think he cares about me?"

"He always had a soft spot in his heart when it came to you." Leah put a hand on Tayla's knee. "But he doesn't look at you like that little girl anymore though." She smiled.

"How does he look at me?" Tayla searched Leah's face for a hint. She knew she was being forward, but she had to know.

"Let's just say that the light I saw in my son's eyes tonight has been missing for a very long time."

"That's the last of them," Malcolm yelled from the corral.

Both women turned to look at them. The animals had been contained and it seemed as if everyone had gotten away unscathed—except for Lester.

Rafe dismounted his beautiful strawberry horse just before he reached the stable. He quickly disappeared inside.

"I think," Tayla started in nothing more but a whisper, "I love him. I think I always have." She realized as she said the words aloud, that it was true.

# CHAPTER NINETEEN

Rafe wanted to spit nails. When he'd seen Tayla fall in the yard with many of the animals still riled up and running around the outbuildings, his heart had nearly sunk into his gut. What had she been thinking coming out like that and off the porch? He patted Lexa on her side and reached for the brush hanging from the nail in her stall. He hoped that brushing down Lexa would help him to regain his wits about him before he went back into the house to face Tayla.

He and Harrison would be headed out to the city in the morning. Lord Darington should be meeting them at the train station. He had to find out what was going on and he didn't trust himself to take Tayla along. The distraction was becoming too much for him to focus and that was dangerous—especially in his line of work.

"Rafe?" Malcolm leaned on the half door with his elbows and peered into the stall at him.

Rafe continued to brush. He was sure there was an explanation to what Tayla had seen. He knew he should give Malcolm the chance to explain, but either way, old wounds had been opened and exposed and he wasn't in the mood to be practical.

"What happened, Malcolm. With Tayla?" he stopped brushing Lexa long enough to look straight in his friend's face. "Who is she running from and how were you there with her?"

"It's a long story. I work for a very dangerous man."

"And he wants to hurt Tayla?"

"Lord Darington won't let anything or anyone stand in his way."

"Of what?" Rafe flexed his hand, then relaxed it around Lexa's brush. "You know what? We need to talk about this later. We've waited this long and as much as I want to know what is the hell is going on, I think we should discuss this with Tayla and Harrison."

"Why Harrison? And since when did you invite your bounties to the table to eat with your family."

"Like you said, it's a long story and he's more a part of this than what you might think."

"Do you think you can trust him?" Malcolm asked. "Most of them will say anything to get you to believe what they want."

"He saved my life."

"Okay," Malcolm said, pushing himself away from the gate and raising his hands. He turned to leave the stables, then stopped and patted the stall gate. "You are better off, you know," Malcolm said.

Rafe shot him a confused look.

"Tessa would never have made you happy."

He did not want to discuss this right now. He had come to terms with Tessa leaving him years ago—or so he'd thought. Why was he still so angry?

"And what, exactly, do you know about what makes me happy?" Rafe met Malcolm's eyes.

"I know you want someone you can trust."

"Trust is something you earn."

"Rafe, I didn't kiss her." Malcolm pushed away from the door and flicked his hands at the air. "*She* came onto *me*. Tayla must have seen us, but if she had stuck around long enough, she would have seen me tell Tessa exactly what I thought about her advances. And I wasn't so polite about telling her exactly what I thought about her either." Malcolm dropped his chin and shook his head. "I didn't tell you because... Well, because she left back to England and I never thought you'd see her again. You'd been hurt enough."

Malcolm had been one of Rafe's best friends for twenty years. He deserved the benefit of the doubt.

Rafe dug the mud from Lexa's hooves. When he was finished, he unlatched the stall gate. Malcolm handed him an apple from the bag hanging above the counter. His thoughts returned to Tayla. He didn't know if he could leave without her. Didn't know if he wanted to. He took the apple from Malcolm and then it hit him. He was falling in love with Tayla.

"Took a long time for me to realize it, but you are right," he said to Malcolm with a clap on the shoulder. "Tessa would never have made me happy."

Malcolm looked at him with a quizzical expression.

"I was the bigger fool for not recognizing it in the first place." Rafe fed the apple to Lexa and shut the gate. "It's hard to believe that I didn't see what was right in front of me. She was beautiful and fun. Our families were friends. I loved spending time with them. Tessa was the logical choice. Every time some other man looked at me with envy, it made me want to hold onto her even tighter. Everything just seemed to fit. The timing, granddad's will, the career, the woman. It all fell into place...just before it fell apart."

Rafe hung the brush on its nail and walked out of her stall. He was ready to see Tayla. He wanted to be near her. Needed her to know she was his choice.

"You know," he said to Malcolm as they turned to leave the stable, "I can still remember how Tessa's laugh made me feel. It was like warm butter laced with honey. But I never—"

"I hoped I'd be able to find you out here." That same buttered honey dripped from the woman's voice with horrifying familiarity.

Rafe whipped around and sucked in a breath at the sight of Tessa Hawthorne standing beneath the frame of the stable's entrance. Her beautiful raven tresses were perfectly coiffed and the snug lavender dress she wore accentuated her very womanly curves. Enough with the coincidences.

"Hello, Rafe," she said with a slight curve to her overly pouted lips.

His throat went dry. It felt as if the last eight years disappeared. He'd loved her once.

"I'll just be in the house," Malcolm said, excusing himself from the stable.

Tessa didn't take her eyes off him. "How have you been?"

How had he been? His head cleared. He tipped his hat. "Tessa," he said as he walked past her out into the yard and toward the house.

She followed. He paused at the pressure of her hand on his arm.

"Rafe," she cooed.

He turned to face her. "Look, Tessa," he said, meeting her eyes and stooping low enough that he hoped his words would penetrate her façade, "I don't know what you're playing by coming here, but—"

She kissed him.

Emotions played with his logic and it took him a moment before he pushed her away from him.

"What the hell was that?" he asked, his anger brimming at the surface.

A flash of color grazed the corners of his eyes and he looked up in time to see Tayla disappearing into the house.

Damn.

"Tayla," he called loudly and started for the house.

"Rafe, didn't you miss me? Even a little?"

That was it. How dare she waltz back into his life after eight years and expect him to have missed her.

"What are you doing here, Tessa?" Rafe demanded, as he whipped back around. His jaw clenched.

"We received a telegram that Tayla was in trouble and had been brought here. Of course I came. She is my baby sister."

No one could have known Tayla would be here. Unless...

"Lord Darington did not want to wait. We boarded the first train and he rented a carriage in the city and we came here straightaway."

"Wait. Lord Darington is here? At Redbourne Ranch? Right now?"

"Yes."

He had to find Tayla. To protect her. If Lord Darington was as dangerous as Harrison and Malcolm had made him out to be, she wouldn't be safe. He started for the house again, then paused. "When did you get the post?" he asked quickly.

"We came as soon as we could. It's only been a few days. A week at most."

"Seven days? Have you been here in the states? Who did you get the post from?"

"Yes. Mother and I have been staying with…a friend of ours in Boston. I'm not sure who the post was from."

"Where is Darington now?

"I'm sure he is with my beloved little sister," she said with annoyance.

Rafe had to find Tayla before Darington did.

Tayla had to make a choice—run away or fight.

She'd seen Rafe kissing another woman—not just any other woman, but her sister, with whom he had once been in love—and had run into the house, up the stairs and into the first unoccupied room she could find.

She should have been thrilled to see that Tessa was here. But somehow seeing her had torn a hole in the new world she'd created for herself. A hole where Rafe had been in her heart.

*Tayla, you are being stupid.* She had realized in the last few hours what her sister was capable of. *You need to give Rafe the chance to explain.*

There was a light knock on the door just before it opened.

"Tayla, dear," Leah leaned into the room, "there are some people downstairs who'd like to see you."

She turned. Leah's reassuring smile comforted her.

"Yes. I saw Tessa. She's outside…*speaking* with Rafe."

"A very handsome lord also awaits you downstairs, waiting for you in the living room."

"A Lord?" *Darington? It had to be.*

"I believe he's your," Leah cleared her throat, "fiancé, dear. From England."

Tayla glanced at the slight washstand mirror. Her cheeks were flushed, but Grace had gotten a new dress for her to put on, place of the soiled one she'd been wearing. Then, she helped her clean up her face and fix her hair. Tayla presumed she looked presentable enough.

"Tayla." Rafe appeared behind Leah in the doorway and pushed the door all the way open. "I know what you think you saw." His baritone voice had an edge to it.

"I guess Tessa found you," Leah confirmed with a nod, looking up at her son.

Rafe's jaw flexed and he stepped around his mother into her room. The warmth of his hand on Tayla's shoulder was nearly too much. She dropped her head and closed her eyes. One lone tear trailed her cheek and she quickly wiped it away. It was time to face her challenges head on. She would fight. For him. She lifted her head to meet Rafe's eyes with what she hoped was a casual smile on her face.

"I understand that Tessa is beaut—"

Rafe grabbed her face with both hands and kissed her firmly, then let her go just as quickly. "You don't understand, but I don't have time to fix that right now. We have to talk."

Tayla breathed out audibly, lifting her fingers to her lips. She glanced up at him, searching his eyes. He was worried.

"I don't remember kissing my betrothed as being a part of our agreement."

Tayla darted her eyes to the voice. A very handsome, dark haired man in a finely tailored grey suit stood just outside the door. His chiseled face played instant havoc on her memories as images flew into her mind with no context. If this man was her fiancé…

Her breaths suddenly became shallow.

"Tayla?" Rafe looked down at her. A worried line creased his forehead.

Lord Darington started forward, but Leah blocked his way

into the room. "Let's move this conversation downstairs," Leah suggested. "Rafe, you too." She met Rafe's stare and lifted her eyebrow. "This is no place for gentlemen to speak with a lady."

Tayla stood up straight and took a deep breath.

Rafe grumbled something under his breath and left the room.

Leah stepped inside and closed the door behind her. "It must be hard," she said, "having two very handsome men vying for your affections."

Tayla smiled, then laughed.

"Are you ready?"

Tayla glanced back at the washstand mirror. *You can do this,* she said silently. She took a hold of Leah's extended hand and together they descended the stairs.

When she reached the bottom of the staircase, Tayla looked back and forth between Rafe and Darington. She didn't have to wonder if the kiss had affected Rafe too. He swallowed hard and narrowed his eyes at her fiancé.

"My lord?" she dipped her head as she addressed him.

He shoved away from the couch where he'd stood with his arms crossed in front of his chest and in two strides made the distance between them. He put his arms around her and lifted her off the ground.

"Darling, why so formal?" He set her back on the ground and gently placed a kiss on her cheek. "I've been so worried about you."

It was warm and sent unfamiliar tingles down her neck to her abdomen. Tayla darted a glance at Rafe, who seemed more stunned than anything. He stood frozen to his place.

"You can't imagine the relief I felt when I received word you were okay." He had her head in his hands, his thumb caressing her lips and her chin. "It's so good to see you." Darington bent his head down to kiss her on the mouth.

Tayla couldn't think. She couldn't let him kiss her. Right now all she knew was that she loved Rafe. But this man was her fiancé. She had to have loved him too.

Was it possible to love two men at once?

She dropped her chin to her chest and the kiss landed on her forehead.

"Let me look at you." Darington pulled her away from him and scanned her from head to toe.

She felt herself blush under his scrutiny. "You are perfect. And you are safe." He looked up at Rafe. "Thank you for that," he said and extended his hand.

Rafe stood his ground.

"Yes, well, right. Thank you," Darington said with a tilt to his head, retracting is hand and rubbing his fingers together.

"My lord, there is something you need to understand," she said as she looked up into his eyes. She guessed he wasn't quite as tall as Rafe, but the two were close.

"Yes, darling, what is it?"

"I don't...I can't..." She didn't know how to say it.

"She doesn't remember you, *chap*," Rafe said matter-of-factly. Tayla nearly choked with laughter at his use of the last word.

"There was an accident," she said after composing herself enough to speak.

"What kind of accident?" Darington narrowed his eyes and then turned them on Rafe. "Has she seen a doctor?"

"I am fine." Tayla spoke before Rafe could. "My memories are returning—though a might slower than I would like."

She was worried. She did not remember much about this man. She couldn't deny Lord Darington was handsome and obviously wealthy, so why hadn't he been able to protect her? Why had she needed to leave her home and come to America? He was her fiancé.

Her fiancé. The idea was still so strange to her. She couldn't quite believe it was real. She stole a glance at Rafe. His face was stoic. Questions filled her mind and suddenly what had seemed so simple moments ago, when Rafe's lips had captured hers, had just become a lot more complicated.

Rafe wanted to punch the *bloke* in his all too perfect face. No wonder she'd fallen for him. His fancy duds painted him in London society, not at a ranch in Kansas. Was he really what Tayla wanted? He watched her for any hint of recognition, but nothing.

If she had wanted a life that came with wealth and a title, that was something Rafe could not give her. He'd missed out on his inheritance a long time ago and the life of a bounty hunter's wife would be anything but luxurious. Could he even hope that she would accept him?

When Darington leaned in to kiss Tayla, Rafe's hands started to itch. He glanced over at Tessa, who'd followed them into the house and leaned against the fireplace, watching, a smug look of satisfaction distorting her otherwise beautiful features. She winked at him.

His stomach turned.

Rafe knew nothing of the man claiming to be Tayla's betrothed, except that he'd placed a bounty on an innocent man. All of his senses were on fire, and in that moment he realized that he could no longer be objective.

"You are perfect," Darington said to Tayla with a smile that Rafe wanted to wipe off his face. Then, he turned to him. "Thank you for that." He extended his hand.

Rafe was wary of the man. Harrison and Malcolm had both told him that Lord Darington was dangerous. He didn't want to shake his hand, and pushed his fingers down even deeper in the pockets of his denims. He intended to do everything in his power to make sure that Tayla remained safe.

Rafe had sent two telegrams when they were in the last town—one to Adrien, letting him know where they were headed and they were safe, and the other to Lord Darington, telling him to meet in Kansas City and he would hand Harrison over. So, why had he come to Redbourne Ranch?

Davis.

He needed to go find Harrison. Then, they could sit down and finally get to the bottom of the enigmatic situation. This was the first time Rafe really wished that Tayla's memory was back.

He realized that the Tayla he had grown to care about over the last couple of weeks may not be who Tayla really was and it pained him to know that she could be leaving.

As if on cue, Harrison walked into the house. "Glad that's over," he said when he saw Rafe. "Your life always this cracked?"

Rafe jutted his head toward Lord Darington.

Harrison looked at the man. "Sorry, are you another of Rafe's brothers?" He asked with an extended hand. He'd already taken two steps toward Darington before Rafe stopped him.

"You!" Darington gasped incredulously and reached for his side. There was no weapon there and he took a step backward. "What's going on here, Redbourne? Why isn't he in custody?"

"Custody? I'm sorry," Harrison replied, "I don't believe I've had the pleasure."

There was a knock on the door. Rafe's mother set down a pitcher of lemonade on the table and rushed out of the room to answer it.

"Never had the pleasure?" Darington snorted. "Coming to my home at all hours of the night. Insisting you should be the rightful recipient of my title. And you've never had the pleasure?" His voice grew louder with each accusation. "You stole my grandmother's music box, kidnapped my fiancée, and destroyed my carriage, and you tell me that you've never had the pleasure? Are you daft?"

Harrison stood up straight, lifted an eyebrow at the man. "*You* are not Lord Darington."

"Excuse me?" Darington pulled his head back. "I most certainly am. Who else would I be?"

Harrison looked at Rafe. "I really need to talk to you in private."

"Okay, just as soon as we're done here," Rafe said in low tones very close to Harrison's ear.

Harrison took a deep breath and spoke, resigned. "I assure you, *my lord*, I have never met you before tonight and I certainly didn't kidnap your fiancée or steal any of your things. I only met

Miss Hawthorne a few weeks ago in Colorado." Harrison had started to sweat again, but this time Rafe didn't think it was from nerves, but anger.

Rafe stepped forward and placed his hand on Harrison's forearm. "Not here," he whispered.

When Harrison relaxed his stance, he leaned against the hearth and pulled his handkerchief from his pocket to dab at his brow. Darington followed suit and relaxed his offensive stance, but neither of them took their eyes off one another.

"So, Lord Darington. In the flesh." Harrison's lip curled and his voice dripped with disdain.

"So, you obviously *do* know me," Darington announced knowingly.

"I thought I'd met you once," Harrison lined his ribcage with one finger, "but it appears I only know you by reputation. You placed a bounty on my head and when I tried to contact you to sort it out, you had your man beat and torture me. I barely escaped with my life."

"You *are* daft."

Rafe let them talk. Having everyone in the same room should bring out the truth of it all.

"Tayla disappeared the same night you came to visit me with your threats. When my men saw you board the ship to America, I realized—"

"That's what I am trying to tell you, old chap." Harrison's voice grew louder. "I did not visit you—"

"I did."

All heads turned. Rafe looked at the archway where a near replica of Harrison stood, a rich brown leather bag strung across his shoulder. Not just brothers. Twins.

"Hello, brother."

Harrison stood up again and with a grin on his face made it over to his brother very quickly. Without warning, he landed a punch directly across Finn's jaw. He sprawled backward and caught himself on the arched doorway before stumbling the rest of the way to the floor. He sat there, stunned, looking up at Harrison.

Tayla gasped and shook her head as if she were recalling something, some memory. She fell back against the arm of the cushioned chair and Rafe stepped forward and guided her down into the seat. He crouched down next to her, his hand resting on her back.

"Another memory?" Rafe asked in a whisper.

She nodded.

"What did you do that for?" Finn asked, nursing a discoloring jaw.

"Because, Finn," Harrison said firmly, "do you have any idea what you've done? How much trouble you've caused me?" Harrison shouted. "What did you do?"

"He died," Tayla said softly.

"You died?" Harrison said loudly to his brother. "Wait." He turned to Tayla. "He what?"

Everyone was silent.

Darington fell to his haunches on the other side of her and placed a hand over hers.

"What are you saying, love?"

"I remember standing by the back door in the library and looking out into the garden. You and he," she said, pointing to Finn, "were yelling at one another." She closed her eyes. "Then he tried to hit you, but you ducked away and knocked him to the ground."

"You were at the window?"

Tayla looked at Lord Darington with wide eyes.

Rafe could hardly watch. He smiled with a small sense of satisfaction when she pulled her hand out from beneath Darington's and leaned more toward him.

"You killed him," she said, barely above a whisper, accusation lining her voice.

"I what?" Darington's head jerked backward. He pulled away from her and stood up.

Rafe watched him closely. His surprise was evident and his shock sincere.

"I apologize that you saw our little altercation, and yes, when he refused to leave the grounds I drew my pistol and shot,

but not him. I shot into the shrubbery. As a warning."
Darington crouched down again and leaned toward her.
"Darling, he gathered his things, taking my grandmother's music
box with him and rushed away—very much alive. I'm afraid that
he got away by stealing my carriage…with you inside it. I've
been beside myself for months."

She didn't flinch this time. She looked at him long and hard.
Rafe had to resist the urge to pull her back.

"You mean…"

"Tayla, darling, I could never kill anyone." Darington
grabbed her hand again. "How could you have thought that?"

"Malcolm."

"Malcolm?" he asked, obviously surprised. "What does
Malcolm have to do with any of this?"

Finn finally pulled himself to his feet and they all turned to
look at him.

"You're not Harrison," she stated flatly. "And you're alive."
She spoke as if trying to convince herself of the truth of it.

"You're telling me," Finn said sarcastically, still rubbing his
jaw.

Rafe ran his hands through his hair. Information was
coming in spades and he wasn't at all sure he liked where the
conversation was heading.

"Malcolm told me I had to run," Tayla whispered, shaking
her head. She stared forward and spoke to no one in particular.
Then she looked at Darington. "He said you would hurt me if
you ever found out I'd seen you that night in the garden."

Malcolm had admitted to Rafe that he worked for
Darington, but why would he lie to Tayla? Rafe hadn't seen him
since he'd left the barn just after Tessa had confronted him and
he wondered where he'd gotten off to. He must have more
information. He wouldn't just tell Tayla to run away for no
reason. There had to be an explanation and Rafe was tired of
waiting.

Tessa pushed herself away from the fireplace and turned to
look at Tayla. "Are you telling me that we left England for
nothing?" she said in a high pitched voice, slamming her hands

against the decorative table in front of her.

Tayla jumped. "I'm sorry," she said after a moment. "I..." she looked at Rafe, then at Darington. "I'm sorry for all of this." She jumped up from the chair. Both men followed suit.

"Tayla," Darington reached up to touch her cheek, "don't go. I don't know what else Malcolm told you, but you know me. You know I could never hurt you."

It took every ounce of strength left in Rafe's body not to grab Lord Darington's hand away from her face and break every one of his fingers.

Tayla looked at her fiancé, but it was Rafe's hand that she found and squeezed, as if she needed his strength. "That's just it," she said with a shrug of her shoulders, "I don't know you. Not anymore."

When she glanced at Tessa, Rafe felt her stiffen and she let go of his hand. "Please," she said to the two of them, "just let me go."

Damn.

# CHAPTER TWENTY

Tayla wasn't sure she could breathe. She needed some fresh air. She flung the front door wide and let it slam behind her as she left. As she skittered down the steps, she ran full force into a man and stopped cold. He was huge.

*He has to be another Redbourne.*

When he turned around, a huge smile touched his quite handsome features. "Tayla," he said congenially, "you're okay." He bent down and hugged her. "But how did you get here?" he inquired as he pulled away from her.

What was it with this family? It seemed like there were so many of them she would never be able to keep them all straight. She remembered his smile and something about him put her at ease.

"Rafe brought me." She took a deep breath.

"What?" He sounded shocked. "Rafe? My brother? Brought you, Tayla Hawthorne, here to Redbourne Ranch?"

Tayla shrugged and nodded.

"Sounds like there is a story in there somewhere. Who else is here?"

"Too many for me to keep track of."

He laughed. "That's my family, all right." He picked up the bag he'd dropped when she'd bumped into him and climbed the stairs. He turned back to look at her before opening the door. "Are you okay?"

"I'm sorry," she said. "I can't do this right now. If you'll excuse me." She saw a light coming from the barn and hoped that she may be able to escape in there for a bit. There was so much to sort out in her head. Memories filled the empty spaces of her mind, but they didn't all fit together nicely.

"Well, hello," Hannah said when she popped her head up from behind one of the horses. "Sometimes they get to be a little too much to take, don't they?" She smiled. "Would you like a glass of fresh warm milk?"

"Thank you."

"I come out here to get away. Eli is rocking Eliza Jane to sleep and I thought I'd take advantage. I honestly don't get much time to myself." Hannah pulled a couple of stools up next to Tayla, motioning for her to sit. "It's peaceful out here—when everybody is inside, that is." She chuckled.

"I made a huge mistake and now I've made a mess of everything." Tayla said to the woman who she knew had once been her friend. "What if my memory never returns completely?"

Hannah waited a moment before replying. She leaned back against one of the stall gates and thought. "Then every day will be a new adventure," she finally said with a shrug. "Life is what we make of it. If you don't have old memories to rely on, then maybe it's time you start making new ones."

That thought hit Tayla hard. Hannah was right. There was no reason she should sit around and lament the old memories. She didn't remember much about her fiancé from before and she just discovered that he'd been searching for her—even though she'd gravely mistaken his character. She owed it to herself to move forward and while she was unsure what that meant right now, she took comfort in knowing she had made a decision. There were a lot of things she didn't remember, but it was time for her to move forward instead of dwelling on the past.

"Remind me how many brothers you have."

Hannah snickered. "I have eight older brothers. All as protective and stubborn as the next...wish they all lived close."

"Some of us do."

Tayla didn't turn around. She was afraid to even look at Rafe. His voice had become so familiar to her, a part of her.

Hannah returned the front two legs of her stool to the ground and stood. "Guess they've discovered us," she said with a wink. "You have stories to tell," she said to Rafe as she left the barn. "I'll be waiting," she called out.

Tayla could feel him getting closer. "Are you all right?" His voice was etched with concern.

"Why does everyone keep asking me that? I am fine. I just needed a little bit of fresh air."

Rafe walked in front of her and sat down on the stool that Hannah had just vacated.

"It's harder than I thought it would be." She swallowed hard.

"What is?"

"To admit I was wrong."

Silence.

"I mean, I was supposed to love him, right? We were...are," she corrected, "engaged to be married. How could I have jumped to such a drastic conclusion?"

"Things have a funny way of working out."

"Working out? Is that what this is? I accused my fiancé of murder and dragged my entire family to America and for what? I am engaged to be married to the Earl of Darington, who is handsome and refined and seems to really love me, and yet I can't make myself stop thinking about a bounty hunter from Kansas. What part of all of that is working out?"

Rafe slid to the edge of his seat and reached a hand out to her face.

"Don't," she pleaded. She loved him, of that she was sure, but she was engaged to someone else. She didn't know if she could stop him from kissing her if he tried and for now, it wasn't right.

"Tayla?"

Rafe's hand fell from her face and she whipped around to see Lord Darington standing in the barn's doorway. She stood up and turned to meet his eyes.

There was hurt there, behind the warmth.

"Will you walk with me, my lady?"

"Tayla," Rafe touched her arm. "I don't think that is such a good idea," he protested.

*Be strong.* She smiled at both of them.

"There will be plenty of time for all of us to talk in the morning. It's been a very long day. I think I would like to turn in for the night."

"As you wish," Darington said with a slight nod.

"I'll walk you in," Rafe said.

"As will I," Darington countered.

Tayla rolled her eyes. She should be enjoying the fact that she had two dashing suitors, but she didn't want to play games. She wanted to start building her life and for that, she had to make a choice. How could she do that without all the facts? Without her memories.

"Come with me, my dear," Leah said. "We'll get you all set up in the twins' old room."

Rafe groaned inwardly. Levi and Tag's room was right next to his.

*Mother,* he screamed in his head with exasperation. "You have no idea what you are doing to me," he said under his breath.

Rafe knew Tayla would be in good hands with his mother. Leah Redbourne loved to fuss—especially over women she saw as potential brides for her sons. He and Raine were the only unwed children left and he suspected even now that his mother was cooking up something. She'd see the fact that Tayla was engaged to someone else as a minor hiccup.

Tayla turned to him, her smile not quite reaching her eyes. "Goodnight."

She was troubled. He couldn't let himself think about what must be going through her head. It *had* been a long day, but there were still a few things he needed to work out.

"Goodnight."

Rafe walked back through the kitchen and opened the back door with one last glance at the empty hallway, then joined Darington on the stairs. He shook his head. His time for distractions had passed. He was missing something and there was no time for mistakes. If someone was still after Tayla, he needed to be cautious and alert—at his best.

It was getting late. The sun had all but disappeared below the horizon. There was nothing more he would be able to accomplish tonight and for the first time in a long time he was home. He just wanted to enjoy the time he had with his family. But something still ate at him.

"How did you know Tayla would be here?" Rafe asked casually.

Darington took a deep breath and eased it out before he responded.

"I received your post, almost a week ago now, to meet you at Redbourne Ranch."

"*My* post? Do you still have it?" A week ago he'd been at Maggie's place. No one outside of the Smokey Sky knew they were there, except...

*Impossible.* He'd sent word to Adrien that he'd found Tayla. He was the only other person who'd known where they were headed.

"It's with my things. Why?"

Rafe had watched Darington closely over the last few hours. He seemed to genuinely care for Tayla. Rafe generally had a keen ability to read people and as much as he wanted to he did not believe that the lord posed a physical danger to Tayla. He'd been wrong before, with Tessa, but somehow he didn't think he was wrong this time. So, if Lord Darington wasn't a danger to Tayla, then why did Rafe still have an ominous knot in his gut? He was missing something and he was sure it was right in front of him.

"I didn't send that post," he finally said.

Darington opened his mouth to say something, then closed

it with a wrinkled brow. "Then who did?"

"That's what I intend to find out." Rafe recapped the day's events in his head.

"What is going on here?" Darington shifted his position on the stairs to face Rafe. "What happened to Tayla? How did she lose her memory?"

Rafe met his stare and understood the man's desire for answers. "Jonas and Lester took her from Longhurst Manor and shot her father in the process."

"Who are Jonas and Lester?"

Jonas and Lester. Somehow, they were a part of the puzzle that Rafe had overlooked. He cursed himself for not talking to them before, when they were still in his custody, but those two ruffians had gotten out of the cellar—something that irked Rafe beyond reason. If Darington wasn't 'the boss' they had referred to and he hadn't been the one to send them to kidnap Tayla, who had? Where was the connection? Rafe thought for a moment and then it hit him with a force to be reckoned with.

Malcolm.

Rafe searched his mind for any other explanation. Malcolm was his friend. They'd known each other for a very long time. Had spent hours every summer at Adrien's feet, listening to his stories. Had spent a year together with the Pawnee, learning the ways of his people—how to hunt, track, kill. They had even liked some of the same girls. Malcolm had been a groomsman at Rafe's wedding.

It was Malcolm. There was no time to mourn their friendship. He'd disappeared just before Darington arrived and could be anywhere. It was no longer just Tayla who was in danger, but his whole family.

"It's Malcolm," Rafe said aloud.

"What is?"

"Don't you remember? Tayla said that he's the one who told her to run from you because you would hurt her. He implanted the idea you had killed Finn in her head."

"I can't believe this. I would have trusted my life to Malcolm," Darington said aloud, though a shocked whisper.

Rafe shifted uncomfortably. He would have done the same. There had to be another explanation, but he couldn't take that chance.

"There are just too many coincidences."

"He must've known we would figure it out. I haven't seen him since the stampede—just before you and Tessa arrived."

"Wait, Malcolm is here on the ranch?" Darington asked disbelievingly.

Rafe nodded.

It took a moment, but Darington shook off whatever shock had ailed him. "What do we do?"

"Go wait in the kitchen. I'll be there shortly." Rafe grabbed Darington's arm as he stood up. "He's dangerous. You'll need to be prepared to protect yourself and others."

Darington nodded with a clenched jaw and headed for his room.

Rafe had to let the others know that danger wore a friendly face. Malcolm Longhurst had an agenda and until Rafe understood what that was, he needed to be prepared. It had only taken a few minutes to gather the others together and explain the situation. Now seated around the table were Ethan, Harrison, Eli, Jameson, Darington, and Finn.

"Why would Malcolm do this?" Jameson leaned forward on his elbows into the lantern's light. "We've known him nearly his whole life. I can't believe that he would betray our trust like this. He's like one of my own sons."

Rafe wanted to believe he was wrong. Wanted to believe that Malcolm had nothing to do with all this, but he couldn't rid himself of the nagging feeling that Malcolm wasn't the same man he used to be.

Thunder rolled across the sky and rain drops fell in succession. A storm seemed fitting for tonight's events. Wind blew through the kitchen window and whipped at the flicker of light coming from the lone lantern on the table. Rafe quickly moved to the window and shut it tight.

"So," Eli spoke for the first time tonight. "If he knew that Tayla had run away, why did put a bounty on Harrison's head for kidnapping her and then hire Rafe to find him?"

Good question. Rafe looked at Harrison with a raised eyebrow.

Harrison cleared his throat. "Because it is possible," he said quietly, "that I am the rightful Earl of Darington. If Malcolm knew that…"

Lord Darington's face was stoic, perfectly masked of emotion. "Malcolm has been in my employ and my closest friend for nearly six years. Maybe he, in some misguided way, was trying to protect me."

"You are too trusting, my lord." A man stepped out of the shadows of the hallway and into the kitchen.

Rafe instinctively reached for his guns and drew.

"Whoa, little brother. It's just me."

It took a moment for Rafe's eyes to adjust enough to make out his identity. "Will?" Rafe returned his revolvers to his holster and stepped forward to embrace the man fiercely. "I thought you weren't coming in until tomorrow."

"Train arrived early and we were anxious to get here."

"We?"

"He's the one who brought me here," Finn said.

"What do you know about Malcolm?" Rafe asked.

"Tayla and her father came to me the night she ran from Darington. She'd said she was in fear for her life because she'd seen Lord Darington kill a man and his henchman had told her to run. What she'd neglected to tell me was that Malcolm Longhurst was his henchman."

Rafe glanced at Lord Darington. He imagined his face would look much the same if someone had falsely accused him of such a crime.

"She would not be consoled or deterred," Will continued, "and said she wanted to go as far away as she could. So, I contacted Adrien. Because of the Hawthorne's history with our family, I thought it best to keep her away from Redbourne Ranch." He looked at Rafe. "I see that worked out well."

Rafe shrugged.

Will lifted a foot to rest on an empty chair at the table and he leaned forward on his leg. "It took a while, but when I discovered that the man Tayla thought she'd seen murdered was Finn, who was very much alive and well, I was naturally curious as to what might have happened and I went to see Lord Darington myself. Imagine my surprise when it was Malcolm who greeted me instead."

"Malcolm pretended to be me?" Darington asked.

Will nodded. "But then, he saw it was me and quickly changed his tune. He told me he was working for you and that you had come to America in search of your betrothed. He said he would be joining you post haste."

"I have not seen him since I left England. He was supposed to be handling my affairs in my absence—not pretending to be me."

"It was not long after that that I received word from Adrien that Tayla had been taken from Longhurst Manor."

"Where is he now?" Ethan asked. "I haven't seen him since we got all the animals settled and put away."

"He was talking with me in the stables until Tessa came out," Rafe said. "That wasn't too long ago."

"Wasn't he supposed to be riding the fence line with you and Harrison tonight? I don't remember seeing him after that fella got shot." Ethan scratched at his whiskers with the backs of his fingers.

"Lester, the man who got shot tonight, was one of the brutes who took Tayla from Longhurst Manor," Rafe told them. "We've had quite a few run-ins with him as we've trekked our way home. He was working for Malcolm."

"So, what do we do now?"

"Stay alert," Rafe cautioned. "He knows us and knows our tactics. He's disappeared, so he must know that we suspect him. We have to be careful. Before you turn in for the night, make sure all the doors are locked and the windows closed. The last thing we need is for him to get inside the house."

Ethan looked out the window toward his little house where a light shown in the living room window.

"Ethan, I'll come with you and we'll bring Grace and the boys here to the main house for tonight. I think it's better if we all stay together.

Ethan nodded.

"Hopefully, this rain will let up by morning's light."

Rafe was grateful that Tayla was safe in her room for the night. He'd had no idea the betrayal he would feel at Malcolm's deception and he worried for the safety of his family.

"Just one more thing," Darington said, getting right up next to Rafe. "Tayla is my fiancée. I love her. No one will hurt her. Do we understand each other?"

Was that a threat? Heat rose in his neck and the muscles in his jaw twitched. Rafe took a deep breath. Tayla was betrothed to him…for now. But he was right. No one would hurt her. He would make sure of that.

Once they were all settled into their rooms for the night, Rafe lay awake in his bed thinking about the woman who slept in the room next to his. He had to admire her strength. She'd endured a lot over the last couple of months and she'd done it with grace.

"Rafe, come quickly," his mother's urgent tone as she knocked on his door brought him to his feet immediately.

He threw on his red button-down shirt, but left it hanging open as he tugged on his boots and hat and grabbed his rifle. His gun belt was still strapped about his waist. When he yanked open his door. The panic-stricken look on his mother's face scared him.

"What's happened?"

"Hurry." Leah took hold of his hand and guided him out to Lottie's room.

"I wanted to check on her and when I took in a glass of water I found her crumpled on the floor."

Rafe pushed the door open. Lottie lay in a breathless heap at the side of her bed. Rafe rushed to her side and lifted her from the floor to the bed. She was still breathing, but barely.

"Lottie?" He set his rifle in the chair at the foot of the bed.

She roused slightly when he called her name. Moonlight filtered into her bedroom casting a soft blue light to her features.

"Mother, will you please bring me that glass?"

Leah must have been standing right behind him as the glass of water appeared in front of him in an instant.

"And will you light the lantern?" he asked over his shoulder.

The warm glow brought little color to the old cook's face, but her lips curled at the corners into a labored smile.

"Señor Rafe," she said through parched lips, though wet with drink, "your friend, Señor Malcolm open cellar. He no good. Cuídate," she whispered, her shaking hands grasping his for reassurance.

She'd seen Malcolm. His heart hurt. Everything he'd feared had been confirmed with one sentence from a dying woman.

He squeezed them gently. "Shhhhh," he coaxed. "Descansate, carina," he said with a heartfelt curve of his lips.

"Señora Leah," she called for his mother.

Rafe let go of her and stood, allowing room for his mother to sit at her side. There was nothing he could do. He didn't think there was anything anyone could do. He'd seen patient's like this while he was in school. She knew she was dying, but she'd made sure he knew there was something wrong with Malcolm.

He glanced at her, his heart full. It wouldn't be long. With an affirming squeeze on his mother's shoulder, he picked up his rifle and moved to the door. His father stood leaning against the frame, watching. Rafe wasn't at all surprised to see him there.

"How is she?" he asked in a voice barely above a whisper.

Rafe shook his head and Jameson dropped his with a nod

of understanding. Rafe put his hand on his father's shoulder for a few moments before leaving the room. He didn't return to his own room, but went out onto the porch to stand in the fresh morning air. He looked across the dark horizon, arms crossed in front of him, over the barn and other outbuildings. He'd missed this place. He finally admitted what he'd known for some time now. It was time for him to stop running from his past and to start building a future.

"Is everything all right?"

Rafe didn't have to turn around to know it was Tayla. He turned his head a little over his shoulder. "No," he said simply.

The light weight of her hand on his arm kindled a fire beneath his skin. He didn't move. She was standing so close to him the soft scent of her newly washed hair incited an inward groan. He wanted to turn to her, to pull her into his arms and promise her all of his tomorrows, but something held him back.

She pressed her body into his back, her head resting against his arm and shoulders. She had no idea what she was doing to him. He relaxed his stance and rested his hand over hers at his side. They stood there together in comfortable silence until Rafe took her hand in his and turned around. He sucked in an unexpected breath.

*She is betrothed,* he reminded himself.

Tayla wore a light night shift, covered only by a shawl. Her hair fell in disarray around her shoulders and the moonlight added an angelic glow to her tresses. He led her to the large wooden swing on the porch that he and his brothers had built for his mother years ago, sat down, and tucked Tayla up under his arm.

An oversized blanket lay on the corner of the swing. He pulled it and wrapped it around her. She snuggled into him and laid her head against his chest.

They said nothing.

Damn she felt good.

Tayla blinked a few times as she opened her eyes to the new morning light. The warmth beneath her head reminded her where she was and she smiled. She knew she should care about propriety, but somehow she could not make herself get off that swing. She closed her eyes again, reveling in the feel of his thigh beneath her head.

"Rafe," a male voice penetrated her revelry.

"Shhhh," Tayla heard him respond.

She opened her eyes again and pushed herself upward. Ethan stood there with his hat low on his head and greeted her with a warm smile.

"Good morning, ma'am," he said, tugging on the front of his Stetson.

"We've gotten most of Lottie's chores done for the morning. Eli's gone into town to send post to the others, and Will is in cooking breakfast," he told Rafe, who removed his arm from around her and stood to stretch. "The night was…uneventful."

Ethan's words were a little cryptic, but Tayla didn't want to think too much about it.

"Where's Hannah?" Rafe asked his brother.

"I don't think she's up yet."

"Think again, big brother." Hannah pushed open the door, the baby in tow. "Uncle Ethan doesn't think we wake up early," she said in a higher pitched voice to the baby. "He doesn't know you actually slept through the entire night last night, does he?" She wiggled her nose back and forth across the baby's.

Rafe and Ethan both laughed out loud and Hannah nudged Ethan with her shoulder. Tayla liked their playfulness.

"I assume my brothers didn't bring a wardrobe full of clothes for you to change into," Hannah said with a smirk, "and thought you might like something of mine to wear."

"Yes, please," Tayla jumped up from the swing, then noticing her improper dress, demurely pulled her black shawl closer around her with a grin.

Hannah took her by the hand and led her back into the house. She stopped short when a bare chested Darington walked out of one of the rooms, his hair damp, and he was using one end of a towel to rough up his dark locks—the other end slung across his shoulders.

Tayla lowered her lashes. "Good morning, my lord," she said without thinking.

"Ladies." He bowed his head, then looked up at her. "Tayla, about that. We have a lot to discuss. I was hoping you might consider returning to England with me." He dropped the towel to his shoulders. "I think you have a better chance of regaining your memory if you surround yourself with familiar things and people."

Hannah dropped her hand, but remained next to her.

He certainly was a very appealing man and fresh feelings of a girl's youthful affection washed over her. Tayla had no doubt that she'd loved this man...once. She opened her mouth to speak when the front door slammed shut. She darted a glance at the entrance. Rafe stood there, a scowl darkening his features. He looked almost dangerous.

"I must say, the cool water was quite refreshing this morning." Darington lifted an eyebrow at Rafe as he sized him up. "You should have a go."

Rafe took a step forward. Luckily, the man Tayla now remembered as Will, Rafe's brother, walked out of the kitchen just in time and stepped in front of him, his hand up and pushing firmly against Rafe's chest.

"Whoa, little brother. We're going to work together this morning. To keep everyone safe, remember?"

"Safe from what?" Tayla asked curiously. Ethan had been a little secretive before on the porch and now Will. What was going on?

Dare exchanged looks with Rafe and Will. When his gaze returned to her, it fell to her chest. She reached up and caressed her pendant.

"The locket. You still have it," he said with awe. "After everything you have been through." He stepped closer to her.

"Dare," she said, stepping in front of him, "stop." When she put up a hand and it grazed his well-defined chest, she regretted the action immediately. He was anything but little.

He took her hand and held it close to him. "You called me Dare." His voice softened. "You remember."

She forced a smile. "I remember a few things, but I just—"

The door slammed shut again.

Little Eliza Jane jumped at the sound and started to cry.

Tayla dropped her hand from Dare's chest.

"Excuse me for a moment, would you?" Hannah asked, casting a meaningful glance at Tayla. "I'll be back shortly."

Tayla stared at the door. Rafe was gone.

Will rolled his eyes and turned back for the kitchen.

# CHAPTER TWENTY-ONE

Rafe shoved his hands through his hair. When he'd seen the heat rise in Tayla's cheeks at Darington's touch, it had nearly been his undoing. He could not sit by and watch the woman he loved fawn over another. He strode toward the stables. Maybe a short ride would be good for him.

*She is betrothed*, he reminded himself for the umpteenth time. *She was never yours to claim.*

It was early yet. The sun had barely peeked over the mountainside. He walked into the stable and Lexa snorted her approval. He tried to summon the anger he'd carried around for Tayla Hawthorne for the last eight years. Tried to hate her, but he couldn't. The fact was, he'd allowed himself to fall for another Hawthorne. He realized it was time to put his past behind him. This time he would have the chance to say goodbye.

He strode back toward the house. As he passed the kitchen window the soft melody of a music box played. Another piece of the puzzle was about to be revealed and he wanted to be there.

"Come on, Harry. I have to know." Finn's voice carried around the open archway.

Dare reached down and captured her hand in his. "Tayla,

darling, I want you to know that I have loved you since the moment we were introduced at the Duke's ball."

She met his eyes, although she didn't know what to say.

"I know you don't remember everything yet…" he paused as if unsure how to proceed.

"I am remembering more every day. I'd love for you to tell me about us. About me," Tayla told Dare with a slight upturn at the corners of her mouth.

He smiled, then shook his head. "There will be time for that. But right now, there is a music box on the table in there that belonged to my grandmother." He looked away from her and swallowed. "I'm told it holds a family secret."

"Dare, what are you trying to say?" She liked saying his name. It made her feel connected somehow.

"Your locket," he met her eyes again, "is a key that opens that box. I'm afraid that others have kept me from the truth for far too long and I think it's time to see just what's inside." He squeezed her hand and then let go.

Tayla's heart began to race. The locket, *her* locket, was a key to a Darington heirloom. She reached up and slid the pendant through her fingers. Until now it hadn't seemed real. She was betrothed to the Earl of Darington. She glanced back at the closed front door, closed her eyes, and breathed.

Dare opened the bedroom door behind him, removed the towel from his neck, and draped it over the arm of a tall backed chair in the corner of the room. He grabbed a white shirt and slid his arms into it. He held out a hand to her.

Tayla looked at it and then up to his eyes. She slipped her hand into his and together they walked into the kitchen.

"If you don't want it, then let me have it. It is our right." Harrison's brother was yelling across the table at him when they reached the table.

"We've never even seen what's inside. Maybe the old woman was senile and her story just that—a story."

Dare cleared his throat and the two men stood up straight and looked at them.

Tayla had no idea what they were speaking about, and by

the tension in the air, she wasn't sure she wanted to.

On the table, between the two brothers, sat a beautifully crafted music box.

"Is this it?" she asked, letting go of Dare's hand and stepping forward.

He nodded.

"Please," she asked, "what song does it play?" Tayla reached out to caress the lid.

No response.

"May I?"

Harrison nodded.

When she lifted the lid, the sweetest melody filled her ears. She closed her eyes and remembered sitting at a piano playing the piece for her father.

Her father.

Visions of the night he'd been shot flashed through her mind. She closed her eyes and shook her head.

The back door to the kitchen opened and Rafe stepped inside. He seemed collected. Tayla rushed to his side. "You said my father was alive. I want to see him. Where is he?"

"I can answer that," Will said as he stacked another flapjack on an already overflowing plate.

In that moment, Tayla realized just how desperately she needed to know about her family. They had all been lost to her for the last few weeks and now that she was starting to remember the things and people from her past, the emptiness she'd felt was starting to dissipate.

"What do you know of my father? Where is he?"

"He is alive, but I am afraid the prognosis is not good. He's been asking for you, but is in no condition to travel."

"You've seen him then?"

"Adrien sent him to my home in Boston along with Doc Simmons. Your mother is with him. The journey has made him very weak. I think it may do him some good to know that you are safe, and well by the looks of it."

"Yes, yes, her father is alive. Can we get back to the box?"

Everyone turned to look at Finn. He was breathing more

heavily than before and had started to bounce a little in place.

"The Dowager said everything we would need to prove our birthright lies in this box."

Tayla had no idea what Finn was talking about. Why would a Darington heirloom be so important to him?

"Darling," Dare turned to her, "may I?"

She smiled and nodded slightly.

He reached around her neck to remove the locket.

"Finn here has been talking non-stop about this box and its contents. How are you planning to open it?" Will asked Dare.

Tayla instinctively brought a hand to her chest to feel the smooth gem in the center of her necklace. When the straps fell away from her neck, she felt a loss she couldn't explain, but she let him have it.

"With this." Dare held up the bottom side of the pendant. He placed the five short spires into five coordinating spots near the bottom of the box.

Tayla could feel the tension immediately fill the room as everyone loomed over her shoulder in anticipation of what would be locked inside the beautiful box.

Dare released a breath and turned.

The music stopped and the clicking sound of metal wheels focused her attention. Then, snap. A small door opened and a rolled piece of paper jutted out.

Everyone just stared at it.

"Well, come on then," Finn said, "somebody has to read it."

Dare pulled the rolled parchment from the box and extended it. "It is a hand written note from the Dowager."

As he read the note, his face nearly drained of color. He looked at Tayla with a horrified expression on his face. The note fell to the table and Dare turned on his heel and walked out the back door.

Harrison and Finn both scrambled to pick up the note. Harrison got it and scanned the message. He looked at Tayla and back to the note. When he had finished reading it, he handed it to Rafe.

"What?" she exclaimed when Rafe looked at her with raised eyebrows. "What?"

Tayla was the Earl of Darington's daughter.
*Impossible.*
But there it sat boldly in front of him, notarized with the red wax crest of Darington.

The Earl of Darington had been a violent man who'd beaten his first wife so severely that she'd died in childbirth. The Dowager had informed her son that the twin boys she'd carried had also died that day along with their mother, but had charged the midwife with raising the boys as her own with her husband, away from the Darington estate at Beckett—a farmhouse just outside of London.

Before he remarried, the Earl'd had several affairs, one of which was with a young Millicent Hawthorne, Tayla's mother, and had resulted in a child. The Dowager had feared what would happen if the Earl ever discovered the girl and had given the woman a lofty sum to convince her husband the child was his and to stay away from the Earl.

"What is it?" Tayla asked again.

How could he tell her? How could he tell her that the life she had just started to remember was riddled with lies? And then it hit him. Tayla was an heiress, the daughter of an Earl. How could he compete with that?

"Why is everyone staring at me?"

"Because you…" What could he say? "You *are* the secret. Well, at least one of them."

"What are you talking about?"

He handed her the note, but couldn't bear to watch her read it.

"Is this some sort of jest?" she asked incredulously. Tears brimmed along the bottom ridges of her eyes. She'd been so strong and now this. "No." She shook her head. "Stuart

Hawthorne is my father."

Lord Darington walked back in the house. Some of his color had returned. He looked calm as he leaned against the counter with his arms folded and his ankles crossed in front of him.

Harrison pulled a folded yellow envelope from the music box. Three birth certificates, a thick silver ring with the Darington crest carved into the top, and two smaller white envelopes were inside. One with Tayla's name scribbled on the outside and the other said, Lord Brick Darington.

Tayla reached out, running her fingertips over her name on the envelope. Her hands started to shake and picked up the note. "I don't want to read this here," she said quietly and backed up through the archway into the living room.

Rafe wanted to follow, but he also understood she needed a moment to herself.

Darington pulled out a chair at the table and sat down. His face had gone ashen white and he stared vaguely at the box, then his eyes moved to the envelope with his name on it.

"Well, Lord Darington," Darington bowed his head curtly at Harrison, "I'm sure we can get all of this sorted once we return England," he said as he examined the documents on the table. He picked up the letter addressed to him and opened it.

Harrison looked dumbfounded. Sweat had formulated on his brow and he rubbed his arms anxiously and then lifted his hand to his face, swiping his cheeks with one hand. He exhaled loudly. "Let's just call me Harrison for now, mate" he said.

Darington leaned onto the table, his fingers massaging his forehead just above the temples as he read the contents of the letter.

"What is it, Darington?"

He looked up at Rafe with a resigned laugh. "I'm the bar sinister who killed Malcolm's mother." He tossed the note to the table.

"That's impossible. Mrs. Longhurst died when I was just a child," Rafe said.

"The night I was born to be exact," Darington affirmed.

Rafe eyed the man speculatively, and he bent over and picked up the note addressed to Darington. He scanned it briefly, then sat down next to the man who'd just had his very foundation pulled out from beneath him.

Ironic. In the moment Tayla discovered she was one of the Earl's legitimate heirs, Darington discovered he was not. Unbeknownst to the Earl, his wife had had a brush with another man that had resulted in her...condition. And, to make matters worse, it had been her carriage that had plowed down Malcolm's mother on the streets of London as they rushed her home to deliver her child—Lord Brick Darington.

Rafe actually felt sorry for his would-be rival.

"I think I'll retire to my room for a bit," Darington said as he pushed himself away from the table and picked up the locket. He shoved it into his pocket and walked out.

Rafe waited until he left and then he re-read the note. Malcolm couldn't have known about this. There had to be another explanation. Rafe would ask him straight out, if he would just show his face. Maybe it was time for that ride after all. Malcolm had to be close. If anyone could find him, Rafe could.

Tayla sat on the couch re-reading her note from her grandmother. It gave Tayla her blessing in marrying Lord Darington and said that even though she already carried Darington blood, Dare did not, and their marriage would be a new beginning. The old woman had not wanted to carry these secrets to her grave and hoped that they would all be able to make peace with what she had done.

Tayla was vaguely aware that Hannah had returned and was speaking with Will near the kitchen entrance. She did not want to look up for fear of the pity she might see in her friend's eyes.

"Come on, Tayla," Hannah said, "let's go get dressed for breakfast."

When she reached the bottom of the stairs, she turned back to Will. "My father," she looked away from him and then back again. "Stuart Hawthorne," she started again, "he'll be okay, right?"

Will looked at her with some semblance of a smile. "I hope so."

Tayla reached up to her locket. It wasn't there and suddenly she felt like a part of her was missing. That locket had been the only thing she'd been able to cling to. The only thing that had brought her hope in discovering who she was. But now that she knew, she wished she could go back. It had been so much simpler when she was just Locket.

She followed Hannah into her room. Hannah set the baby down in the center of her bed and opened her wardrobe. Dresses of all color jumped out at her and she stood, mesmerized, by the sheer number of dresses Hannah owned. She had a brief flash of her own wardrobe and realized she'd had many dresses to choose from as well. Suddenly, she felt guilty for all the luxuries she'd enjoyed as a Hawthorne.

Hannah pulled three different styles and colors—all of which seemed the more appropriate and less elegant sort—and in turn, placed each one up against her and looked from her face to the dress and back again. She quickly dismissed the first two, tossing them onto the bed, careful not to cover her baby. When she put the last one up to her, Hannah smiled.

The baby started to fuss.

"Here," she said draping the fabric over Tayla's arms. "And take these." Hannah pulled some white underthings from the drawers in the wardrobe. "And these," she said, topping the pile with a pair of black boots.

The baby was crying now.

"I'm sorry if the shoes won't fit. I have strangely large feet. My brothers can hardly stop teasing me about it. She picked up the little girl, but the child did not stop crying. "She must be hungry. Join you in a minute?"

Tayla nodded and turned out into the hall. When she finally reached the twin's room, she pushed open the door with her foot and carefully set everything down in the chair next to the bed. As she looked at her reflection in the tall wooden washstand, she couldn't help but wish she was at home in front of her own vanity.

Enough, she told herself. There was no use pining over what couldn't be. She pulled the dress from the chair and held it up to her in the small mirror. She couldn't see much, but was just happy to feel like a woman again.

With a quick shake of her head, she quickly stripped of her night shift and donned her new attire. She stood back as far as she could to try to get an idea of how she looked in her reflection. She hoped the blue tulips on the otherwise soft ivory color of the material, would bring out the blue in her eyes. She wanted to look her very best.

She reached for the brush that had been placed on the washstand, next to the water pitcher and basin last night after Leah had helped her wash her hair.

"I think youse done up enough there, girly."

Tayla whipped around to see Lester standing behind the door with his hand covering a struggling Hannah's mouth. The baby was no longer crying, but Hannah's eyes were full of sheer panic.

"Lester. What are you doing here?"

"Unfinished business," he replied with a snarl.

"One scream from me and five men twice your size will be at my door."

"I wouldn't do that if I were you. See." He flashed a gun he was holding at Hannah's side, "I would hate to see things get messier than they need to be."

"What do you want, Lester?"

There was something wild in his eyes. Like he was desperate for something and that scared her. She'd seen what he would do when provoked when he shot her father and didn't want to take the same chance with Hannah and her baby.

"Well, darlin', I've got a job to do and if it doesn't get done, I don't get paid. And if I don't get paid, people are gonna die."

Tayla's eyes were drawn to the droplets of blood that now

stained the floor.

"You wouldn't want that, now would ya?" He stumbled.

"You're hurt, Lester. Let me go get Rafe and he can help you." Maybe she could talk some sense into him.

"It's a cause a Redbourne that we're in this mess to begin with." Lester spat on the floor. "If'n he'd taken Davis to the boss like he was supposed to, this'd all be done with and I'd be spending some of that money on good liquor and a whore of my choice."

*Dolt.*

"How far do you really think you are going to get?" She had to think. "I don't know if you realize that you are threatening Rafe's little sister."

Lester shrugged. "So? That supposed to mean something to me?"

"What do you think Rafe will do if you harm her? Not to mention her other six brothers, her husband, and her father—all of which are twice the size of you and many of them in this house right now."

"Nothing's going to happen to her, if you do as you're told."

"What do you want?" she asked again.

"You." His answer was simple. His leering gaze made her skin crawl and she shuttered in disgust.

She swallowed hard. "Let them go and I will come with you."

"I'm not as stupid as you must think. The moment I let them go, she'll run and get all them folks you mentioned and I'll be a dead man." He shook his head. "No. I think we'll just take them with us." He shifted his weight and grimaced at the movement. His bandages were soaked in blood and the color was quickly draining from his face. If she could just stall him.

Just as Rafe reached the stables, Eli pulled up in the wagon.

And he wasn't alone.

"Look who I found wandering around the train station." Eli jumped off the buckboard, reached into the back, and pulled out two large carpet bags.

Now, here he stood. Adrien Longhurst looked more alert than he'd been a few weeks ago when Rafe had last seen him. His eyes weren't red and bloodshot, and he seemed almost spry.

Adrien climbed down off the seat, careful to avoid putting too much pressure on his bad leg. He must have been worrying himself sick over losing Tayla to Jonas and Lester. How was he going to tell his friend and mentor about his only son?

"Adrien, old friend, to what do we owe the pleasure?" Rafe extended his hand to Adrien.

"When I got your message, I wanted to see for myself that she was all right and offer my apologies that I hadn't protected her like I should have."

"I'm sure she'll be glad to see you. Let's get you inside. Was my family expecting you?"

"I'm afraid not. I sent word ahead, but it seems that my telegram is among those Eli collected from town this morning." He leaned on his cane with both hands in front of him. "I've got a room at the Gold Dust Hotel."

"Mother isn't going to let you stay in town. You know that."

"Will you tell Grace I'll be in as soon as I unhitch the wagon and brush down the horses?" Eli asked as he took a hold of the team's reins and started making his way to the barn.

"Yep."

When Rafe opened the front door, he looked up to see Tayla descending the stairs. Her cheeks were flushed and her hair spilled in loose tendrils over her shoulders, down in front of her breasts. When she met his eyes, warmth flooded his chest.

He dropped the bags he held to the floor and couldn't stop himself from gaping. He had to fight to keep his jaw from dropping. She was beautiful. He had a new appreciation for Hannah's taste in clothing.

"Are you coming down for breakfast?" he asked.

She turned around as if going back upstairs.

Something wasn't right. Her eyes kept shifting from side to side and through her smile he read the apprehension that laid there.

"I'll be down shortly," she said with only a slight quiver to her voice. "Have you seen Hannah? I was hoping she could help me with my hair."

The not too distant sound of the baby crying was quickly muffled and lost. Had he imagined it?

"She's probably in the kitchen…or her room," he added.

Tayla nodded.

She took the next step up, watching him from the corner of her eye.

Bare feet. She had been on her way down, he was sure of it.

Rafe stopped in front of the kitchen doorway and turned back to Tayla. She had stopped in front of the twin's room and watched him.

"Rafe," Eli yelled from outside. "Come quick."

He stole another glance at Tayla. Her face still bore a smile, but it looked rehearsed.

What now?

Tayla took a deep breath and closed her eyes when Rafe ran out the door. He was always so perceptive and she worried that she wouldn't be able to fool him.

"Is he gone?" Lester asked in a quiet and raspy voice from behind the door.

"Yes," she said curtly.

Lester peeked his head out from the door quick-like. When he emerged, he still had Hannah's head cradled in his arm. Hannah was bouncing the baby to try to keep her quiet.

Lester flicked his chin forward. He wanted her to go down the stairs. She took each step slowly, Hannah and Lester only one step behind. Lester's back was all but plastered to the wall as he descended. When they reached the bottom of the stairs she took a step toward the front door.

It burst open and Eli ran past her and into the kitchen.

Lester had ducked into the hallway that led to Jameson's study. He motioned for her to come back to him.

She darted a quick glance at Hannah, silent tears streamed down her face.

The look on Lester's face scared Tayla even more than before. He was like a trapped animal with nowhere to go. She had to give him an out. A place to run.

Lester laid his head back against the wall and grimaced. "This was supposed to be an easy job."

The sudden commotion from the kitchen sent Jameson, Will, Ethan, and Dare running out the front door.

She hadn't seen Grace or the children this morning and with Leah still in Lottie's room, there would be no one left in the kitchen. At least she hoped.

"Run," she said to Lester, meeting his wild stare straight on and pointing to the back door through the kitchen.

He didn't seem to comprehend what she was telling him.

"Now's your chance. I promise not to scream. Run!" she said more loudly.

As if that had been all the encouragement he needed, he shoved Hannah away from him.

Boom.

A loud crack nearly deafened Tayla and she fell to the floor gripping her ears.

The muffled sound of the baby crying filled her head and she watched in horror as Lester's body fell forward, lifeless. She looked up to see her savior.

Adrien Longhurst stood with a pistol raised and smoking as he leaned on his cane for support. He rushed forward to Hannah, set his cane against the wall, and hunched down to collect the baby.

"Hannah, my dear, are you okay?"

"Adrien?" Hannah asked with an air of disbelief. "Oh, Adrien." She fell into him, sobbing. "It was awful."

# CHAPTER TWENTY-TWO

Jonas laid face first on the seat of the buckboard behind the house, convulsing. Rafe reached for the man. His skin was cold to the touch and his breathing was labored and irregular. Rafe pulled him from the buckboard and laid him on the ground. Within moments, all movement stopped. He was dead.

Rafe stood and threw is hands through his hair—an action that was becoming all too familiar. He kicked at the dirt and leaned up against the buckboard. A canteen of spilled liquid lay at his feet, which he thought odd.

He reached down and picked it up, bringing the rim to his nose. Instantly, he turned away. The odor coming from the canteen was anything but pleasant.

Jimsonweed.

He had learned a lot from his time spent living with the Pawnee. Detecting poisons was one of them. It seemed as if Jonas had consumed a tea that had been concocted with Jimsonweed leaves or nectar. The tribe he and Malcolm had lived among had used the plant in moderation for some of their spiritual quests. It was said to have awakened the spirits enough for communion, but could only be used sparingly. Someone hadn't been very sparing with the poison in this tea.

He didn't like this one bit. It was too close to home. To the people he loved. If Malcolm had done this, Rafe had no doubts that he was still somewhere on the ranch. How had Jonas gotten back onto the ranch without him or his family noticing?

Unless…

He never left. So, where was Lester? Rafe glanced up and noticed they were directly beneath the room Tayla had slept in—or at least where she was supposed to have slept. He only allowed himself a fraction of a moment to remember the sweet smell of her hair as she'd laid on his lap in the swing.

Boom.

A gunshot came from inside the house. Rafe's heart vaulted from his chest. He looked down at the lifeless Jonas, then at Darington. A dead body wasn't going to go anywhere. At once both men dashed toward the door, closely followed by Harrison and Will.

Once inside, Rafe scanned the room and immediately his eyes were drawn to the place on the floor where Lester's lifeless body laid, a look of shock still plaguing his dead features.

Tayla stood against the wall in the hallway with her hands over her mouth. The look in her eyes was a combination of fear and horror. Rafe wanted nothing more than to pull her into his arms and tell her how happy he was that she was safe, but it appeared that Darington had had the same thought. They both froze mere feet away from her. Tayla's brow wrinkled as her gaze shifted from one man to the other as if she were unsure where to go.

Tayla looked down at the fresh corpse and color drained from her face. Rafe reached out to steady her.

"What in the hell happened in here?" He turned to his mentor and friend. "Adrien?"

"That man was holding Hannah at gunpoint," he tossed a disinterested hand toward Lester. "When that smart little lady there," he nodded at Tayla, "told him to run, he pushed Hannah far enough out of the way that I had a clean shot."

"But how did…" Rafe started. "Never mind," he dismissed his thought. He knelt down next to the body and put his ear up to the man's chest. He looked up at a room full of expectant stares and wiped the sweat from his brow with the back of his hand. "He's dead all right."

Adrien set Hannah away from him and picked up his cane.

"I think you'll find this very interesting," he said making his way to the bags resting near the couch. Two crumpled papers sat at the top of his things and he handed them to Rafe.

"Wanted posters?" Rafe looked up, confused. "I've never seen these before. Where did you get them?"

"There were a lot of them hanging on the walls down at the train station. I recognized them from home. I'd seen them hanging around in town a few days after Miss Hawthorne and her father came to stay with me. I thought you might be interested."

"Malcolm," Rafe called, an impatient tone lining his voice. He waited.

No response.

"Malcolm," he called louder this time. "I know you are here. Let's talk about this."

It had gone too far and now, two men were dead.

Still, no response.

Rafe glanced over at Tayla who stood as if frozen to the spot. He watched her until her eyes finally found his. He needed to reassure her somehow. To let her know it was going to be okay, but he couldn't do that until he found his old friend.

"Malcolm!" Rafe screamed as he turned in circles, scanning the corners of the room.

Everyone now stared at him, expectation lining their features, asking him what they should do, begging him to tell them everything was going to be all right. But the truth was, he didn't know.

"Are you saying that Malcolm is here?" Adrien took a step toward Rafe, surprise evident in his voice. "Malcolm? My son? He's not in England?"

Rafe met Adrien's questioning eyes and answered with a quick shake of his head.

"What does he have to do with this?"

The side door, near his father's study, opened and Malcolm walked inside the house, slapping his gloves against his denims.

Rafe reached for his guns, resting his hands at his sides. He had to be careful. Malcolm stood just a few feet from Tayla.

"Marty said you've been hollering for me." He looked at Rafe expectantly. "What is it?"

Rafe narrowed his eyes at the man, but didn't say anything. That was...unexpected.

"Where've you been? Haven't seen you since the stampede last night," Rafe inquired as he took a small step toward them.

Malcolm's eyes trailed to the dead body lying at Rafe's feet. "Rafe," he said quietly, "what's this?"

Adrien moved around Rafe to look at his son. "Malcolm, did you have something to do with this?"

"Father?" Malcolm's eyes grew wide, but his brow furrowed. "What are you doing here?"

"I could ask you the same thing." Adrien lifted his cane. "This is a far cry from London."

"Yes. It is. And I will tell you all about it later, but first what is going on here?" He pointed to the floor. "Is that man...dead." He swallowed.

Rafe didn't know what he was playing at, but a part of him hoped that Malcolm was innocent of all the wrongdoings Rafe had come to believe him capable over the last few hours.

Adrien looked down and tsked.

"He attacked Hannah. And Tayla." Rafe relaxed his stance a little, but a small glint of light through the window reflected off the pistol at Malcolm's side and Rafe flexed an itchy hand. "Do you know him?"

"Should I?" Malcolm asked, barely glancing at the corpse.

Everything in his head told him he should trust the man. That maybe there'd been a grace misunderstanding. Maybe Malcolm was innocent. But his gut...

Darington took a step forward.

"My lord. I didn't realize you had arrived. I would have met you at the station. I guess you see that Miss Hawthorne is safe."

Darington raised a brow and cleared his throat. "Mr. Davis has some very interesting things he's told me about you, Malcolm," he said with a nod at Harrison.

Rafe looked between the two men. What were they talking about?

"I'm sorry, my lord, but who?" Malcolm started to breathe a little faster and his eyes darted from one person in the room to another.

Harrison stepped up next to Darington. "Me." He lifted his shirt to expose the long, jagged scar on his gut.

Rafe remembered something Davis had said when he'd first shown him the scar. *But after spending a few damaging moments with him, I realized the error of my ways.* He'd been speaking of Lord Darington. Rafe needed to get his family out of this room. Now. A wall of tension had erected itself in front of him and he feared he wouldn't be able to contain the aftershock if it tumbled.

"Ladies," Will called to Hannah and Tayla as if reading his thoughts, "you've been through quite an ordeal this morning. I wonder if you might accompany me into the kitchen and I'll make you some tea."

Hannah rushed toward her brother, but Tayla hesitated. She glanced at Rafe and he forced a smile. She returned the gesture and took a step toward Will.

"Maybe we should take this outside, son," Adrien placed his hand on Rafe's arm.

"He's not your son, old man." Malcolm spat, his façade breaking in an instant. He reached out, grabbed Tayla by the hair, and pulled her back toward him.

She screamed.

Rafe darted forward, but in that instant, Malcolm had drawn his pistol and backed into the wall with Tayla in front of him. She lifted her hands in attempt to pry his fingers loose from her scalp. He released her hair, but held his gun into her side. She didn't move. Color had returned to her cheeks, however, and when she caught his gaze, the panicked look that had occupied her face moments ago turned calm.

Malcolm chortled derisively. "My whole life it has been, Rafe this and Rafe that. You excelled at everything. Everyone was so taken with you. My own people. Even my father preferred you over me."

"Malcolm." Maybe he could reason with him. "This isn't you. Let her go." Rafe reached out his hand and opened his palm. "We're brothers."

"But you have enough of those, don't you?" he said with a sneer. "But, you know, you're right. I am not Malcolm Longhurst anymore," he said with a satisfied smirk. "My name is Lord Darington."

"Excuse me," Darington started forward, but Rafe stuck out his arm to block his way.

"Just ask your friend, Beckett there. Or Davis. Or whatever you call him. He'll tell you."

"Why are you doing this, son?" Adrien asked. "Did I not provide for you? Make sure that you wanted for nothing?"

"I wanted my mother and because of him," he spat the last word at Darington, "I never knew her."

Darington opened his mouth to defend himself.

"Don't bother," Malcolm said. "I am leaving and Miss Hawthorne is coming with me. After all," he shrugged, "she is my fiancée."

"You are daft, Longhurst. You'll never get away with this." Lord Darington told the man who held her captive.

"That's where you're wrong, my lord."

His breath reeked of stale cigars and gin.

Tayla's mind raced. When she met Rafe's eyes, she knew that he would try anything to save her—even if that meant risking his life in the process. She could not let that happen. There had to be something she could do.

"You see, no one knows you. You've been a bit of a recluse for so long that it was easy to pass myself off as you."

Tayla stomped on his foot.

He screamed out in pain and relaxed his grip on her.

She bolted.

He caught her by the arm and lifted his gun at Rafe. "Another trick like that, Miss Hawthorne, and I'm afraid I'll have to hurt the man you love."

She looked at Rafe. "It's okay, Lord Darington," she said quietly to her captor. I will not fight you." Even as she spoke to Malcolm, she was unable to tear her gaze away from Rafe.

Malcolm opened the door next to Jameson's study. "If any of you try to follow us, I will not hesitate to hurt her. Do you understand, *brother,*" he said disdainfully.

Rafe shook with anger. Heat rose in his neck and face. His hands balled into fists, then stretched near his weapons.

"Just to make sure we understand each other." Malcolm lifted his gun and aimed. Tayla brought down her elbow on his arm. When the shot fired, she held her breath.

Darington went down. Malcolm jerked her outside and slammed the door behind them. Her arms flailed as she pounded against him, fighting for release. The wagon waited for them at the back of the house. He kicked Jonas's lifeless body aside and waved his gun at her.

"Get in."

Tayla closed her eyes, then grabbed a hold of the seat railing and heaved herself up onto the bench. She looked around. The yard seemed awfully quiet. There were no hands roaming the property. A few animals dotted the ranch, but most were nowhere to be found.

Malcolm climbed up on the seat beside her and whipped the team horses to a start with a hard, quick slap of the reins. The buckboard jerked forward. She held onto the edge of the wooden seat and braced her feet against the front of the wagon to keep herself upright.

Guilt filled her mind as she thanked God that Rafe had not been the one shot. Two men were dead and she had no idea how badly Dare had been hurt, but she knew he was in good hands.

She'd seen how Rafe had taken care of Jake's leg at Maggie's place and how he'd been with Marty on the trail back to the ranch—wrapping his ribs with bandages and caring for his cuts and bruises. He was going to make a wonderful doctor. She needed to tell him that.

*Please don't let him die*, she pleaded silently.

Several times Malcolm darted a glance over his shoulder to make sure that no one was coming for them. Tayla couldn't turn around. She was afraid she would see the dust kicking up into the air and afraid of what Malcolm would do if that happened. After a while, he slowed the pace of the horses.

"There are a lot of benefits to being married to an Earl, you know."

"I must have thought so…once." She didn't want to make small talk with him.

The man was delusional if he thought she was going to marry him. She looked down at the ground as they rode. She wondered how badly it would hurt if she simply jumped off. The idea left as soon as it was formed. He would just turn around and come after her. There was nowhere to run. No, she would have to wait until they got into town. The town's people would not let him take her. Certainly, someone would help her.

It was then that she noticed the small leather satchel that had fallen from his pocket onto the bench. By the size and shape of it, she guessed it contained his valuables, maybe even the train tickets he'd purchased.

A plan quickly formulated in her mind. She would have to do it. Now.

# CHAPTER TWENTY-THREE

Shards of red and metal flew everywhere.

Rafe reached out to catch Darington as he fell backward and to the floor. He tried to tell himself that Malcolm had not aimed for him, but somehow it just didn't ring true. Rafe helped Darington lay back. A small red pool had started to form through the man's trousers.

"Hannah, I need water and rags." He'd said those words too many times in the last few days. "And some of mom's poultice," he added. "Will, I'm going to need my bag. You know the one. It's out in my saddle in the barn."

Will nodded and ran for the door.

"Rafe, you need to go after Tayla. I've never seen Malcolm like this before." Darington winced. "He could hurt her."

Rafe didn't need to be told the kind of danger Tayla was in right now. He knew Malcolm and now, more than ever, understood just what he was capable of. "Shut up and stay still." He pulled his blade from the strap on his leg. He would have to cut the material away to see the damage. The fabric tore easily and Rafe gingerly folded back the sticky layers.

He fell backward onto his rear end and leaned against the couch with a relieved laugh. Tayla's pendant, still in Darington's pocket, had taken the brunt of force, and the bullet had ricocheted to the right and had only penetrated half an inch into the fleshy part of his hip. He took a deep breath.

Harrison stared at him as if he'd gone mad.

"I'm glad you find this humorous," Darington said, "but it stings like hell."

His moment of relief passed with the thought of Tayla out there alone with Malcolm. Rafe knew just how impulsive a man he could be and now, it seemed, all reason had left him. He moved to his knees and reached down for the chain that held the remnant of what was Tayla's locket and held it up.

Will burst through the doors in a pant. "He'd got them all tied up in the barn."

Rafe looked up. Anger quickly replaced relief. "Is everyone okay?"

"As far as I could tell." Will tossed him his bag. "Do you need me?"

"We need to go after them, Will."

"I know."

"Go!" Rafe instructed.

"How bad is it?" Darington asked.

"You'll live."

Hannah returned with the supplies he'd requested, and without the baby.

Rafe quickly stuck his knife into the mixture his mother had concocted for cleaning the many scrapes and scratches her children had accrued over the years and wiped it clean with a towel. Then, he turned to Harrison. "Davis, I need you to grab the bullet when it reaches the surface."

"What?" Darington lifted his head.

"Oh, I couldn't possibly—"

"He has Tayla, Harry," Rafe pleaded. "You can do this."

Harrison pursed his lips, then crouched down next to him and waited, a bead of sweat trailing the side of his face. He nodded. Rafe placed a hand on one side of the wound and eased the tip of his knife into the wound. Blood gushed. Hannah patted the area with a dampened cloth. Rafe slid his knife in a little further, deep enough to get under the little metal ball. He lifted slowly and without hesitation Harrison grabbed the bullet the moment it came to a head.

Harrison blew out and held the bullet in the palm of his

hand for the wounded man to see. Darington laid his head back
on the floor and closed his eyes.

"Thank you."

Rafe barely heard the words as he was already half way out
the door. He whistled. Lexa came. *Thanks, Will.* His brother
knew him all too well.

It was time to get his woman.

Tayla swiped the leather satchel from the buckboard's
bench and tossed it as hard as she could into a hedge of brush
by the wayside. Malcolm pulled the team to a stop in a hurry. He
stood up, teeth grinding together and face redder than a beet,
and he swatted her across the face with the back of his hand
before jumping down. There was no time to think. She blinked
through the tears, grabbed the reins, and slapped them hard.
The horses bolted, just as they'd done before.

A shot buzzed past her head and several more sounded. She
rode straight ahead long enough that she was sure he could not
have caught up on foot and then she swung the team wide until
she was facing the direction they had come. She expected to see
Malcolm in the distance, but there was no sign of him.

Redbourne Ranch should be a straight shot ahead, but
without knowing where Malcolm had gone, she was leery of
taking the shortest route. She eased the horses forward. She'd
had no idea whether or not she'd be able to control the team,
but to her relief she'd done it. The sound of her heart in her ears
had still pounded in a steady, rhythmic beat.

The early afternoon was decorated with blankets of storm
clouds and the ground was already riddled with puddles from
yesterday's rain. If it got much wetter, Tayla was fearful that she
may not be able to guide the wagon wheels through the mud.

She scanned the countryside, watching for the slightest
indication of Malcolm. He couldn't have just vanished. An odd
creaking sound came from behind her. She whipped around.

Malcolm stared at her with cold, murderous eyes. Gooseflesh traveled down her arms. She looked around for anything she could use as a weapon. She slapped the reins harder and the horses jutted forward on cue.

She jerked her head backward. Malcolm had fallen against the side of the buckboard, but still moved forward. Her chest tightened and her breathes came more rapidly. She looked back again, he was almost in reach.

The loud whinny of a horse pulled Tayla's attention behind her to the side. Rafe had caught up to them. Tayla's heart nearly jumped from her chest. Bam. Rafe jumped from Lexa into Malcolm and they both tumbled off the wagon in a throng of fists. The buckboard rocked unnaturally from side to side. Tayla thought it might tip over. It took her a moment to gain control, but she was finally able to pull the horses to a stop. She jumped off the seat and started to run toward them, then thought better of it and stopped midstride.

Malcolm and Rafe circled each other, fists up.

"You have to let her go, Malcolm. It's over."

Tayla could barely hear their words, but couldn't take her eyes off them.

"I can't do that. I've worked too hard," Malcolm countered.

One drop. Then two. The heavens broke and rain slammed down on top of them, nearly blocking her view. She couldn't lose him. Not now. Not after everything. She loved him.

Lexa brushed up against Tayla's arm and she rubbed her neck. "Come on, girl," she said as she mounted the large strawberry roan. She clicked her heels into the horse's flanks. Memories flooded her mind with ease and she welcomed them, focused them.

"Rafe!" she screamed out over the pounding rain.

If he'd seen her, she couldn't tell as his focus seemed perfect. She was so close now. He had to see her.

Rafe shook his head, water whipping out from his sopping locks of hair and he landed a punch squarely in Malcolm's jaw, sending him sprawling backward to the ground. He looked up, grabbed onto the saddle horn as she passed, and hauled himself up behind her. He urged Lexa even faster.

The feel of Rafe's warm body behind hers sent a different kind of jolt through her body. The rise and fall of his chest caressed her back and his hot breath on the back of her neck sent tingles through her belly.

He was safe.

When they reached the outer edge of Redbourne Ranch Rafe finally slowed their pace and Tayla allowed herself to relax into him. This is where she belonged. This was home.

Malcolm wouldn't be back. At least not tonight. Rafe suspected that he'd had a plan to escape all along and would be on his way back to England before long. He smiled as he thought of the bravery it had taken for Tayla to climb up on his monstrous horse and head straight into the danger. In the rain, her dress was soaked and clung to every curve. He had to direct his thoughts in a different direction, but when she leaned back against him, it was nearly his undoing.

Rafe reached an arm beneath hers and helped her slide to the ground. She turned around and looked up at him, her wet tresses framing her beautiful face, and he felt it.

He was home.

Ranch hands darted from one outbuilding to another. Rafe dismounted.

"You outdid yourself today, my friend," he whispered as he ran his hands across the horse's neck. "Thank you." He handed Lexa's reins to Judd, who nodded and took the horse into the stable.

He turned back to the house. Tayla still stood at the foot of the stairs watching him. He took a deep breath and had to remind himself to put one foot in front of the other. The closer he got, the faster he moved until he reached her and in one fluid movement shoved his hands into her hair and under her jaw, bringing her lips to his. She responded eagerly to his touch, to his kiss. He slid his hands down her arms and around her waist, pulling her more tightly against him and for a moment, everything around them stilled into a quiet blur until it seemed they were the only people on earth.

When he broke their kiss, Tayla bit her lip and smiled. "It's about time," she said with a laugh.

"Marry me, Tayla Hawthorne," Rafe pleaded with everything inside of him. "My heart is yours." He smiled and wiped a stray lock from her face and tucked it behind her ear. "My life," he whispered as he lowered his head again toward her. "My trust. You are my match in every way and I love you." His lips grazed hers in sweet surrender.

"Yes."

# ABOUT THE AUTHOR

KELLI ANN MORGAN recognized a passion for writing at a very young age. Since that time, she has devoted herself to creativity of all sorts—moonlighting as a cover designer, photographer, jewelry designer, motivational speaker, and more.

Kelli Ann is a long-time member of the Romance Writers of America and was president of her local chapter in 2009. Her love of and talent for writing have opened many doors for her and she continues to look for new and exciting opportunities and calls to adventure. She feels very blessed to have a talented husband and son who inspire her on a consistent basis.

Her novels are on the sensual side of PG—without graphic love scenes. Great romance novels are those that make you feel the spectrum of emotion, that leave you wanting more, and it is her hope that every time you crack open one of her romance stories, that you walk away inspired, uplifted, and with a love of romance.

www.kelliannmorgan.com